ALEXANDER SÖDERBERG

The Other Son

TRANSLATED FROM THE SWEDISH BY
Neil Smith

VINTAGE

1 3 5 7 9 10 8 6 4 2

Vintage
20 Vauxhall Bridge Road,
London SW1V 2SA

Vintage is part of the Penguin Random House group of companies whose
addresses can be found at global.penguinrandomhouse.com

Penguin
Random House
UK

First published in Vintage in 2016
First published in Great Britain in 2015 by Harvill Secker

First published with the title *Den Andre Sonen* by Norstedts, Stockholm,
in 2014

A CIP catalogue record for this book is available from the British Library

ISBN 9780099575924

Printed and bound by Clays Ltd, St Ives PLC

Penguin Random House is committed to a sustainable future for our
business, our readers and our planet. This book is made from Forest
Stewardship Council® certified paper.

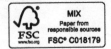

PROLOGUE

THE VEHICLE WAS DRIVING FAST, SWERVING WILDLY, ACCELERATING AND BRAKing erratically. Sophie couldn't hear properly. Everything was muffled, as if she were underwater. The ambulance sirens blaring out into the dark night sounded dull and distant.

A harsh, cold blue light kept swirling in and out of the space around her. She was lying on a stretcher, strapped down, as she felt the ambulance lurch.

She tried to look around. The back of the ambulance felt like a tunnel, as though it had been stretched. Everything was like a feverish dream.

She could see Jens, which made her feel more secure. He made his way towards her. Dully she heard him try to comfort her, tell her that everything was going to be all right. But she didn't believe him. Because his whole face was saying the opposite. He radiated anxiety and sorrow.

She whispered the name of the person who had stabbed her with the knife, repeating the name to Jens twice.

There was a paramedic beside her, working hard and intently.

She looked down at herself, managing to raise her head ever so slightly. The blanket tucked tightly around her was covered in blood.

He had twisted the knife inside her; she remembered that. First he had thrust it into her as deeply as he could, then he had twisted it, to and fro, to cause as much damage as possible, to kill her.

An itchy chill enveloped her, a nausea made more oppressive by an immense physical weakness that seemed to emanate from her neck or somewhere around there. That was followed by a dizzying sense that she was upside down, weightless, in an altered state, that she was at the point of toppling over a cliff, a boundary, and losing everything. Sophie couldn't hold on. The chill was getting worse, cutting through her whole being, and she started to shake, the shakes radiating through her entire body, hard and uncontrollable. The paramedic was above her, holding her body down onto the stretcher with all his weight, trying to keep her still. She looked into his eyes and saw fear in them.

And then she realised what was happening. Sophie heard herself say 'No' several times. *No, dear God I can't do this, not now . . .*

She realised she was about to die.

PART ONE
FOUR WEEKS EARLIER

FOUR WEEKS EARLIER

1

(ISTANBUL)

THE COFFEE WAS SWEET, BLACK AND TREACLY.

Sophie left it untouched, as did Aron, who was sitting beside her in the lavish room listening to Basir, the fat Turk opposite them on the other side of the desk, as he tried to haggle and gain the upper hand.

Behind Basir's bulky frame sat his silent bodyguard. Wiry, swarthy and alert, he sat there observing everything. The bodyguard had searched them brusquely and thoroughly before the meeting began. Everything was fine now. Basir smiled at them as if they were old friends. But they had never met before. Basir was a front, the weapons were destined to end up somewhere else. Where didn't matter. But he was important because he was the one they were negotiating with. Basir was very talkative. He babbled and chattered as if the sheer quantity of words he uttered would improve his position, rather than what he was actually saying.

Sophie interrupted him.

'We'll send the goods through, and you'll have to get them out,' she said. 'Everything has to go smoothly, otherwise it could all grind to a halt. And if it grinds to a halt, there's a greater risk of mistakes happening.'

Basir dismissed her concern with a wave of his hand.

'I know this city. I know everyone, the police, customs officers, transport officials. This is my city; everything will be fine, trust me.'

The room was ostentatious, overblown. Everything was dark red – thick carpets, long curtains, big, heavy furniture, brass ornaments all over the place.

'So what do you need us for, then?' Sophie asked.

His smile wavered slightly.

'You've got the weapons,' he said.

'And we'll supply them in small consignments over a period of four months. That's how we're going to do this.'

'And we'll pay after each consignment,' Basir said. 'That's the best way, believe me,' he repeated.

'I believe you, but that isn't what's going to happen.' She smiled.

Basir looked offended. 'Isn't it?'

A phone rang twice in a neighbouring room.

She said calmly, 'You pay in one instalment, for everything. Payable now.'

He glanced quickly at his watch.

'What if it does grind to a halt, if something happens? If we lose a consignment?' he asked.

Sophie smiled.

'Are you in a hurry?' she asked.

He pretended not to understand.

'You looked at the time,' Sophie explained.

'I do that occasionally. Don't you?' His laugh sounded false and put-on. Almost like a cough.

He wasn't what she had been expecting, Basir. According to the people who had helped set up the deal, Basir was supposed to be a reasonable man. Calm, straightforward and uncomplicated, with a degree of honour in his approach to business, the nature of his business notwithstanding. But this man was quite different from that.

'Yes, when I'm in a hurry,' she said.

'Well, I'm not in a hurry.' He laughed again.

Everything felt very peculiar. Sophie glanced at Aron to see if he was feeling the same as she. He was busy studying Basir.

'What was your question?' she asked the Turk.

'Yes, what was my question . . . ?' he muttered, slightly bewildered, as he cast a glance at his bodyguard, who replied quietly in Turkish without taking his eyes off Aron.

'If we lose a consignment . . .' Basir said.

'You won't,' Sophie said. 'You just said so, because you know everyone. You know what goes on in this city. It's yours.'

'True.' He laughed again. He was getting more nervous.

Sophie considered the situation. She had a feeling that he saw these negotiations as something to be endured, and that he wanted to get away. That his reasons for sitting there were quite different from hers. That this wasn't about doing business at all. Because if it were, this wasn't the way it was done.

'So, what do you say, Basir?' she asked.

He pretended to think. Beads of sweat had broken out on his forehead. He was off-balance.

'Let's do as you say, then,' he said. 'We pay you now; you arrange to send us the weapons as you suggested. That's probably best.'

Just like that? She could feel Aron's electrified reaction beside her. He felt the same as she.

The bodyguard adjusted his position on the chair. Aron noticed.

'Thank you, Basir,' she said.

'Stay and have coffee with us,' he said.

The mistakes were coming thick and fast now. You didn't drink coffee after a deal. Not with a man like this. You drank it before. And they had already done that. Stillborn chat that didn't go anywhere.

She turned to Aron. He was staring at Basir, reading him like an open book.

'Aron?' she asked.

'I know,' he said quietly. They heard heavy footsteps on the stairs outside the closed door. Steps that were making their way up towards them.

The bodyguard reached for the gun in his shoulder holster. Aron threw himself at him as Sophie rushed towards the door behind them. No key, just a handle. She grabbed hold of a chair and wedged the back of it under the handle. The bodyguard was out cold. Aron had moved on to Basir, and had him on the floor. A lead paperweight on the desk took care of the thickset Turk.

Heavy thuds against the door.

They were on the fourth floor. No way out apart from the door.

Aron grabbed the bodyguard's pistol, tipped the desk over and

aimed the gun at the door. Sophie crouched down next to the door. The blows got heavier. The door was about to give way.

At a signal from Aron she pulled the chair away and the door flew open.

Aron fired several shots in quick succession, moving the pistol a few centimetres from side to side, until the magazine was empty and the gun started to click. Then he vanished behind the desk.

Silence. Gunpowder, the smell of cordite. Sophie stared at a point on the floor, trying to focus. Her heart was pounding so hard in her chest she thought it must be audible throughout the room.

Suddenly Aron was at her side, pulling her to her feet and tucking her behind him.

'We're going down; stick close to me. When I say stop, you stop. When I say move, you move.'

They left the room, stepping over a dead body in the doorway. There was another one lying on its back farther down the stairs. Sophie tried not to look. Aron picked up a pistol beside the body and moved on cautiously. He gave her quiet instructions. A few minutes later they reached the ground floor. There was life outside, mopeds, motorbikes, people.

He told her to wait while he checked the street. Then he waved her to him.

The smell of exhaust fumes hit her as she emerged onto the street.

They melted into the crowd and began to walk away quickly. She turned around after a while and found herself meeting the gaze of a man who was making his way towards them through the mass of people. A big man, almost six feet tall, swarthy, moving quickly and determinedly.

'Aron!' she said.

He had seen the man too and grabbed Sophie by the arm and began to run, then he let go. Sophie stayed close to him. Adrenaline was coursing through her body, shielding her from strong emotions. She just had to get away, get to safety.

They hurried through an alley crowded with people, forcing and shoving their way through. She glanced back behind her; the man was gaining on them. He was quicker, more agile.

A large square opened up at the end of the alley.

'Out there,' Aron said.

But it was completely open. She wanted to object, say that they should try to hide, but Aron had already set off and she hurried after him.

Out in the open square he stopped abruptly, then quickly gave her clear instructions: 'We're splitting up. Get to the airport and go home. Make sure no one follows you, and don't try to contact me. I'll contact you!'

Aron was focused. He always was whenever things went to hell. He took out the pistol, sank down on one knee and took aim at the man as he emerged into the square.

'Get out of here, now!' he snapped at her.

Aron aimed and squeezed the trigger, but the gun just clicked.

The adrenaline that had carried her this far began to fade. Fear and anxiety were creeping up on her, taking over. Her breathing was heavy and laboured as she ran off towards the far side of the square. She glanced back and saw Aron run towards the man and attack him with military precision, raining blows and kicks on him before they fell to the ground.

She carried on to the other side of the square. Streets, faces coming towards her, strong smells. Sophie didn't know where she was going, just that she was getting away. She ran for twenty minutes through a maze of narrow passageways and alleys.

She came to a restaurant that opened onto a lively pedestrianised street, relatively empty inside. She went and sat down at a table in the gloom at the back of the restaurant, where she had a good view of the room and the street outside. Still trembling, down to her very core, she ordered some water.

She wondered if Aron had got away OK or if the man was hunting her now. Sophie tried to think. They had been planning the meeting for a long time. Minutely, everything checked in detail. The people, the location, the circumstances. They had analysed, scrutinised, tried to predict everything. It had felt like a secure operation for them. So secure that Aron had for the first time left the hiding place in Spain where he was watching over Hector. This deal was going to be big. And they needed the money.

But things had turned out very differently. Why?

A waiter brought her a bottle of water and a glass, put them down on the table in front of her, then walked off. She unscrewed

the bottle, didn't bother with the glass and took deep gulps straight from the bottle. She put it down and tried to catch her breath.

She had been doing this for six months, doing as she was told, doing everything Aron told her to do. Travelling around and meeting Hector's business partners – criminal, manipulative, untrustworthy people whom she despised, most of them grown men with the mind of a child, unpredictable, impulsive and ultimately extremely dangerous. The main purpose of her travels was always to calm the situation and reassure people that Hector was fine and was directing operations from his hiding place. But that was a lie. Things weren't good, and Hector wasn't directing operations from his hiding place. He was in a coma, a deep coma after he and Sophie had been attacked when they were making their way from the airport in Málaga to Hector's father's house in Marbella six months earlier.

Aron was running the organisation now, among other things. But Ernst, Leszek and she herself were all helping. Everything to keep the sinking ship afloat. Her role as a sort of outward face of the organisation stemmed from the fact that no one else could take on that role. Aron and Leszek were both highly intelligent. But they were men of action, violent men. Ernst was extremely logical but was socially inept, incapable of dealing with people. So Sophie ended up doing it, and she was good at it.

But she hated the position she was in. She was frightened. Frightened when she went to bed at night, frightened when she woke up. She didn't want to be, she wanted to be free. But she had no choice. Hector had bound her to his organisation before he got shot. She was a threat to them; she knew too much. Which was why Aron had put her in the position she was now in. As long as she was working for them, she was involved, part of everything, an accomplice. Which meant that she was controllable, less of a threat. And everything depended on Hector. Her fate was in his hands, even when he was lying there out of reach in his coma. Hector liked her. Aron knew that. If it hadn't been for the relationship between Sophie and Hector, Aron would have driven her out into the woods and shot her long ago; she was convinced of that.

Sophie was trapped, and would be until Hector woke up. If he woke up . . .

And if he died? Then, in all likelihood, so would she.

Four hours later she was on her way home. Istanbul disappeared beneath her as the plane climbed. The city was vast, stretching out in every direction.

Sophie held her hands tightly clasped together.

She landed at Arlanda Airport in Stockholm, and showed her fake passport at customs. She passed through the arrivals hall, emerged into the cold January air and got into a taxi.

The security arrangements were always the same. She would make great detours to get to wherever she was going. Today was no exception. She changed taxis twice. No one was following her. That was the rule she had to stick to.

Eventually Sophie arrived home at her apartment on Eriksbergsgatan. She and Albert lived there under false names. They had left their villa out in Stocksund a few months earlier. All things considered, that apartment might well be the safest place for them.

He was awake even though it was late, and rolled his wheelchair out into the hall when she came in.

'Hi, Mum.'

'Hello, Albert,' she said.

He didn't ask where she'd been; he never did. A tacit agreement between them. The less he knew, the safer he was.

'I'll make some tea,' he said, and rolled into the kitchen.

She followed him, and sat down on a stool. She hid for a while, pretending to leaf through a newspaper on the counter.

From the corner of her eye, he seemed like he could have been a little boy. But he wasn't. Almost seventeen. A teenager, careful about his appearance, sporty, keen to do all he could to live as normal a life as possible in spite of his spinal injury.

But obviously life was different since he had been run down by a car six months earlier: he had fewer friends, but Anna was still there. Sophie could see the love between them, it was real. That was more than enough for her. But there was something else, too. A sadness that he couldn't handle, that she couldn't handle, that they couldn't talk about.

'Green or black?' he asked.

'Black, please,' she said.

She let it live inside her. Sometimes it grew and swelled up, becoming immense, taking so much space that on a few occasions she had been physically forced to throw up. She knew that nothing could make it disappear. It was always there, firmly anchored in every aspect of her life – her guilt. Because the consequences of her actions were the reason why he was sitting in that wheelchair. Her fault. *Indirectly*, a more kindly disposed person would say. But directly or indirectly, the result was the same when it came to her son.

Her fault . . .

Sophie had been playing a devious game. Imagined she could control the situation. But she couldn't. On one side she had a police officer, Gunilla Strandberg, who wanted her to inform on Hector Guzman, who was on the other side. Sophie had tried to find a path somewhere between the two of them, had tried to do the right thing. But the police were corrupt. There was no right option. It led to Gunilla's gorillas driving into Albert when they tried to kidnap him in order to blackmail Sophie. He broke his back, so high up his spine that he would probably never get out of that wheelchair.

Her fault . . .

Sophie went on leave from her work as a nurse at the hospital to take care of Albert at home. Her guilt and grief went hand in hand, and seemed to grow as time passed. She had figured out that she shouldn't fight it, just let it grow, as part of her. A sick part that had the paralysing power to take control of her entire life at any time.

But it was very different for Albert. To start with, after the accident, she had been amazed at the ease with which he seemed to accept his fate. But that had changed as everything became routine and commonplace. When he realised the consequences of his injury. Old friends who kept their distance and became oddly polite. The loneliness, isolation, the feeling of not being part of things.

She could see how vulnerable he was. And finally the inevitable happened. Despair and grief crashed into his life two months after the accident, becoming large and powerful, terrorising him day and night as he struggled against them in silence. But the battle was unequal and unfair. Albert gave up and surrendered. She wanted to tell him not to give in, to try to hold it all at bay, at a distance. But how

could she tell him? He had to find his own way and deal with this himself. Sophie let him be, and suffered in her own inability to help him. And from having put him in this position.

Her fault . . .

So there she sat, Sophie Brinkmann, with her beloved son, Albert, about to drink tea. Earlier that day she had negotiated a weapons deal, people had been shot around her and she herself had only just escaped with her life . . .

There was no longer any logic to life. Everything was upside down.

The kettle whistled on the stove, and Albert rolled over and lifted it off. The whistling soon stopped.

'Do you feel like a game?' he asked as he poured the steaming water into two large cups.

He meant chess. She always lost.

'Definitely.' She smiled.

2

(BIARRITZ)

HE WAS FAIRLY TALL AND WELL BUILT, WITH THE PARTICULAR LOOK OF SOMEONE who spends his days in the sun. A mixture of lines and wrinkles on his skin, along with an overdose of sun in his eyes – a freshness, a sort of natural joy.

The working day was over and Eduardo Garcia moved along the side of the ship from the bow towards the stern. There he boarded an open boat that was tethered to the larger vessel and pulled on a windbreaker and life jacket. It was January. The daytime temperature was around ten degrees Celsius, but the wind from the sea was hard and biting.

He pulled away and headed at speed over the rolling swell towards the French mainland, and Biarritz.

Eduardo Garcia lived a peaceful life. A life he had consciously chosen.

His real name was Eduardo Guzman, although he had been using his alias for an eternity now. He left Spain and Marbella in his late teens together with his girlfriend, Angela. They set off to France and Biarritz for the surfing. They discovered that they liked it there and settled down. A new life, a new name, a new country.

Now, so many years later, they had two boys and steady jobs. He was a marine biologist, Angela a legal assistant at a small law firm in the city. The only change in the make-up of the family was Hasani,

a stocky Egyptian bodyguard who had knocked on their door six months earlier. Hasani had been sent by Eduardo's father, Adalberto Guzman. Things had kicked off in Stockholm. Eduardo's brother, Hector Guzman, had been run down by a car at a pedestrian crossing in Stockholm by a rival group. That was all Eduardo knew. And he didn't want to know more. He had kept his distance from his father's and brother's affairs.

Eduardo saw his sons on the pier as he approached land, along with Hasani. A comical sight. The big Egyptian, always in a smart jacket, together with the two happy boys with their schoolbags over their shoulders.

Eduardo raised his arm and waved. The boys waved back eagerly. Hasani joined in, but in a more reserved way, as if he understood that Eduardo's wave wasn't meant for him.

Eduardo walked with his sons up through the city, away from the harbour, hand in hand through the streets that took them away from the tourist areas. This was what happened every day, the same routine. The children came to meet him after school, then they went to have something to eat and drink and later got some groceries and went home to prepare the evening meal. Hasani was always a few steps behind them.

The boys suggested the Lord Nelson. They liked the aquarium with its live fish and lobsters. Eduardo said no, he wanted to sit outside, despite the time of year and fairly cool temperature. He often went to the same place, in a small square. There were plenty of people milling about and Eduardo and the boys sat down at one of the outer tables. Hasani sat down two tables away.

When Eduardo beckoned the waiter over and was ordering the usual, two bottles of orange juice and a coffee, his mobile phone rang in his trouser pocket.

'Sí?'

It was Angela, letting him know she was going to be late, that someone was on the way to value the house and that Eduardo would have to let them in.

They'd discussed moving to something larger. Eduardo wanted the valuation. But he also wanted to sit outside the café for a while.

'OK,' he said, and ended the call. He waved to get Hasani's attention.

'Take the boys home and then let the estate agent in; I'll be along soon.'

The boys protested but Eduardo didn't listen. He wanted them to be with Hasani the whole time. Because even if there wasn't any visible threat, he knew Hasani was always a valuable extra precaution.

The boys left with Hasani, heading off across the square. Eduardo watched them go, smiling at their body language, which made it abundantly clear that they thought they were being treated unfairly. He smiled even more when they abruptly forgot the injustice and started chasing each other instead.

The coffee and bottles of juice arrived on a tray. The waiter looked over at the boys.

'Shall I take their drinks back in?'

Eduardo shook his head.

'I'll take them home with me, if that's OK?' he said, then gestured towards a newspaper that was rolled up under the waiter's arm. 'Could I borrow that for a bit?'

Eduardo drank his coffee and skimmed the main headlines, failing to find anything remotely interesting, then turned to the sports pages and checked the football news.

A bicycle was approaching. A multi-gear bike, its wheel making the characteristic ticking sound. Eduardo looked up from the paper. The cyclist stopped just across from him, next to the row of tables closest to the square. The man who got off the bike was short and had a rucksack on his back. He sat down at a free table next to Eduardo and nodded when their eyes met. The man was pale, with cropped hair, and there was something familiar about his eyes . . .

Eduardo smiled at him and went on reading his paper. He found the list of international league tables, scanned it and frowned at Málaga's lack of progress. He didn't want to have to support Barca or Real; for him it was Málaga or nothing.

A gust of wind swept across the square, catching the top edge of the paper and folding it down, fluttering silently.

At the same moment, he heard the ticking sound of the bicycle. Eduardo looked up at the cyclist, who left on his bike and disappeared. Eduardo turned his attention to the paper again.

Then an image forced its way into Eduardo's consciousness, an image of the cyclist. An image telling him that something wasn't right, that something was missing. His gaze moved to the table where the man had just been sitting. What had he seen? Had the man looked smaller when he left? Was something missing? Had he forgotten something? A jacket? No, something else. He leaned over. The rucksack was there under the chair. But it seemed alive somehow. As if Eduardo could see something that wasn't visible, some sort of life inside it that would soon make the rucksack move.

The speed of a feeling is perhaps slightly quicker than the speed of light. So Eduardo had time to feel a nanosecond of gratitude. A brief but warm and intense feeling of gratitude that the hand of God had led his two beloved sons away from the hopeless situation that engulfed him in that instant and blew him to pieces.

The heat from the brutal, intense explosion vaporised everything in the vicinity.

Everything that had previously been Eduardo Garcia vanished into infinite nothingness.

3

(STOCKHOLM)

THE UNDERGROUND TRAIN RUSHED THROUGH THE TUNNEL.

The carriage was half-full of passengers. Most were busy with their mobile phones. A few were talking quietly among themselves. Some were staring into space. A woman a few seats away from Sophie was talking on her phone, conducting a character assassination of a friend in an innocent voice.

Sophie leaned her head against the cold glass.

She wanted to call someone and just talk. About nothing. Just be ordinary. But that was impossible, because she wasn't ordinary.

Sometimes she forced her way back into it. Into being *ordinary*. As if to provide herself with an alibi. Only temporarily, often dinners where ordinary people got drunk, where ordinary men got too close and sought ordinary or not-so-ordinary attention, affirmation perhaps, possibly just love. She could never figure it out.

And no one questioned her right to be or not to be in that world. All the *ordinary* people treated her with a mixture of distance, consideration and exaggerated respect. She, Sophie, the widow with a son in a wheelchair; the label had become her defence. And that was how she wanted it, to protect Albert and herself. Isolated, no close ties, nothing but a shell, impersonal in a personable way – anything to stop people from wondering and asking questions.

At Östermalmstorg she got off and walked through the streets around Stureplan for a while, checking she wasn't being followed.

Then she hailed a taxi and gave the driver an address in the city centre.

As they approached the roundabout at Sergels torg she leaned forward.

'Hang on,' she said. 'I've changed my mind. Can you go around the roundabout twice, then head up Sveavägen towards Frescati?'

The driver glanced at her in the rear-view mirror. 'Sure, lady. No problem.'

Sophie turned around and looked out the rear window. As usual, no one was following her. Sophie faced the front again. She was constantly on her guard.

Outside: traffic, people, cars and an indistinct reflection of herself in the window. Sophie looked away.

The taxi stopped at Kräftriket by some handsome old brick buildings, some of which were attached to the university on the other side of the motorway.

She paid the driver in cash and went into a three-storey building that contained a number of small businesses. She walked up the stone steps to the first floor and opened an unfamiliar door, then walked along the corridor lined with empty, unfurnished offices and a small, glass-walled conference room. She noticed that someone had written some mathematical calculations on the whiteboard in black marker.

At the end of the corridor Sophie opened a door and walked in.

'Sorry I'm late.'

Ernst Lundwall didn't answer; he was concentrating on a sheaf of papers. Leszek was sitting alone on a chair farther away.

'Hello, Leszek,' she said.

He didn't answer either. There was nothing impolite about that; it was just that he never said hello.

She sat down at the table in front of a mobile phone.

Sophie looked at the men. Ernst, Hector's legal and financial adviser, who had an almost unbelievable grasp of the Guzman organisation. He was an awkwardly intelligent person with a pronounced lack of interest in other people.

And Leszek Smialy, Adalberto Guzman's bodyguard for many years. Now at her side as some indeterminate mixture of bodyguard, probation officer and warden.

She looked around the room. She had never been there before, would never go there again. That was always the way with these meetings, which took place regularly once each week. Always in a new location, the details of which she was informed about a few hours in advance.

The phone on the table in front of her vibrated. She waited a couple of seconds before picking it up and answering.

'Yes?'

'*Who else is in the room?*' Aron's voice.

'Leszek and Ernst.'

'*Is the speaker on?*'

She switched the phone to speaker mode and laid it flat on the table. There was a slight hiss, possibly because the reception was bad up in the mountains of southern Spain, where Aron was calling from.

There was a crackle, then Aron's voice again: '*Hector's brother, Eduardo, was murdered yesterday in Biarritz.*'

The room grew darker. *Hector's brother.* She had never met him . . . Eduardo, the marine biologist from Biarritz, she knew that much, married to Angela, two sons . . .

'What happened?' Leszek asked.

'*A bomb in a café.*'

Silence.

'Was it meant for him?' she asked.

'*We assume so.*'

She looked at Ernst and Leszek. Ernst showed no reaction. Leszek, on the other hand, looked grief-stricken, as if all the air had just gone out of him. She was aware that of the three people in the room, he knew Eduardo best. He had sent Hasani to Biarritz on Adalberto's orders to protect Eduardo and his family last year, after Hector had been knocked down at a pedestrian crossing in Stockholm by the Hankes. That had been the starting shot for everything, and led to Hector being admitted to Danderyd Hospital, where Sophie worked, and where they met for the first time.

'And the children? His wife, Angela?' she asked.

'*They're safe. Hasani has moved them.*'

'Who did it?' she asked.

The loudspeaker crackled, then the noise disappeared when Aron's voice came back.

'*The same people who tried to kill us in Istanbul.*'

'Hankes?'

'*Who else?*'

'Why now? Why Eduardo?' Sophie asked.

'*You tell me . . .*' Aron said thoughtfully. Then his voice became clearer and he said, '*Ernst? Skip everything that isn't urgent right now. What's critical?*'

Ernst adjusted his glasses.

'First, Don Ignacio is putting us under pressure again. He wants to expand and is being quite aggressive, asking for Hector. He wants to talk to him in person.'

Ignacio Ramirez, or Don Ignacio as he was usually known. A drug baron from Valle del Cauca in Colombia. An old business acquaintance, principally of Adalberto Guzman, Hector's father. The biggest fish they ever dealt with, by far.

'*What have you told him?*'

'The same as usual: that this is what the agreement looks like, for security reasons.'

'*Does he believe you?*'

'No, and I think we've dragged it out as far as we can now.'

'*What else?*' Aron asked.

Ernst picked up a document and began to talk about other business. To start with, the forged-goods industry in which they invested a lot of money in fake groceries, designer labels and medicine; then people they were trying to extort information from in companies listed on the stock market. About drug smuggling, weapons, about the cold war between their organisation and other factions, about securing their assets and ruining other people's. Acquiring market share, getting rich by any means possible. Murder, blackmail. Striking hard and without mercy against anyone who got too close. Never questioning right and wrong. Just racing at full speed until you hit something without a safety belt. At which point you might be forced to consider things more thoughtfully. Something like that.

Sophie switched off and thought about her own concerns.

She missed Hector. She wondered where he was in his coma.

Could he think? Dream? If he could, she knew he would be missing her, too. She had felt loved by Hector Guzman. Unconditionally. He had raised her up, awoken something inside her. But she hadn't been able to return his love. He had too many hidden sides. And she didn't feel able to love them all. And now his brother was dead. Hector didn't know about that. His whole family, apart from one sister who lived in Madrid, was gone. Her heart ached for him . . .

Aron's voice crackled over the feeble loudspeaker.

'*Sophie? Pick up the phone.*'

She woke up from her thoughts and switched off the speaker-phone function.

'Yes?'

'*How are you, Sophie?*' Aron asked.

The question surprised her, it wasn't like Aron.

'I'm OK.'

He was silent for a moment, then said, '*You did well in Istanbul.*'

'Thanks, Aron,' she said.

Then he reverted to his professional self again. '*I want you to arrange a meeting with Don Ignacio.*'

'What for?'

'*Calm them down. We need them on our side, but we can't expand, not now. Ask them to be patient. Raise the price if you have to. We need time to figure out what's happening to us calmly, so make sure they're calm. It's important that we've got them on our side . . .*'

She wanted to argue, saying that she could not do the things that they asked of her. That she was the wrong person. But it was her lifeline. As long as she filled a function . . .

'Where shall I meet Ramirez?'

'*You'll have to go to them, ask Ernst to arrange it.*'

He sounded stressed.

'Colombia?' she asked.

'*That's where they live.*'

4

[STOCKHOLM]

THE BODY WAS LYING ON ITS STOMACH ON THE PARQUET FLOOR, A KNIFE STICK-ing out from between the shoulder blades. He was naked, or almost naked, except for a pair of white sports socks on his feet.

Detective Inspector Antonia Miller considered the sight in front of her. Almost no blood where the knife had penetrated. And his position? She squatted down and looked at the body from different angles. Had he been stabbed in his bed while he slept? Perhaps he'd woken up and fallen to the floor before finally dying? Unless he was stabbed on the floor . . .

She was blinded by the flash of a camera, followed by several more in quick succession. Forensics was taking for ever to document the scene. Antonia stood up and looked slowly around the room. One picture: Elvis as a bartender, with Dean, Humphrey and Marilyn at the bar. On the other wall, above a chest of drawers, a framed poster behind dirty Plexiglas, a basketball team, lots of stars and stripes, pre-printed autographs – Harlem Globetrotters, 1979.

A pine bookcase containing some old *Dirty Harry* and Charles Bronson films, as well as a few porn films, mostly featuring transvestites.

Antonia read from her small notebook, which was bent from being in her back pocket. The dead man had no name. The owner of the apartment was a woman who apparently had another twelve properties in the city and out in the suburbs. Probably a front.

'I'm done,' the forensic technician said, and left the room.

'Thanks,' she muttered.

The footsteps behind her changed. She turned around.

Her boss, Tommy Jansson, was standing there staring at the body. He had brought the weather inside with him; at least it felt like it, the cold and the melted snow on the shoulders of his black leather jacket.

He had also brought something else with him: his stressed anger, his constant companion.

Tommy pointed behind him with his thumb and whispered irritably, 'This damned street is one-way. I came from the wrong direction and had to park and walk two blocks!'

Tommy stared at Antonia. Perhaps he was expecting a response, a sign of agreement, some display of sympathy. But he got nothing.

'What are you doing here, Tommy?' she asked instead.

It was a good question. He rarely came to crime scenes any more.

'Heard it on the radio, was in the area,' he muttered in reply. He pointed at the corpse. 'Can you take this one, Antonia?'

'Yes, I'm here, aren't I?'

'All the way, I mean,' Tommy said.

'Yes.'

'You're always saying you have too much to do,' he went on.

'No, I'm not,' she said.

Antonia and Tommy left the apartment at the same time. The old lift mechanism creaked as it made its way down to the ground floor.

Antonia Miller and Tommy Jansson in a confined space. They didn't get along. Didn't have much to say to each other as they stood on their own in the creaking lift. Thank God she knew his wife was dying of motor neuron disease.

'How's Monica?'

Tommy's eyes were fixed on the floor, then he looked up and stared at her as if to discern a motive for her question.

'No change.'

His reply was so abrupt that she felt a stab of guilt in her guts.

They reached the ground floor. Tommy slid the internal grille

aside with a rattle. He pushed his way out ahead of her. 'Ladies first' didn't apply when he was in charge.

The snow had turned to hail as they stepped out into Sofiagatan.

'Might see you this evening,' she said.

'Maybe,' he said blankly, then cursed the weather and headed off to the right.

She watched him go, then looked up at the dark, cold sky that was firing small icy bullets at them. Antonia steeled herself and headed out into the grim weather, hurrying to her car and throwing herself into the front seat. The hail got stronger, banging hard against the metal roof. She sat there for a while before turning the key and starting the engine. The heater worked hard to clear the condensation from the inside of the windscreen. Then she drove away, passing Tommy, who was walking quickly along the pavement, close to the walls of the buildings, his hands stuck deep in his jacket pockets, his body language ample evidence that he was suffering.

Antonia didn't even entertain the idea of giving him a lift to his car.

———

HIS FIRST NAME WAS PRONOUNCED LIKE THE MEASURE OF DISTANCE, OR THE first name of an American jazz trumpeter. But his parents didn't have American roots, nor were they particularly fond of jazz. They were diplomats, and thought it was important to have an 'international' first name. The whole Ingmarsson family were diplomats, and had been for generations. They all had un-Swedish names, like John, Catherine, Sandy, Ted, Sam, Molly. Miles's younger brother was called Ian, and had named his own children Sally and Jack. A pervasive Scandinavian Kennedy complex ran through the entire family: success, white summer houses, yachts, ambitious side-partings, always on the ball and the fantastic ability never to show the world around them a hint of what was going on inside them. They demonstrated a form of surface tension where cocktail conversation and other banal talk about nothing held their lives in check.

Miles had also been a diplomat. But he had been lost in that world right from the outset. He understood nothing of the collective social rules that everyone else seemed so comfortable with.

His career ended up going backwards. He started high, then clambered quickly but surely downwards. From the embassy in Ankara, to Skopje in Macedonia, then Chisinau in Moldova, before ending up in Khartoum in Sudan, where his post was so vague that no one really knew what it involved.

His family tried to give him advice about the future. Miles couldn't bear it. Changing career was his only escape, and he applied for a job as far away from the Foreign Office and Diplomatic Service as he could imagine: the police.

His family stopped talking to him. Their disappointment was immense, as was his feeling of liberation.

Miles Ingmarsson was now forty-five, wiry and in pretty good shape, thanks to his habit of doing sit-ups and push-ups before going to bed. He had dark hair with streaks of grey, his face and eyes reminiscent of an old-style film star. But the way he looked was mostly overshadowed by his posture, which was weighed down by an invisible sadness that not even Freud would have understood, and certainly not Miles himself.

He had a serious addiction to strippers. It was only around them that he was able to relax. The warmth exuded by feminine company, just being allowed to look for a while – breasts, curves, the essence of femininity . . . It wasn't about sex. More a sort of warped compulsion for security that he had never managed to find anywhere else. And God knows he had tried – everywhere and everything. Alcohol, hash, food, exercise, gambling. Nothing worked as well as striptease. He went to the strip club five times a week, all year round.

Now he was sitting there at a table in a dark corner, staring at a thin woman with silicone breasts as she performed a pole dance to cheap, electronic, eastern European music. She was very bad at it. He felt like telling her she didn't have to dance, that she could forget all that and just stand there, maybe just move a bit . . .

His mobile phone vibrated in his jacket pocket.

'Yes?'

Tommy Jansson from National Crime wanted to know what he was doing.

'I'm having lunch,' Miles replied.

'Do you want to come and work for me?'

The woman spun around the freshly polished pole far too fast and with very little balance.

'OK,' Miles said as he continued to watch the entertainment.

There was always a moment of shame involved in leaving a strip club in broad daylight. Seven seconds of what it took to open the door, step outside, close the door again and walk off, soaking up the looks on the faces of anyone nearby: *a perv.*

Miles pushed through the snow that had been falling heavily all morning. Now it was lying there, shoved up onto the pavements for pedestrians to kill themselves on, so motorists could pass unimpeded.

Keeping close to the walls, he fished a cigarette out of his pocket, stuck the filter tip between his lips and lit it with his Zippo. He sucked the smoke in as he walked, allowing it to burn holes in his lungs before letting it out again. Then two quick, deep drags, one after the other, to calm the craving and give him a destructive sense of pleasure.

He had spent the past few years in the Economic Crime unit, where he investigated uninteresting cases that rarely led anywhere. Which was fine: he never had to feel involved.

But now Tommy Jansson had called. Tommy wanted to meet, Tommy wanted a chat. There was a 'blue-light' evening at that pub in the Klara district in the city centre where all the cops hung out. And tonight there'd be ambulance staff and firemen as well. They all met up and drank themselves senseless in the middle of the week. Miles had been a few times, didn't like it. The paramedics were retarded, the firemen either stupid or gay – or both. And his *colleagues*, as a certain type of cop insisted on calling other officers, were so far removed from Miles's sensibilities that he felt nauseous in their company. But Tommy wanted to meet there, and he was going to offer Miles a new job. It was probably time to move on. Miles had a feeling that he was dying a little bit with each passing day. And he'd had that feeling for a very long time.

———

The smell of sweat, cheesy pop music from the '70s, flat beer on tap and lighting that was far too bright – the prerequisites for a blue-light evening. Miles made his way through the sea of people.

Tommy was sitting farther in at a table with some other senior officers. That corner was reserved for them, the top cops. Occasionally an ignorant newcomer would wander over and sit down there, and it always ended in deep embarrassment. Everyone there wanted to show that they knew the rules. Lots of booing and shouting.

Tommy held up his right hand when he saw Miles. Ingmarsson sat down and gestured for a beer. They plodded through the social crap, which went quickly, seeing as they were both completely hopeless at it. Then Tommy got to the point.

'Do you want to take over a murder investigation?'

'Which one?'

'Trasten.'

'Trasten?' Miles asked.

'The restaurant in Vasastan. The gangster shootout last summer. When Hector Guzman fled the country,' Tommy explained.

Miles nodded. No one could have missed that one.

An honest-to-God bloodbath in Vasastan six months earlier, at the Trasten restaurant. Four dead. Three killed in the restaurant, Russian gangsters. Two shot and killed in the restaurant, one tortured to death in the kitchen. The police also found parts of a dismembered body in the freezer. This turned out to be a harmless local petty criminal, Leif Rydbäck. Not long after that, the lead investigator, Gunilla Strandberg, was murdered by one of her colleagues, Lars Vinge. A really screwed-up story. The newspapers wallowed in theories and the questions just kept piling up, even within the investigation. The police were casting about; they had nothing to go on, seeing as the central character, a hitherto unknown major-league criminal, Hector Guzman, a Spaniard based in Stockholm, had vanished from the face of the earth after the shootout.

'Why?' Miles asked.

'Because I need a different detective.'

'Why me?'

'Because you've been around a while, you know the ropes,' Tommy said.

'No, I don't.'

'Yes, you do.'

'What's the catch?' Miles asked.

'No catch, I just want to replace the current detective with you.'

'What's the catch?' Miles asked again.

'Don't be so fucking critical of yourself. We've got a lot going on, you can get a promotion. And I need her elsewhere.'

'Her?'

'Miller, Antonia Miller.'

Antonia Miller. She was good, according to what he'd heard.

'When?'

'Soon,' Tommy said, taking a deep swig from his glass of beer.

'I'm in the middle of a load of cases at Eco,' Miles said. 'I can't leave the others in the lurch; not now.'

Tommy stifled a hiccup.

''Course you can. They're all a bunch of damned socialists up there, the whole lot of them. I'm pulling you out of there.'

Their paths had crossed now and then over the years. They were half friends, you could probably say. They hadn't met for a while, and Miles thought Tommy seemed different somehow, more acerbic.

'What about Miller?'

'Don't worry about her,' Tommy said gruffly.

A waiter appeared with a sloppily poured beer and put it on the table, spilling some in the process.

Miles took a gulp of his, while Tommy took three deep swigs.

'Do you want another one?' Tommy asked.

Miles shook his head. Tommy belched.

———

ANTONIA WAS STANDING A SHORT DISTANCE AWAY AT THE BAR. SHE SAW TOMMY and another man but didn't think too much about it. She and Tommy saw each other pretty much every day, worked together and argued about all manner of things. That was how it should be. Tommy was her boss. But their relationship was wrecked, for some reason. He'd changed in the past few months, with mood swings – a very short fuse, caustic and arrogant. He was micromanaging her, getting in the way of her work. And he reeked of a hangover pretty much the whole time. Probably because of the stress of living with a wife with

a fatal disease. Even so, Antonia was sick to death of trying to adapt to his bad qualities. Not that she could deny that she had some of her own. It was obvious Tommy thought she was a nuisance, a lot of people thought that. That she was trouble, too eager, too pushy. What was she supposed to do about that? Give in and back down?

Antonia had grown up in a loving home. That was how she remembered it anyway. But in that love there had also been a fear of the truth. Lots of whispering and hushing when she approached adults having a conversation. Maybe her parents were just scared that so-called reality was too cold and raw for her gentle little ears. In itself it didn't actually matter. What did matter was that because of the whispering that surrounded her when she was growing up, she had developed an almost obsessive need to know things. Whatever it was, she needed answers in order to carry on living and breathing.

And she had found many answers over the years. That had accelerated her career, and she was recognised as a good detective. But Tommy had started to whisper when she approached. And she wanted to know why.

She looked at the men over in the corner again. The dark-haired one stood up, shook hands with Tommy and left the table. He walked in her direction, and they looked at each other as he passed. She recognised him: he worked for Economic Crime. One of the thousands of disillusioned men she had seen coming and going. What marked him out from the crowd was the way he dressed. Jeans, black oxfords, a smart shirt under an expensive lambswool sweater. A thin beige coat over his arm. There was something tiresomely stylish about him . . .

Antonia looked around among the police officers, firemen and ambulance staff, looking for Ulf in the crowd. Ulf was the only reason she had come. He was a brawny surveillance officer from Ludvika, in the backwater of Dalarna, taciturn but decent. She didn't find gym-trained cops attractive. But what she did find attractive was that he was so focused about sex, was kinky in an unthreatening way and kept his mouth shut, and he was kind, deep down.

She caught sight of him, and their eyes met. They had a drink together, with nothing to talk about. Then they took a taxi back to his tidy two-room apartment in Sundbyberg, with scented candles in the bathroom.

5

(VALLE DEL CAUCA/STOCKHOLM)

SOPHIE WALKED OUT INTO THE ARRIVALS HALL WITH ITS ROW OF CAR-RENTAL
desks. She presented her reservation at the correct desk and was
soon sitting behind the wheel, heading towards the city of Cartago,
southwest of Pereira.

The window was open, heat was flooding in and her sunglasses
allowed her eyes to relax in the bright daylight.

This was a routine job, like all the other trips she had made over
the past six months. She was going to calm people down and re-
assure them that everything was under control. She was good at it;
it had become something of a talent.

She wondered if she was going to see Alfonse, was seeing him
in her mind's eye. Alfonse Ramirez, Don Ignacio's nephew. He had
been at Trasten . . .

Six months before, late summer. She and her boyfriend, Jens, had
been pursued through the centre of Stockholm by Russians he had
sold weapons to. The Russians were wired and violent. They wanted
their money back, and they wanted to kill him. They fled in a car
but had nowhere to go. She had called Hector: he was in a business
meeting at the Trasten restaurant in Vasastan. Ernst Lundwall, Hec-
tor's adviser, was there, Alfonse Ramirez was there and the restau-
rant's owner, Carlos Fuentes, was there. She and Jens arrived. The
Russians showed up, waving their guns, and they beat Jens until he
was more dead than alive. They were about to start shooting when

Mikhail Asmarov and Klaus Köhler burst in and opened fire on them, saving the lives of Sophie, Jens, Hector and the others.

Blood, brain tissue, gunpowder smoke and silence. Those were her clearest memories as she lay on the floor with Hector on top of her, protecting her. Then Alfonse Ramirez's bloodlust when he managed to persuade the two men not to shoot the gang's leader, the vile Dmitry. Alfonse and Hector had finished him off in the kitchen, and took their time over it. Alfonse Ramirez was beaming like the sun when he emerged.

Sophie and Hector fled in his private jet to Málaga, and drove off towards Marbella, where Hector's father lived. The restaurant's owner, Carlos Fuentes, then snitched to Hector's nemesis, the German magnate Ralph Hanke. Hanke's men caught up with them on the motorway and shot Hector, causing him to slip into a coma.

Her memories were crystal clear.

Sophie took her sunglasses off, she needed light.

A church bell was chiming three o'clock in the afternoon when she parked the car in the little square in the centre of the city. She had been told to wait there for a taxi. She barely had time to think about it before it came driving up along the narrow street.

The driver didn't speak to her, just drove around the city looking in his rear-view mirror, then he made a call on his mobile, muttered something and hung up.

After a while he stopped on a busy street outside a restaurant and gestured to her to go in. She did as she was told, and inside the door a man took her gently by the arm and led her between the tables, through a kitchen and out through another door into an empty back street. Another taxi was waiting for her there, its back door open, and she slid in, the door closed and the taxi drove off. It went on like that. Sophie switched cars three times before she found herself sitting in a silver Cadillac that sped her along a motorway at high speed.

A pickup with wooden crates on the back was passing her window, anxious chickens clambering on top of one another in the crates in a fruitless and impossible attempt to break out.

She was struck by a sudden sense of unease, a premonition that she shouldn't be there.

The Cadillac turned off the motorway and headed into a forest. The trees were spread out and sunlight filtered through the foliage.

They came to a security lodge and a barrier across the road. A thin man with an automatic rifle over his shoulder came out, raised his hand in greeting and lifted the barrier. The Cadillac drove in. She noticed a camouflaged sniper on a small hill among the trees. He was lying on the ground, tracking the car she was in with his gun.

They emerged from the forest, where the road improved and eventually wound its way up towards a cream-coloured little castle with pillars, statues, fountains and lush rectangular lawns.

The driver opened Sophie's door and she got out. The view was immense. Dense, verdant vegetation below her, as far as the eye could see. Mountains in the distance, and a heavy, moist heat weighing everything down.

A dark-haired man in grey trousers and a white shirt came towards her from the entrance.

'Sophie?' he said.

They exchanged a firm handshake. Ignacio Ramirez was faceless in an inexplicable way, impossible to describe. The smile on his lips looked genuine, but there was something different about his eyes, something false, perhaps. His black hair was dyed, his skin pallid and the stomach bulging under the white shirt bore witness to indolence and a bad diet.

'Come,' he said, gesturing away from the building with his hand.

Don Ignacio invited her to sit in an electric golf cart, then drove off through the grounds, pointing and explaining things as they went. They passed a compound containing a solitary giraffe that stood there staring at nothing in the company of a few zebras and two hippopotamuses. The animals looked thoroughly depressed. Tennis courts, a swimming pool with a waterfall, a helipad with a helicopter on it. Armed guards everywhere.

She watched him from the corner of her eye as he proudly steered the electric cart through his pale imitation of Disneyland. It was soulless and empty. Full of a negative energy that was so strong she could almost smell it. And in that energy was something that reminded her again that she shouldn't be there, to get away, run. This place was dangerous, it could make you sick, it was infectious.

———

They were sitting in a large living room. Stone walls, pale-grey granite, large thick windows, all held together by solid pale wood. The sofas were wide, deep, expensive. The room was reminiscent of a North American hunting lodge; they could have been in an exclusive ski-resort. Sophie was sitting on the edge of one of the deep sofas, Don Ignacio on an armchair.

A waiter in a white jacket and black trousers came in with drinks and nibbles, put them down on the table and discreetly left the room.

Don Ignacio reached for the glass bowl of nuts.

'We'll wait for a while,' he said, and began eating the nuts.

A door opened at the far end of the room. Sophie saw Alfonse Ramirez walking slowly across the floor towards her. His smile was radiant white, his skin light brown, his hair black. He threw most of the world into shade, he was that sort of person: *all lights on me!*

'We know each other,' he said to her, keeping his huge smile intact.

No, they didn't, they didn't know each other at all, apart from the fact that she had been present at Trasten when he beat one of the Russians to death in a state of genuine joy.

She stood up and Alfonse gave her the customary double kiss on both cheeks, then sat down in the corner of the sofa and threw his hands out.

The men in front of her were neither friends nor enemies. They were longtime business partners of Hector's organisation, and they paid more to Don Ignacio than they earned from selling his drugs. That was the way it was for everyone who did business with him. If you wanted out, you died.

'Stockholm,' Alfonse said. 'That's where things happen!' Then he chuckled and let his laughter fade away before switching his expression from delight to empathy.

'How is Hector?'

'He's fine.'

Alfonse nodded. 'Good to hear. I've been worried. My uncle, too.'

Alfonse gestured towards Don Ignacio, who didn't look particularly worried. His blank look suggested that he considered everything apart from himself to be of a definitely secondary nature, and entirely unnecessary.

'And now you're here, Sophie,' Alfonse said.

She took his words to mean that she should explain why she had come, but Alfonse held up his hand to her.

'Now you're here,' he repeated. 'To reassure us, to tell us that everything is as it should be. Perhaps you're going to ask for more time, perhaps tell us a tale of how you're up and running again, that our dealings will soon be back in action.'

She turned cold and had an immediate sense that this was heading in a direction that she couldn't control, and with which she wasn't at all comfortable.

His attitude was different now.

'But we know everything,' he went on. 'We know you've approached a lot of Hector's business contacts, have reassured them that it is business as usual, under control, that Hector is in hiding but is working at full capacity. That's what you've been saying. You've asked for time and understanding, you've promised even greater successes once things have calmed down and returned to normal. That's been your task, and you have done it well.'

She smiled in an attempt to play it cool and tried to object, but Alfonse Ramirez raised his forefinger.

'But perhaps Hector Guzman is dead? Or so badly wounded that he can't speak for himself? Perhaps Aron is struggling to keep your little enterprise afloat? Am I on the right track?'

Alfonse fell silent. Don Ignacio went on eating the nuts, slower now, one at a time, as if the first handfuls had sated his hunger.

She tried again.

'You're painting a rather unhappy picture.' She smiled. 'But it isn't true. Everything is carrying on the same as usual, even if Hector has to stay in hiding. There's a warrant out for him, and we aren't taking any risks . . .'

Ignacio and Alfonse stared blankly at her. Ignacio said, 'Hector's brother, Eduardo Garcia, died tragically in Biarritz a couple of days ago.'

The room grew darker. How could they know that? The urge to flee was getting stronger. But she remained seated, holding the sofa with her hands, trying to keep steady.

Alfonse continued in a monotone. 'Someone wants something of you, someone wants to say something.'

He looked at her with his ice-blue eyes.

'You must have someone in mind, Sophie?' he went on.

'It doesn't matter,' she said. Her voice caught, and she cleared her throat quietly.

Alfonse smiled.

'Don't be scared. Who?'

'There are several possibilities. Hector has a lot of enemies.'

'But the most likely?'

She gave up.

'The Germans,' she said.

'The Hankes?'

An almost imperceptible nod from Sophie.

'What is the story with Hector and Ralph Hanke?' Alfonse asked.

'I think you know, Alfonse. Why do you ask me?'

'Please tell us,' Don Ignacio said.

Everything felt very scripted, each one knew when the other should take over.

'It started innocently with competitive bids on a legal construction project in Brussels between Ralph Hanke and Hector's father, Adalberto Guzman. It escalated beyond everyone's control and took an upturn, when one of Ralph's men did a hit and run in Stockholm, where Hector was hurt and hospitalised. Adalberto and Hector answered shortly after by attacking Ralph's son Christian Hanke. Everything went wrong. Christian's girlfriend died . . .'

'And in the end?' Don Ignacio asked.

In the end . . .

Sophie was sucked back to the events on the motorway between Málaga and Marbella, six months earlier. Two people on a motorcycle chased her and Hector. They shot straight into the car. Hector was injured, went into a coma. It was a planned assault, Adalberto was murdered in his home in the same moment.

'In the end,' she said. 'They killed Adalberto Guzman.'

'So they won, didn't they, the Hankes?' Don Ignacio leaned back.

She didn't even shrug, just sat there and waited.

'What is going on, Sophie, why the Hankes now? If you're just guessing?' he continued.

'There's something they want,' she said.

He raised his eyebrows.

'"*There's something they want*,"' he repeated theatrically, crossing one leg over the other.

Sophie noticed his low black shoes, worn and dirty, the socks that were too short, a length of pale shin exposed.

'What do they want?' he went on. Now he sounded like a schoolteacher trying to elicit a prepared answer.

'Everything, they want everything, I guess.'

Ignacio clapped his hands in a short round of applause.

'Yes,' he said, as if she had given the right answer. 'They want everything.'

Ignacio leaned forward and whispered, 'Now listen carefully, woman . . . We helped the Hankes to find Eduardo Garcia in Biarritz.'

The cold that washed over her cut into her.

'And I understand that you only just escaped with your lives in Istanbul the other week?' he went on.

She realised she was staring at Don Ignacio. He acknowledged her stare with a look of amusement.

He scratched the corner of his mouth with three fingers, still staring. 'Do you understand what we're saying? Do you understand the process of this conversation, the language? Can you appreciate what we're saying? Is the picture clear to you?'

'Istanbul?' she whispered.

Ignacio nodded.

'Istanbul,' he said thoughtfully. 'You were lucky there. It was you and Aron, wasn't it?'

'What do you mean, lucky? Were you involved?'

Ignacio shrugged.

'Not involved, but aware. We knew the plan.'

'What plan?'

'The Hankes have been looking for you, just as you have been looking for them. That was their best chance.'

She made it clear that she didn't understand.

Ignacio scratched the back of his neck.

'They were in control of the whole situation, right from the start,' he said, in a voice almost devoid of emotion.

'But we set up the deal, found Basir. The whole thing was arranged in absolute secrecy, only a few of us knew anything about it . . .'

'They have their tentacles everywhere,' he said.

She was trying to understand.

'And the purpose?'

'I don't know. They probably wanted to get Aron. But it didn't turn out that way . . .'

' "Get"?'

'Yes.'

'And me?' she asked.

'You?' Ignacio wondered with amusement.

'I'm sitting here. What are you going to do with me?'

He pondered for a moment, then laughed.

'Good question . . . The Hankes obviously have a goal behind all this, they want to get rid of Hector and seize control of everything he's got, and we're helping them with that.'

He coughed, then went on. 'Now, take this back home and explain it sensibly to Aron or whoever's making the decisions now. Come back with a constructive proposal that includes total capitulation. That's what you need to do.'

Ignacio Ramirez stood up, and Alfonse followed suit. They left the room.

The world outside the window of the plane was pale blue to start with, endless and cold. Then it became dark and closed.

Ignacio was working with the Hankes, they had killed Hector's brother, Eduardo, wanted to get rid of Hector. And she was supposed to persuade Aron to fall to his knees and surrender everything they had. Which was never going to happen. Aron would fight to his dying breath; he was like that, down to his very marrow.

People would die.

She had to find another way, somehow.

6

(SONORA, MEXICO)

JENS STOOD UP IN THE CARGO HOLD OF AN OLD RUSSIAN ANTONOV AN-12 THAT was cruising west at an altitude of 8,000 metres.

The plane, around fifty years old, was being driven forward by four roaring Soviet turboprop engines. The noise level in the hold was unbearable.

In the good old days the Communists had managed to squeeze one hundred angry and fully equipped paratroopers into a machine like this. Now there was only Jens. He, and four crates of stolen goods lashed to the middle of the floor.

The crates belonged to an American Special Forces unit that had helped itself to some of the assets of the Ba'ath Party leadership during the first wave of the ground invasion of Iraq in 2003. Mostly gold and jewellery, art, museum artefacts, drugs, weapons and an awful lot of cash. Everything had been packed up and buried in the desert east of Baghdad. Years had passed, the war had ended and the time had come to dig up the treasure and get it out of the country. Jens had been contacted, and was given the job. He had gone to Baghdad, slinking around under constant fear of car bombs, and transferred the crates from one war to another: Afghanistan. There they had been buried once more. And more years had passed.

A month ago he received a call. The Special Forces unit had finished fighting, and wanted the goods back in the USA: *Take the goods to Mexico, we'll get them into the States from there.*

A lamp flashed on the wall of the cargo hold. The pilots wanted something. Jens made his way to the cockpit.

The captain and co-pilot were Georgian. Taciturn, proud and constantly smoking hand-rolled cigarettes.

'We'll be landing in forty minutes,' the captain said. 'Then we'll have four hours to unload, refuel. Then we leave.'

The Georgians would be heading home. Final destination: Batumi, on the Black Sea. Jens was going with them. He might get off somewhere en route, he didn't know yet. That was what his life was like, constantly on the move, a compulsive urge to keep going, to keep working, tempt fate, experience new things. But it wasn't as good as it used to be. He no longer gained the same satisfaction from it. The excitement didn't give him the same rush, and the life he had chosen as a smuggler had started to seem repetitive, uninteresting, even dull.

It shouldn't be like that. But that was how it felt, which made him feel rather sad. What was he going to do after this? Nothing could match the life he had lived over the past twenty years.

The co-pilot offered him a roll-up. Jens took it, even though he'd given up a while back. He lit the cigarette with the co-pilot's gold lighter, then slid into the glazed nose section.

It was pitch-black outside and the cigarette tasted of hay and caught angrily in his throat. The plane was lurching in the wind, the roar of the engines rose and fell, the panelling rattled and clattered and the rivets creaked. But Jens was used to it, and trusted in God and a bit of goodwill to hold the plane together.

They had left Dushanbe two days before, crossing Turkmenistan and Turkey, then following a southwesterly arc across Africa, flying the last stretch on fumes before refuelling and spending the night in western Algeria. Then an unsteady and turbulent flight across the Atlantic to Central America.

It was solid night outside. Jens rolled with the pitch of the plane and tried to see any landmarks but could make out nothing but the weak flash of the plane's navigation lights and clouds drifting past.

Eventually they approached the ground with all lights extinguished. He could see a few lights on the ground below them, but otherwise everything was dark. That was good. They were arriving

without clearance – the plan was to come down on a landing strip without being noticed, then take off again.

The wheels unfolded from the body of the plane. There was a creaking, banging sound before they locked into position. The increased air resistance was noticeable as the machine forced its way forward with its engines roaring at top speed.

Jens could see the contours of the ground, mountains on either side etched against the dark sky, narrow roads, trees, small villages. Occasionally a few houses clustered together, vanishing quickly beneath him. The Mexican countryside, nothing more, nothing less.

The ground levelled out and the co-pilot opened the flaps to maximum. The air resistance increased still further and the plane seemed to just hang in mid-air. There was a makeshift barely lit landing strip beneath them. The Antonov tilted forward slightly. Suddenly it dived thirty metres and then levelled out again. The noise of the engines disappeared as the co-pilot eased off the acceleration. They hovered silently for a few seconds before the wheels hit the ground. There was a hard thud, then another brief, soundless period of flight before another thud, then gravity kicked in and held the plane to the ground. The machine raced across the uneven surface and the roaring sound came back as the pilot reversed the engines and the plane braked in a cloud of sand and dust. They came to a halt, slightly askew, and the engines were switched off. Silence, except for a whining tinnitus sound in Jens's head.

When the plane came to a halt, Jens crept out of the nose. The co-pilot was already standing by the loading ramp, and he pressed a button on the side of the plane. The entire rear section of the plane opened up like a massive jaw.

The air that streamed in was warm, soft and dry.

Mexico, he'd never been to Mexico before . . .

The headlights of three vehicles approached along the landing strip. He glanced at his watch. The Americans were clearly early. Time to get going. Jens and the co-pilot loosened the straps from the large crates.

The vehicles stopped abruptly below the ramp. A gang of armed Mexicans in modern military uniform stormed into the plane. The co-pilot was hit first. Before he could come up with anything practical, Jens was struck on the cheek by the butt of a rifle, then again on the side of the head and collapsed.

7

(STOCKHOLM)

LESZEK WAS DRIVING. SOPHIE WAS SITTING BESIDE HIM IN THE PASSENGER seat. They were heading out of Arlanda Airport, towards Stockholm. He was clutching a mobile phone to his ear.

'I've just picked her up,' he said.

Sophie heard Aron's voice crackle quietly in Leszek's ear.

Would she lie to them now? . . . Or would she tell the truth? How Hanke and Ramirez collaborated to unreservedly force Hector down on his knees, once and for all.

Either way, truth or lie, the consequences would be enormous, in both directions. The truth would lead to prolonged violence and death, a scorched-earth strategy. The lie, on the other hand, would lead to more lies, procrastination and her loneliness and powerlessness. Because who would she have on her side if she chose the lie? No one, absolutely no one. She'd be all alone.

Leszek angled the phone towards her.

'Off you go,' he told her.

Sophie watched the road ahead. Travelling fast to an unknown future.

'Sophie?' Leszek said.

She looked at him.

Did she even have a choice?

The lie . . .

'As expected,' she said in a slightly louder voice than usual.

Aron said something, and Leszek repeated it to Sophie: 'What do they want?'

'For us to expand.'

Three people in the same conversation. Two speaking, one acting as a go-between. Aron thought that led to fewer misunderstandings.

'And what did you reply?' Leszek asked Sophie.

'That we'll hold back on that,' she replied.

'Did they accept that?'

'Yes.'

Aron asked Leszek a question.

'Just like that?' Leszek asked Sophie.

She nodded. 'Yes.'

'The price?'

'The same.'

Aron's voice from the tiny speaker, Leszek mediating: 'Why?'

'We got on well,' she lied.

Leszek listened, then asked Sophie a question: 'Are they calm?'

'Yes, I think so,' she lied once more, looking out the side window.

Out-of-focus fir trees flashed past.

'Anything else?' Leszek asked.

'No,' she whispered.

Leszek and Aron exchanged a few quiet sentences, then Leszek ended the call and concentrated on driving down the motorway.

She sat there, staring at nothing, trying to maintain the relaxed air she hoped she was exuding. She would have to think twice about everything she said from now on.

'Angela and the children are on their way here with Hasani,' Leszek said. 'They're going to stay with Daphne and Thierry until we know what's going on.'

Sophie saw a train running parallel to them, racing along the rails at the same speed as the car.

Leszek's tone changed. 'Tomorrow?' he asked.

At first she didn't understand the question.

'Your schedule?' he clarified.

Her schedule, of course, the never-ending fucking schedule.

It was a daily routine with Leszek, the daily schedule, her schedule. The intrusive system of surveillance that he never let up on,

which was utterly incompatible with any sort of private life. It was all about what she was going to do, where she was going to be and when, whom she was going to meet, and so on. Sometimes more general, sometimes tiresomely detailed. Every step she took was mapped and controlled by him. He made spot checks. Leszek could show up anywhere without warning, could suddenly call and check where she was and ask her to go to a location close to where she had said she would be.

It was stressful, but she had got used to it and didn't complain. She never complained.

Sophie kept her eyes on the world outside, nudging aside some hair that had fallen across her forehead.

'Home in the morning,' she said in a monotone. 'Laundry, then driving Albert to his exercise class in the afternoon. Out to Daphne and Thierry, meet Angela and the boys.'

Sophie avoided herself in the mirror, focusing instead on her shoes until the lift stopped at her floor.

From the hall she could hear laughter from the living room. She put her bag down on the floor and went in.

Albert was sitting on the sofa with Anna on his lap. She was facing him, cooing, talking and giggling as he tickled her. She stroked his hair and they kissed.

Anna felt Sophie's presence and quickly got off Albert's lap. The two youngsters tried to stifle a sense of embarrassment. Sophie laughed at Anna's peculiar posture as she stood there in the middle of the floor, not knowing where to go, and at the panicked smile that Albert often adopted whenever he felt uncomfortable.

'Hello,' Anna said with forced cheeriness to hide how awkward she felt.

Sophie chuckled, then went over and hugged first Anna, then Albert.

She unpacked in her room, leaving the fake passport and her three phones in her handbag. Three phones, three numbers. One general phone for Sophie Brinkmann, open to everyone. The

second had a number known only to a few people, mainly Leszek and Aron. The third was a simpler model, with ordinary buttons, a small screen and no fancy features. She had been given that one by Jens. It hadn't rung in six months, but she carried it with her wherever she went. It lay there quietly in her handbag, fulfilling no function other than a sort of vague hope that it might one day make a noise. She looked at it every now and then.

Jens had gone away without saying goodbye, he just left, sending a bland text message. The days had turned into weeks, the weeks into months. She wanted to think he was weak, that he had let her down, but she couldn't. She just wished that bastard phone would ring.

Sophie showered, changed into jogging trousers and a blue tennis top, then went into the kitchen. In the pantry she stared at the never-ending supply of home-made blackberry juice.

She poured some in the bottom of a glass, filled it with ice from the ice maker in the fridge door, then topped it up with water.

Albert and Anna were laughing again in the living room.

On the kitchen counter she prepared a pie crust. She pressed the crumbly dough into an ovenproof dish, forcing it up the sides.

Her options ran through her head . . . Ruin Hector's remaining businesses so there was nothing left for the Hankes to take? Could she do that? No . . . Talk to Leszek? Would he understand? No . . . Try to talk some sense into them? But who? . . . Contact all the groups she had visited over the past six months and persuade them to hand themselves over to the Hankes and Ignacio? . . . No.

There were no options.

Sophie started to cut some apples into pieces. Albert had liked apple pie as a child. These days it wasn't as delicious. But she clung to it so she could still feel like a mother.

8

(MÁLAGA PROVINCE)

THE RAZOR SLID THROUGH THE WHITE SHAVING FOAM ON HECTOR GUZMAN'S cheek, gently, with a practised gesture, before moving on to the skin between his nose and top lip. The process was accompanied by the wheezing sound of the respirator, the subdued bleeping of the heart monitor, the sinusoidal curve showing his ECG, and the drip that was slowly running through the rubber tube to the needle attached to the back of his right hand.

The moment Hector had slipped into his coma, security arrangements kicked in. He was moved in secret to this farm in the mountains, hooked up to machines and looked after day and night by a nurse, Raimunda.

She was sitting there now on the edge of the bed as she finished shaving him, and she wiped his face, first with a warm, damp flannel, then with a dry towel. Then she rubbed some moisturising cream into his cheeks and neck.

Farther away in the large room Sonya sat on a sofa reading a book. Sonya Alizadeh, always at Hector's side, like a sister to him. She was Iranian; her parents had been business partners of Hector's father, and they had been murdered in Switzerland when she was young. Adalberto Guzman took her under his wing and she grew up as part of Hector's family in Marbella.

On the floor by her feet lay Hector's father's old dog, Piño.

Aron was leaning over the large mahogany dining table.

The atmosphere in the room was tranquil. They were waiting, just as they had been for six months.

The entire table was covered with notes and scraps of paper taped into place, complete with Aron's personal annotations. This was how he liked to work. It was all about their business, their partners, enemies, costs, expenses, profits . . . He was like an officer in a bunker, trying to develop a strategy and stick to it, doing all he could to hold Hector's empire together even though it was gradually disintegrating. But one thing was more important than everything else: the Hankes. He had paid agents out there. They were searching and hunting, then reported back. They were looking for Ralph Hanke and the traitor, Carlos Fuentes . . . the bastard who had told the Hankes where Hector was after the incident at Trasten. That bastard was the reason Hector was in his current state. Aron was going to kill Carlos. He had promised himself that, and had whispered it in Hector's ear more than once. Aron was convinced Hector had heard him, deep down where a little flame of consciousness was flickering. And that gave him strength.

Aron knew that the Hankes were doing the same thing, trying to find them. And they had managed to lure him into the open with that deal in Istanbul. Aron cursed himself for that. Now everyone was dug in on both sides, aware of what would happen if they showed themselves. After the shootout in Marbella when Adalberto Guzman was killed and Hector wounded, things had been quiet. Nothing on the radar. Then suddenly a bleep. A faint echo of someone or something. Almost invisible. They would check – usually it was nothing. But Istanbul . . . Aron and Sophie had walked straight into the trap. That mustn't happen again.

There was an acid shower installed above the table, in the form of three showerheads fastened together. If anyone approached, or if their cover was blown, Aron would only need to back three metres away from the table, pull the little chain and a thin cloud of tiny acid crystals would obliterate everything.

He examined his two-dimensional world, leaning on the table with both hands. He usually stood like that. Building up images, planning, trying to understand.

Don Ignacio. A longtime business partner. A rapacious business partner. Unreasonable, dictatorial, insane. A drug baron who had

oppressed Hector's organisation for years, sucking money from it. Impossible to negotiate with, impossible to walk away from . . .

Why did he back down?

Aron turned to Sonya.

'Why did he back down?' he asked her.

Sonya didn't answer. She was used to him asking questions without actually wanting an answer.

'Sonya?'

She looked up from her book. 'What?'

'What's he like?' Aron asked.

'Who?'

'Ignacio.'

'You've met him yourself.'

'Towards women?'

'What do you mean?' she asked, putting the open book down beside her.

'What's he like towards women?' Sonya wasn't following him. Aron went on: 'Men behave differently towards women, don't they? Some flirt, some do other things. Maybe some don't even care at all?'

'You're very narrow in your analysis of relationships, Aron,' she said with a smile.

He threw up his hands in irritation.

Sonya thought about the question for a few seconds. 'Which one of those categories does Ignacio Ramirez fit into?'

'Yes.'

'He doesn't care at all,' she said.

'How do you mean?'

'He isn't interested. Feminine wiles don't work on him. Some men are like that, believe it or not.'

She went back to her book.

Sonya's words took root in Aron's head. *He doesn't care at all.* But Hector did, at least when it came to Sophie Brinkmann. He had cared as much as it was possible to care, all the way. Hector had fallen in love with her. And consequently had become less cautious.

What had she said? What had happened at Don Ignacio's that had made the Colombians so calmly stop demanding more? Because that was what they always did; it was in their nature. And if it wasn't

48

possible to charm Don Ignacio, why would he let Sophie go home with a guarantee that everything could simply carry on as usual?

After all, that wasn't why he had sent her there; he could never have dreamed that it would have gone as well as that. He had sent Sophie to show Don Ignacio and Alfonse that they were listening to their demands. And Aron had been counting on the fact that she would come home a wet rag, roughed-up and dejected, to pass on a list of mad and unacceptable criteria for their ongoing collaboration. Because that was how Don Ignacio worked. That was how he did business. Always, without exception. But not this time, evidently. *Why?*

His mind was whirring; there was no clear structure.

The table again. The whole of his universe was laid out there. Aron was stiff with concentration, trying to reason with himself.

And suddenly, out of nowhere, a different thought forced its way in. Purer, clearer. Less opaque, easier to understand: *Sophie.*

A beeping sound from one of the machines by Hector's bed interrupted Aron's thoughts.

Raimunda flew up from her chair and hurried over. Aron stared. Sonya stared.

Raimunda examined the machine.

'What is it?' Aron asked impatiently.

She didn't answer, but lifted Hector's eyelid.

'Raimunda!' he said sharply.

She turned around.

'I don't know. It might be a sign,' she said.

'A sign of what?'

'That he might be with us.'

9

(STOCKHOLM)

THE BOYS SITTING ON THE SOFA ON EITHER SIDE OF THEIR MOTHER LOOKED SAD.
Their mother was also sad, but she seemed to have run out of tears.

Sophie was sitting opposite them, perched on the edge of the seat of an armchair. She looked at the elder of Eduardo and Angela's sons, the seven-year-old, Andres. The boy was picking at his fingers. The younger one, Fabien, was shut off, clinging to his mother, unwilling to look at Sophie or anything else in this strange new world.

They were sitting in the living room of Daphne and Thierry's villa, out in the suburbs to the south of Stockholm. Hasani was sitting on his own on a chair over in the corner. He was quiet and relaxed, his gaze focused slightly below everything, as if that were his way of keeping his senses alert the whole time. *If you don't look at anything, you see everything.*

Daphne came in carrying a tray with a carafe of juice and some glasses. She put it down on the coffee table and served the boys first, then Angela, and Sophie last.

'Have you got everything you need?' Sophie asked.

Angela made an effort to smile. 'We're staying in the basement. Daphne and Thierry are giving us everything we could ask for.'

Sophie looked at the devastated family: the boys seemed somehow hollow, empty and alone in their grief.

Sophie gave Daphne a look she understood.

Daphne went over to the boys and spoke to them in French: 'Come with me, I'll show you the workshop. Thierry's got all sorts of funny things in there.'

Andres looked at his mother, who indicated that it was OK. He took Fabien by the hand and the boys got off the sofa. Hasani stood up from his chair and followed them and Daphne out into the garage.

Angela's smile faded. She was pale and brittle. Nothing could be controlled; the world was a lethal place. That much was clear from her eyes.

'Is Hector alive?' she asked.

'Yes.'

'Where is he?'

'I don't know,' Sophie said. A lie that didn't make any difference.

'It's his fault,' Angela said.

Sophie said nothing.

'If it wasn't for Hector, Eduardo would still be alive. We picked France and Biarritz to get away from all this.'

Angela was struggling to control her feelings, but they slipped out anyway.

'I almost felt relieved when I heard Adalberto had died,' she said. 'Not because I'd wish that on anyone, he was Eduardo's father, after all, my father-in-law – but it lowered the risk for us. Do you understand what I mean?'

Angela looked weighed down by guilt.

'Yes, I understand,' Sophie said.

They could hear laughter from Daphne and one of the boys out in the workshop.

'Who did it? Who killed Eduardo?'

'I don't know.' Lying came automatically now.

Keys in the lock of the front door, a door opening and closing.

Thierry appeared in the living room. He always had the same cheerful expression on his face. He was holding a bag of groceries in each hand.

'Hi,' he said. 'Daphne and the boys?'

'In the garage,' Sophie said.

He looked at the two women, and perhaps he noticed the sombre mood.

'Come with me,' he said. 'Help me prepare dinner.'

The three of them stood in the kitchen. There was a lot of food, all of it vegetarian. Thierry gave them instructions on how to prepare it all. Halfway through the chopping and slicing Daphne and the boys came back, with Hasani following behind them. The boys were happier, and they sat down at the kitchen table together and were given something to drink and crayons and paper to draw on.

Daphne and Thierry. Smugglers in Hector's organisation who used the cover of a shop in Stockholm that sold ethnic artefacts. They were currently a dormant resource, now that everything had ground to a halt in Hector's absence. They seemed to be enjoying it, living the quiet life in the suburbs for a while.

Daphne kissed Thierry on the cheek and helped a bit with the food but mostly stood close to Thierry making small talk. They were always like that. Sophie watched them discreetly. They appeared to be naturally in love, whatever that meant.

Everyone ate dinner together at the kitchen table in silence. It wasn't oppressive, the silence among them, just no one felt any need to talk. Hasani picked at his vegetables, and the boys noted his reluctance. When he tentatively asked if there was any meat, the atmosphere lightened and they started laughing. Angela got up and fried a piece of steak for Hasani. A quiet, hesitant conversation developed, and soon they were all chatting. Everyone but Sophie. She kept her distance, reluctant to get too close.

But the atmosphere around the table affected her nonetheless, and she couldn't help seeing the boys' temporary happiness, Angela's smile, Daphne and Thierry's warmth and Hasani and his fondness for meat. They were all individuals who wanted nothing more from that moment than to feel a bit of human camaraderie.

But she knew something they didn't know: she knew who had killed the boys' father. She also knew that she couldn't tell anyone, because the consequences would be uncontrollable. She saw it all the time: Aron's progress, the risk-taking, the proximity of violence . . . And that was how everything would develop. Aron would fight to

the last. Leszek would follow him. That was just the way it was. Predetermined, decided by fate . . .

Andres and Fabien were laughing so hard now that they almost spat their food out.

Sophie looked at the boys, unaffected by their laughter. Just as she was considering giving up everything, something began to grow in her mind. The germ of an idea. The last of all ideas, the one that really shouldn't be there. The people around the table laughed, and the thought inside her pleaded and begged to be allowed to live, if only for a short while.

Sophie ate, trying to ignore the idea. But it was impossible. The idea grew too strong, taking clearer shape, assuming a face.

Ralph Hanke's.

10

(BERLIN)

LOTHAR TIEDEMANN WAS RINSING VEGETABLES UNDER THE KITCHEN TAP. HIS mother, Franka, was working at the kitchen table. She usually sat there, counting and sorting. She was clever and smart, and he felt a natural pride in her.

He turned the tap off, then began to chop the vegetables for a salad. The window to the courtyard was open. Down below, children were playing football, a neighbour was beating one of her carpets and over on the playground there was a moped constantly revving its engine in a sand pit.

They spent a lot of time together, Lothar and Franka. Mainly because they enjoyed it, but also because Lothar didn't have any brothers or sisters, or a father. Franka's face was always radiant, and she seemed happy and grateful about something that he, at seventeen, never quite understood. They didn't live anywhere particularly nice, one of Berlin's southern suburbs. She worked as an accountant, and saw to it that he always had everything he needed, even if it meant her going short. They didn't have much money. But she was always smiling, as if she took pleasure in the simple fact of living. She was naturally beautiful, with her long blond hair. Men occasionally courted her, but she wasn't interested. Perhaps she thought she had everything she could wish for, and a new man didn't seem to be part of that.

She made a joke. She was always making jokes. Lothar was about

to turn towards her when he suddenly saw a man standing in the kitchen. A short man in dark clothes, with a shaved head. He was pale, and his eyes were small and close together.

'Lothar?' the man asked.

Lothar looked uncomprehendingly at his mother, then back to the man, nodding automatically when he heard his name.

The man raised a pistol fitted with a silencer and fired a shot. The weapon made a puffing sound, and Franka Tiedemann was left with a hole in her forehead.

The paralysing effect of shock left Lothar immobile. The man took a few steps forward and pressed the silencer to Lothar's forehead. With the other hand he drove a hypodermic needle into Lothar's arm and injected him with the contents. His legs gave way instantly and Lothar collapsed to the floor, unconscious.

The man sat down on a chair next to Franka's body and waited patiently. His name was Koen de Graaf, and he was twenty-nine years old. His lack of height and the somewhat compressed nature of his face was due to his mother's persistent consumption of alcohol and heroin during pregnancy. His pale looks were genetic.

Koen looked at Lothar as he lay on the floor. To begin with, he had doubted that the boy really existed. It had started as a rumour. Ralph Hanke had searched half the known universe in his hunt for any sign that could tell him if Hector Guzman was alive or not. Koen was his right-hand man in that enterprise. And two months ago one of their sources told them he had heard about the possible existence of an illegitimate child that Hector was said to have fathered. It sounded too good to be true.

Hector Guzman's son . . .

Two men came into the apartment, each carrying a large wooden box. They cleaned up the kitchen, lifted Franka's body into one of the boxes and put Lothar in the other one.

Koen checked the apartment one last time, then they carried the boxes down the stairs and loaded them into a waiting van.

They drove several hours on the Autobahn, then turned off at an isolated rest area. The two men pulled out the box containing Franka Tiedemann's dead body, took a couple of shovels and headed off into the dark forest. Koen went to the rest area's public toilet.

He sat down with his feet on the toilet lid. The room stank of

urine and excrement, the lamp in the ceiling was feeble. He worked quickly. The rubber tube round his upper arm, the syringe already prepared. He found a vein, pulled the plunger back slightly and drew out a little of his own blood. Whoosh – blood and heroin in a beautiful, pale-red mixture. Then into his system with the whole thing. He counted backwards from twenty before untying the tubing and letting the syringe fall to the floor. The heroin had kicked in properly by the time he got to four. Koen made his way out and back to the van, managed to get in the cab and leaned back.

The other two men returned and they drove off.

The headlights of the oncoming traffic formed a soundless symphony. Koen drifted south along the Autobahn, with beautiful music playing in his veins.

11

(SONORA)

THE SUN WAS BLAZING FROM ITS ZENITH. HE WAS LYING IMMOBILE ON HIS back, vultures circling high above in the blinding sky. His throat made a whistling sound as he breathed, his skin was sunburned, painfully tight.

Jens turned his head and saw an infinity of flat, hard-packed sand, stones and in the distance . . . mountains etched softly against the hard blue sky. With an effort he managed to raise his head . . . Everywhere, stony nothingness.

They had left him there, whoever they were, to die in the middle of the desert. They hadn't even been willing to spare him a bullet. Would he have preferred that? A bullet in the head instead of this? No, he never wanted a bullet in the head. But this was fucking awful.

Jens tried to stand up, but it was as if he were stuck in quicksand. He gave up and rested his head on the hot ground again. His body temperature kept on rising. He shut his eyes and drifted through fevered dreams, hallucinating, coming to once more and realising the extent of his predicament with a little more clarity . . . This time he really was beaten.

Fear of death hit him hard and without mercy. Now he *did* just want a bullet to the head. He felt affronted at having to lie there, didn't want to die in emotionless darkness. Jens wanted light, begged for it. And it came to him in small doses, in the form of images and smells. Mum and Dad, his family and childhood. Fragments, things

that had evidently meant something . . . the smell of English tea, sleeping between clean sheets, freshly cut grass . . . And in the midst of all that warmth, Sophie Brinkmann's face appeared . . . She was close, he wanted to reach out and touch her . . . feel her. But Jens couldn't reach her. Maybe he never had. They had met one summer when they were young. A genuine infatuation. It scared him, he didn't know what to do with it. He left her without a word and just disappeared. The years passed, but Jens never forgot her. They bumped into each other by chance last year . . . She was in a hopeless position, caught between helping the police and helping Hector Guzman. Jens helped her out. They grew close again. But that closeness scared him. The closer he got to her, the harder it became. And Jens ran away, the way he always did.

The vision of Sophie vanished, taking everything else with her . . . Only Jens was left. *Alone* . . .

The paradox was striking. He had worked single-mindedly to look after himself all his life, to be free from having to rely on anyone else . . . But now he didn't want to be independent, he didn't want to be alone, not now.

Night came, and with it biting cold. It cut into him. He would freeze to death if he stayed there.

With an immense effort he managed to stand up on unsteady legs and stumble forward through the dead landscape. The night sky was clear, the Milky Way was lit up above him. He followed it, shivering, arms wrapped around himself, knowing he was going to die.

12

(STOCKHOLM)

ANTONIA COULD FEEL HERSELF SMILING. NOT A HAPPY SMILE, BUT AN EMOTIONally misleading smile that hid her disappointment.

'I don't understand. This is a bad idea . . .'

Tommy rocked back on his desk chair, his arms folded across his chest.

'Well, this is what's going to happen,' he said.

'Why?'

'Because that's what we do sometimes, reallocate work, reorganise.' Tommy stopped rocking. 'You've got four murder investigations, Antonia. That's too much, even for you. So I'm taking one of them away from you. There's nothing odd about that.'

'Why Trasten, why not the latest one, Blomberg? Or one of the old ones?'

'Because you can make a difference to the Blomberg case. It might even get to clearance. And we need clearances.'

'The Trasten case is closed.'

Tommy stroked his moustache out of habit.

'Not in this lifetime.'

'Why do you say that, Tommy?'

'Because I do.'

She didn't have time to respond.

'I have to consider the statistics,' he continued. 'And the statistics

from Trasten are bad. The investigation isn't going anywhere. And the more time passes, the harder it gets.'

'I don't believe that,' Antonia said.

He didn't answer.

'Who's taking over?'

Tommy put his hands on the desk. The first sign that the conversation was approaching its conclusion.

'Miles Ingmarsson,' he replied.

So that was his name, she remembered. The introvert from the Economic Crime unit.

'Why him?'

Tommy searched for something on his desk. 'Why you, why me, why anyone? This isn't about the individual.'

'What is it about, then?'

'It's about who's available.'

'There are hundreds of others, hundreds better than he is.'

Tommy kept pretending to look for something among his papers.

'Not available,' he said.

'I'm available.'

'Good,' he said dismissively, and made a move to stand up.

She was unwilling to let it go.

'Just one question,' she said.

Tommy waited.

'Ingmarsson. Is it because he's good, or because someone has to investigate Trasten even though you don't think it's going to lead anywhere?'

He had to think through her question one more time.

'That's not what I said,' he replied.

'Yes, you did.'

She saw him lose his thread. He started acting superior again.

'Do you know what, Antonia? Stop arguing. This isn't some fucking trade union where you and I are supposed to reach some sort of compromise. I'm the one who makes the decision, and me alone. I'm your boss and we investigate murders. You can either do as I say or look for a new job. Your choice.'

Tommy wiped his mouth, then went on: 'Right, time to start the weekend.'

A fake smile, a sigh and Tommy stood up.

Antonia spun around on her office chair, biting one of her fingernails. Tommy was a damned idiot. She hated having to act subordinate, especially when something was obviously completely wrong . . . and aimed directly at her. Antonia felt like breaking something. But she held back and waited until her colleagues went home for the day. She wasn't finished with the Trasten investigation yet.

The office was deserted when she put the two Trasten murder investigation files on the desk in front of her. There were masses of papers, documents, photographs. She lifted them out, lining the edges up with the palms of her hands so they were neat.

Then she went over to the photocopier and switched the big white machine on. A fan started up, and the machine sounded odd, as if something inside was loose, trying to find its place. She waited patiently until it calmed down and the lights on the control panel were all glowing evenly.

Antonia made a copy of the entire investigation. The machine swallowed up her documents and spat them out again just as quickly.

The plans of the Trasten restaurant, statements, forensic medical reports, ballistic evaluations. Pictures of the Russians found dead in the restaurant. Information about Leif Rydbäck, a Swedish repeat offender whose body parts were found frozen in the restaurant kitchen, many of them already processed through the mincing machine. A passport photograph of Hector Guzman, who in all likelihood had been in the restaurant when the murders took place. Plenty of witnesses who weren't witnesses, because no one had seen anything. Records of bullets from weapons that didn't exist, fingerprints from people who didn't exist, DNA samples that didn't belong to anyone. But Antonia, as the detective on the scene after the shootings, had found Anders Ask and Hasse Berglund there, chained to a radiator in the restaurant's office. At first she didn't know who they were, and managed to ask them some quick questions. Berglund showed her his police ID, and Anders Ask claimed he was working freelance, and that they were watching Hector Guzman, who had been in the restaurant but had since vanished.

Then a short report appeared from the copier, an excerpt of an interview she herself had conducted with a nurse who had got to know Hector when he was a patient at Danderyd Hospital: Sophie Brinkmann. The woman hadn't had anything to say. Her son was in a wheelchair, she was a widow, she was reserved . . .

More details were spat out into the photocopier tray, all circumstantial, without any real foundation. That was what the investigation was like. She skimmed the pages, interpreting them, trying to read between the lines, trying in vain to see something that wasn't there.

More pages kept coming steadily. It was hypnotic. Antonia thought she could hear distant sounds. Cries from the other side. Voices that wanted to be heard, and laid to rest.

The photocopier stopped and just sat there gasping for breath until the fan fell silent and it died altogether.

Antonia picked up the bundles, put the originals back in their files, placed the copies in a plastic bag that she stuffed into her handbag and left police headquarters.

TIME SEEMED TO WEIGH HEAVILY ON HIM THESE DAYS. IT WAS SO HEAVY AND unmanageable he could never ignore it. If he did, it felt like he was suffocating. So the only thing Tommy could do was rush away from it. And rushing away from time was something you did by constantly keeping busy, keeping on the move.

Tommy Jansson sat in his car, parked on the road in front of his terraced house with his engine switched off. The air in the car was warm and dry and full of problems.

He left the car, walked the few steps up to the door.

The hall with its fabric-texture wallpaper. Tommy hung his leather jacket up on a hook in spite of Monica's endless nagging to use a hanger. He slipped into the bathroom.

His bulging stomach had got bigger, he couldn't see *it* when he peed any more. *Young Mr Jansson*, he had always called it. Back when he and Monica were able to make jokes, *Jansson's Tempta-*

tion. And they used to have fun, most of the time, it was the glue that held them together. A sort of affectionate humour with a lot of warmth and lightness that acted as a backdrop for their shared, if tacit, conviction that life was actually difficult – dangerous, even. But the backdrop had collapsed when Monica's illness was diagnosed. The humour and warmth disappeared. All that was left was confusion, gloom and a large portion of bitterness.

Monica was sitting in the kitchen, being strong and ill. He hated her I'm-strong-and-positive charade. Tommy couldn't bear it, just as little as he could bear her illness.

She did crosswords, drank coffee, tried to do normal things. But her right hand no longer obeyed her, her speech was becoming slurred and she couldn't walk without the help of crutches, although she refused to use the walker the nursing aide had given her.

'Hi, Tommy.'

Her pronunciation was thick and heavy. She was smiling, but only with half her mouth. It tore at his heart – he loved her so much.

He filled a mug with coffee and sat down at the kitchen table, talked about nothing, drank the coffee, helped her with her crossword without actually being any help. Then she said his name in that soft, pleading way. *Tommy.* An attempt to sound loving, with the implicit plea, *Please, Tommy, listen to me.*

And he knew what was coming. Practical things he ought to know about when she could no longer do them, and later, when she died. She had figured out what he needed to do in various situations, like buying food, the budget for the girls' clothes, their menstrual cycles, contact with their teachers. It was a long list. He couldn't deal with that sort of thing, and he stood up.

'Where are you going?' She gave him a beseeching look.

He didn't answer as he made his usual escape to the basement.

Tommy sat down at the little desk in the workshop, fished a quarter bottle of transparent alcohol from a drawer and struggled to swallow a few swigs. The horrible taste of gin. He put the bottle back and pulled a folder out of the same drawer.

Bank withdrawals from accounts held with banks based in shady regimes. Two in western Africa, one in the Middle East. Expensive as hell, but hidden and safe from tax. The amounts were large, and unreal.

Six months earlier, in a apartment on Södermalm, Tommy was with two colleagues, Gunilla Strandberg and Lars Vinge. Tommy had shot them both. Vinge hadn't been much of a problem; he was a wretched little man, a nobody who'd run himself into the ground. The 'suicide shot' to his temple had felt almost like an act of mercy. Gunilla had been worse. A friend, a colleague, an ally. She was the one who had paid in the money that had been in those accounts. Gunilla had been corrupt for years. Together with her brother Erik, she had embezzled money from the cases they worked on. Tommy had had no idea. He had been tipped off by Lars Vinge, who wanted justice and some advantage to his career in exchange for the revelation. The old Tommy had thought that sounded reasonable. But Gunilla approached him with a counter-offer . . . He should have dismissed it as the solid, honest cop he had always been. The new Tommy was born there and then, when he realised that the money she was offering him could change things, primarily Monica's illness.

And when the new Tommy was born, the old one died. It happened fast. And the new Tommy started to think. It had been unavoidable; they would never have been able to share the spoils. He knew her, he knew his new self. The appeal of a new arrangement seldom lasted very long.

It wasn't about the money, more about fear, his own warped fear. He had realised it with the passage of time. His fear of Monica disappearing. What the hell was he going to do without her? Who would look after him when he got old? Who would make sure the girls didn't marry idiots? Who the hell was going to do the cooking? And buy his clothes? Who was going to be sociable when people came over? Who was he going to talk to after work so he didn't find himself in an eternity of silence? Monica was his lifeline, in every conceivable sense.

So when he found out about the money, he saw his chance. The pair of them, Gunilla and Lars Vinge, died in Lars's apartment, and Tommy made it look like a personal dispute: Vinge shot Gunilla, then himself. He took the money she had accumulated over the years, and set about his mission at once. Tommy contacted researchers and specialist doctors in the USA, France, Japan . . . everywhere people were conducting research into motor neuron disease. They all said the same thing: no medication, no cure. But financial help would at

least speed up the eventual discovery of drugs that could delay the illness, and at best find an actual cure. Tommy took this on board and began the laborious task of withdrawing all the millions from the bank accounts and sending them anonymously to organisations all over the world. His working life was now constructed around his frantic efforts to plug any holes that might end up linking him to the murders of Gunilla Strandberg and Lars Vinge.

Tommy leaned forward and stared at the amounts on the bank statements. There wasn't much left now. Half a million kronor in cash buried out in the garden behind the shed. One and a half million in Africa, just over a million in the Middle East. And those banks had negative interest rates. They charged for hiding the money. The rate was based upon an index of dictatorships. The fewer dictatorships there were in the world, the higher the negative interest was, more or less. And the interest was mounting. Soon the money would all be gone . . .

Tommy could feel a slight pressure on his chest and took shallow breaths, rubbing his face with his hands, letting his palms cover his eyes like blinkers. Darkness. He breathed slowly and the darkness was dark, fucking dark. Was this where Monica was heading?

There was a knocking sound on the ceiling. Monica's crutch on the floor up above. She needed help to get to the bathroom.

13

(STOCKHOLM)

THE WOMAN'S BACKSIDE WAS AT EYE LEVEL. THE G-STRING WAS BARELY VIS-
ible. She was holding the pole with her right hand and leaning forward. Their eyes met, upside down. Miles Ingmarsson looked away.

There were only three other men there, spread out around the room with as much distance between them as possible. He recognised a couple of them, but recognition wasn't encouraged. Total anonymity was the aim.

The girl on the shiny pole was named Sanna. She was new, thirty-something, older than the other girls, different. He wasn't sure in what way – the way she moved, perhaps, or her manner? Her long legs, maybe? No, it was something else, something he couldn't put his finger on. She wasn't the type, she shouldn't be there.

The woman unsettled him, and strippers didn't usually have that effect on him. But this one was different.

Miles looked at Sanna, her cropped blond hair, red lips, milk-white skin . . . There was an underlying sense of joy in her, the world was evidently a decent place . . .

His phone vibrated in his jacket, and Miles swallowed and answered.

'Yep.'

'*Hi, Ingmarsson.*'

It was Tommy again. He knew exactly when to call.

'Hi, Tommy.'

'How's it going?'

'Oh, OK.'

'What does that mean?'

'No idea.'

Tommy coughed into Miles's ear.

'What are you doing?' he asked.

'Having lunch,' Miles replied.

'Where?'

The signal kept coming and going, Miles guessed Tommy was in his car, on a hands-free device.

'City centre.'

'Is it good?'

'What?'

'Your lunch. Is it good?'

'Yes, I suppose so.'

A loud car horn. Presumably from the traffic around him.

'What are you having?'

'What am I having?'

'Yes, what are you having?'

Miles laughed. 'You ask some odd questions, Tommy.'

'There's nothing odd about asking what you're eating, is there? What's so odd about that?'

Sanna was squatting down, legs wide apart, and was sucking on her thumb for far too long, in and out, in and out.

'No, I suppose it isn't.'

'So?'

'Pasta,' Miles lied.

'Pasta. That's good, Ingmarsson.'

'Yes.'

'Is it à la striptease?'

'Sorry?'

'No, no sorrys. Is pasta à la striptease on the menu?'

It was as humiliating as being kicked between the legs. Ingmarsson wiped under his nose.

'You could say that,' he mumbled.

'Do you think I care?'

'No, I don't.'

'That's right. But others might.'

Sanna was on her back, thrusting her crotch towards the ceiling, her black thigh-high boots reflecting the lights.

'*So lie low, Ingmarsson.*'

'That's what I'm doing,' Miles said.

'*No, you're not.*'

He didn't quite follow.

'*You've asked for things . . . You've requested material from the archive.*'

'Doesn't anyone working on an investigation do that? I need to gather all the available material before I can get to work . . .'

Sanna raised her backside and her underwear came off.

'*Forget it.*'

'Forget what?'

'*Everything. Forget about the investigation.*'

Her underwear was spinning around her forefinger, slowly and beautifully. In his head he could hear the sound of rotor blades from some old Vietnam film, *whop, whop, whop*. Then she let go. They sailed off into the darkness. Miles watched them.

'What?'

'*Just sit there and pretend to work, don't make any effort.*'

'Why?'

'*Because I say so. Gunilla and Erik Strandberg were investigating Hector Guzman, as you know. Which led to the shootout at Trasten. But they buggered the whole thing up. If you make any progress, you'll be tarnishing their memory; that's pretty much it. I don't want that. They were good friends, and good police officers.*'

Sanna was squatting down in the middle of the stage, legs wide apart again, showing Ingmarsson absolutely everything.

'*Cops protect cops, don't they?*' A pause. Tommy Jansson cleared his throat. It didn't quite work. His voice sounded gravelly when he spoke again: '*Besides, who the fuck cares, Ingmarsson? Three dead Russian gangsters . . .*'

A sharp cough from Tommy, this time it worked.

'*And Hector Guzman,*' he said. '*some Spanish mafioso who's fled the country or is burning in hell. What more could we ask? In my opinion, our citizens are safe and the case was concluded a long time ago; it concluded itself. There's no point wasting resources and a load of taxpayers' money on this. If you get me?*'

No, Miles didn't get him. 'What are you saying, Tommy?'

'*Go through the motions. Come up with something, I don't know what, but remember that you're a police officer, Ingmarsson. A police officer who goes to porn clubs day after day after day. How the fuck do you think that looks?*'

Miles just squeezed the bridge of his nose between his thumb and forefinger and shut his eyes.

'*Especially now all the lunatics in this country have gone and become feminists. You'd be hung out to dry. Unless . . .*'

Tommy left a dramatic pause.

'Unless what?' Miles asked. He still had his eyes closed.

'*We're cops, Ingmarsson. I protect you, you lie low. We help each other, old-fashioned cops' honour, OK?*'

Miles didn't answer.

'*Good, Ingmarsson, that's more like it,*' Tommy said, and ended the call.

Miles opened his eyes and sat there with his phone in his hand, feeling depressed. '*Cops' honour*' – *what the hell?* He put his mobile back in his jacket pocket. This wasn't how he remembered Tommy Jansson. But people changed, presumably. Tommy had been friends with the Strandberg siblings, Gunilla and Erik, good friends, Miles knew that. So Tommy must have his reasons – he had implied as much when he gave him the job. Miles had realised at once that there was something funny about it, because why else would he have been given a murder investigation? There were a million better cops than him, eagerly sitting and waiting for an offer like that.

Well . . .

The choice was fairly easy. He realised he could just as easily sit on his backside at Violent Crime drinking bad coffee as sit on his backside at Eco and listen as his older colleagues falsified and exaggerated stories about some golden age of policing that had never existed.

And perhaps there was something in what Tommy said. Cops protect cops. And Ingmarsson wasn't about to stop going to strip clubs to look at Sanna, not a chance . . .

Sanna?

Miles woke from his reflections to find that he was alone in the room. The old men had gone, the show was over. He looked towards

the stage and was blinded by a sharp spotlight. Miles squinted and put his hand horizontally above his eyes. *Sanna . . .*

She was just standing there in the middle of the stage, her left hand on her hip, wearing those thigh-high black boots, otherwise naked in the sight of Ingmarsson and God.

'Finished for today,' she said. Her dialect was from the north of Sweden, beautiful, good, kind . . .

Ingmarsson stared at her, and now he saw her more clearly, the line of her jaw, her mouth, her eyes . . . Everything was beautiful individually, fantastic in combination, divine as a whole.

After a magical eternity she broke into a little smile, turned around and left the small stage in a way that would make any man fall to his knees and beg for mercy.

IT WAS PAST LUNCHTIME. ANTONIA WAS STANDING IN THE LIFT AS IT RACED downwards. Her mobile rang.

'Yes?'

'*Antonia Miller?*' a male voice asked.

'Yes.'

'*Reuterswärd, Security Police.*'

She dug around in her pocket for a cough drop.

'Hello, Security Police,' she said.

She found one and popped it in her mouth.

'*You're investigating the Conny Blomberg murder?*'

'Yes.'

The cough drop clicked against her teeth.

'*In line with our protocols, I wanted to get in touch to say that we've been keeping an eye on him over the years.*'

The lift doors opened and Antonia got out.

'Tell me.'

'*His case is no longer classified now that he's dead, so if you need any of our material, get in touch.*'

The sun was shining as she emerged onto the street.

'Why do you have material on him?'

'*We shouldn't have, really. But he was involved with people we were interested in, so he fell under our surveillance automatically.*'

He was deemed to be of low-grade interest, but he's been in our system ever since. This was a long time ago.'

'What do you know about him? Conny Blomberg?'

Antonia was walking along the pavement, the lunchtime rush going on around her.

'According to his file, Conny was a promising footballer in Norr-köping in the '80s. He landed himself with a knee injury and kids at the same time. He started drinking and smoking dope, then bailed out when he realised he couldn't look after his family, pretty much. He left the provincial idyll and came up to Stockholm, partied hard and quickly ended up in the wrong company. Was put away a few times for minor offences, then his crimes got more serious, as did the punishments.'

A brief silence.

'He liked hash and transvestites,' Reuterswärd concluded.

'Who doesn't?' Antonia said drily.

Reuterswärd didn't share her humour. 'Well, anyway, I'll send over what we've got, it might help you make a start.'

'I have to ask something,' Antonia said.

'Yes?'

'Are you always this considerate?'

'How do you mean?'

'I've never heard of the Security Police calling us to volunteer their material.'

Reuterswärd lowered his voice slightly.

'Well, it does happen,' he said.

'But?'

'But that's not why I called. It's mostly that ,there's a peculiar coincidence.'

'What?' she asked, growing tired of talking to him.

'Sometime last year, towards the end of the summer, if I remember rightly, a former colleague called me here at the Security Police. Anders Ask. He asked about one of the members of that gang, Leffe Rydbäck.'

Her world stopped. Ask . . . Rydbäck. She knew those names. Rydbäck slaughtered. And Anders Ask, who worked for Gunilla and later committed suicide . . .

'And?' she asked.

'It was Rydbäck you found cut up in pieces at Trasten, wasn't it?'

'Yes, that's right.' Antonia tried to sound indifferent.

'That's not really a coincidence, but I just thought you should know. That's mainly why I called. An interesting quirk of fate, perhaps. After all, he and Conny were in the same gang.'

'What did Anders Ask say to you when he called, why was he asking about Rydbäck?'

'He didn't specifically ask about Rydbäck. He asked about someone else in the same gang, someone we'd been trying to pin down a few years before. A man named Håkan Zivkovic.'

HÅKAN ZIVKOVIC'S OFFICE WAS IN A BASEMENT ON LUNTMAKARGATAN. HE RAN a security business.

Dark '70s wooden panelling on the walls, green wall-to-wall carpet. A dead cactus on top of a metal filing cabinet. And Zivkovic himself, sitting at a walnut-laminated desk. On the wall behind him there was a picture of Sitting Bull. WE WILL NEVER FORGET YOU was printed beneath it in ornate silver writing. Above the old Indian chieftain an unleashed bull flew across the sky.

Håkan Zivkovic gestured towards a visitor's chair from the '90s, chrome with a woven seat. She sat down, asked about Conny Blomberg and watched the man in front of her. Deep-set eyes in a coarse, angular face with a solarium tan. A *Top Gun* haircut, streaked with grey. His arms one size too big for his T-shirt, bulging muscles.

'We used to meet in prison, Conny and me, every so often,' Håkan said. 'The first time was in '89. When we got out last time, we did a bit of work together. I set up this security business, he did a few small jobs for me, then it just sort of dwindled away, you could say.'

Håkan Zivkovic should have looked big and tough. But instead he made a rather cretinous impression. Possibly because of his weak chin, or the suspicious but stupid way his eyes kept looking for a threat that wasn't there. Perhaps it was simply the smell. He smelled of fabric softener.

'Leffe Rydbäck?' she asked.

'What about him?'

Antonia waited coolly. Håkan tried to match her coolness, but she noticed that his eyes continued to dart around.

'What do you mean? He died six months ago. Murdered, chopped up, everyone knows that, it was in the papers.'

'Who killed him?'

'Why are you asking me?' Now he sounded like a child who had been accused of something.

'Why not, Håkan?'

He didn't answer.

'Was it Anders Ask?' she went on.

It was as if he blinked without actually blinking, then he touched his nose with his finger and pretended to think.

'No, I don't recognise the name.'

He was a hopeless actor.

'Are you sure?'

'Yes.'

'Might Leffe ever have mentioned that name?'

He looked at her with exaggerated steadiness. 'No, I don't think so, I'd have remembered that.'

'Why? Why would you have remembered?'

'Anders Ask, it's an unusual name.'

She laughed. 'Anders is an unusual name?'

His face began to twitch.

'No.'

She allowed a few moments of silence to torment him a bit more, and it worked. He almost looked mournful.

'But?' she said.

'Together . . . "Anders" and "Ask", that's the sort of thing you remember.'

Antonia laughed again. 'You're very funny.'

He tried to smile back.

'I heard that Anders Ask contacted you last autumn,' she went on.

'I don't know anything about that,' he said.

She smiled. 'Yes, you do, Håkan.'

'No, I said.'

'Are you nervous, Håkan?'

'What do you mean?'

Antonia softened her voice. 'I don't mean you any harm, I just want answers.'

He bit his cheek. 'You're a cop, and you're asking weird questions. I don't like that.'

It didn't sound very convincing. She looked at him hard. Håkan Zivkovic looked pretty pathetic sitting there. Not that it mattered at all. What mattered was his utter inability to hide the fact that he knew what she was talking about.

'Anyway, they're all dead,' she said. 'So why the hell are we sitting here talking about them?'

She waited a few moments.

'Are you on the side of the Indians?' she eventually said.

Zivkovic didn't follow her. Antonia nodded towards Sitting Bull. He turned around and looked at the picture. 'Obviously.'

'Why?'

'The white men took their land!' There was conviction in his voice.

They parted with a handshake. It hurt.

Antonia spent the rest of the day in her office, pretending to work. When her colleagues walked past down the drab corridor at five o'clock a few of them wished her a good weekend.

Antonia drove back to Luntmakargatan, parked and watched in her rear-view mirror as Zivkovic left the office at six o'clock.

She crossed the street, holding the lockpick like a key in her hand. She shielded the door with her body. People passed by behind her, completely unaware. Fourteen seconds to get the door open, enter the dark office and close the door behind her.

She quickly got used to the darkness, then set to work. She hunted through the filing cabinets and leafed through the address book on the desk, all under the watchful gaze of Sitting Bull. He looked seriously pissed off, probably with good reason.

Antonia photographed each page of the address book with her mobile, then did the same with the Rolodex. She recognised a few of the names: petty criminals, fences, dealers and pimps.

Nothing of interest.

14

(STOCKHOLM/MUNICH)

'WHERE ARE YOU GOING?'

'Doctor's appointment.'

'Where?'

'The Karolinska.'

'What for?'

'A mammogram.'

'How long?'

'I don't know. It always takes longer than you expect.'

Sophie was standing in the kitchen with the phone to her ear, answering Leszek's questions.

'You need to give me a time.'

'Afternoon, five o'clock.'

'Before then?'

'I'll be at home, might go shopping.'

'Call and tell me if you do,' he said, and hung up.

She looked at her watch. She had to hurry. Sophie switched her mobile phone off and stuffed it into her handbag.

Her heart was pounding in her chest.

Downstairs a taxi was waiting to drive her to Stockholm's Arlanda Airport.

An SAS flight would carry her to Munich.

Then a beige Mercedes would take her from the airport into the city.

She wasn't supposed to be there; it was enemy territory, the home turf of the Hanke family. She had spent two days thinking about how to make contact. In the end she simply picked up the phone, called Ralph Hanke's office and introduced herself by name. His secretary said he was busy. Two hours passed before he called her back.

The security arrangements that met her when she got out of the taxi at Marienplatz were thorough and careful. She was driven around for an hour: two cars, a local bus and finally a taxi. She was taken all over the place before finally being dropped off in front of a house in the city's most exclusive residential area.

The façade of the building was white, as was the short flight of steps that led up between two stone pillars to a door painted shiny black.

She stopped abruptly. Doubt crashed in on her like a thunderclap.

'What the hell am I doing?' she heard herself whisper.

The urge to run was trying to pull her away. But she knocked on the door.

A man she didn't recognise opened it and led her into a large, arched hallway.

There were three armed men standing inside, weapons raised, looking agitated. The doubt she had felt outside was replaced by an all-pervading sense of fear. Were they just going to grab her now? Kidnap her and use her for blackmail?

Sophie was searched thoroughly by the man who had opened the door.

'I'm here to see Ralph Hanke,' she said in as firm a voice as she could muster.

No one replied; the men acted like she didn't exist, but one of them muttered something inaudible into a radio.

Sophie was led into sitting room, large and airy, with tall windows and a group of sofas in the middle of the room on a huge Persian carpet. In the middle of the coffee table there was a large vase of fresh flowers – lilies, roses, peonies, a sea of blue Himalayan poppies, even a few orchids.

She sat down on the edge of one of the sofas and looked at the flowers, trying to find some calm in the beautiful arrangement.

Coming here had been a huge mistake . . .

'I can't tell you what those flowers are. But perhaps you know?' a voice beside her said.

She looked up.

Ralph Hanke was gazing down at her. His black-grey hair was neatly combed, with a stiff side-parting; his smile was white, his nails recently manicured. He was wearing beige trousers, black shoes, a pale-blue shirt and a dark-blue cardigan, and smelled of eau de cologne, something spicy and masculine.

'Yes, I do,' she said quietly.

Ralph Hanke's handshake was warm and brief. He sat down opposite her.

Another man came into the room. A suit, tousled hair, glasses from the '90s. He evaded her gaze.

'Roland Gentz,' he said, and sat down on one of the armchairs.

Roland Gentz. Ralph's right-hand man.

Ralph Hanke, a German businessman who ran a clandestine criminal empire. The man who had ordered the murder of Adalberto Guzman, who had sent gunmen to kill her and Hector while they were driving to Marbella from the airport, who had recently seen to it that Eduardo Garcia was blown to pieces in Biarritz. He was the root of all evil . . .

'I'm glad you've come,' Hanke said. 'I gather that your meeting with Don Ignacio went much as expected. Now you're here with an answer to our proposal. Very sensible. Let me tell you a little bit about our work—'

His left hand was open on his lap, the fingers splayed and bent slightly inwards, a sign of arthritis, of age. And Roland Gentz, unkempt, traces of shaving foam by one ear. Two men sitting there, two old men.

'I'm not here to give you a reply,' she said tentatively.

Ralph gave a surprised smile at having been interrupted in the middle of a sentence.

'I'm here to ask you to reconsider your proposal. To think again,' she went on.

Her heartbeat was thudding in her chest and neck.

His smile faded. The German businessman's grey eyes looked over at her glassily.

'I'm here without anyone else's knowledge,' she said. 'I've come

to ask you to look at this from a different perspective, to think long-term.'

The same mute look from Ralph Hanke. Then suddenly another expression. Something old, tired, almost ill. Only for a few moments, ash-grey and listless, *disappointed*. Then he became focused.

'Go on,' he said.

Sophie was nervous, needed to swallow.

'After Adalberto's murder and Hector's flight, the organisation has shrunk, business has decreased significantly. There are only crumbs left. What you want to take over is no longer of any real value.'

'What *do* you have today, do you think?' Roland asked from his armchair.

She knew that he was bound to know, so there was no point in lying.

'We've got insight into a number of stock-market-listed Swedish companies. We trade in that information via investment companies. Nothing big, but the numbers are growing, slowly but steadily—'

'Why slowly?' Roland interrupted disinterestedly.

'We need to be careful.'

She gulped, then went on in a voice she wished wasn't so thin. 'We're developing a market for forged goods. That could be big. We're still profiting from investments Adalberto made a long time ago, but that's not much.'

'Such as?' Roland gave her no opportunity for reflection.

'A percentage of takings, smuggling from Morocco, black-market money from construction, money laundering, collaborations with the Italians and other groups in Europe ... weapons smuggling, protection rackets, and so on.'

' "And so on"? And you call that "crumbs"?' Ralph Hanke said.

'Yes, comparatively speaking.'

'Compared to what?'

'Compared to you and Don Ignacio.'

He was staring at her, back to his usual colour.

'And your outgoings?' Roland asked.

She tried to speak in a neutral voice.

'Mainly to Don Ignacio; he costs us sixty per cent of what we

earn on his supplies. A lot of rolling contracts, percentages for protection, bringing the goods in. And standing payments to the justice system here and there, especially in Spain. And of course a lot of expenses associated with our expansion into the fake-goods industry.'

The expression on Ralph Hanke's face . . . empty, impossible to read.

'And you say you've come here with no mandate?'

A nod from her.

'No one knows you're here?' he went on.

She didn't want to sit there any longer

'Are you brave or just foolish, Sophie?'

'Does it matter?' she replied.

'What do you want?' he asked.

'I want you to back off.'

Ralph Hanke looked at Roland Gentz. Roland's face was blank.

'Where should we back off to?' Ralph asked.

'It's going to grow,' she said. 'It's going to get bigger. Take over then.'

He came close to shrugging his shoulders. 'I can do that myself, get it to grow.'

'That's one way of looking at everything,' she said.

A half smile from him.

'It's my way,' Ralph said.

There was a muffled sound of traffic out in the street.

'Leave it alone,' she suggested.

'Leave what alone?'

'Us, the people around Hector.'

Hanke didn't even need to think; he had an answer to that. 'I need to know where Hector and Aron are. Give me their location and I promise that nothing else will happen to anyone.'

He wiped his mouth, his arthritic hand clearly exposed.

'I don't know where they are,' she said.

Tapping on the parquet floor.

'Can you find out?'

'No.'

Ralph Hanke leaned back in the sofa, realised his arthritic hand was visible and hid it.

'Do you regard yourself as disloyal for coming here, for going behind Hector's and Aron's backs?' he asked.

She didn't answer.

'Or perhaps you're not going behind their backs?'

She remained silent.

'Is he alive?'

Sophie nodded.

'How can I be sure that's true?'

Sophie remained silent.

'What do you need, Sophie, to get Hector to hand himself over to us?' Roland asked.

'Nothing.'

'Meaning?'

'Nothing. I can't do it.'

'What *can* you do?'

'I can give you more than you'd get if you went in and took over now. If you're patient, if you wait.'

'How long?'

'How long can you wait?'

Ralph shrugged. He suddenly seemed completely uninterested in the whole meeting.

'Anything else?' he asked.

She twisted the ring on the ring finger of her right hand subconsciously.

'I know about pretty much all the activities of Hector's organisation. Take whatever you want, I'll help you, on condition that there's no violence.'

'You took a huge risk in coming here,' Ralph said. 'I don't know if you're brave or just foolhardy. But here you are. And we know that you were in Istanbul with Aron.'

Ralph fell into thought but stared at her the whole time.

'Should I ask you to stay here with us?' he mused, almost to himself.

Sophie hid her fear by looking away from him and staring down at her lap. Her left hand twisted the ring on her right ring finger. She could feel him still staring at her.

'No,' he whispered, and leaned back.

And with that, the meeting was over. Roland stood up and gestured

for her to follow him. She remained seated for a few seconds, then stood up.

There was a car waiting in the street. She got into the back seat. The car began to roll through Munich.

Sophie put her hand to her mouth.

Fuck . . . fuck . . . fuck!

Roland Gentz sat back down on his chair, Ralph Hanke on the sofa.

'What's her role in all this?' Ralph asked.

Roland gave the question a few seconds in his head. But instead of answering he posed another question: 'Was that Hector talking? Were we listening to Hector?'

Ralph reflected. 'No, not the way I saw it.'

'So who was it, then? Aron? Herself?'

Ralph and Roland considered this, without arriving at a conclusion.

'What was she asking for, really?' Ralph asked.

'She was asking for a respite,' Roland replied.

'Can she be useful? Does she know all about the business?'

'No, not the way she's trying to make out. But with enough pressure she could still be useful.'

'Her son?' Ralph asked.

'Albert.'

'He's all she's got?'

'Yes.'

Ralph's eyes were focused on a point on the floor.

'So she comes here and asks for more time. Time for them to gather their strength and hit back against us. Unless it really is the way she says, and she's trying to avoid violence and conflict?'

'She's a nurse,' Roland said.

'So she's got nothing to give us?'

'No, not as the person she's pretending to be, anyway.'

'But?'

'You mentioned her son,' Roland said.

A thought flashed into Ralph's head.

'Do they know that we know?' he asked.

'How do you mean?'

'Do they know that we know? That we know more about them than they know about us? That we've got hold of Hector's son, that we know what their group looks like, we know their business is treading water.'

'No, I don't think they know all that.'

'But they'll know later this evening?'

'Yes, Ralph, later this evening they'll know.'

'So, should we go ahead?'

'Yes, we should,' Roland whispered.

'Are you sure Koen can do it?' Ralph asked.

'He ought to be able to.'

'How stupid is he?'

'Relatively.'

'But?'

'He's got some sort of warped father complex. Wants our favour, wants approval, affirmation.'

'Let him have it then. Call him, explain, help him,' Ralph said.

'Hmm. Shall we bring Carlos in?' Roland asked.

Ralph thought for a moment, then nodded.

Roland got up from his armchair again, walked across the floor and opened the door to the next room. Ralph heard Roland say a few short words. Then he went back to his chair. Behind him came Carlos Fuentes. The Spaniard, the traitor who had previously worked for Hector. Large, bald, unbuttoned white shirt, loose linen trousers, barefoot. He sat down on the sofa opposite Ralph, where Sophie had just been sitting. One arm along the back of the sofa. There was something smug about him, as if he felt this all revolved around him.

'What do you think?' Roland asked.

Carlos shrugged his shoulders.

'Did she come here of her own accord?' Roland pressed.

Carlos Fuentes had lost weight. Not so much from his body as his face. It hung loose, and there were large shadows cast under his eyes.

'I don't think so,' Carlos replied.

'Why don't you think so?' Roland asked.

Carlos threw his hands up in exasperation. 'She was just a nurse.

Hector was in love with her. And she was there at my restaurant in Stockholm when everything kicked off.' He cleared his throat and went on: 'So no, she didn't come here of her own accord, then.'

'What makes you say that?'

'I've never seen Hector in love, except with her. They're close, he trusted her; he must have sent her, no question.'

'Why?' Roland asked.

'You could see for yourself. Was she threatening? No, she was cautious, quiet . . .'

'Why?' Roland asked again, calmly.

'Because they want time. She said so straight out.'

'Will they give us anything?'

Carlos had one hand inside his shirt, stroking his chest.

'No,' he said.

'Because?'

'Because I've told you time and time again . . .'

He was uncouth and blunt, the Spaniard.

'That Hector won't give up?' Roland asked.

Carlos nodded, repeating the words quietly. 'That Hector won't give up.'

'But what if he's dead? Perhaps Aron's in charge? Or someone else,' Roland said.

'Does it matter?' Carlos said.

Ralph Hanke didn't feel like sitting and listening any longer. He stood up and left the sitting room.

Roland did the same, neither of them deigning to look at Carlos Fuentes.

Roland stopped on the way out and said, 'You'll be moved now, Carlos. This house is no longer safe. Get ready, you'll be picked up within ten minutes.'

Their steps faded away towards the hall and front door.

'I don't like the food anyway,' the Spaniard called.

But as usual, the men weren't listening to him. The front door closed with a loud slam, then the house fell silent.

If it had been up to Carlos, he would have held the nurse, forced her to say where Hector was, with every available means. Because one thing was certain: if Hector was alive, he would kill Carlos Fuentes the moment he caught a whiff of his scent.

KOEN DE GRAAF CAUGHT A TAXI FROM THE AIRPORT TO THE CENTRE OF STOCK-holm, to a multi-storey car park on Regeringsgatan. On the fourth floor was a nondescript silver-grey Mazda.

The key was under the mat in the rear footwell. He got in the driver's seat and read the message on his phone. Three lines from Roland Gentz:

The shop on Västmannagatan.
Sophie Arlanda.
Ernst.

Koen typed Västmannagatan into his phone and the GPS searched for satellites.

He leaned over towards the glove compartment. It contained a white envelope. He opened it and took out a piece of silver foil and a small bag of heroin.

Koen prepared the drug with a practised hand, heated the foil from beneath with his lighter and the heroin quickly began to bubble and boil. He breathed in the fumes, held them inside him, releasing nothing but transparent air when he breathed out again.

Something that hadn't felt good suddenly improved.

He followed the GPS and drove, high on heroin, through Stockholm's morning traffic. This was what his life was like. Regular jobs for Ralph, and always a precisely measured amount of smack to keep his addiction and emotional life under control. That was good, it meant he did his job better.

He parked outside the right address on Västmannagatan and leaned back.

His mobile phone rang in his jacket pocket.

'*Get going,*' Roland Gentz said.

'I need the nurse's flight number. Have I got time?' Koen asked.

'*Just get to Arlanda and follow her the minute you see her.*'

Roland gave Koen Sophie's flight details.

'And then bring that old man with me?'

Roland was silent for a moment, then said, '*Yes. I sent you a list, didn't I? Is it too much for you?*'

'No.'

'*Are you sure? You need to concentrate, Koen. Can I rely on you?*'

'Yes!'

He sounded like a teenager.

Roland sighed. '*Listen. This is a chain of events, Koen. Everything has to work just-so. Can you handle it? Give me an honest answer.*'

'Tell me again,' Koen said sluggishly.

'*Once you've finished the job in the shop, that will send everyone running. They'll go to ground and gather in the same place. That's what we're hoping. You need to find out where, that's the priority. You do that by following Sophie from the airport. Do you get that?*'

'I get it,' Koen muttered.

Roland spelled out the rest: '*Then, when you're finished, you bring that man back here to us. You're very important, Koen. Both Ralph and I are very appreciative of all that you do.*'

A flash of happiness ran through Koen as he ended the call; then he yawned, wiped his face with his hands and opened the car door. He went around to the boot. It was empty. On top of the spare tyre under the floor was a jack, a wheel brace and a Mini Uzi with an extended magazine. He tucked the weapon inside his jacket and crossed the street towards the shop.

Koen looked in the window. It was small and fairly unassuming, and contained beautiful things. Strongly coloured textiles, spears, shields, ceramics – all sorts of things – old, ethnic, historical.

A little bell rang when he opened the door.

He saw a dark-skinned woman with a lot of thick hair. Proud, attractive. Behind her stood a man, tall, sinuous, smiling. The man was standing on a stool, rearranging things on one of the top shelves.

'Hello,' they said to Koen in tandem, cheerily.

He felt welcome, and realised he was smiling as he opened his jacket and pulled out the Uzi.

The man on the stool threw himself instinctively at the woman, landing on top of her and shielding her with his body.

Koen fired. And everything became very ugly.

SOPHIE PAID THE TAXI DRIVER IN CASH AND WAS JUST GETTING OUT OF THE car when her mobile rang. She answered.

'*Daphne and Thierry have been murdered, they were shot in their shop an hour ago . . .*'

Sophie headed for the door, her legs still carrying her even though she had fully understood what Leszek had just told her.

'*Sophie?*'

She managed to tap in the code, open the door with her back and walk across the narrow carpet leading to the lift.

'*Sophie?*' Leszek asked again.

She opened the door to the lift.

'Angela and the boys?' she asked, pressing the button for her floor. The lift began to rise.

'*They're safe. Where have you been, Sophie?*'

She tried to pull herself together. 'Nowhere. What happened?'

'*They were found on the floor. Thierry had his arms around her, he was trying to protect her. There were a lot of shots, that's all I know.*'

An image conjured up by Leszek's words flashed through her mind. She tried to suppress it. Leszek went on talking and she tried to listen in spite of the panic that was assaulting her from all sides. Leszek clarified the situation to her. *Everyone could have been exposed.*

She understood what that meant. *Run!*

The world came back. Sophie made a call to Albert as she unlocked the door and the security gate inside, but it went to voicemail. She hurried into the bedroom and opened the cupboard. From the back she pulled out her pre-packed case. It contained all she needed for a few days, as well as her real passport. The fake one was already in her handbag.

Without looking back she left the apartment, headed down the stairs and left the building.

Sophie hurried towards Birger Jarlsgatan. Albert's voicemail felt like a hopeless echo as she tried to call him again and again.

She looked up the number of the school and reached an automated menu that asked her to press a button to be put through to

the right place. She pressed the first option, which turned out to be the principal's office. It rang a few times, then the call was cut off. She phoned those of Albert's friends whose numbers she had in her mobile. She called Anna. She sounded calm, friendly. No one knew where he was.

Sophie got hold of a taxi and jumped into the back seat. Gave the driver the address of Albert's school. She felt horribly frightened. The outside world looked sharp, as if all the angles were wrong.

She prayed to God that they didn't get stuck in traffic. She should have prayed to God about Albert as well, but she didn't dare. It was as if her prayer would make the situation more real, more dangerous. It already was, of course, but she was unable to handle that.

KOEN DE GRAAF HAD FOLLOWED HER BACK TO HER APARTMENT FROM ARLANDA. And he had waited until she emerged again. She was in a hurry, with a suitcase in her hand. News of the murdered couple had already reached her.

Now he followed her taxi as it wove through the city traffic, heading south. She would lead him right where he wanted to go.

ALBERT'S SCHOOL WAS ON SÖDERMALM.

Sophie pulled the heavy door open and was met by the smell of school: pencils, linoleum, stone and something elusive that was found only in academic buildings. She hurried through the corridor, past the classrooms, windows in their doors, all the rooms empty, no one in sight anywhere. It was late in the afternoon, perhaps all the lessons were over?

She stopped to catch her breath and listened. The silence echoed emptily. Sophie tried to make out any sound at all. Far away in a muffled universe she heard slippery sounds, a hint of voices shouting. A gymnasium.

Sophie headed down the main staircase and made her way along a long passageway towards two large doors. She threw them open.

A group of youngsters was playing basketball in half of the hall, while a few more sat on the stand. Towards the other end of the hall Albert was practising throwing a ball at a hoop in his wheelchair while a friend caught the ball and gave it back to him.

She walked around the free-throw line, smiling with relief at Albert's friend, Marcus.

Albert looked at her in surprise, and Sophie did her best to maintain her smile.

'Are you ready?' she asked softly.

'Ready for what?'

'Ready to set off first thing tomorrow morning?'

Albert looked at her curiously.

'Where are you going?' Marcus asked, standing there clutching the basketball to his chest.

'Rehabilitation,' Sophie said.

Marcus looked thoughtful.

'We've got a few things to sort out, are you ready?' she asked.

Albert was avoiding her gaze.

'See you,' Albert said, and pushed himself away from Marcus.

'How long are you going to be gone?'

'Three weeks,' Sophie interjected.

Leszek drove up outside the school, braked sharply, got out and quickly helped Albert into the car with a practised hand, then put the wheelchair in the back. They drove off fast.

Sophie and Leszek talked quickly in low voices: what were the arrangements, was everyone safe, then details – mobile phones, computers, other traceable items. Albert asked questions from the back seat, his voice loud, but they didn't get through; no one was listening to him. They just carried on working through everything between them in a very focused, concentrated way.

'What's going on?' Albert shouted.

Leszek and Sophie went on talking.

'Mum!' He was yelling now. They stopped talking. She turned around.

'We have to go into hiding,' she said.

'Why?'

'We just do.'

'Mum?'

A pleading look in his eyes.

'Two people have been killed.'

He tried to make sense of what she'd just said. 'What?'

She didn't answer.

Albert looked down, struggling with all the questions that came into his mind. 'Who?'

She remained silent. Leszek took over.

'Daphne and Thierry,' he said.

'There's nothing for you to worry about, Albert,' she said in a feeble attempt to sound calm.

'How can you say that?' he asked bitterly.

Then he turned his head away.

Sophie was struck by a flash of realisation. What the hell was she trying to do, acting as the protective mother?

She turned back towards Albert.

'I'm sorry, Albert,' she said. 'I'm not thinking straight at the moment. This is serious, we need to go into hiding. There's a secure apartment waiting for us. That's where we're heading now.'

He looked at her.

'OK,' he said quietly.

———

BEHIND THE WHEEL OF THE MAZDA, KOEN WATCHED AS THEIR CAR STOPPED halfway along Norr Mälarstrand. Sophie got out, Leszek got the wheelchair out of the boot of the car and quickly unfolded it and helped Albert in. They headed towards a door, Leszek tapped in a code and they disappeared into the building.

Koen made a note of the address on his phone and sent it to Roland. This was going really well. Roland and Ralph would be pleased.

Now there was just old Ernst left . . .

THEY REMAINED SILENT IN THE LIFT AS IT CARRIED THEM TO THE TOP FLOOR.
Leszek opened his jacket, drew a pistol from his shoulder holster and
let it hang down by his leg.

They reached the top floor. Leszek got out first, followed by So-
phie and then Albert. He unlocked the door and looked inside, then
held the door open for the others.

'It's OK,' he said, gesturing them inside.

Everyone was there. Leszek introduced Albert to Angela, Hasani
and the boys.

Sophie found a quiet place in the passageway between the kitchen
and dining room. She crouched down and breathed through the
sleeve of her sweater with her head bowed. Paralysed with a despair
that stopped any tears from coming, just a pain in her throat, a ter-
rible pressure in her chest and, beyond the physical, a sense of guilt,
guilt, guilt. Daphne and Thierry dead . . .

She wished she could stand at the edge of the world with her back
to everything, facing away from everything and everyone . . . She
wanted to make herself stand in the corner and never leave, if she
could find such a corner . . .

'Sophie?'

Leszek's voice calling for her. She took several deep breaths, try-
ing to hide the truth somewhere inside her and hit the Reset button.

Hasani was leaning against the sink when she went into the
kitchen. Leszek was looking out the window, and he turned around.

'How secure are we here?' she asked.

'Secure, for now,' he replied.

'What do we know?'

'Nothing.'

'Has everyone been contacted?'

Leszek nodded. She could see he was shaken up.

'Right now you and Albert need to make sure your family and
friends are calm. We don't want them to start looking for you. Give
them some sort of plausible explanation.'

Leszek hadn't finished.

'Whoever did this has a goal,' he said. 'And he'll carry on killing
until he reaches that goal. Understood?'

'Yes,' she said weakly.

'So from now on nothing gets done without serious thought. Everything has to go through me and Hasani.'

The wooden floor creaked as she walked towards Albert's room.

Andres and Fabien were blissfully unaware; they were running around chasing each other with their shoes off, sliding on the polished parquet floor. They were enjoying themselves, and their happy cries formed a distant background of noise, no matter where you were in the apartment.

Albert was sitting on the bed, his legs out straight in front of him. She went into his room and sat down beside him on the edge of the bed. He waited for her to say something. But she merely took his hand in hers. She leaned over and hugged him, holding him tight.

'I love you,' she whispered.

'I love you too, Mum.'

———

SILVER AND GOLD SIGNS WITH COMPANY NAMES NEXT TO THE DOORWAY ON Mäster Samuelsgatan. Koen pressed all the buttons on the intercom except one. The door buzzed and he went in. The lift took him up to the third floor. He knocked on a tall white door, which was opened by a man who was getting ready to leave.

Koen recognised him from photographs.

'Ernst Lundwall?' Koen asked lazily.

'No,' Ernst said.

'Yes,' Koen said, showing him the submachine-gun under his jacket. Ernst took a step back, and Koen walked in and closed the door behind him.

'Ralph Hanke wants to see you,' Koen said, pointing the weapon at Ernst. 'You need to pack some things,' he went on, pushing Ernst farther away from the door.

15

(STOCKHOLM)

MILES HAD A FUNNY FEELING IN HIS STOMACH. A TINGLE, HE'D HAVE SAID IF HE were a child. But he wasn't, he was grown-up, and the time for tingles was long gone. But whatever it was, it was directly connected to Sanna, who was performing onstage in front of him.

Hers was the last performance of the evening. As usual, he was sitting in the darkness at the back of the room. He thought she was moving differently, as if she was bored and tired.

Miles didn't like evenings. Different people came then, people who shouldn't be there. That evening there were three drunk thirtysomethings in cheap suits. The plastic badges they had been given at their conference or sales fair or wherever they had been were still dangling from corporate straps around their necks. The men were talking loudly in an Örebro accent and laughing exaggeratedly at bad jokes.

Miles looked at Sanna again. Yes, she probably felt much the same as him, didn't like evenings, didn't like country hicks and drunks and loud talking.

A bachelor party tumbled in. There were three of them as well, but these seemed to be made of sterner stuff. They had an empty shopping trolley with them, which bounced noisily down the stone steps.

The groom-to-be was wearing a filthy wet T-shirt, a nappy on top of his jeans and had a condom on his head that was horribly stretched across his forehead, giving him very odd eyebrows and an unnerving stare. The groom's friends were each drinking from

a bottle of Koskenkorva. Miles guessed that they had come straight from the Finland ferry, and all three were close to passing out. But they could at least stand up. The groom yelled something indistinct and threatening at the room. One bottle flew through the air and hit one of the men from Örebro in the head. The man fell, hitting his face on the edge of the stage, then just lay there. Then the shopping trolley raced across the room.

The bachelor party set their sights on the two remaining visitors from Örebro, who didn't stand a chance.

Once they had been dealt with and couldn't be beaten any more, the young men set about some of the defenceless old pervs.

Miles had been on his way out, but stopped. An old man was being beaten up. Something happened inside him. Maybe it was the sight of a defenceless man being attacked, maybe a sense of total injustice, that what was happening was simply wrong.

Without being able to stop himself, Miles strode over, pulled the condom from the groom's head, grabbed him by the hair and punched him repeatedly in the eye, cheekbone and temple with his right fist. The blows were steady and hard, and the man's legs gave way and he fell to the floor. Miles leaned over towards him.

'Don't get married,' he leered.

One of the groom's friends, possibly his best man, came towards Miles. He was angry, drunk and ugly.

Miles pulled him to the floor and smashed him in the face with his left hand. When he was done, he looked around for their other friend. But the third one was just standing there, rocking drunkenly and glaring at Miles, gesturing to indicate that he was done for the day. He sat down hard on a chair and threw up.

Miles helped the old perv up from the floor and led him off towards the stairs. A whispered *thanks* as they parted on the street outside.

Miles lit a cigarette and took a few drags. It tasted incredibly good. What had just happened? He had never hit anyone like that before. It had been easy.

He inspected the knuckles of his right hand. He had even enjoyed the fight.

With his hands in his pockets and the cigarette still in his mouth, Miles walked away.

Someone appeared alongside him. Sanna looked just like she did

onstage, although she had clothes on now. A pair of sneakers, jeans, top, coat.

'Hi,' she said.

Her eyes flashed.

'Hi,' he said.

They walked a few steps.

'That was unpleasant,' she said.

'Yes,' he said.

She stayed by his side. 'You're a regular, aren't you?'

'You could say that,' Miles said.

'For me, or just in general?'

'In general, but you're good,' he said.

'You don't stare like the others,' she said.

He turned to face her. 'Really?'

'Where are you heading?' she said.

And with that, Miles stopped. A glimpse of paradise. Everything made sense, right there, right then.

'Home,' he replied.

'Shall I finish the show back at yours?'

He didn't even need a moment to consider. Miles nodded.

'Yes, if you like.'

Miles and Sanna set off towards Nybroviken, walking side by side. They got on the tram outside the Royal Dramatic Theatre, stood and held on to the straps. Catching each other's eye was evidently quite amusing. At Skansen they got off and walked over to the houses on the other side of the road.

She stripped for him on the living-room floor, at a greatly reduced rate. To the accompaniment of an old jazz record. There was no thrusting. She just stripped really well.

Then they drank strong tea, played Yahtzee on her phone, told stories about their lives, happy memories, things they liked.

She fell asleep on his sofa. Miles covered her up, put a soft pillow under her head and set his alarm clock for half an hour earlier than usual.

He wanted to make it nice, wanted her to feel at home.

He wanted it to be perfect . . .

16

(MUNICH)

SHE WAS A PSYCHO. HE LIKED PSYCHOS; THEY WERE OFTEN COMPLETELY UNIN-
hibited in bed, and got turned on by old men like him.

But not this one, she was asexual. She just lay there like a glove and soaked it up. It was as if he was assaulting her. Which he was, but it was OK, because they'd agreed to terms, there was an understanding: she was a whore, he was a customer.

At least that was what Carlos Fuentes convinced himself of as he lay there on top of her with his tongue in her ear, mumbling dirty words and working with determination towards climax.

Carlos Fuentes finished and rolled off, gasping for breath. Once he was breathing normally again he got up from the bed, then put on a pair of slippers and a paisley-patterned silk robe.

'The money's on the bedside table,' he muttered, then left the bedroom and went downstairs to the kitchen. He was always hungry after sex. There was a bottle of Chablis in the cooler. Foie gras, spiced German sausage and smoked salmon in the fridge. He could eat it all with his hands; things tasted better then.

He entered the kitchen – sterile and modern.

The fridge was huge, like a wardrobe. Carlos tucked the bottle of wine under his arm, then carefully picked out a night-time snack.

'Carlos?' A woman's voice, whispering and sensual.

He turned around.

Sonya Alizadeh was smiling at him.

'Sonya,' he said with a gasp.

Sonya Alizadeh, at Hector's side throughout all the years that Carlos had worked for him.

And then he realised.

'Wait a minute . . .'

A truncheon hit him in the temple. Carlos slumped, and the wine bottle fell to the floor and shattered. Sonya hit him again and all his muscles went limp as he fell flat on the floor.

Sonya pulled off her black rucksack, sat astride him and quickly pulled out some zip ties and bound his hands and feet. Then she fished out a thick roll of tape, put a strip over his mouth, then wound it twice around his head and bit down to cut it. Sonya stood up and shook out a transparent body bag next to him.

The woman from Carlos's bed came into the kitchen and went and stood by his feet, and Sonya stood by his arms.

At an invisible signal the two of them lifted the heavy man onto the body bag. Sonya put an oxygen mask over his face, attached it to a small tube of oxygen and zipped the bag shut. She stood up again and looked down at her handiwork.

'That'll do,' she whispered to herself.

She handed the woman an envelope. Its thickness suggested a lot of money. The woman opened it and counted.

'Are you a user?' Sonya asked. 'Is that why you do this?'

The woman looked up from the envelope of money with a smirk. 'What do you think?'

'Give it up,' Sonya said.

The woman snorted derisively and put the envelope into her handbag.

Together they quickly carried the body bag out to an SUV in the sleepy back street. Once they'd heaved the body into the back of the vehicle, the woman turned on her heel and walked off down the pavement.

Sonya closed the door, got in behind the wheel and drove off.

17

(MUNICH)

THREE ROOMS IN A ROW, A KITCHEN AND A SMALL BATHROOM. IT COULD HAVE been a home if it weren't for the surveillance cameras in the ceiling, the barred windows and the locked doors.

Ernst was standing by a window, looking out. He was at a farm, isolated, palatial, exclusive. There was clearly a lot of land – there were horses and fields out there. Stables, barns and – in the distance – a gatehouse.

Koen had driven him to Arlanda. Together they had taken a flight to Munich. Koen kept close to him the whole time. A car was waiting for them when they arrived, and Ernst had been sedated. He had woken up alone in a large bed in this room, watched some German television, had some food and waited, pacing around nervously.

There was a knock on the door, then a key was inserted into the lock and turned. A tattooed, dark-haired man leaned in and looked around the room. He backed away, held the door open and Ralph Hanke walked in, accompanied by Roland Gentz and a younger man Ernst recognised from photographs: Christian Hanke, Ralph's son, his heir. He was in his mid-twenties, with curly black hair and ice-blue eyes.

'Do we need to introduce ourselves?' Ralph asked.

Ernst shook his head.

The three men sat down on the group of sofas. Ernst remained

where he was by the window. He got the impression that they were stressed.

'What have you got to tell us?' Ralph asked.

Yes, he sounded stressed.

'I don't know,' Ernst replied.

They stared at him. His answer was unacceptable, he realised that. As long as he had something to give them, he would be kept alive. Then they would kill him and bury his body somewhere, probably out in those fields. And Ernst Lundwall didn't want that. So he needed to play this right and give them a little at a time. Betray Hector? Yes, that was unavoidable if he wanted to live.

'What do you want to know?' Ernst asked, and cleared his throat.

'Where is he?' Christian asked.

'Who?'

'Who the hell do you think?' he roared.

The room became tense.

'I don't know where he is,' Ernst replied, pushing his glasses up his nose and trying to keep his voice steady.

'Who does know?' Roland Gentz asked.

'I'm mostly involved in Hector's business affairs. I'm his adviser. But I don't talk to him any more.'

'Who do you talk to?'

'Aron. And Leszek, to a lesser extent. Sophie Brinkmann also attends our meetings from time to time.'

'What do you do?'

'I look after the legal side of things, provide advice and suggestions, I draw up contracts, I'm in constant contact with our business partners, official and unofficial alike.'

'Carlos?' Christian said.

Ernst didn't follow.

'Carlos?' Christian repeated very clearly.

'I don't know. Haven't seen him for six months. He disappeared, betrayed Hector. You're the ones who've got him,' Ernst said, confused.

'You don't know?'

'What?'

'He disappeared last night,' Ralph said. 'We need to know who took him.'

'I don't know,' Ernst said. 'I don't get told about that sort of thing. That's not my role in the organisation, I'm more—'

'Like Roland?' Ralph said, pointing at Roland Gentz.

'Sorry?'

'You're like Roland. Would that be a fair comparison?'

'Yes, like Roland, you could say,' Ernst replied.

'Then it's probably best for the two of you to talk to each other? What are Christian and I doing here?'

Ernst didn't know how to reply to that.

Ralph went on. 'You're here to give us information and redirect Hector's business affairs and partners in our direction. You can speed everything up. Make sure you do a good job, to save your friends unnecessary suffering. And yourself.'

Ralph stood up and Christian followed suit, then they left the room.

Ernst and Roland were left alone. They were the same sort. There wasn't much to say. No friendship, no enmity. Just two of the same sort of people who were expected to come up with something.

'Aren't you going to sit down?' Roland asked.

'I'd rather stand.'

'Sit down, Ernst,' Roland whispered.

18

(STOCKHOLM)

He stopped that night and did ask, 'We need to know who gave him.

ANN MARGRET WAS FIFTY-FOUR, WITH BLEACHED BLOND HAIR AND SIGNS OF heavy tanning-bed use, and had been through a messy divorce. She had skinny legs, a flat backside, a protruding stomach and she thought George Clooney was sexy.

Tommy looked at her as she stood waiting at the bus stop, their meeting place. He pulled up in front of it.

He leaned over, opened the door on the passenger side.

'Hi, Tommy,' she said in her affected, smoke-damaged voice when she got into the car.

'Hi, Maggie,' he said.

She giggled excitedly at the fact that he had given her a nickname.

'How are things?' he went on, pulling out into the traffic.

'Oh, things are fine,' she twittered hoarsely, pulling a bundle of papers from her handbag.

Ann Margret looked up to Tommy in an unhealthy way; she did to all men in managerial positions, she wanted to make them happy, and he exploited that.

Ann Margret was a civilian employee within the police. Years of reorganisations had moved her around inside the bureaucratic machinery. She had been a senior secretary, an assistant in the Coordination unit, an auxiliary in the command centre, a clerk for the Violent Crime and Economic Crime units and an administrator for the forensics team. These days she was working as an assistant to an

analyst in the CID's Surveillance unit. She still retained the competencies and permissions she had acquired in her previous positions, giving her almost total access to the police authority's databases, with greater insight and more access to the organisation than she herself was aware of.

There's something about Antonia Miller or the investigation that isn't right, he had told her. *Check what she's been doing on her computer, scan her searches, any progress in the case and keep me informed.*

And Ann Margret had done as she had been asked, flattered by the secret mission. And now Tommy had added Miles Ingmarsson to her surveillance.

He glanced at her.

The woman was a complete idiot. And she wasn't exactly beautiful, either. Her sunglasses covered her face. Her hair was freshly brushed, but she'd forgotten about the back. Tousled from sleep. The dark roots of her natural hair colour were showing close to her scalp, but the rest was bleached yellow. She smelled of cheap sweet perfume, a mild hangover and the acrid stench of a recently smoked cigarette.

Ann Margret leafed randomly through her papers and began the run-through: 'Antonia Miller is busy with the Conny Blomberg case. Nothing new to report there. Miles Ingmarsson doesn't appear to be doing anything at all, he seems a bit of a dead loss.'

She laughed, a smoker's laugh. Tommy tried to smile.

Ann Margret carried on in the same hopeful way she usually did during these informal meetings. She read out Antonia's and Miles's search histories, both on the Internet and in the police's internal systems. She told him what phone calls they had made, and about their digital activity in general.

And Tommy always concluded with something along the lines of: 'Ann Margret, I can't tell you any details, but you're a star. What you're doing is very important. You'll definitely be rewarded for it, I can promise you that. But for the time being, all this has to stay between the two of us. This is what working undercover is like – little signs, especially the ones that seem arbitrary, can ruin an investigation. Bear that in mind.'

And she would nod solemnly, reaffirming her oath of confidentiality and her loyalty.

This business of manipulating people really isn't so difficult, he thought.

He let her out by an underground station and headed home. He felt relieved. The situation was just as he had hoped, just as he wanted. Antonia was occupied with her new murder. Ingmarsson was getting used to his new role and was doing nothing. *Perfect*.

At home, in front of the terraced house, he sat for a while in his car, as he usually did. He could see his daughters, Vanessa and Emelie, through the kitchen window. They were standing side by side by the counter, already so grown-up.

Ten years ago things had been different, they had been different, he had been different, everything had been different. He danced and sang with them, he had struggled against their reluctance to let the day end when he read them a bedtime story, he had performed magic tricks, had made them laugh at made-up tales. When the girls got a bit bigger, he had taken responsibility for their homework, started to get them interested in better food, tried to bring a bit of quality to everyday life. Sometimes they travelled, Monica would put together a photograph album, summers were long and happy.

Then it had all ended.

There was a smell of food in the hall when he stepped into the house. Monica was sitting on a chair in the kitchen, tired, staring blankly into space. He leaned over and kissed her on the forehead. Their daughters were preparing food. But there was one more person in the kitchen. A person who shouldn't have been there.

'Hi, Dad, this is Mattias,' Vanessa said. She was beaming, and looked infatuated as she stood by the counter chopping fruit.

Tommy looked the young man sitting at his kitchen table up and down. Bad posture, ponytail. He didn't even stand up.

'Hello,' Tommy said, trying to sound friendly.

'Hello,' Mattias said. His voice was exaggeratedly self-confident. 'So you're the policeman?'

Mattias laughed; he evidently had no respect at all. Vanessa didn't know how to behave. She tried to laugh, looking at her dad uncertainly.

'What are we having?' Tommy asked.

'Something easy tonight. Fried cod.'

'Then?'

'Fruit salad,' she said.

He cast a glance at Mattias, who was still sitting while the others stood. Everything suddenly felt very dark. His daughter shouldn't have a boyfriend like that. Christ, his family ought to be aiming higher than that.

They ate dinner. Mattias was studying to be an ethnologist, had left-wing genes and had an opinion about everything and answers to most things.

Mattias asked Tommy how he thought the police should deal with demonstrations. He had been in one recently, apparently.

'The police act in line with regulations,' Tommy mumbled. He had no desire to get into a debate with this cock-sucking ethnologist.

'Violently attacking defenceless youngsters?'

Monica tried to give Tommy a calming smile.

'I don't know,' Tommy said, clenching his teeth.

'You don't *know*?'

Mattias laughed again.

Tommy looked at Vanessa and saw her predicament, and his heart ached for her.

19

(MÁLAGA PROVINCE)

A TWO-DAY DRIVE, FROM THE SOUTH OF GERMANY TO THE SOUTH OF SPAIN.

Sonya was tired and worn out by the time she parked the SUV in the yard in front of the house.

Aron went to meet her. Together they lifted Carlos Fuentes out and laid him down on the ground in the body bag. Aron crouched down and looked at Carlos through the transparent plastic as he lay there in his robe, the oxygen mask over his nose, his eyes wide open. He unzipped the bag and took the mask off, revealing the taped mouth beneath it. Carlos was breathing jerkily through his nose, and was trying to say something. Aron stood up.

'Take him inside.'

Hector was lying in bed in the middle of the room, connected to his life-support machines. Aron was already in the room, and Carlos was pushed in behind him by Sonya. The tape over his mouth recently ripped off.

'Just listen to me,' Carlos pleaded.

Aron turned around, slapping him hard and fast. Carlos lost his balance, was about to say something, but Aron hit him again.

'Sorry!' Carlos screamed.

He was trembling as he stood there in his loose-fitting robe.

Sonya shoved him towards Hector's bed from behind. Carlos tried to avoid looking at Hector.

'Look at him,' Aron said.

Carlos did so, briefly, then looked down again.

'Look at him,' Aron repeated.

Carlos resisted, then raised his head again.

Hector's respirator wheezed quietly. Carlos's breathing was heavier.

'How did you find me?' he whispered.

'Pimps,' Sonya said.

Carlos turned to her with a questioning look.

'It wasn't hard,' Sonya said.

'That's what you are, Carlos,' Aron said. 'Right down to your marrow. A john.'

Carlos stared at them.

'What do you want to know?' His voice was weak and brittle.

'The Hankes.'

Carlos cleared his throat.

'They're nervous,' he began.

'What about?'

'About everything.'

'What are they doing?'

'They're looking for you,' Carlos said.

'What do they know?'

'I don't know.'

'You must have told them something?'

'No, nothing of value. I don't know anything.'

'Don't lie.'

Carlos blinked, thought feverishly, then rubbed his eyes hard.

'They're in hiding,' he said.

'Where?'

'Here and there. Ralph and his son keep moving around, are rarely seen in public, never together.'

Carlos saw an opening.

'You need me, Aron,' he whispered beseechingly. 'Send me back to the Hankes, I'll keep my ears open and report back to you!'

Aron didn't answer, just took him under the arm and dragged him out of the house.

They stopped at the back of the building, at the edge of the forest.

Aron let go of Carlos, took the pistol from the holster on his belt and aimed it at Carlos's head. He fell to his knees, muttering something about mercy, panting and spitting.

'I know more!' Carlos said hoarsely.

Aron lowered the pistol slightly, away from Carlos.

Carlos thought frantically. Then he stood up and tried to run. But he was so terrified that he stumbled pathetically and fell in a heap. Aron took a few steps towards him. Carlos sat with his legs beneath him, muttering about the Virgin Mary, something about his mother and that life had been unfair.

Aron wasn't listening, and aimed the pistol at the back of the Spaniard's head.

'Wait, wait, wait!' Carlos screamed, holding his hands in the air. All of a sudden he was furious.

'Wait, I said! What do you need to know, Aron?'

Anger and dread coursed out of Carlos. Aron couldn't bear to look at him.

'You need to know all sorts of things . . . Aron?' He sounded humble now, running his hands over the ground for some reason. Carlos's brain was working at top speed. He thought of something. 'What was said once they were alone in the room!'

He repeated the same sentence again.

'What room?' Aron asked.

'The room! After she left. What was said in there afterwards!'

'When who left what room, Carlos?'

'The meeting with Ralph, what was said after she left.'

'What meeting, and after who left?'

'The nurse!' Carlos squealed.

Aron's eyes narrowed and he lowered the gun. 'The slightest lack of clarity now, Carlos, and I'll shoot you in the knees, then the arms and then the stomach, so you bleed to death very slowly.'

Carlos was breathing hard. 'When the nurse was in Munich!'

'What are you talking about?'

Carlos made an effort to get his breathing under control and gulped.

'The nurse, Hector's woman, Sophie, the Swede!' he said. 'She was in Munich, she met Ralph.'

'When?'

He searched his muddled mind. 'About a week ago.'

'Go on,' Aron said.

Carlos couldn't shake off the feeling of panic. 'I don't understand.'

'What was she doing there, the nurse?'

Carlos ran his hands over the ground again.

'Talking,' he said. 'She was there talking to Ralph and Roland Gentz.'

'And?'

'I barely heard them, I was in the next room.'

'Go on, Carlos!'

Carlos scratched his arm hard, it looked painful.

'Something about giving what you had to the Hankes, that she could help them with that. That she wanted time, that things would grow and get bigger, and then the Hankes could take over everything. Something like that.'

Aron listened, and Carlos searched for more, cursing himself for not remembering anything else. The something popped into his mind.

'They talked about a son!'

'A son?'

'A son, someone they'd been looking for for a long time and had found at last.'

'Did Sophie talk about that?'

'No, this was earlier.'

'Who talked about it?'

'One of Hanke's men, I heard him talking on the phone.'

'When?'

'I don't know, a week or so before Sophie's visit. I don't remember.'

'Whose son? Was a name mentioned?'

Carlos shook his head. 'No, I don't know. But I can find out!'

Aron's eyes were empty and glassy. Carlos held both his hands out.

'Wait, Aron! I know other things.'

He muttered short words, trying to sound helpful. But he had nothing to say. Instead it was just rambling nonsense that didn't mean a thing.

Aron aimed the barrel of the pistol at the Spaniard's head. Carlos wet himself, covered his face with his arms and screamed, asking with anguished madness where he was going to be buried.

Two loud bangs from Aron's pistol. A flock of birds took off from a tree. The echo of the gunshots faded over the valley.

Carlos's body lay limp on the ground in front of him. Disgust at what he had done gathered in Aron's mouth. He spat, not at Carlos, but alongside, as if the taste were unbearable, and then he kicked sand and grit over the blood next to Carlos's head.

He pulled out his mobile, took a photograph of the body and went back towards the house.

Sonya was standing on the veranda as he approached.

'Aron?'

He stopped and turned towards Sonya without looking at her. 'Let Piño out. And get ready to leave.'

'Where are we going?'

'France. The house in Villefranche,' Aron said.

He continued on into the house.

In the dining room he glanced at the table, all the pictures, his entire world. Now it had all changed dramatically.

Aron went over to the wall, hesitated, then pulled the chain that hung down from the ceiling, left the room and closed the door behind him.

From the other side he heard the hiss of the showerheads above the table. A million microscopic drops of acid forced their way out of the tiny holes, forming a gentle mist that slowly settled on the table, destroying everything on top of it and leaving just an unrecognisable grey sludge behind.

From an open safe in his bedroom Aron took out a worn old notebook and leafed through it until he found what he was looking for. He keyed the digits into his mobile with his right forefinger. It was a Berlin number, belonging to Franka Tiedemann, mother of Lothar, Hector's son.

They had sent money to her every month for seventeen years. At first she had turned it down, but Hector had carried on and Franka realised it was pointless trying to object and had opened an account

to cover the cost of Lothar's education. The money was paid in via dummy accounts in the name of dead people by someone with power of attorney, all to conceal its origins. Every other month Aron would speak to her over the phone. He would ask how they were, about Lothar's progress, his general well-being. Franka always answered dutifully, but no more than that. She had made it very clear to Hector right from the start: stay away from Lothar, you're dangerous. Hector knew she was right, and had therefore done as she asked, but kept his eye on them as best he could. He had always had a suspicion that something might happen to the boy, in spite of the fact that he had done everything in his power to conceal his existence.

The voicemail beeped in Aron's ear.

'Franka, you know who this is. Call or contact me however you think best. But I need to hear from you urgently.'

Aron ended the call. He felt Sonya's presence behind him.

'What did Carlos say?' she asked quietly.

Aron blew the air out of his lungs and stared blankly ahead for a while as he pieced together fragments of his conversation with Carlos.

'That Sophie might have gone over to the other side. And that they might have Lothar.'

'Might and might?'

'Yes, might and might,' he replied quietly.

'Why "might"?'

'Because it was Carlos saying it.'

'What if there's some truth to it?'

Aron had no answer. He stood up, started to walk back inside.

'Leszek and the others?' she asked.

Aron stopped at the door. 'I'll contact him, just give me a bit of time.'

Aron scratched the back of his neck, staring hard at nothing and remained standing in the doorway, as he wanted to ask her something without quite managing to find the words.

'What are you thinking, Aron?'

'I don't know.'

'If what you said is true, then we're all in danger, especially those of us who've been closest to her. Leszek, Angela and the boys, Hasani. Aren't they?'

Aron had got stuck on one particular thought. It didn't lead any-where. He looked at Sonya, and as if he hadn't heard what she said, he went on: 'You can call Raimunda now, and tell her to come back home.'

Three hours later Aron, Sonya and Raimunda left the house in the mountains together with Hector, and began the marathon journey towards the south coast of France and the house in Ville-franche. They drove non-stop, Aron was nervous. Nervous about Hector's condition in the back of the SUV. But also worried. The 'signs' that Raimunda had seen. The fact that Hector was showing signs of brain activity meant that he might one day wake up. How would they handle that? Would they be able to do everything right during the critical moments of his reawakening? And what would Hector be like? Different?

Usually Aron would have taken everything in his stride; that was the key to his success. But he couldn't find any comfort at all. Every-thing was dangerous now.

Seventeen hours later they arrived. The house was large, luxuri-ous, located on a hill with a view of Cap Ferrat and the Mediter-ranean.

They settled in.

20

(SONORA)

THE BED JENS WAS LYING IN WAS SOFT, THE SHEETS WHITE, THE PILLOW FAR too big. He felt dry everywhere, in his throat, his mouth, his eyes. His skin and lips were burning.

A tractor was rumbling in the distance, there were hens clucking beneath the window and on the radio a male voice was talking very fast.

A woman came in, stared at him in surprise, put a hand to her chest and muttered several quick sentences in Spanish, almost as rapid as the voice on the radio. She said something to Jens and pointed up at the ceiling . . . unless she meant heaven. The woman was very expressive, gesticulating wildly, her facial expression constantly changing: she looked happy, then surprised, then astonished.

Jens didn't understand any of it.

'Where am I?' he whispered in English.

The woman kept on chattering and didn't seem to have understood his question. She filled a glass with water, talking non-stop, then abruptly left the room.

Jens reached for the glass of water, his body aching, and drained the contents in one gulp. When he put the glass back on the bedside table he discovered that the fingertips of his right hand were stained. Each finger bluish-lilac, ink . . . fingerprints.

With a sudden sense of urgency he went to get out of bed, but something tugged at his ankle, sending a flash of pain up to his knee.

He threw the covers back. His foot was chained to the metal frame of the bed. Jens tugged at it, trying to find a way to get free, but the cuff was firmly attached.

Car tyres on the gravel outside the window, hens shrieking and flapping to take cover, then the car stopped. Doors opened and closed, footsteps on the gravel, he thought he could count two people. They walked quickly up a flight of steps; an outer door opened, then the sound of shoes approaching his room rapidly.

Two men came in. One in civilian clothes, an ivory shirt, a vest visible beneath it, a gold-coloured police badge around his neck. He was accompanied by an officer in uniform.

The man in the suit indicated that the uniform could leave. The man found a chair and pulled it across the floor towards the bed.

'You were lucky,' he said to Jens as he sat down on the chair. He fished a packet of cigarettes from his jacket pocket. 'How are you feeling?'

Jens didn't answer.

The man took out a cigarette and made a gesture as if to ask whether Jens would like one. Jens declined.

'You were found by one of those paragliders,' he said, lighting the cigarette. He sucked hard three times, and only half the smoke came back out. 'He contacted the people in this village, and they picked you up. You were in a very bad way: dehydrated, almost dead. A doctor came and took care of you. And now you're awake.'

Two more drags.

'My name is Guillermo Mendoza,' he said. Another drag. 'And who are you?'

'No one special.'

'Nor me, but I need to know.'

'What for?'

'Because I'm a police officer.'

'Have I done something?'

Mendoza shrugged. 'I don't know.'

Jens looked at him. *Guillermo Mendoza* . . . There was something appealing about the man, a sharpness, intellect, something simultaneously good and intelligent that he hid behind a weary gaze and a cloud of smoke.

'Why am I being held captive in bed?'

'Where are you from?'

'Here and there.'

Mendoza scratched his chin. 'How long have you been in Mexico?'

'A while.'

'How did you get into the country?'

'Doesn't matter. How much can I pay you to look the other way while I get a head start out of here?'

Mendoza reflected, stroking his cheek. 'Well, I don't know . . . Nothing, really.'

'Name your price.'

Mendoza saw that his cigarette had burned down to the filter, and stubbed it out on the floor with his shoe. 'No, I'm sorry.'

He had reacted to the bribe as if Jens were offering him a second-hand car he didn't want to buy. He pulled the packet of cigarettes out again, and pointed quickly at Jens.

'But, in answer to your previous question as to why you're chained to the bed . . .'

Mendoza tapped out a cigarette and put it between his lips.

'We took your prints.'

He lit it.

'We ran them through all our databases, but we couldn't find your identity anywhere.'

Two deep drags, one after the other.

'But?' Jens asked.

'An alarm went off somewhere.'

'Where?'

Mendoza fixed his gaze on Jens, then gestured towards the ceiling with the hand holding the cigarette.

'Far up to the north. Sweden . . . Stockholm.'

21

(STOCKHOLM)

SANNA WAS MAKING SPAGHETTI WITH CLAM SAUCE, THE FAN ABOVE THE STOVE was whirring, the kitchen radio was playing Sonny Rollins.

Miles was sitting at the kitchen table, leafing through a boat magazine and looking at her. She was beautiful, and she made good food for him. That was better than anything.

She lived with him now. For a while, she had said. It had started with the sofa, then a mattress on the floor of his bedroom, like she was just a friend staying the night. Last night she had crept under his covers. They lay together and talked in the evenings in the dark. Sometimes they got up and watched a film in the middle of the night, a comedy, perhaps; she said she liked comedies. They laughed at the same things. Sometimes she stripped for him. That was wonderful. So wonderful that he didn't dare ask any questions. He just let it happen, so that he could look at her, have her to himself.

She was humming something to herself over by the stove. An old dance tune. He wanted to stop time, stay like that forever. Sanna turned around as if she had heard his thoughts. She smiled.

They ate the food and Sanna talked about growing up in Malmberget, in the far north, about her first car, a Volvo. About the first time she had sex, and the first time she got drunk. She said she didn't give a damn about the northern lights, mines, politics or anything else the people up there got excited about. She liked being cheerful,

grateful and happy. That she tried to be like that as much as possible. That she knew things always got better if you worked for it . . .

'Miles,' she said suddenly.

'Yes?' he said. She was different, serious, cautious.

'You're a police officer.'

He couldn't tell if it was a question or a statement.

'You're good,' she said.

Her eyes were honest, alert, almost intense.

'What is it, Sanna?' he asked.

'Promise you'll never hurt me,' she said quietly.

He didn't understand, but said, 'I promise.'

Then it was as if the conversation had never happened. They ate in silence.

22

(STOCKHOLM)

THE DAYS WERE DIFFICULT FOR ALL OF THEM. NO ONE WAS ALLOWED OUT FOR long. One by one they could take short walks with either Leszek or Hasani by their side, or take a short drive in the rental car. But apart from that they had to stay holed up in the apartment. Not doing any of the ordinary everyday things, like being in contact with their friends, or like going to a restaurant for a meal or out to the cinema. But something else developed in this isolated existence. A sense of community, of solidarity.

Sophie and Leszek had left the city to buy food at a shopping centre far away, beyond the suburbs, in the middle of nowhere. These days they went shopping at places she had never heard of, and never the same place twice.

Leszek steered the big shopping trolley; she walked in front and loaded it with the things they needed, things they didn't need.

There was subdued music playing in the shop, and she listened to it unconsciously as she picked things out and felt normal for a while.

Then she heard a distant peeping sound, the same signal three times in succession. At first she didn't react. The noise was thin and nondescript. But it went on spoiling the background music.

'Sophie?'

She turned around and saw Leszek trying to get her attention, pointing at her handbag in the trolley. At first she didn't get it, then

the signal rang again, simple and monotonous. *Jens!* The phone that only Jens had the number to . . .

Sophie hurried over; the sound was coming from deep inside her handbag. She pulled the bag out and stuck her hand in, feeling for the phone. Too many things. She looked down, and there was something lit up in there.

The light went out just as she answered.

'Hello?'

Nothing but silence.

No, no, no . . .

Leszek was giving her a quizzical look.

'Who was it?' he asked.

Sophie held up the phone. He didn't get it.

'It's the phone Jens gave me,' she said. 'You said it was OK that I kept it.'

Leszek remembered, nodded his head, whispered: 'Yes, it's OK . . . Was it Jens?'

'I don't know,' she said.

She checked the phone; there wasn't much of a charge left.

They carried on through the shop, but she had no idea what she was putting in their trolley.

Ten minutes later it rang again. Sophie answered instantly.

'Jens? Hello?'

'*Coming to Sweden Wednesday. I got caught. Being handed over to the police. Coming from Mexico City, probably via the USA, but I don't know. They still don't know who I am. I mustn't be handed over . . . They matched my prints to Trasten . . .* '

The call cut off. He had been whispering, sounded stressed.

Her heart was beating fast and she felt a rush of joy.

THE SNOW COVERED SMELLS AND SOUNDS. IT WAS A THICK WHITE EVERYTHING that lay there sleeping like a well-meaning but heavy dog.

The air Leszek breathed in as he was walking through the evening darkness along Norr Mälarstrand was clean. He had the earphones from his mobile in his ears, his hands in his jacket pockets. The phone rang three times at the other end before Aron answered.

'Yes?'

'Jens Vall is on his way to Sweden from Mexico, police escort,' Leszek said.

'*Jens Vall?*' Aron said in surprise.

'He's asking for help,' Leszek went on.

'*When?*'

'In two days.'

'*What's it about?*'

'He's in custody over there. When the Mexican police ran his fingerprints through the system it set off an alarm from Trasten.'

'*And now he's being transferred to Sweden?*'

'Yes.'

'*And he'll be questioned about Trasten?*'

'In all likelihood.'

'*That mustn't happen.*'

'No. Of course not.'

'*So you've already thought of something?*' Aron said.

'Yes.'

'*Tell me.*'

'Somewhere between the airport and the city.'

'*Why?*'

'Open space, fast exit.'

'*OK. Plan to break him out with Sophie and Hasani. Two cars. When you're done I want you to travel with Sophie. Hasani drives Jens.*'

'What difference does it make?' Leszek wondered.

'*Just do as I say.*'

Something was going on.

'Aron?'

'*Once you free him, you leave the apartment.*'

'Tell me.'

'*No. Not now. You'll get a call from me.*'

'And then?'

'*Then you'll find out who's going to be left behind, and who's going with you.*'

23

(STOCKHOLM)

THE MAN IN FRONT OF HER WAS NORTH AFRICAN, A PROSTITUTE, IN HIS THIR-
ties, and the tears running down his face were fat and full of regret
and sorrow.

He kept sniffing between sentences as he explained how he had
stabbed Conny Blomberg in the back with a blunt old knife he found
in a drawer.

The motive was jealousy, apparently, or at least that was what
Antonia guessed as she listened to the man's story. But it was un-
clear and confused. Perhaps there wasn't a clear motive, just a sud-
den impulse during an evening of far too many drugs and too much
extreme sex.

The man kept crying and saying he was sorry, over and over
again. Antonia waited patiently for him to stop. But he seemed to
think that if he kept talking, explaining and making excuses for
long enough, the murder of Conny Blomberg would become less
wrong.

She had heard hundreds of similar monologues over the years,
and could never figure out if the perpetrators were talking to her, to
their victims or simply to their own consciences. But it didn't really
matter at all.

Antonia called two uniformed colleagues, who came and got the
man and took him back to the cells.

She stood in the doorway of the interview room and watched as

the remorseful murderer and the police officers disappeared down the corridor.

She leaned her head against the door frame. *Fuck . . .*

Antonia ought to be happy. Every police officer's dream, a solid confession from a perpetrator. Case closed. But she felt deflated . . . again. The same way as when Tommy had taken the Trasten investigation away from her. Then something cropped up in the Conny Blomberg investigation. A coincidence, a link to Trasten . . .

Some of the names led back to Trasten. Leif Rydbäck, parts of whose body were found at the restaurant, had belonged to the same gang as Blomberg, along with Håkan Zivkovic. Anders Ask, the police officer who had contacted the Security Police, had worked with Gunilla Strandberg, the detective who was investigating Hector Guzman and was later murdered by Lars Vinge . . . It was all very thin and circumstantial. But then, it usually was . . .

Antonia started walking back down the corridor to her office.

The Conny Blomberg case was concluded. She should have been happy about that.

She sat down on the chair, her shoulders slumped. She gathered everything to do with the case and prepared her report for the prosecutor. Something in the corner of her eye. Miles Ingmarsson was standing in the doorway with a cup of coffee in his hand.

'That was easy,' he said.

'Yes . . .'

Miles let out a quiet 'Congratulations'.

Antonia raised her eyebrows and adopted her work smile.

'Thanks,' she said.

Miles was on his way out. She felt she should reciprocate his gesture of friendship.

'How are you doing, Miles?'

He paused.

'Fine,' he said.

Miles scraped one foot along the floor.

'Well,' he said, and left.

Antonia did her best to understand.

She finished her work, reluctantly put Conny Blomberg in her out-box, all the while with a gnawing, tickling, burning sensation that it wasn't quite finished yet. Conny's death, the man's confession,

the link to Zivkovic, Tommy's power games. And now Ingmarsson. Had he been smirking at her? Was he making fun of her? Was God making fun of her? Was it all a big fucking joke? Was everything going to be whipped away from her every time she got close to a breakthrough? Was she doomed to live her life in a limbo of ignorance?

Antonia Miller leaned back in her chair, feeling her stress levels rise. Her anger gnawed at her nerves. But then an idea began to take shape.

Antonia took out her notepad from the desk drawer. She leafed through until she found the page where she had written down all the numbers and names she had photographed from Håkan Zivkovic's address book. She had recognised most of them. The list consisted of half of Stockholm's small-time gangsters.

She grabbed a blank sheet of paper from the printer and started work on a fake story that she wrote using a pencil, a lot of imagination and a few of the names from the address book.

The fake story was based on drugs, whores and murder, the fact that Zivkovic's name cropped up everywhere when she asked about Blomberg, and that he was the prime suspect for a load of minor offences, which when taken together became big and ominous and would lead to plenty of years in prison. Something along those lines.

Antonia read through her work, and when she was happy with it she dialled Zivkovic's number. He answered, and she told him the basics of the fake story. He denied it completely, truthfully and in all honesty – she knew him now.

Antonia suggested they meet up. Håkan was breathing heavily down the phone.

'*Please!*' he said.

She didn't feel the slightest pang of guilt.

Håkan Zivkovic looked pale. He was sitting on his desk chair, his biceps bulging under his T-shirt, Sitting Bull staring out sternly behind him.

'You're a fucking bitch,' he said, picking at one of his molars with a toothpick.

She didn't answer, and just stared at the Sioux chieftain instead.

'Give me everything you've got and I'll let you go. Mess with me, and I'll keep getting you for minor offences, a few at a time.'

His eyes were glowing with loathing.

'What do you want?' he grunted.

Thank you . . .

'You know something. About Anders Ask and Leffe Rydbäck, that's what I want.'

His eyes seemed glued to her, as if he were seeing something he'd never noticed before. He laughed.

'Shit, woman. You're buzzing with fucking curiosity!'

She wasn't prepared for that.

He laughed again, almost with relief. 'That's true, isn't it?'

She couldn't let her mask slip now. She nodded.

'And you think you can show up here and threaten me just so you can get what you want?'

She said nothing.

Håkan was radiating controlled aggression, which made him dangerous, and it scared her.

He lowered his voice.

'Let's turn this around,' he said. 'Instead of you threatening me, why don't you give me what you've got?'

'What do you want?' she said.

'I want a free pass,' he said hoarsely, with the toothpick hanging from the side of his mouth.

'A what?'

'A free pass. I want to be able to do something illegal and get away with it.'

'What are you talking about?'

'Are you deaf or something?'

'There's no such thing as a free pass, surely you know that?'

'There is now!'

He was stubborn.

'And protection,' he said.

'I can give you protection, but not the *free pass*,' she snapped.

'Call it what you want, but I'm going to need money to get away with. And I need a lot of it. And when I get it, I'm going to need protection. Help me with that, and look the other way.'

If she understood correctly, he was asking for big things, impossible things.

'I'm a police officer,' she said, trying to make it sound impressive.

He snorted, and he was probably right to. Håkan had seen through her at once. He knew she was prepared to pay, and pay a lot.

'Maybe you haven't got anything,' she tried.

He burst out laughing this time, and tossed the toothpick in the wastepaper basket under the desk. 'You seemed pretty sure about that when you called.'

'Tell me,' she said.

'If you give me what I want.'

'If you give me what *I* want,' she countered.

Håkan Zivkovic rubbed his cheek with his thumb, emphasising his weak jawline.

'It doesn't really matter anyway,' he muttered.

'What?'

'Ask and Rydbäck, you said?'

She nodded.

'Now, that's a crazy fucking story,' he said quietly, his thumb still on his chin.

She felt a glimmer of hope.

'Do you promise to help me?' he said.

'I promise.' She swallowed.

He thought for a moment.

'A businessman was being blackmailed. He contacted me and Leffe Rydbäck for help. After a lot of work, we figured out who was blackmailing him: Hector Guzman and Aron Geisler,' he said.

A gentle feeling of happiness washed over Antonia. She was right, she knew she was right.

'What sort of blackmail?' she asked.

He shrugged. 'The usual crap. The man worked for some big stock-market listed company. They wanted inside information, so they could use it to buy and sell shares.'

'And Anders Ask?' she asked.

'It was him who gave us their names. It felt like a happy coincidence.'

Håkan went on: 'So Leffe and I went home and worked out a plan, then a few days later we went around to Hector's house. We waved our pistols about, told them to stop blackmailing our client, that's usually enough.'

He lowered his voice: 'But they were made of sterner stuff, Guzman and Geisler.'

Håkan stared ahead of him. 'I realised pretty quickly that we were out of our depth, we didn't stand a chance.'

'What happened?' she asked.

'We were overpowered. Hector Guzman forced me to watch while Aron Geisler shot Leffe through the heart. Without a moment's hesitation, cold as ice. Boom! Leffe died right in front of me.'

Antonia listened, wide-eyed.

'He looked so fucking terrified before he died, Leffe. He was a nice guy.'

'Then what?' She tried to keep her voice steady.

'They let me go. I walked out.'

Antonia studied the look in his eyes; he was difficult to read, Zivkovic. One moment he acted like he had learning difficulties, driven by impulse and mania, only to switch suddenly to self-control and common sense.

'Why did they let you live?' she asked.

Håkan was lost in his own thoughts.

'As a witness, I suppose,' he said. 'To let people know what sort of people they were. What they were capable of.' He ran his forefinger under his nose. 'I'm just waiting for them to appear and pick me up.'

A vacuum cleaner started up on the floor above. The noise broke the silence, giving her the chance to absorb all that she'd been told.

She had an answer: Aron and Hector had murdered Leif Rydbäck in Hector's home, probably dismembered him there and then moved the body parts to the restaurant. The body parts she had found when she arrived shortly after the shootout.

'Anything else?'

Håkan looked at her in surprise. 'What?'

'Anything else, have you got anything else to tell me?'

A bitter smirk. 'Are you kidding?'

'No,' she replied coldly.

'Forget it.'

'Why?'

He flared up. 'Now it's your turn to help me, like we agreed.'

'Yes, with protection. I'll help you with protection if you need it, nothing else.'

Håkan's disappointment turned to anger almost instantly. His impulses took over. He pulled out a pistol. It must have been fixed under the desk. The barrel was pointing right at her forehead.

Antonia instinctively raised her hands. 'Put the pistol down!'

For a second she saw a flash of doubt in him, as if threatening her with the pistol had been an impulse that he couldn't control. He kept hold of the pistol in his right hand but lowered it a little. If he fired she would still die, but having the barrel aimed at her chest instead of her face somehow made the situation feel less threatening.

'Put the pistol down, Håkan,' she tried again. It was pointless. He'd crossed a boundary, a transgression that couldn't be undone. And he knew that himself, which made everything twice as dangerous.

He leaped to his feet, went around the desk and pulled Antonia up from her chair, keeping his pistol trained on her the whole time. Håkan ran his left hand over her body and under her jacket.

'I'm not armed,' she muttered.

'Let's go,' he said, shoving her in the back.

Antonia stumbled, and he shoved her towards the door again. 'What?'

'We're leaving!' He sounded extremely agitated.

She stopped and turned around.

'Hang on a moment,' she pleaded.

Håkan Zivkovic screamed, 'We do what we agreed!'

Saliva sprayed from his mouth. Antonia stared ahead of her in horror as he shoved her towards the door.

They were sitting in her car as she pulled away from Luntmakargatan, heading towards Sveavägen. Håkan kept the pistol aimed at her in his right hand. With his left he was stuffing himself with some old Rohypnol that he'd saved up, *roofies* as they are sometimes known, a reliable old small-time crooks' drug that made

him feel unafraid and violent, should the need arise. He swallowed them down with an energy drink. Then he told her the plan. It was simple. Håkan was going to three addresses: a bank in the city, a tobacconist that offered bets on the horses and finally a currency-exchange office in Värtahamnen, close to the ferries to Finland. And that's where he'd vanish. Antonia just had to drive, wait outside and listen to police radio and if necessary try to mislead her colleagues. With each robbery she would get to hear a bit more of what he had to tell her. Then, when he felt ready, they would part company. That was his idea of what was going to happen. Hers was to get away at the first opportunity. Probably at the very first robbery. Or possibly the second.

'OK, start talking, Håkan.'

He swallowed the last of the energy drink.

'Three months ago I got a big job,' he began. 'A stuck-up cow who was getting divorced wanted proof that her husband was being unfaithful, so she could negotiate a better settlement. I'd been chasing the old man around the city, filming him, but hadn't come up with anything useful.'

Håkan checked that the pistol was fully loaded.

'I realised I needed to shift things up a level. So I got in touch with a guy who knows all about surveillance to ask for help.'

The drugs were kicking in, she could tell.

'Who?' she asked.

'His name's Harry. We talked on the phone, and I ordered microphones, and asked for help installing them.'

Håkan bit one of his thumbnails.

'So Harry and I broke into the rich old guy's house, set up a few microphones. When we were done, I suggested going for a drink nearby.'

He spat out the nail.

'One drink turned into several. Harry was drunk and started babbling about Trasten and all that. Obviously he didn't know I'd met Guzman. But he kept going on about a job that had some connection to it. I was drunk, I don't remember exactly what he said, but he did mention a name.'

'What name?'

'A name that was in the papers.'

'Yes?'

Håkan smiled.

'No. When I come back out,' indicating that she should park in front of a bank. He tucked the pistol in his belt.

'No violence,' she said.

'Wait here' was all he replied.

'Tell me the name,' she asked again.

'No, I told you, when I come back.'

'Cut it out, Håkan. Tell me the name now. That's how it works: you give me the information before you go in, otherwise I drive off.'

He considered this, his eyes darting around.

'Give me the name.'

He was searching for the truth again, his eyes cutting through hers. Christ, this guy had serious trust issues.

Håkan said nothing, just opened the car door and got out.

'Håkan!'

He turned around and put his hand on the car roof, leaned over into the car, then hesitated.

'Lars Vinge,' he said.

'The police officer?'

'Yep.'

Håkan was already walking away.

'Wait, Håkan! What did he say, what did Harry say about Lars Vinge?'

Håkan pulled a balaclava onto his head. 'Stay tuned for the next instalment.'

He headed towards the bank.

'How do I get hold of Harry?'

Håkan didn't answer, just marched coolly and steadily towards the entrance. Antonia watched as he stuck his hand down between his stomach and trousers, turned around and pushed the heavy glass door open with his back and slid in. Was he smiling at her?

She desperately wanted to drive away, call her colleagues.

Then she heard shots from inside the bank, three in rapid succession from the same weapon. She heard screaming as all hell broke loose.

She could see the backs of the people inside the bank as they sat down. Hostages.

No . . .

A few minutes later she heard the sound of police sirens approaching. She looked over to see if Håkan was on his way out, but couldn't see anything. Antonia started the car and did a U-turn over to the other side. She stopped there as two patrol cars came racing up with lights and sirens and parked across both ends of the road, effectively shutting off all traffic in front of the bank. More police cars arrived from all directions, everyone wanting to get involved.

She was in the middle of everything, and showed her ID to a uniformed policewoman who was clearing the street outside the bank of civilians. She grabbed a pair of binoculars from a patrol car, took cover behind it, leaned on the roof and zoomed in on Håkan, who was wandering around inside the bank with his balaclava on, shouting and making demands that no one could hear. The hostages were cowering on the floor.

The National Rapid-Response unit showed up. Desperate to do a bit of real-life shooting. They took up covered positions and aimed their semi-automatic rifles towards the bank. Håkan had to open the door to shout out his bizarre demands for a helicopter and free passage to some obscure country far away. The cops took their chance and shot him in the hip, the backside, the base of his spine. He spun around and collapsed, his legs paralysed. Screaming, Håkan used his hands to drag himself inside the bank again. She followed him through the binoculars, saw his useless legs, the trail of blood he left behind him, saw his pathetic attempts to keep moving.

Antonia switched focus to look at the frightened faces of the people sitting on the floor inside the bank. Then back to Håkan. He had stopped dragging himself, and was lying on the floor like a wounded baby seal. He tugged the balaclava off. Antonia saw him give a hopeless smile. It seemed to be aimed at one of the cashiers. She was wearing a cornflower-blue dress. She'd wet herself badly. Håkan Zivkovic said something to her, put the barrel of the pistol in his mouth and fired. The wall behind him turned red, the noise reached Antonia half a second later. The cashier threw up.

She called Ulf; he had the day off, had a slot booked in the communal laundry and was going to be working that night. They

met in the laundry where he was ironing his T-shirts when she walked in. The whole thing happened on top of the tumble dryer. It lasted one hundred and twenty seconds. They gasped in each other's arms, her sitting, him standing. Antonia wanted to stay in that embrace, just be there for a while. But they didn't have that kind of understanding. Ulf pulled away.

MILES HAD BEEN LUCKY TO GET HOLD OF A PATROL CAR. MOST OF THEM HAD been allocated to a bank-hostage drama over on Sveavägen. The pair of cops in the front seats looked like Laurel and Hardy. Miles didn't know their names, and didn't care, either. One large with a double chin, the other small and wiry.

He was sitting in the back seat, reading through the document again. The man he was going to pick up at Arlanda had no formal papers. The fingerprints the Mexicans had run through the system had set off an alarm with Interpol, then bounced on to Europol, where they triggered an automatic response to the number of Miles's case, the Trasten investigation and ended up in Miles Ingmarsson's email because he was listed as the lead detective.

It could be anyone, a guest who ate dinner at the restaurant a long time ago, a waiter . . . Or someone else. Possibly one of the suspects, even if that was highly unlikely.

The custody unit at the airport was a miserable place. Custody units were always miserable, no matter what they looked like. The officer on duty was a girl in dark-blue trousers and a pale-blue shirt. She didn't say much, just pointed to a pile of documents on a table and left Miles to it. He signed everything.

She returned with a large, blond, suntanned man in his forties whose hands were cuffed.

'Thanks,' Miles said, then took an authoritative grasp of the man's upper arm and led him out of the custody unit.

A plane thundered overhead as they headed towards the police car.

'Miles Ingmarsson, police inspector,' Miles said, trying to make himself heard over the noise of the plane.

The man didn't answer.

The uniforms were sitting in the car, drinking coffee from flasks.

'Let's get going, then,' Hardy said as Miles and Jens got in the back seat.

They forced their way through the taxis and set off back towards the motorway. The radio was playing hard rock. On the motorway Hardy turned the volume up.

'Turn it down,' Miles muttered.

Hardy looked away from the road and into the rear-view mirror. 'Sorry?'

'Turn it down!' Miles said again.

Hardy turned the volume down.

He tried to look at Miles in the rear-view mirror again.

'I just didn't hear what you said, sir,' he said.

Sir?

Then everything happened very quickly. A loud cry from Hardy, swearing from Laurel, then a lurch as the police car braked sharply. Miles was thrown forward, bracing against his seat belt. They were rushing towards a construction area that had been set up in the left-hand lane, in the middle of the motorway. A few yellow cones and a bit of tape, it looked very amateurish. A van had stopped across the right-hand lane.

The crash was unavoidable. The police car smashed into the van, pushing it forward. Glass shattered and flew through the air, metal crumpled, someone screamed, the dashboard bent and snapped with a bang; there was a smell of burning, and something acrid, like acid. The van broke free from the police car and toppled over. Their speed slowed. Miles saw the world outside indistinctly through the crazed glass of his window. They were sliding forward along the motorway, towards the right-hand shoulder. He had a few happy seconds in which to think everything was going to be fine, they were going to be all right. Then something came rushing towards them from behind. An infernal noise, a car horn combined with the piercing shriek of rubber tyres braking sharply at high speed. Miles braced himself. Then came the bang. Like an explosion. It was deafening, and at the same second the immense force made its way through the car. The whole vehicle was thrown forward. Miles was weightless for a moment, then found himself flying forward . . .

The driver of the car behind came crashing in through the rear window, hitting the back of Miles's head with some part of his body before smashing into the shattered dashboard between the two police officers.

The ruined police car bounced off the edge of the road and came to a halt facing the drop at the side of the motorway. Then everything went quiet.

There was a ticking sound, the turn signal, perhaps, or the noise of the overheated engine. The wind was blowing gently through the broken windows of the wrecked car. Laurel and Hardy were moaning in pain and confusion. Otherwise nothing. It was almost peaceful.

Miles Ingmarsson was hanging forward in his seat belt, and from the corner of his eye he could see two men approaching the car. They were carrying weapons. Miles tried to warn the two officers in the front. He couldn't make a sound, couldn't breathe. Something was blocking his airway. He hit Laurel on the shoulder, but the policeman just sat there and didn't react. The men were approaching the car from opposite sides.

The suntanned man beside him undid his seat belt and glanced at Miles.

'Are you OK?' he asked.

Miles guessed his face was turning blue.

'What is it?'

Miles raised his chin and pointed at his throat. The air had run out. He closed his eyes, he was suffocating. Sounds became muffled, the world was dark, Miles didn't want to die. He started to jerk as his body screamed for oxygen, and the jerks turned into convulsions. About then, Miles slipped into unconsciousness.

Miles opened his eyes. He was lying outside the car, coughing and gasping for breath. The suntanned man was sitting on top of him.

'Good! Thought you were going to die.' He smiled with his white teeth, and patted Miles on the shoulder. 'I'll take this as payment.'

He dangled Miles's key to the handcuffs. He stood up and quickly disappeared from view.

Miles turned his head and watched the man and the two others hurrying away from the police car. He took several slow, deep breaths, then rolled over onto his back and looked up at the sky, where he saw thick white clouds against the blue, and realised that life was finite. And that he didn't want it to be, because he hadn't had time to do anything yet. After all, he'd only just met Sanna.

ACCORDING TO THE PLAN, THE POLICE CAR SHOULD HAVE HAD TIME TO STOP. But it hadn't.

Sophie had been sitting in the getaway car and watched the accident happen in the rear-view mirror as the police car crashed into the van, then was run into from behind.

It had taken much longer than expected. But they all appeared in the end. Leszek, Hasani and Jens. All in one piece.

Leszek hurried to her car, Hasani and Jens jumped in the rental car alongside. She caught a glimpse of him, their eyes met, he smiled. She wanted to reach out to him.

Then they drove off.

Sophie headed for Stockholm.

Her heart was thudding so hard that she felt physically exhausted. She wanted to pull off and leave the motorway, hide somewhere. But Leszek ordered her to carry on. They drove along the motorway, painfully slowly.

Sophie wished she had Jens with her rather that Leszek. She wanted to talk to him, look at him . . .

Leszek turned the radio on. A hostage drama on Sveavägen meant that half the city was closed off.

'We were lucky,' he said.

As they approached the building on Norr Mälarstrand Leszek's phone rang. He answered, listened, said little. He was facing away from her. She got the impression something was up . . .

The call ended.

'Who was that?' she asked.

He didn't answer, just bit one of his cuticles, which was unlike him.

'Leszek?' She tried to sound normal.

He turned towards her, and the look on his face made her blood run cold. Disappointment, derision, something impenetrable.

'What is it?' she managed to say.

He pointed at a free parking space close to the door. She parked the car and switched the engine off.

Leszek remained in his seat and held his hand out to her.

'Give me the key.'

'What for?'

'Just give me the key, Sophie.'

She pulled the key out of the ignition and gave it to him.

'Get out of the car,' he said.

'Leszek, I don't understand.'

But she did understand. This was about her. They knew something.

'Just do as I say.'

She stared at him. 'No, I'm not going to. Who was that calling, Leszek? Who did you just speak to on the phone?'

She tried to play the game, to get a hint of what was going on. What did they know?

But Leszek didn't answer. He simply pulled out his pistol and laid it on his lap. His voice was slow, threatening, restrained but aggressive.

'Get out of the car. Now, Sophie.'

He raised the pistol a centimetre from his leg, it was pointing at her.

'What are you doing?' she whispered.

Nothing she said seemed to have any effect on him.

Sophie opened the car door and got out. She walked across the street towards the entrance.

As she tapped the code in she turned around and saw Leszek drive off again in the car.

The lift made its way slowly upwards.

She entered the apartment.

'Hello?'

No answer. She hurried to Albert's room.

He was sitting on his bed, his big headphones over his ears, sketching on a pad. He saw her and pulled the headphones off.

'Hi,' he said.

'Where is everyone?' she asked.

He thought for a moment. 'Leszek and Hasani are with you. Angela and the boys are out. Where have you been?'

'Where are Angela and the boys?'

'Out somewhere, I don't know.'

'When did she leave?'

'Fifteen minutes ago, maybe. Someone called, then she took the boys and left.'

'Where to?'

'I don't know,' he said irritably.

'Who called?'

'I don't know. Mum, what is it?'

She turned around and walked out.

In the hallway she took out one of her mobile phones from her handbag and called Hasani's number. The call didn't go through. She tried Leszek's number, but his mobile phone was just as dead.

Jens? She pulled out her other mobile phone, the one only he knew the number to, checked that it was working, that the volume was switched on, that the battery was charged. She put it back in her bag.

In the kitchen she got a glass off the shelf near the sink, turned on the tap and let the water run until it was so cold it hurt. Sophie tried to think. Tried to figure out what had happened, if they knew anything – and, if so, what?

The water gushed from the tap. The noise suddenly sounded far too loud. Like in a dream. And beyond it there was another sound somewhere, harder, farther away. She turned the tap off.

Something clicked. The front door closing?

'Hello?' she called out.

She tried to listen.

'Hello?' she said again, much quieter this time. As if her own voice had scared her.

She went out into the corridor.

There was a man standing there. In the middle of the hall floor. Short, dark clothes, shaved head. Hands in his jacket pockets, head thrust forward, crooked eyes that were staring at her.

Fear landed heavily in her stomach. She hurried towards Albert's room. The man was close behind her, and grabbed her hair and dragged her to the floor.

'Albert!' she cried, even though she knew he couldn't do anything, he was sitting there paralysed on his bed.

'*Mum!*' he called back.

The man sat on top of her. His crooked eyes were clearer now, asymmetrical in a pale face.

He was working efficiently, holding her down with brute strength. There was something in his hand: a folded handkerchief. He pressed it into her mouth as she tried to scream. He held her nose tight. Out of reflex she opened her mouth, and breathed in through the handkerchief. Strong, bitter, chemical. She felt giddy instantly. She had time to see him shake out a black cloth sack, which he pulled over her head and tied around her throat.

Everything went black.

PART TWO

24

(STOCKHOLM)

A STRAY DOG WAS RUNNING AROUND, SNIFFING ANXIOUSLY AMONG THE DEAD and buried.

Antonia was standing in Västberga Cemetery looking at the stone beneath which Lars Vinge lay buried beside his parents.

Why was she standing there? Because she wanted to understand something? Hear something – a whisper, voices from the other side? But nothing of that sort came to her. Only that morning's events, which didn't want to leave her consciousness. The chaos at the bank on Sveavägen. The shot, Håkan Zivkovic's skull exploding, the blood on the wall.

Antonia sighed.

The stray dog scampered around in front of her.

Was she standing here among the dead in the hope of coming to terms with everything?

No . . .

She just wanted to know. Just like she did on all the other days of the week.

Antonia walked away and got back in her car, putting it in reverse. The stray dog pissed on Lars Vinge's grave before wandering off.

She drove back to the station, sat down behind her desk and read through the report on his death.

Vinge had shot himself in the head six months ago with a stolen

weapon in an apartment on Södermalm after murdering his boss, Gunilla Strandberg. There were plenty of convincing statements from forensics experts and medical officers. Suicide, nothing more, nothing less.

But it felt shaky. She had felt as much the first time she read it. There ought to be more there. There always was in other investigations. Official details, bureaucratic nonsense, references and all manner of information about things no one would ever be interested in. But not here, not with Lars Vinge.

Antonia leaned back.

Where was all the information about bankruptcies, relatives, his estate, debts? There wasn't even some of the most basic information, such as where his belongings had been archived. Lars Vinge's employment file ought to have been there as well, and all the details of his employment history. But there was nothing like that. Was it just a matter of sloppiness? Or was it more deliberate?

Antonia opened a search engine on her computer. There were eight companies and individuals who dealt with the belongings of dead people in Stockholm. She called each of them in turn, introducing herself and giving them Vinge's name and ID number, and said the same thing to them all: 'It's urgent.'

MILES HAD A DRIP IN HIS ARM AND WAS STARING UP AT A BLANK WHITE ceiling.

A grey-haired doctor came in. White coat, blue trousers. He was reading some notes.

'You've got three broken ribs, concussion and numerous scratches and bruises.'

He moved on to the usual questions: *How are you feeling, any memory loss, anxiety?*

Miles answered *OK, no, no.*

'I'll prescribe some painkillers, something for anxiety and some sleeping pills, in case you have trouble sleeping.'

'But I don't feel anxious,' Miles said.

'This is Sweden, everyone's anxious,' the doctor muttered.

'Nurse will give you some pills on your way out, until you get to a chemist.'

 The staff room smelled of scorched coffee when Miles got back to the station. He filled his cup.

Antonia Miller came in and got a mug from the cupboard.

'What happened?' she asked.

He recognised her curiosity. It was always there, like some destructive torment.

'I don't know. A prisoner breakout.'

She looked tired. There was something brittle about her, and her eyes were blazing.

'How are you doing?' he heard himself ask.

'How am I doing?'

She sounded as if he'd accused her of something.

'Yes, how are you doing, Antonia?'

'I'm fine. You?'

'Absolutely fine,' he replied.

She looked doubtfully at the injuries to his face.

'Who is he?' she said.

'Who?'

'The guy from Mexico.'

'No idea.'

'But this must mean something?'

'Not necessarily. Maybe he was just a guest at the restaurant, or one of the staff. That could be why the alert sounded when his prints popped up.'

She almost snorted.

'But he was broken out of custody?' she said.

'Yes, people get all sorts of ideas in their heads these days. There's not necessarily any connection.'

He smiled, a past master at dismissing objections.

She met his smile, happy mouth, angry eyes. 'What do you mean by that?'

'No more than I said.'

'What did you say, then?'

'That there's not necessarily any connection.'

She was on the point of exploding but tried to hold everything in.

'What did he look like?' she asked.

'Nothing special,' he replied.

'How does that look, then?'

'Like nothing much,' he said.

She scooped coffee into the filter.

'Lars Vinge,' she said quietly.

He stopped.

'What?'

'Lars Vinge,' she repeated.

He didn't know who she was talking about, and said, 'Who's that?'

'Lars Vinge, he worked for Gunilla on the Hector Guzman investigation. The man who shot her, then himself . . .'

Miles looked at her with distaste. 'This is depressing, just let it go, for God's sake.'

'Let what go?'

But Miles merely walked away.

That, together with Miles's dismissive attitude and her own inability to control herself, made her see red. She marched after him.

'You're pathetic, Ingmarsson. And soon you'll be a laughing-stock. You know that, don't you?'

He stopped.

'What are you doing here?' she went on.

An irritated smile crossed his face. 'I'm doing my job.'

'No, that's exactly what you're not doing. Are you pliable, Miles? Is that why you're here?'

She struggled to stay calm.

'I don't know what you're talking about,' he said.

'Yes, you do. When anyone needs to empty the bucket of shit, they call you. And you do the shitty job. You've been brought in here specifically not to do anything. I'm not stupid. How are you going to keep the lid on this incident?'

'You look after your own cases and I'll look after mine.'

He kept on walking.

'Yours? You've only got one, and it's a joke,' she said.

'You're a very unpleasant person,' Miles said.

Back in his office Miles sat down on his chair, regretting his last words to Antonia. He didn't like being bitter and mean.

He stared out through the window, the sky was blue, the clouds were white, aeroplanes were flying around up there, and somewhere beyond the atmosphere the universe began, and beyond the universe there was evidently nothing.

He could see her from the corner of his eye, she was standing by the door.

'We protect the good from the bad,' she said. 'We do it because we believe in it. And while we do it, we protect each other. We help each other and we all work towards the same goal. And you know why?'

She knew he wasn't going to answer that, so she went on.

'Because we police officers have chosen to do this over any number of other good things.'

She pointed behind her with her thumb.

'Everyone in this corridor has made sacrifices. So who the fuck are you, Miles Ingmarsson?'

She marched into his office, put a mug of fresh coffee down on his desk and walked out.

He stared at the mug of coffee, took hold of it and drank a sip. It was perfect.

Miles left the office later that afternoon and walked home alone through the city. The pain in both his soul and his ribs was constant and severe. His injured face scared people he met. He smoked three cigarettes in a row and kept his feelings locked up. He was fine with that, he'd been brought up to do that whenever his emotions got too much.

Sanna was home.

She looked normal: no make-up, jeans and a top. He liked that. But he liked it just as much when she looked like a whore. Sanna was perfect, however she was.

'How are you doing?' she asked, touching the wounds on his face carefully with her forefinger.

'It's fine.'

Sanna searched his eyes. 'No, it's not.'

He slumped on the sofa and she sat down beside him. Miles talked about the breakout and the car crash. Sanna looked horrified. She patted his cheek tenderly. Her gentle touch released the tension, and Miles sighed.

Fifteen minutes later she was standing in front of him, hand on hip. She was posing very nicely, dressed up as a maid, with fishnet stockings and a skirt that was far too short. Her breasts were squeezed tight and her lips were redder than a Communist star. Sanna turned around and walked steadily towards the hall. She pulled one of his beige coats from its hanger and put it on.

'See you,' she said, and disappeared.

The front door closed with a bang.

Miles listened to her footsteps in the stairwell until they faded away.

He stared at the ceiling. The car crash came back. The feeling of suffocating, the cold, brittle anguish.

That near-death experience had been of no value at all. Just horrible, in every possible way.

Music from the radio in the kitchen, melancholic and beautiful; it hurt, cutting a breathing hole in what Miles was trying to smother.

He made to get up from the sofa, but the pain in his ribs was instantaneous. He tried again and got to his feet with a short yelp of pain. He went out to the kitchen and turned off the damned radio.

He leaned against the kitchen counter and stared down into the sink, silvery in a surprisingly ugly way. His breathing was fast and shallow, his heart was beating faster and weaker. The doctor was right, everyone was anxious. He found the pills the nurse gave him at the hospital.

He took a painkiller.

He took a tranquilliser.

He took a sleeping pill.

Miles waited a minuite, nothing happened. He took one more of each again.

Artificial reassurance forced its way through.

Emotional vacuum . . .

Miles stretched out on the bed, his breathing becoming deeper and steadier.

The phone rang solemnly beyond walls of tiredness and emotional numbness. His eyelids closed.

The ringing phone was far away. Miles slipped into a black, medicinal torpor.

The phone rang again.

25

(STOCKHOLM)

SOPHIE OPENED HER EYES. EVERYTHING WAS BLACK; THERE WAS CLOTH OVER her face. She was lying on the floor, her hands taped together behind her back. Something in her mouth . . . the handkerchief. She managed to spit it out. A headache was cutting through her head.

'Albert!' she cried.

A phone rang some distance away in the apartment.

'Albert!'

The phone rang again. She recognised it now. Jens's phone.

Sophie struggled and tugged, but her arms were held tight by the tape. She screamed in frustration and pushed herself back across the floor with her feet until she hit a wall, then pressed upwards until she was standing.

She felt her way towards the hall with her back-tied hands. She managed to get hold of the strap of her handbag on the chair, and pulled it behind her as she hurried blindly towards Albert's room.

Beside his bed she sank to her knees and leaned forward, but could feel nothing but sheets; the bed was empty.

'Albert,' she said, even though she knew he wasn't there. *Abbe . . .*

She had to get the phone out in case it rang again, and she managed to stick her taped hands inside the bag. She rummaged around with her fingers. There it was. Sophie took it out carefully and put it behind her so she could reach it with her fingers.

Then she sat there on her knees, tied up and blind. There wasn't anything else she could do.

Time passed; there were no sounds at all, she guessed it was night. Tears came, she was frightened.

The mobile phone rang again.

Sophie managed to press the Answer button. A muffled voice in the distance.

'Jens, I can't hear you. You've got to come!'

Her voice was loud, almost a shout. She gave him the address and code for the door.

'They've taken Albert! I'm tied up!' she went on.

She could hear his voice but not what he was saying.

'Don't hang up!' she cried, terrified of being alone.

He didn't, and his voice kept her company for twenty minutes until she heard the heavy white wooden door open and Jens came rushing into the apartment.

'I'm in here!' she called.

He entered the room and first untied the cloth sack from around her neck and helped take it off. Then he sat down behind her and cut the tape from her wrists. She glanced around Albert's room. His things were still there, but the wheelchair was gone.

'Look for Albert,' she said as she got up. She went from room to room, leaning against the walls for support. The substance on the handkerchief that had drugged her was still in her system; she was having trouble keeping her balance, her headache cutting through her forehead and into her eyes. She searched manically through the apartment.

'There's no one here, Sophie.'

Jens was behind her.

She stopped in the living room.

'You need to sit down, Sophie.'

She turned towards him.

'Why did you call me?' she said.

Her suspicion was obvious.

'In the middle of the night, Jens?'

'I'm still on Mexican time, I couldn't sleep.'

'So you called me several times?'

'Yes, I did.'

'Why?'

'Why are you so suspicious?'

'Why, Jens?'

Jens tried to read her.

'Your friend Hasani drove me into the city after you freed me. His phone rang; suddenly he was in a hurry, and he let me out. I thought it was odd. I made my way home but couldn't shake the feeling that something was wrong, so I called you. But that doesn't matter right now. Sophie, tell me what happened.'

She did, as best she could. From start to finish.

How she had been working for Aron since she and Jens last saw each other. How she had recently contacted the Hankes after she found out that they and the Colombians were working together against Hector. The fact that she was doing it in secret, without Aron or anyone else knowing what she was trying to achieve. That her meeting had resulted in Daphne and Thierry being murdered. She told Jens about the phone call Leszek had received in the car, how she had made her way up to the apartment and found only Albert there, then how she was attacked and Albert taken.

'Hector?' Jens asked.

'Still in a coma.'

'Aron?'

'He's in charge.'

'What does that mean?'

'He makes sure things keep working.'

'And are they?' Jens asked.

'No.'

He tried to understand.

'Why didn't you go to him first? You went to the Hankes? What were you thinking?'

'Aron isn't himself. He's stressed and edgy, impossible to reason with. I knew he'd start a small war if I told him what I knew. And he would have lost, everyone would have lost.'

'How much did you know?' he asked.

'The Hankes and Ignacio Ramirez are working together to get rid of Hector and take everything he's got. They murdered Hector's brother Eduardo and tried to get Aron in Istanbul at the same time. That was how they started.'

'But how did you know that?'

'I was in Colombia shortly after Istanbul. It was supposed to be a routine meeting with Ignacio and Alfonse Ramirez. But it turned out to be their way of communicating with the organisation, through me.'

'What did they say?'

'That we should lie down and give up, give the Hankes everything, Hector included.'

Jens thought for a while.

'And you went home and said nothing?'

'There would have been a bloodbath . . .'

They looked at each other. Only now did she really see him. He was the same as before, a bit older, maybe, but it suited him. She could see empathy in him; he radiated it as if he really did understand her position, her dilemma.

'Do you regret it?' he asked quietly.

She knew he didn't mean any criticism. As usual, he was straightforward and undaunted when things got serious.

'I can't think like that. You can see that, can't you?' she replied.

'Yes, I understand. And it was wrong of me to ask,' he said. 'You made a decision that felt right at the time. And it was, in spite of everything. Because there was no alternative. I would have made the same decision, Sophie.'

His words were some comfort to her.

'I think Aron knows about Munich,' she said.

'So he moved everyone, afraid for their security now that you've been to see the devil incarnate?'

She let him continue.

'And now he's taken Albert as a bargaining tool,' Jens said. 'As long as Aron has him, you can't do anything. Does that sound plausible?'

'It sounds plausible,' she said.

'But why didn't they take him at the same time as they must have taken the others, Angela and the children, before you got home?'

She had no answer to that.

'And why didn't they just kill you?' Jens said.

She thought about it. Perhaps he was right, perhaps he wasn't. It

didn't matter any more. Albert was all that mattered, getting him back as soon as possible.

'The man who took Albert, the one who drugged you, did you get a good look at him?'

'Yes . . .'

'Did you recognise him?'

'No.'

'Are you sure? Think about it, have you ever seen him before anywhere? With Hector, with Aron, in the background? Is he one of theirs?'

She searched her memory. Trying to identify anyone next to Hector. No, she was sure she'd never seen the man before. But a different face came into her mind. A woman she had first met at Hector's birthday celebrations. The woman stayed close to Hector. She was extremely beautiful, and Sophie had felt oddly jealous. Then they had met in the house in Marbella, where Adalberto was killed . . . when Hector was shot.

'Sonya . . . ?' she said out loud to herself.

Sophie quickly dug out the number, got up and paced around the room, waiting impatiently for her to pick up.

A woman's voice answered.

'Sonya!'

A brief silence.

'*Sophie?*' Sonya replied in surprise.

'Where's Albert?'

'*We're not to talk. Hang up and don't call me again.*'

'Where's Albert?'

'*I'm hanging up now.*'

'Wait, please, Sonya.'

She waited, and Sophie breathed out.

'Just explain what's happened, and where Albert is. Tell me what you want me to do.'

'*No, I'm not going to explain, and we're not to talk any more.*' Sonya paused before going on in a low voice: '*But I swear to you that I don't know where Albert is. I hope nothing's happened to him. Don't call again.*'

The call ended. Sophie stood there with her back to Jens, with the mobile phone in her hand.

'She didn't know where he was?'

'No, that's what she said.'

'Do you believe her?'

She turned to him. 'Yes.'

'So who's taken Albert?'

'The Hankes,' she said.

'Can you be certain?'

'No.'

'So what are you going to do?'

'They'll be in touch.'

'Why would they be in touch?'

'They want something. That's why they've taken him.'

She tried to sound convincing, not least to make herself believe it.

'You're not that naïve, Sophie,' he said, then went on: 'This is Ralph Hanke we're talking about. If he's taken Albert, he's not going to make you an offer and then hand Albert back.'

She looked at him.

'Ralph Hanke takes,' Jens continued. 'That's his skill. He knows how people who haven't got anything work. It's all about pressing people down and shaping them, nothing else . . . Look at the murders. Eduardo – why him? Daphne and Thierry? A brother, a married couple. None of them belong to Hector's inner circle. Hanke just wants to show he can do whatever he wants. It's a form of language, Sophie. Otherwise they'd have killed you in Munich . . . They want something by taking Albert.'

'They want Hector,' she said.

'And if you give him Hector? Which I doubt that you could actually do. What happens then?'

She didn't answer.

'Is he going to give Albert back? No, Ralph Hanke doesn't give anything back.'

It was blunt, and chilling.

'We have to go and get him,' she said.

Jens nodded.

'We do,' he said.

'Just you and me?' she asked.

'It'll be difficult,' Jens said.

'Have you got anyone else who can help us?'

'Not off the top of my head. You?'

Sophie thought. Her eyes grew bigger.

'Yes, I think so,' she said.

HE WOKE UP IN THE SAME POSITION HE HAD FALLEN ASLEEP IN. ON HIS BACK, on top of the bedspread. No Sanna beside him. Night outside the window.

Miles searched through the apartment. She hadn't come home.

His mobile phone was on the kitchen table. Five missed calls, all from Sanna. Three messages in his voicemail.

He called her, but her phone was switched off.

Miles checked the messages.

'*Hi, it's me, can you come and get me at the club? I'll wait here.*'

She was speaking in a tone of forced calm.

The next message followed.

'*They're closing soon, the place will soon be locked up. I can't walk out of here on my own. Please, call me.*'

Miles could hear an unmistakable anxiety in her voice.

Then another message, the call made by mistake. A scraping sound as she walked, her voice, muffled by the fabric of her pocket. The words were unintelligible, but the pleading tone was clear enough. He heard a male voice, complaining, loud, high-pitched, agitated, wounded, intense . . .

The line went dead.

THE TAXI STOPPED OUTSIDE SOPHIE AND ALBERT'S APARTMENT ON ERIKSBERGSGATAN.

The lift up.

Sophie unlocked the door and walked through the apartment to the guest bedroom. There, in a cupboard, up on a shelf behind a box of winter gloves – a wooden casket. She took it down, opened the lid. An old napkin, white and crumpled. There was a phone number written on it in firm handwriting, written by a man who had prom-ised to return a favour to her.

She dialled the international code for Germany, then the number on the napkin.

A male voice answered with a German *hallo?* after three rings.

'Klaus?' she asked.

'*Who wants to know?*' the voice said in German.

'An old friend,' she said quietly in English.

'*Klaus isn't here any more,*' the man said in English.

'Do you know where I can find him?'

'*He's passed away.*' The voice was subdued. '*Who am I talking to?*' he asked again.

'What happened?'

'*The cancer got him in the end.*'

Sophie felt a wave of grief. She could see the man in front of her, Klaus Köhler. Wiry, dangerous, different . . . and sensitive. He was one big paradox. He'd arrived in Stockholm together with the big Russian, Mikhail Asmarov, and they had both worked for Ralph Hanke. They were planning to put Hector under pressure. It didn't go as planned.

They kidnapped Hector, drove him out into the woods, put a gun to his head and made demands. Aron, Sophie and Jens followed. Aron shot Klaus in the stomach. Hector and Aron wanted to leave him to die there, bleed out in the forest. But Sophie didn't listen to them. She stopped the bleeding temporarily, demanded that they drive Klaus to the hospital. They did it reluctantly.

She would meet Klaus Köhler two more times. In the chaos that followed, everything became increasingly blurred. Enemies and friends became friends and enemies. Mikhail Asmarov came with Klaus to her and Jens's hideout. Klaus was hurt again. This time a bullet in his shoulder. She helped him again. The third time it was Klaus's turn to help her, and indirectly Hector and Aaron, when he and Mikhail stepped into Trasten at the right moment and fired their weapons against the Russians who were about to kill them all.

Klaus made her the promise there and then.

You've saved my life twice, Klaus had said, then wrote his number on one of the restaurant's napkins before walking away.

'When?' Sophie asked the man on the phone.

'*Two months ago.*'

'Had he been ill for long?'

'*Yes. But it was diagnosed too late.*'

'Who are you?' she asked.

'*My name's Rüdiger. I lived with Klaus.*'

'I'm sorry,' she said. It sounded hollow.

A pause.

'*Is that a Scandinavian accent I hear?*' he asked.

'Yes . . .'

'*Then I think I know who you are.*'

'Who am I?' she asked.

'*You're the woman who helped him, the nurse. Aren't you?*'

She didn't answer.

'*Thank you, Sophie,*' he said, as if they knew each other. Several seconds passed before he went on. '*What did you want to talk to Klaus about?*'

'I wanted to ask for help,' she said quietly.

'*What with?*'

'It doesn't matter now.

A pregnant pause.

'*Goodbye,*' Rüdiger said, and hung up.

MILES SLIPPED INTO THE STRIP CLUB. THERE WERE JUST A COUPLE OF POOR, lonely jerks waiting for the morning show.

He headed straight for the curtain that was off-limits to people like him.

A heavily made-up woman with fiery red hair, thigh-high boots, a leather corset and a bullwhip in her hand was walking towards him along the corridor on her high heels.

'Do you know where I can find Sanna?' he asked.

'You're not allowed back here.' She had a strong Finnish accent.

'Do you know where I can find Sanna?' he asked again, frustrated.

'Why?'

'I need to get hold of her.'

The woman looked at him carefully. 'You're a regular here?'

He nodded again.

The leather mistress brightened up.

'Well, sure! We always give each other's addresses to customers who sit and stare at us all day long. All we ever dream of is that one of you will one day discover us and get in touch.'

The Finnish accent made her sarcasm even more biting.

'I actually know her. I want to talk to her . . . We're living together.'

She held his gaze. He looked away, dug out his wallet and showed her his police ID.

'That doesn't make it any better,' she said.

Miles realised it was pointless and put his ID away.

'If you see her, tell her Miles is looking for her.'

He walked away.

The Finnish woman called after him. 'How well do you know her?'

Miles stopped and turned around. 'What?'

'How well do you know Sanna?'

Miles thought. 'Fairly well.'

She waited for more. 'That doesn't mean anything to me. Tell me something about her.'

'Tell you something about her?'

She knew he'd heard her, and said nothing.

'She's a good cook,' he said, but could hear how hollow that sounded.

The woman confirmed as much with an unimpressed stare.

'She likes comedies,' he mumbled. 'She lights candles, buys flowers when she can. When she's by herself and in a good mood she sings old Swedish pop songs.'

Miles searched his memory and more images appeared.

'She's allergic to nickel. She hits me hard on my upper arm when she laughs, she's very good at French, good pronunciation . . .'

He shrugged, thinking it all sounded silly.

The Finnish woman stood there motionless; there was something bitter about her, as if she were giving him a last chance. Miles scratched his head.

'She grew up with her mum and dad in Malmberget. They were Communists,' he said.

He rubbed the back of his neck, then went on.

'Sanna thinks they loved her but their political convictions meant they sometimes neglected her—'

'Sanna's in Södermalm Hospital,' the leather-clad woman interrupted.

Miles looked up. 'Sorry?'

She knew he had heard.

'Her ex was here yesterday after work. He beat the shit out of her.'

She walked off. Miles tried to make sense of what the woman had told him.

'Who? What's his name, the ex?' he managed to say.

The Finnish woman stopped, turned around, but seemed to hesitate.

'Roger Lindgren,' she said.

She stood there for a while with one hand on her hip.

'You're such fucking pathetic little cunts, all of you.'

She said this with genuine disgust, aimed at the entire male gender. He wanted to say he wasn't one of them. But of course he was.

Her stiletto heels clicked hard on the floor as she stalked off and disappeared behind the curtain to the strip club. A smattering of thin applause greeted her as she walked onstage and cracked her bullwhip in the air. Synth drums from 1986, Samantha Fox singing 'Touch Me'.

She lay there, unconscious and badly beaten. Her jaw was broken, the lower half of her face hidden by bandages, her eyes bruised and swollen beyond recognition, traces of dried blood.

Part of him wanted to walk away; another part wanted to stay, stay and keep watch.

Staying with her won.

He fetched a chair, pulled it to the side of the bed and never took his eyes off her. He didn't cry. Everything was dry and revolting.

Hospital apparatuses hummed in the room. Miles wanted to lean forward and whisper something in her ear, tell her he was there now, that he'd never give up. But he didn't. Instead he just sat there staring at her, as if he were being forced to. As if some stronger power

were holding him there. Look at this, look and see how it feels, Miles Ingmarsson.

The Finnish woman at the strip club was right. He was a little cunt.

Miles had always wanted to believe that his nonchalant attitude towards life and the people around him gave him a sort of neutral alibi for everything and everyone: an in-between person, neither good nor bad, neither kind nor mean. Just drifting past everything without any responsibility. As if he had convinced himself that the reality he lived in was a sort of mixture of extremes. And that if he balanced precisely on the knife's edge, he would be immune to most things. But Miles Ingmarsson wasn't immune to anything. Not to mortal dread: the car crash had proved that. Not to love: Sanna had proved that. Not to fear: the previous evening had proved that.

And not to hatred, as the person who had done this had proved.

26

(MOSCOW)

MIKHAIL ASMAROV HURRIED DOWN THE ESCALATOR IN THE UNDERGROUND. HIS BIG BODY MOVED quickly; people scattered to make way for him.

There were four men after him, and there were probably more on the way. He had drowned their boss in the bath, in his lover's home. It was problematic, half-political. He had been given the job by another freelancer who was close to the police. That was how the cops commissioned murders. So now he had a mafia group after him, and soon the police as well. The lover had talked. Mikhail regretted giving in to an attack of mercy. He should have drowned her, too.

The underground train was standing at the platform. Was he going to make it? He heard the little signal and the driver's voice inside the train. Mikhail took a huge leap into the carriage just before the doors closed.

He saw his pursuers reach the bottom of the escalator as the train began to move. Panting, he made his way back through the carriage to an empty seat. He sat down breathlessly. Now every fucker in Moscow knew he was on this train.

The train rattled through the tunnel, and glitches in the electricity supply meant the lights in the carriage kept flickering. Mikhail could feel his pistol against his ribs.

A little girl was playing a violin at one end of the carriage. It sounded good; she knew what she was doing. Mikhail looked

around: children, adults, old people. There'd be a bloodbath if he stayed where he was.

The train ground to a halt at the next station. Mikhail scanned the sea of people going past but had no chance of knowing if anyone was waiting for him.

The doors opened and he dived into the people on the platform, cruising around the big, square marble pillars as he hurried towards the escalator.

On the other side, on the escalator taking people down to the platform, two men had just got on and were heading towards him. Mikhail thought he recognised one of them. He put his hand inside his jacket.

The man caught sight of him when they were almost level. The moment of recognition was unmistakable. Mikhail pulled his pistol from its holster, shot and hit the man in the side of the head, then ducked down for cover.

People started screaming and trying to get away in panic on the escalators. He heard pistol shots firing blindly behind him. Mikhail crouched down, then glanced up; he was almost at the top of the escalator. At that moment his mobile phone rang, caller unknown, and he answered with a grunt.

'Yes?'

'Mikhail?'

'Yes?'

The top of the escalator was close now.

'Rüdiger here.'

'Hang on, Rüdiger.'

Mikhail stood up and ran up the last few steps and through the hall. He reached one of the exits and took it, hurried along a pavement until he found a door that was open, ran through a corridor and found himself in a back yard. High-rise apartments all around him, sky up above. Mikhail stopped, held his phone up and gasped: 'Yes?'

'It's Rüdiger.'

'Yes, so you said.'

'Are you busy?'

'What do you want?'

'*The nurse called.*'

'Who?' Mikhail was still out of breath.

'*Hector Guzman's woman, Sophie . . . Sweden.*'

Mikhail added Rüdiger's words together, and after the equals sign a woman's face appeared in his mind. She was beautiful, kind and good, he remembered. And completely wrecked after the shootout at Trasten.

'And?'

'*The debt you inherited from Klaus. She needs help.*'

Klaus had been lying on his deathbed, emaciated and pale, full of guilt and other crap. He had tried to make amends for his past before the devil came to get him, because he was going to; no one doubted that, least of all Klaus himself. So his promise to Sophie had been important to him. She had saved Klaus's life twice in a short space of time, and that had evidently softened his heart.

Klaus had asked Mikhail for help, and Mikhail had taken on the debt in exchange for €40,000.

'What with?' Mikhail asked.

'*I don't know.*'

'It'll have to wait, I'm busy with other things right now.'

'*That wasn't what you agreed. Klaus was clear about that.*'

'Klaus is dead. And I'm busy. I'm sorry, Rüdiger, not now.'

'*Why would you say that about Klaus, Mikhail? You promised him. And you were also handsomely rewarded. Now the woman is asking for help. Keep the agreement. Do the right thing. That's all Klaus wanted.*'

Rüdiger was as measured as a teacher. Mikhail massaged his bull neck and looked around, surrounded by buildings. It was a fitting metaphor. He was trapped in Moscow. And the longer he stayed there, the closer the walls would press in on him.

'OK, I'll contact her,' Mikhail said and hung up.

He walked across the yard, through the building and out onto the street on the other side of the building. Then down into the underground again. They wouldn't look there again for a while. He needed to get out of Moscow without being spotted; that was his first goal.

27

(VILLEFRANCHE)

ARON WAS STANDING ON THE TERRACE LOOKING OUT OVER THE SEA AND CAP Ferrat.

The electronic gates down at the end of the garden swung open and the seven-seat family Jeep came driving up the hill.

Aron left the terrace and went down to meet them in front of the entrance.

Angela was leading Andres and Fabien by the hand.

'I'm Aron, welcome. Long journey?' he asked.

Angela nodded. She looked drained, anxious, no energy at all.

He said hello to the boys, smiled and tried to make light of the situation. Sonya came to his rescue and helped Angela and the boys inside the house.

Leszek and Hasani were standing in front of him, and he gestured that they needed to talk without delay.

In spite of the chill in the air, they sat down at a secluded table at the back of the house. Raimunda brought cups and a flask of coffee. Aron and Leszek watched as Hasani put five sugar lumps in his cup and stirred it with the spoon.

They started talking.

'Is there any truth in it?' Aron asked.

The question was aimed at Leszek. He answered with a shrug, cautious as ever.

'It's like this,' he began. 'You call and tell us to come, all apart

from Sophie. Without her knowledge, without saying anything to her. We do as we have been told. She is suddenly all alone, scared, possibly worried for her life, who knows. But she has betrayed us. So she does something drastic and says her son is missing, to get our attention and sympathy.'

Aron nodded. But Leszek wasn't finished.

'That's the conclusion one comes to first, the most probable. But perhaps there is some truth in what she says,' he went on. 'I've lived at her side. She's never lied, never tried to distance herself from us, never tried to gain any personal advantage. Instead, she has done whatever we have asked her to. And she has done her best.'

'She was in Munich with the Hankes,' Aron said. 'She gave us false information after her meeting with Ignacio and Alfonse. And now something unlikely about Albert going missing the moment we leave her?'

Leszek lowered his head, even he couldn't get away from the inevitable.

'Hasani?' Aron asked.

Hasani stirred his coffee again.

'I don't know her, so the little I've seen can't really be taken to mean anything.'

He stopped stirring.

'I saw the grief in the boys' eyes when Eduardo was taken from his family,' he continued. 'I was a guest of Daphne and Thierry when they were murdered. So if she has anything at all to do with . . .'

He didn't say any more, just raised the cup to his lips and drank his sweet coffee.

ANGELA SHOOK OUT THE CLEAN SHEETS. THEY HUNG IN THE AIR FOR A MOMENT before sinking onto the mattress.

The two boys, Andres and Fabien, were asleep on the bed, the window was ajar. Angela had heard fragments of the men's conversation down below. Aron's questions, Leszek's answers, Hasani's comments, their tentative tone of voice. They were talking about Sophie, and they were talking about treachery.

Angela realised that this was how it was going to be, that Aron

and the others' desire to protect her and the boys wasn't the whole truth. She knew too much. So even if the threat against them disappeared, the situation wouldn't change. She and the boys would always have to live a life of undefined captivity.

Hasani wasn't on her side any more, he was on theirs. Maybe he had been all along, but now it was obvious.

Angela wanted her husband back, Eduardo; she wanted to carry on living life the way it was meant to be . . . She put a pillowcase on one of the pillows.

'Are they asleep?'

Angela turned around.

Sonya was standing in the doorway, looking at the sleeping boys.

'Have you got everything you need, Angela?'

Angela realised she was clutching the pillow like a teddy bear.

'Yes, thanks,' she said, and finished putting the pillowcase on.

Sonya was about to leave when the men's voices outside the window reached her. Suddenly she looked anxious, walked back into the room and over to the window and looked down. Then she closed and bolted it.

'Have you been listening to what they're talking about?'

'No, I've just been standing here thinking about other things.' She smiled sweetly and believably.

Sonya was about to say something, then changed her mind and walked out.

Angela's shoulders slumped.

She was frightened. She was going to get herself and her boys away from there. She would ask for help.

And she knew whom she was going to ask.

28

(MUNICH)

ALBERT WOKE UP IN A NARROW BUNK.

He looked around the room. The ceiling and walls were covered with soundproof rubber. There were no windows.

The room was sparsely furnished. Apart from the bed he was in, there was just a small table and a chair in the middle of the floor.

His wheelchair was beside the bed. Albert looked above his head, where there was a metal pole with a handle on a chain. It looked like they'd thought of everything.

The last thing he remembered was waking up in a car, and the man with the strange eyes had drugged him again, just like he had in the apartment on Norr Mälarstrand. A hard grip around his neck, the handkerchief against his nose and mouth, the strong, bitter smell. Albert had time to notice from the road signs that they were in Germany.

He heaved himself out of bed and into his wheelchair. There were two doors in the room, one of which was cut into the rubber and had no handle. The other one was an ordinary wooden door that led to a small bathroom, with a disabled-friendly toilet, basin and shower.

He wheeled himself over to the door with no handle and tried to bang on it.

The hours ticked by. The lack of windows, of a horizon and any concept of time, made him anxious. And the room was so small.

Mum? What had happened to his mum?

He felt panic growing. He just wanted to know where he was, to hear another person's voice. Anything at all . . .

Albert closed his eyes and tried to find a place inside himself, a calm place. But he couldn't.

The hours blurred together and he drifted between dream and reality as he sat in his wheelchair in one corner of the room. The feeling of panic was there the whole time. It just kept growing, and he found himself gasping for breath.

Albert started to shout, then scream. It made the panic worse. He stopped and sat still in his wheelchair, arms wrapped tightly around himself.

The sound was barely audible . . . something metallic. At first he thought it was in his mind, or some remnant from a dream. But it was there, just below him on the floor, halfway along one of the longer walls. A rattling sound, as if someone was running an object up and down a small grille – a high-pitched sound.

Albert lowered himself to the floor, listened, tried to identify where it was coming from, then pulled off some of the insulation and found a small ventilation hole at ground level. The sound became clearer. He put his mouth to the hole.

'Hello?'

The rattling continued. Albert called out again. Then it stopped. A voice, somewhat distant, words in German that Albert didn't understand.

'Who's that?' he asked in English.

A moment's silence. Then the voice replied in the same language.

'I'm Lothar, who are you?'

Albert relaxed a bit, the sound of another person's voice calmed his panic.

'I'm Albert. Are you locked up like me?'

'Yes,' Lothar replied.

'Why are we here?'

'I don't know. Where are you from, Albert?'

Albert got the impression that the voice belonged to a young man, perhaps someone his own age.

'From Sweden, Stockholm. I'm sixteen. How old are you, Lothar?'

'I'm seventeen, from Berlin.'

Albert lay there by the hole, trying to figure out his next question.

'Where are we?' he asked.

'I don't know, in Germany, I think. The south, maybe Bavaria.'

'Why do you think that?'

'The food they serve.'

'They?'

'Yes, whoever they are.'

'How long have you been here?'

'A few days. You?'

'I don't know, I just woke up. Have you met anyone, seen anyone?'

'No, they bring the food in when I'm asleep. I haven't seen or heard anyone.'

'What happened to you? How did you get here?'

'They killed my mum,' the voice said quietly.

Those words changed everything. The brief conversation with Lothar had made Albert forget how serious things were. Now the realisation crashed back in on him with full force.

'They broke into our apartment. Killed her, drugged me, brought me here,' Lothar said.

Albert stared in front of him. She was dead. His mum was dead . . .

'Albert?'

'Yes,' he managed to say.

'What happened to you?'

'They broke into our apartment, drugged me.'

'Was anyone there with you?'

'My mum,' he said.

29

(STOCKHOLM)

ANTONIA HAD TWO CASES LEFT TO WORK ON. THEY WERE HOPELESS – OLD AND forgotten. There was nothing to investigate, and no suspect would ever be brought to trial. All the evidence had long since been cleared away or messed up.

The phone rang.

'Yes?'

'Hi, this is Jerry Karlsson again.'

'Hello, Jerry Karlsson,' she said, without having any idea of who the man was. He seemed to realise.

'I had a call from you the other day. I work with probate cases.'

'Probate?'

'The estates of people who've died.'

She remembered.

'Lars Vinge?'

'Yes, sweetie.'

'And you've got something for me?'

'Yes.'

'Where? What?'

'In the basement of the building I live in.'

Jerry Karlsson had trouble with his hips, and limped slightly on his right leg. He'd been retired for a few years now, his fair hair

was almost yellow, and his thin face was adorned with a large, crooked nose. A sergeant in the Life Guards and a former light-weight boxer, he told her as they walked down the concrete corridor in a basement on Metargatan. He was friendly, cheerful.

'How long have you been doing this?'

'A few years. I'm always buying up estates and house clear-outs. Usually I sell them off at once, make a bit of profit in the process. But some people don't have anything. People are generally fairly poor, especially the dead.'

Antonia's and Jerry's steps echoed along the corridor.

'In cases like that I store the belongings until they've built up. Then I sell the entire contents of the store. If there's no interest, I do-nate the whole lot to charity once a year. You're in luck; all this old rubbish will being going soon, it's been here for six months. Nothing of value.'

He stopped at a metal door and pulled out a key ring worthy of a janitor.

'How about you, sweetie?' He found the right key with a prac-tised hand.

'Nothing special.'

Jerry turned the key in the lock and pulled the door open, gestur-ing for her to enter.

Antonia stepped into an enclosed room. The fluorescent light flickered and hummed for a moment before turning on properly. She saw a ton of different storage areas divided by wooden frames cov-ered with chicken wire and by plastered walls.

The man limped through the labyrinth until eventually he stuck a key in one of the padlocks.

'This used to be two storage spaces, but I got rid of the dividing wall. After you,' he said, opening the mesh door.

She looked inside. The space was three metres by four in size, piled full of belongings from floor to ceiling.

'This is all Lars Vinge's?'

Jerry read a handwritten note.

'No, three different estates in this store, but only their loose ef-fects, no furniture.'

'But one of them is Vinge's?'

Jerry glanced at the note again.

'Yes, according to my notes, that's the case. But there's no proper organisation in here, so I don't know what was his.'

Antonia looked at the mountain in front of her. Boxes, plastic bags full to bursting. Clothes, books, paraphernalia, clutter, odd bits and pieces . . .

'OK, thanks. Can I just start looking?'

Jerry gave her the thumbs-up and left the basement.

Antonia stifled a sigh and looked around at the mess.

She pulled out a big moving crate. Clothes, women's clothes. She closed the lid again, sat down on it and slowly began to go through everything in front of her. First she looked through the books; people sometimes tucked things inside them, notes, money. It was time-consuming, dusty. She felt through the clothes, looked through cutlery and kitchen equipment, moved two framed posters.

Behind them she found more moving crates, containing more clothes, books and bed linen.

It was tiring work, made all the more difficult by her underlying belief that she wasn't going to find anything.

The hours rolled past, and she was drowning in clutter.

Antonia was struck by the fact that there was nothing personal. No letters or notes, no photographs, no mementos, nothing that gave any clue as to what sort of person Lars Vinge had been. Everything seemed to have been cleaned up.

After five hours Antonia had been through the whole of the storage room, bit by bit. She was tired, thirsty and in need of a pee. The working day was long since over. She called Jerry on his mobile phone, and he offered to let her use his loo upstairs.

She went up. Jerry offered her some fruit and something to drink, showed her his trophies from his boxing career, standing dusty on a top shelf in his living room. Then she went back to the basement and started again from scratch, carefully and methodically going through everything one more time.

Jerry was kind enough to show up with a flask of coffee and some shop-bought buns, then limped off again.

It was past eleven in the evening when she heard a lovely sound. She had missed it before when she had pulled out all the front pockets of all the trousers she found. Before starting the second time she decided to shake all the clothes properly. It fell out of the back pocket

of a pair of jeans . . . there was a flash as it flew weightlessly through the air, followed by a wonderful metallic tinkling sound as it hit the concrete floor, like the note from a tuning fork – an A, perhaps, in a strangely high octave.

Antonia looked at the key, then bent over and picked it up. Yes, she had been right. It was the key to a safe-deposit box.

30

(STOCKHOLM/MUNICH)

'*SOPHIE, TELL ME WHAT YOU NEED, AND I'LL SEE IF I CAN HELP YOU.*'

These words, spoken by Klaus Köhler's boyfriend, Rüdiger, were odd; he sounded like a bank clerk who wanted to talk about pension arrangements.

Then Rüdiger explained that Klaus had kept the promise he had made to her at the Trasten restaurant six months ago by passing it on to Mikhail Asmarov before he died.

Mikhail Asmarov . . .

Something cracked inside Sophie and she almost broke down.

'Does Mikhail still work for the Hankes?' she asked.

'No, not after the incident in Stockholm. He's been freelance since then.'

Mikhail Asmarov wasn't the kind of person who helped others. He was a machine, a violent machine. She had seen that several times, perhaps most clearly at Trasten, when he and Klaus shot and killed the Russians who were after Jens . . .

'*What do you need, Sophie?*' Rüdiger repeated.

Sophie gave him a brief summary of the situation, that her son was missing, that the Hankes probably had him. That she needed all the help she could get if she was going to be able to find him and get him to safety.

'*If the Hankes have got him, you should start in their back yard, in Munich. I'll tell Mikhail to meet you there.*'

Sophie and Jens made their way out to the western suburbs, where a Greek named Socrates sold half-reasonable second-hand cars. Jens looked around, checked the engine block, the colour of the oil, the wear on the tyres, but didn't pay much attention to anything else. He bought an Audi loaded with horsepower. Handshake, key in hand, key in the ignition, the engine sounded capable of killing someone.

Jens headed south. Sophie leaned her head against the window, her thoughts clouding her vision.

'Is what's happened to Albert your fault?' he asked after a few dozen kilometres.

Something lurched inside her.

'No,' she said abruptly.

But her curt reply didn't help. His question hung there inside her for a long time.

Your fault . . .

'Albert got sick when he was four,' she said without explanation.

He looked at her.

'What?'

She didn't repeat herself.

'We were out in the archipelago, Albert and I, on an island, we were cut off. We were renting a place out there. No telephone, no neighbours, just a cottage on a small island. David had gone into the city; he'd taken the boat, and was going to be coming back the day after next. It was towards the end of the summer. That evening Albert had an allergic reaction. He swelled up and started to have trouble breathing.'

The memory was vivid. She went on: 'He got worse, started to fade. I shocked him with cold water, gave him mouth-to-mouth, shouted at him, held him in my arms out there in the darkness, blowing air into his lungs, but nothing helped. The life was just slowly draining out of him, and there was nothing I could do. He was so small and helpless. I held him tight, kept him warm, didn't want him to be freezing when he died. Because I was sure he was going to die.'

The world rushed past outside.

'So I prayed,' she said. 'For the first and last time in my life, I prayed, for real. From the depths of somewhere inside me, I prayed for help. I swore I would devote the whole of my life to God if He helped my child. That's how I felt at the time, and I understood the consequences of my promise.'

Sophie put one hand over her eyes, then removed it and said, 'And the swelling disappeared. The allergy faded. Albert got some colour back in his face, his breathing stabilised and he slept soundly in my arms.'

Thinking about it brought images into her mind.

'But I didn't keep my promise. I forgot it, I carried on living my life just as I had before, self-absorbed in pointless worrying and all the stupid little problems of daily life. Then I got that call, last summer, telling me that Albert had been run over. And I prayed, not in the same way, but I prayed for help again, I demanded it. And it came again, from somewhere. Even though I hadn't kept my promise. I won't get that kind of help again.'

'Do you believe that?' he asked, glancing at her.

'Yes, I do,' she replied quietly.

'Completely?'

She waited before replying, 'No, but part of me does.'

'The part that wants you to feel guilty?'

Now she looked at him. He was almost smiling.

Munich by night. They saw the city lit up in the distance as they approached from the northwest. Their hotel was outside the city centre, a short distance from the motorway, where no one lived and nothing happened.

Sophie and Jens walked side by side towards the long wooden reception desk, weekend bags in their hands, a couple just passing through.

Jens checked in as Sophie waited, looking around. A piano bar. The pianist, a happy man with a big nose, was playing 'Do You Know the Way to San Jose?' a little slower than the original, a little calmer, in a more easily digested two-four time.

Some restaurants, another bar in the distance. Quite a few people

around. Men and women with plastic badges around their necks. There was probably a conference venue nearby, hotels close to those tended to look like this one. And the guests tended to look like these.

Some distance away, in one of the small groups of sofas, she saw him, Mikhail Asmarov. He was sitting with his back to her: large, thickset, calm, motionless.

Sophie felt happy to see him again. But Mikhail Asmarov shouldn't conjure up feelings of happiness. He was a remorseless killer, he was lethal, he was the opposite of everything she believed in. But a smile flitted across her lips regardless, she felt it. Possibly just relief at having him on her side now, at having someone on her side.

Jens came up behind her and put his hand gently on her arm.

'Come on,' he said quietly.

They walked towards the lifts. And as if he had eyes in the back of his head, Mikhail stood up and walked towards them without looking at them or meeting their gaze. He passed a key card to Jens, who slipped it unobtrusively into his pocket.

There was a jacket tossed across the bed as they stepped into Mikhail's room.

'Shall we talk?' Mikhail's voice was gruff, even when he spoke quietly.

Mikhail walked farther into the room, pulled out a chair from the desk and gestured to Sophie to take the armchair. Jens found a place by the windowsill and leaned against it.

Mikhail sat with his arms on his knees, his legs wide apart, testosterone leaking out of him.

'I know the Hankes are in hiding,' he said. 'Ralph and his son, Christian, are rarely together, for reasons of security.'

'Do you know anyone close to them?' Jens asked.

'Perhaps.'

'Can you ask?'

'No.'

Mikhail looked at Sophie, as if he was trying to remember her better.

'Sophie,' he grunted.

She didn't answer.

He scratched his neck with his thumb. 'Has life been unfair to you?'

The question could have been sarcastic. But this was Mikhail asking. There was no possible subtext. She thought about his words, twisting and turning them a few times, but only came to one answer.

'Yes,' she said. 'Life has been unfair to me.'

His eyes drilled through her. She got the impression that the question had been asked to test her. To test her honesty, perhaps, her attitude, her position. Who was she in all this, a self-pitying mother?

'Have you changed?' he asked.

'What do you mean?'

'It looks like it.'

'Probably, then,' she said.

For a moment his eyes looked friendly, as if he understood her, then he looked away and became his usual brusque self again. Mikhail stood up, picked up the jacket and pulled out a folded map from the inside pocket. He unfolded it on the bed.

The map showed Munich and the surrounding area, with black marks in various places, circled addresses, arrows at the corners of the map pointing outwards. He put his finger in the middle of the map, central Munich.

'These are the properties I remember from back when I worked for Ralph Hanke. A few are offices, some are residential, some are safe houses, others just properties they own for no apparent reason; a lot of them are empty.'

Sophie pointed to the arrows leading away from the city.

'What do these mean?'

'Three estates. Summer houses, hunting lodges, castles . . . I don't know what they're called.' Mikhail coughed hard enough to raise his blood pressure. 'But they're a good size,' he went on. 'They're secluded and are surrounded by a lot of land.'

He looked at Jens and Sophie.

'But that's just here,' he continued. 'He's got property all around the world.'

'So this is where we start,' Jens said.

'OK,' Mikhail said, trying to switch his head to planning mode. It looked like it was painful. He rubbed above one eye with his forefinger. 'Do you have weapons?' he went on.

'No.'

'Men?'

A shake of the head.

Mikhail raised one eyebrow.

'You and me against the Hankes, without weapons?' he asked.

Jens looked at Sophie, then back at Mikhail.

'Yes,' he said.

Sophie and Jens dropped their bags in their rooms, then went down to the lobby, where they were met by an easy-listening hell as the pianist ran through 'Strangers in the Night'. He'd started singing as well, which really wasn't a good move.

They ordered food from the bar menu.

'Thank you, Jens,' she said as they ate. 'Thanks for helping me.'

He kept eating and didn't reply.

'But do we have any other choice?' she asked.

He looked at her quizzically.

'Is there any other way we can do this?' Sophie asked.

Jens shook his head. 'No.'

31

(STOCKHOLM)

THE DOORBELL RANG. FAR TOO LATE FOR A WEEKNIGHT. ANTONIA PULLED HER robe around her, went out into the hall, and opened the door. She wasn't expecting to find Miles Ingmarsson standing there.

'Hello?' she said.

'Hello,' he said.

Silence.

'Do you have a minute?'

'What for?'

'A chat.'

'A chat about what?'

'Are you going to let me in, or what?'

She made tea. Miles sat at the kitchen table, looking out through the dark window.

'Is this south-facing?' he asked.

Antonia put loose tea in a strainer. She wasn't expecting small talk.

'Yes, south-facing,' she said.

'Must get hot when the sun's on it.'

Antonia turned towards Miles. She could either be accommodating or dismissive. She'd rather have been dismissive and told him to

stop talking shit, but for some reason she didn't. Instead she softened up and relaxed.

'Yes, it gets really hot in here, especially during the summer.'

They looked at each other. He was smiling slightly, perhaps grateful that they were now, after a bit of meaningless chat, more on the same level.

Antonia put two cups and the teapot on the table. She sat down opposite him.

'OK, this is my kitchen, and you're sitting in it, Miles Ingmarsson, in the middle of the night.'

'It's not the middle of the night.'

She wasn't going to argue with that. Miles weighed his words.

'I need your help,' he said.

'How?'

'I need to find someone.'

'Who?'

'The ex-boyfriend of a girl I know.'

'Why?'

'That doesn't matter,' he said.

'Yes, it does.'

Miles hesitated.

'Assault,' he said.

'Of her, the girl you know?'

'Yes,' he said quietly.

Antonia could see desire, honesty, commitment. Qualities she hadn't thought he possessed.

'I presume you've tried to find him yourself?'

'Mm.'

'And?'

He shrugged. 'I have a name, but I haven't managed to get any further than that.'

'So you've come round to see me, a homicide detective, in the middle of the night? Why?'

'It's not the middle of the night,' he repeated in a quiet voice, pursed his lips, then scanned the kitchen without really looking.

'It has to be you,' Miles went on.

'Why?'

'Because you're a police officer.'

She snorted.

'What are you, then?'

He evaded her searching look.

'I'm not the same. You said so yourself.'

Antonia almost got the feeling he really meant what he said.

'And when I find him?' she asked.

'You give him to me.'

Worry lines on her brow. Ingmarsson's expression remained blank.

'And what are you going to do to him?'

'Don't worry about that.' She was on the point of going on when he shook his head and met her gaze. 'Don't worry about that,' he repeated, more firmly this time.

She tried to read between the lines. Miles Ingmarsson was serious about this. He was on his way towards something, and couldn't be stopped.

'You wouldn't come here empty-handed, would you?' she asked.

'Of course not.'

'So?'

'If you help me, I help you,' he said.

'Let's hear it.'

'You're desperate for answers about Trasten,' he said.

'What can you give me?'

'What do you need?' he asked.

A weight lifted from Antonia Miller's chest. She tried to hide how happy she felt.

'What have you got?'

He was just as cool in his reply.

'Nothing. No more than what you had when I took over.'

She was almost taken aback.

'Anything?'

'Tommy Jansson made it very clear that I wasn't to investigate.'

'What?'

'Our colleagues clearly messed up, Gunilla Strandberg and her group. Tommy doesn't want to sully their memory.'

'Did he say that?' she asked.

'Yes.'

'Do you believe that?'

He shrugged.

'Does it matter?'

She snorted in surprise.

'Does it matter?!'

Miles didn't answer.

Antonia tried to understand the man in front of her. His passivity. She couldn't. She poured the tea.

'I'm not just interested in Trasten, Hector Guzman and so on,' she said.

'What else are you interested in, then?'

'Our colleagues. The ones in charge of the case. The ones who died. The ones Tommy says he wants to protect.'

'Why?'

'Never mind the whys.'

'What do you want?' Miles asked.

'Lars Vinge. The truth.'

'Yes, so you said.'

'I'm saying it again.'

'Suicide,' Miles said.

She shrugged.

'Start there anyway,' she said.

'Give me a reason.'

'A little bird whispered that name in my ear.'

'What else did the little bird say?'

'That he was on the side of the Indians.'

'Where's the little bird now?'

'Dead.'

'How?'

She shrugged again.

'Little birds die.'

Miles raised an eyebrow, waiting for more. But Antonia didn't go on. Instead she drank her tea, then got up and walked out of the kitchen.

She came back and sat down again.

'The woman, the one who was assaulted, does she mean a lot to you?'

He averted his gaze, mumbling.

Antonia wasn't so sure, she had trust issues engraved deep in her personality. But on the other hand, she was also a risk-taker.

So she took a chance. She put a small key on the kitchen table and pushed it towards him so it was in between them. The key was flat, silver-coloured.

'What's that for?' he asked.

'A safe-deposit box.'

'Whose?'

'Vinge's,' she said. 'If we're in luck . . .'

Miles leaned forward and picked it up.

'Where did you find it?'

'It was among the things Vinge left when he died.'

'Are you sure it's Vinge's?'

'No,' she said drily.

Miles looked at her quizzically.

'It was in a storeroom. It contained the belongings of three different people, all mixed up.'

'And some of them were Vinge's?' Miles asked.

Antonia could see how sceptical he was, and nodded curtly.

'Which bank?' he asked.

'No idea.'

'What box number?'

'No idea.'

He thought some more.

'And he's been dead a while. So if he had a safe-deposit box, surely it would have been emptied by now?'

'I doubt it,' she said.

'Why?'

'Because,' Antonia continued, 'all that sort of thing, his financial affairs, details of his estate, assets, debts . . . it's all been got rid of.'

'Which means?' Miles asked.

'That someone doesn't want them to be touched.'

'Which means?' Miles asked again.

'That they may not have been touched.'

Miles held the key up to the light, inspecting it.

'This is virtually impossible,' he said.

'You don't have much faith in yourself, do you?'

'Only idiots have faith in themselves,' he said. 'Are you serious about this?'

He was right; she realised that the odds were pretty long, but she stood her ground.

'Help me open Lars Vinge's safe-deposit box and I'll help you find your guy.'

He tried to read her.

'And if I don't succeed? Which I'm probably not going to?'

She shrugged.

'Then I don't find your guy.'

A noise behind them. Miles turned around. A well-built man wearing jeans and a football T-shirt with the Real Madrid insignia appeared in the kitchen.

'Hello,' the man said amiably.

Miles stood up.

'I'm Ulf,' the man said in a Dalarna accent.

'Hi, Ulf,' Miles said, then left.

He lit a cigarette out in the street and checked his watch. It was the time of day when he usually visited Sanna in secret. He walked through the city towards Södermalm Hospital, his fingers toying with the safe-deposit key in his pocket as he walked.

At the hospital he went up to Sanna's ward . . . then stopped, concealed in the corridor, listening.

The night staff were in the staff room, as usual at this time. Miles took off his shoes and crept along the corridor, past the coffee-drinking nurses to Room 9. There he carefully opened the door and slipped inside.

The lights had been turned out for the night. He picked up a chair and moved it to the side of the bed, lit the bedside lamp and angled it away from her. Enough light to see her by. And Miles did what he always did when he sat beside her. He looked, and looked, and looked.

Five hours later he woke up, bent forward and stiff. The sun was up, Sanna looked the same. He had his toothbrush in his coat pocket.

Miles washed his face and brushed his teeth in the bathroom; this was his home now.

He left Sanna and the hospital and headed for work.

He was the first person to arrive. The lights flickered wanly as he walked down the corridor.

He tapped in his old user ID from Economic Crime.

The screen was blank for a moment, as if the system were looking for something. Then Eco's internal home page. They'd forgotten to delete him from the system. Miles knew where to look; this was his world, Economic Crime's databases.

He fed in Lars Vinge's ID number and got a list of relevant pages, most of which were relatively useless. He found his way to the right page and found information about bank transactions. There was a current account – a savings account at a bank on Södermalm – and a safe-deposit box associated with that.

Miles relaxed. Everything had gone smoothly. Then the anti-climax as his doubts returned and he realised there was nothing to be happy about. He had the key to a safe-deposit box. That was all. Miles couldn't get at the box with just the key. For that you needed a key, the specific number of the box, an accepted form of ID for Lars Vinge and confirmation of identity from a bank employee who would have the second key.

32

(MUNICH)

THEY HAD CHECKED OUT THE VARIOUS ADDRESSES THROUGHOUT THE CITY. ALL of them exclusive and unreachable. This was the way to do it. Start slowly, be careful, work through the list, take care not to miss anything along the way.

Jens came back, opened the car door and got in beside Mikhail, who pulled away. No one said anything; they were all unhappily aware that their search wasn't getting anywhere.

They struggled back towards their hotel through the city traffic.

'There's one more place,' Jens said thoughtfully.

'Where?' Sophie asked.

'Mikhail, you know the one. The house in the suburbs,' Jens said.

'Which house?' Mikhail asked.

'The terrraced house, where you took my guns last summer after you stole my car on Jutland. When you, Ralph and Christian all showed up.'

Mikhail remembered, then shook his head.

'That house was always empty, we only ever used it in emergencies.'

'How do you mean?'

'In emergencies,' Mikhail said once more.

'How do you mean?' Jens repeated.

Mikhail glared at Jens, as if to suggest that he ought to know better than to ask.

'How do you mean?' Jens didn't seem to care.

'You remember the man in the garage.'

Jens did remember. The dead man who had been lying there, sliced open, on top of Jens's crates of weapons, his throat cut, the congealed blood. A calling card from Ralph Hanke.

'That's what we used the house for,' Mikhail said.

'Then let's go,' Jens said.

'What for?'

'Because we're checking everywhere,' he said.

The house, one of many in a street where there was no variation.

They sat in the car and looked at the building: dark inside, no movement, nothing.

Jens opened the car door and got out. He walked across the narrow street and up to the front door. He tried the handle. Locked.

Mikhail sighed.

'Come on,' he said to Sophie.

They crossed the street. Mikhail headed towards the garage, whistled to Jens, walked up to the garage door and pulled at it a few times until the lock gave way.

There was a creaking, grinding sound as the rusty springs in the door settled and the small wheels came to a rest in the narrow grooves.

They peered into the gloom as a damp, musty smell hit them. A garage without cars. They searched it, nothing. Dead.

The dark basement steps led upwards.

The hall on the ground floor was silent and deserted. Jens and Mikhail checked the kitchen and the two other rooms on that floor, then they all headed up the stairs to the top floor.

The man was lying on his side on an unmade bed with his clothes on – stonewashed jeans and a yellow T-shirt. He was dirty and unshaven, and had curly black hair. Southern European, perhaps, maybe north African. In his thirties. On the floor beside the bed

were several candles, spoons, lighters, two syringes, some old drinks cans and sweet wrappers. By the foot of the bed a pistol, silvery, partly rusted, old and tired. Mikhail walked over and picked it up, checked the magazine: fully loaded. He put it in his jacket pocket.

The three of them stood there looking at the prostrate body. The man was completely fucked. His mouth was open, dribbling saliva, and his breathing was slow. The sounds coming from his throat were dry and rattling. Sophie went over to the man, sat down next to him and felt his pulse. It was weak, his skin clammy.

'Who is he?' Sophie asked.

'I don't know,' Mikhail said. 'One of Hanke's guys, on the way out, I guess.'

'On the way out?'

'This is what he usually does.'

'What?'

'Among the lower ranks they're nearly all addicts,' Mikhail said.

'Why?'

Mikhail kept his eyes on the man.

'When Hanke no longer needs them, he gives them a little push over the edge, raises the dose. That way he can't be held responsible for what happens. They kill themselves. He did that with a few guys when I was working for him. People say he did the same with his first wife, Sabine, Christian's mother.'

The man lay there, enjoying his misery. He wasn't going to make it any further than this. His heart would get weaker, then he'd die of an overdose.

Mikhail rubbed his nose.

'I'll wait here until he wakes up,' he whispered.

Jens took Sophie by the arm and led her out of the room and down the stairs.

They sat down at the kitchen table as the walls made quiet creaking sounds. A few cars passed by outside the thin window.

Muffled noises from upstairs . . . a conversational tone, calm questions, calm answers. The voices got louder. It wasn't Mikhail she could hear mostly but the other man. He sounded upset . . . angry . . . scared. Mikhail kept talking; she couldn't make out the words, just distorted sounds making their way through the walls and floor to the kitchen.

Then a hard thud, followed by a stifled scream. A cry of pain from behind a closed hand.

Sophie looked up at Jens. He shook his head slowly.

More thuds, and the ceiling above them shook. The man cried out in pain.

Sophie flew up, but Jens grabbed her wrist. She tried to pull free but he caught her in his arms and held her tight. The assault upstairs went on. The thuds grew heavier and more regular, methodical and rhythmic. Then it was suddenly completely silent.

Heavy steps on the staircase. Jens let go of Sophie.

Mikhail came into the kitchen with a vacant look in his eyes.

'There's a boy out at one of the farms,' he said. 'A teenage boy.'

Mikhail walked out of the house.

33

(STOCKHOLM)

ANTONIA WAS WAITING AT THE COUNTER AT THE DRY CLEANER'S. THE RADIO was playing pop music. A woman's voice farther inside the premises was singing along.

Antonia rang the bell on the counter. The singing stopped.

Marianne came out.

'Hello, Superintendent,' she said. There was a faint but detectable note of sarcasm.

'Was that you singing, Marianne?'

'Yep.'

'It sounded good.'

'Thanks.'

'Are you offering coffee?' Antonia asked.

'No,' Marianne said. 'But there's water in the tap; come on through.'

She went back into the depths of the laundry.

Marianne Grip, Assar Grip's wife. Assar, one of the big gangsters in Stockholm back in the 1980s. Vanished without a trace. Marianne was trying to keep the organisation going, mainly to help the youngsters. She seemed to take an odd sort of responsibility for them, as if she were their mother.

That was how Antonia had first met her. By chance. She liked Marianne, and felt that she liked her back. She turned a blind eye and left Marianne alone. And asked for favours every now and then.

They walked back to a very small kitchen.

Marianne was used to these meetings of theirs, and waited for Antonia to explain why she was there.

'Two things,' Antonia said.

'There are always two things,' Marianne said.

'First a man, in his thirties. He beat up his ex, a stripper. His name's Roger Lindgren. I've looked, but I can't find anything except a PO box.'

Marianne's face wasn't giving anything away. Antonia went on.

'And I need an ID card for a dead man. New picture, but otherwise the same information.'

'Does the dead man's driver's licence still exist?'

'No.'

'Passport, any other form of ID?'

'I'm afraid not.'

Antonia took out four passport photos of Miles Ingmarsson and passed them to Marianne, who looked at them.

'What's the ID card going to be used for?' Marianne asked.

'You don't need to know that.'

'Yes, I do.'

'Why?'

'If it's going to be scanned electronically, it'll be difficult. If it's only going to be looked at manually, that makes things easier.'

'It's only going to be used manually, I think,' Antonia said.

'You think?'

'Yes, I think.'

'So that's as good as saying you don't know?'

'Yeah, pretty much.'

Marianne held Miles Ingmarsson's passport photograph up to Antonia.

'Good-looking guy. Don't you think, Antonia?'

'No.'

Marianne cracked into a smile.

'It's always good to see you, Antonia.'

'It's good to see you too, Marianne.'

'So, how are you?' Marianne asked.

'Not sure, I never have time to think about it. You?'

'I'm fine.'

'And your daughter, Ester?'

'Oh, she's fine too. Her dad would have been proud. Sometimes I have to pinch myself; here we are, thirty years on, and we can talk about absolutely anything, her and me. Things are going well for her, she means the world to me.'

'What's the trick?' Antonia wondered.

'Mother and daughter?'

'Relationships in general.'

Marianne shrugged. 'I suppose you just have to be honest and true to yourself and the people you love?'

'Is that enough?'

'More than enough.'

'Is it really that simple?'

Marianne thought for a moment.

'In practical terms, no.'

'So?'

Marianne shrugged again.

'No idea. Why? Are you having relationship trouble?'

'No.'

'Are you even in a relationship?'

'Sort of.'

'Who with?'

'A colleague.'

Marianne waved the passport photograph of Miles Ingmarsson.

'Is this him?'

'No, someone else. His name is Ulf.'

'Mm.' Marianne nodded. 'Ulf, you say. And what do you want with him?'

Now it was Antonia's turn to shrug.

'So what's he like?' Marianne asked.

'He's kind, sensible and afraid of intimacy. A lot like me, really.'

'Minus kind and sensible,' Marianne said.

'Yes, minus kind and sensible, obviously.'

'You deserve love, Antonia. Grab it if it appears.'

'If it appears, I promise I'll grab it. And how's business?' Antonia asked.

'Can't complain. A lot of people out there are fighting for survival these days.'

'True.'

There was something very likeable about the woman.

'The guy who beat up his ex is obviously free of charge,' Marianne said. 'The ID card will cost, both money and favours.'

Antonia took her hands off the back of the chair.

'I'm a police officer, so my salary isn't great.'

Marianne stood up.

'Like I'd care about that! You could always join us, Antonia. You've got a natural talent for it.'

Antonia laughed at the compliment.

'Do you know what my husband used to say?' Marianne went on.

'Yes,' Antonia said.

'Let's hear it, then.'

' "If a storm breaks out, don't shit yourself." '

'Exactly.'

'But Assar wasn't the one who came up with it,' Antonia said. 'He stole it from Max von Sydow in that film . . .'

'Maybe, but Assar stole everything. And then he thought it was his. That's why he was so easy to live with.'

34

(MUNICH)

CHRISTIAN HANKE FOUND HIS FATHER AND ROLAND GENTZ IN ONE OF THE estate's big reception rooms. They were sitting talking in front of a blazing fire, and they turned towards him when he came into the room.

'We're not supposed to be together,' Ralph said.

'Never mind that now,' Christian replied.

'What's happened?' Gentz wondered.

'One of our men has been found beaten to death in one of our safe houses.'

'Where? Who?'

'I don't know, it doesn't matter. But it does mean that we're going to have to rearrange things.'

Everything stopped for a brief moment.

'Are they here?' Ralph asked.

'We can't be sure. But that, together with Carlos's kidnapping . . .'

'What are you thinking?' Roland interrupted.

'Move one of the boys.'

'Where to?'

'Colombia. To Don Ignacio, we'd be safe there.'

' "We"?'

'I'm going too,' Christian said. 'You two should consider your own security as well.'

'Take Lothar,' Ralph Hanke said. 'Hector's son is more important, leave the other one, the Swedish boy, behind.'

'I was thinking the opposite,' Christian said.

———

ALBERT WOKE UP TO FIND STRONG ARMS LIFTING HIM FROM THE MATTRESS, putting him in his wheelchair and pushing him out of the room.

He had time to register a corridor, doors leading to other rooms, a guard's room with a window.

It was night, pitch-black, when he emerged from the building. Albert tried to look around, to get some idea of where he was.

He was quickly lifted into a blacked-out minibus parked there with its sliding door open. He was placed on a seat, then the man who had so abruptly pulled him from sleep disappeared and the door closed electronically and perfectly, without a sound.

There was total silence in there. Albert was alone in the minibus, fighting the suspicion that he was all alone now. No dad, no brothers and sisters . . . no mum.

The driver's door opened and the silhouette of a man got in behind the wheel. Then the sliding door opened again and two other men got in. Albert recognised one of them.

'Ernst!' Albert was relieved, unbelievably relieved. But Ernst avoided his gaze and sat down two rows in front of him, behind the driver.

'You and Ernst are not to talk to each other,' the other man said. He had sat down in the same row as Albert, one seat away. 'My name is Christian.'

The sliding door closed and the vehicle pulled away into the darkness.

'Ernst, is my mum alive?'

Ernst didn't move, he just sat there staring ahead of him.

'Ernst!'

'Stop talking. And no Swedish,' Christian said.

'Ernst, you fucking idiot, answer me!'

'I don't know,' Ernst said with a sigh.

'What are you talking about?' Christian asked in English.

'None of your fucking business,' Albert replied in Swedish.

'Ernst, what are you talking about?' Christian asked.

'The boy wants to know if his mother's alive,' Ernst replied in English.

Christian composed himself, then looked at Albert.

'Your mother's alive. Put your seat belt on.'

'Where is she?' Albert retorted.

Christian leaned over, pulled the seat belt across Albert and clicked it into place.

'I don't know.'

'Of course you do.'

'No, I don't.'

'Does Ernst know?'

'No, Albert, Ernst doesn't know either.'

Albert leaned his head against the window. He ran a hand through his hair. Tears sprang to his eyes.

194

35

(STOCKHOLM)

HIS BODY WAS TELLING HIM IT WAS THE OYSTERS HE HAD EATEN THE PREVIOUS day.

Tommy Jansson clung to the toilet seat and his vomit was torrential.

He had fallen asleep on the basement floor last night, hammered on gin. But it wasn't the gin that had made him sick, he was sure of that. He understood what happened when he drank. It was the oysters, or some sort of stomach bug.

His phone rang in the pocket of his robe. It was Ann Margret.

'Miller's and Ingmarsson's search histories and computer records are in your in-box now.'

'Thanks, Ann Margret,' he managed to say politely.

Tommy pulled the cord of the light in the basement and the solitary little bulb came to life. He went over to the desk and switched the computer on, then checked his email. Ann Margret had sent Antonia Miller's and Miles Ingmarsson's Internet histories as attachments. He printed them out and started to skim through Antonia's online activity, both internal and external. It was a long list, the searches varying from work-related to private. She had bought books and clothes on the Internet. She had read *Dagens Industri* and *Svenska Dagbladet* online. She seemed to be the sort of person who typed impulsive questions straight into search engines. Blood types? How is tarmac made? House clearances in Stockholm? How

many people have been to the moon? Who was the second president of the USA? Procedure for opening a safe-deposit box? Best slalom skis? Easy pasta recipes? Sex toys from the chemist? Stephen King bibliography?

A lot of questions. Tommy skimmed the list for names. Lars Vinge appeared several times. He saw other names he didn't recognise. Why Vinge? And why now?

He switched to Miles Ingmarsson's records. Much thinner. There were searches for old sailing ships, men's clothing from Jermyn Street in London, recipes. What things cost. Names, names and more names, as well as other nondescript searches for safe-deposit boxes, a restaurant's business hours. More names, more sailing ships, tobacco, old books.

Tommy felt like a drink. He opened the bottom drawer of his desk, and there it was – happiness, transparent and reliable. A big bottle of gin from a shop on the German border. He took the bottle out and drank a few cautious mouthfuls, enough to turn the greyish tone of the world into something reminiscent of the way things used to be, a bit like when he was a child.

Tommy carried on reading. Fucking sailing boats the whole time. A swig of gin. Another sequence of names: Roger Lindgren. Herbie Hancock, the Blue Note Years . . .

An alarm went off somewhere in the back of Tommy's head. He looked back and checked the previous name he'd just read, *Roger Lindgren.*

He leafed through Antonia's list, running through it with his finger. Yep, there it was. Roger Lindgren was there as well.

Tommy found a pen and circled the name on both lists. Who the hell was Roger Lindgren? He checked on his computer but couldn't find anything interesting.

He put the lists down side by side. Then he compared everything carefully and thoroughly. It took time, it took gin and it took a lot of effort. When he was finished there were three common denominators between Miles Ingmarsson's and Antonia Miller's search histories.

Roger Lindgren.

Lars Vinge.

Safe-deposit boxes.

Fucking hell.

Tommy called every informant on the police payroll that he could think of.

'Roger Lindgren?'

'*No idea.*'

Four calls to four crooks before he got an answer.

'*There's a gyppo from Trångsund of that name. He's a real arse-hole, if I remember correctly, cooks meth, hits women.*'

'Where does he live?'

'*Where he lives? How the fuck should I know?*'

'Can you find out?'

'*I'll get back to you when I've got something.*'

Twenty minutes later the phone rang.

'*Roger Lindgren's fucking a divorcee who works in the Cultural sector; she lives in Vasastan.*'

'Whereabouts in Vasastan?'

'*Hagagatan . . .*'

36

(MUNICH)

SOPHIE WAS LYING ON HER STOMACH, HER BINOCULARS AIMED AT A FARM FOUR or five hundred metres below her. Jens was lying beside her, taking photographs through a telephoto lens.

She could see movement. Several men outside the building. It was big. Old – 150 years, perhaps – long and wide. Recently restored without looking modern, half-timbered. Some distance away was a brick stable block, and beyond that some white-fenced paddocks and a few horses.

'Can you see anything?' Jens asked.

She looked.

'Well, there's a few men moving around outside the building.'

'Are they armed?'

'I can't tell.'

Jens put the camera down, marked their position on a map spread out next to him, noted the distance to the farm, glanced up at the sun behind him and then back at the farm again and made a note of the time and the position of the sun.

His mobile phone buzzed and he passed it to Sophie, then went on writing.

'Nothing at the other farms, according to Mikhail,' she said.

'In which case he has to be here,' Jens said. 'Come on, let's head back.'

'We're staying,' she said.

He stood up, shaking his head.

'No. We're going back to the hotel. You can't do anything here, not now.'

Sophie looked down at the farmhouse, where Albert might be. So close . . .

He held out his hand to Sophie. She took it reluctantly, and he helped her to her feet. They walked away, towards the car.

Sophie turned around several times. The idea that she was leaving her son, letting him down, weighed heavy on her. She'd lost count of the number of times she had felt like that.

37

(STOCKHOLM)

THE MAN WAS HIGH AND GLASSY-EYED WHEN HE OPENED THE DOOR OF HIS apartment on Hagagatan, dressed in jeans and a white T-shirt.

'Roger Lindgren?' Tommy asked.

'Who are you?'

His voice was far too high to belong to a tough guy.

'I'm a cop,' Tommy said, shoving Lindgren hard in the chest. Lindgren almost fell, but looked amused, as if he'd been beaten up so many times in his life that nothing really mattered any more.

Tommy drew his service pistol and grabbed Lindgren's collar, then dragged him into the living room and pushed him down onto a chair.

'Who are you?' Tommy asked.

'You just said my name,' Lindgren squeaked.

Tommy hit him over the head with his pistol.

Lindgren's face shone with hatred and contorted pain.

'Who *are* you?' Tommy asked again. Another blow with the pistol. This time aimed at Lindgren's ear and temple.

'My name's Roger, and I . . . Tell me what you're doing here!' He pressed one hand to the ear that had just been hit, and blood seeped out between his fingers.

'Antonia Miller?' Tommy said.

'What?'

'Antonia Miller? Have you had any contact with her?'

'No! Who the fuck is that?' Roger yelped, scared he was about to be hit again, which happened. This time on the hand that was protecting his ear.

'I don't know who that is!' he cried.

'Miles Ingmarsson?'

Roger tried to defend himself.

'I've never heard of him!'

Another blow. Across his face this time. Hard as hell.

Lindgren tried to parry further blows. This wasn't good. Tommy was getting a strong feeling that the guy really didn't know.

He looked around the apartment.

'Do you live here?'

Roger's nose was bleeding.

'Yes, from time to time.'

'What a fucking dump.'

'Thanks . . .'

'Why is your voice so high?' Tommy asked.

'Don't know, it always has been.'

'You sound like a pathetic little girl.'

Roger wiped his nose and didn't bother to respond to Tommy's remark.

'What's your connection to Miles Ingmarsson and Antonia Miller?'

'I don't know who they are.'

Tommy was annoyed. He sniffed the air. Something acrid, strong, chemical.

'What's that smell?'

'Nothing.'

Tommy glared angrily at Roger.

'That's a fucking stupid answer.'

He dragged Roger up and pushed him ahead, holding the pistol against his back.

A closed door.

'Open it,' Tommy said.

Tommy jabbed the barrel of the pistol hard in his back. Roger did as he'd been told.

Behind the door, a plastic curtain. Behind the curtain, a kitchen. The chemical smell was stronger. Darkened windows, heat lamps, equipment. A de-luxe meth kitchen.

'I don't know what this is,' Roger said without sounding very convincing.

'I can understand that,' Tommy said. 'What with it being your kitchen and everything. How the hell would you know?'

'It's not my kitchen.'

'Whose is it, then?'

'The girl I live with.'

'But if I had to guess . . . amphetamine?'

'Looks like it,' Roger said.

Tommy thought for a moment.

'Is this the reason . . . ?' Tommy mused out loud, and looked at the meth kitchen.

'The reason for what?'

Tommy abandoned his theory. It must be something else that had got Miles and Antonia on Roger's trail.

'OK. Here's what we do, Roger. This sort of thing carries a whole lot of years. I want you to call me at once the minute you hear from Miles Ingmarsson or Antonia Miller.'

Roger nodded eagerly.

'You do understand how much fucking power I've got, don't you?' Tommy said, scratching his cheek with tip of the barrel of the pistol.

38

(MUNICH)

MIKHAIL WAS SITTING AT THE DESK IN THE HOTEL ROOM, ON TOP OF WHICH LAY SCREW-CUTTING equipment, heat-insulating tape, wire and bullets.

He attached a home-made silencer to the barrel of the pistol, held the weapon up and weighed it in his hand.

'I'll have to get in close,' he muttered to Jens, who was looking through the pictures on his camera.

'We'll aim for the main entrance,' Jens said.

They sat there planning for a good hour. Sophie listened with half an ear to the men's discussions as she tried to calculate their chances of success. That was something neither Jens nor Mikhail seemed willing to do. Maybe that was the difference between her and them, their antipathy towards caution and reflection.

Sophie and Jens left Mikhail's room and walked back down the corridor towards their own rooms.

'Will it work?' she asked Jens.

'That's a very big question,' he replied.

They walked down the corridor.

'We just need to get into the house quickly, gain the upper hand,' he went on reassuringly.

'What can I do?'

They stopped outside Jens's door. He put his key card into the slot and the little light glowed green. He pushed the heavy door open.

'Nothing. If it were up to me, I'd lock you in your room until this was over.'

'Why do you say that?' she asked.

'I'm worried,' he said.

'About what?'

'About you,' he said.

'Why?'

'I'm not going to be able to protect you all the time tomorrow.'

'Have I asked you to?' she said.

He didn't answer, and she regretted saying it.

'You always do that,' she said. 'Protect me. And I'm very grateful.'

'You're worth protecting,' he said quietly.

Sophie looked at Jens carefully as he stood there holding the door to his room open. She had known him so long. Since her late teens, when a summer in the Stockholm archipelago had been the start of a romance between them. The first romance that had really meant anything to her. Maybe it was love she had felt then. Everything had been so different. They had thrown themselves into love with beautiful ease and great seriousness, full of faith in a secure, safe future that made everything seem solid, permanent. Eternal, maybe. But that future was long since gone. They split up at the end of the summer. He just vanished. She had been badly hurt, and the scars were still there. Every injury she had ever suffered was like that. They never healed.

'Do you still recognise me from years ago, Jens?' she asked.

He didn't answer.

'Am I a different person from when we met the first time?' she went on.

He slowly shook his head.

'No, you're not.'

'Why do you think that is?'

He tried to read her.

'You're the person you are now because you have to be. Stop worrying,' he said.

She looked at the floor, then up at him. Instead of turning away and going to her own room, she walked past him into his room and turned around inside. Jens let the door swing closed behind him and walked over to her. She made a tentative gesture, nudging his hand. Jens pulled her to him and they kissed.

Jens was gentle, she remembered that. Sensitive. It had surprised her at the time, when they were young. Gentleness and caution, together with an emotional self-confidence, had made their time together special then. It was the same now, a lifetime later. She let herself drown in the feeling.

They undressed each other and were suddenly lying naked in bed. Sophie sat astride him. She groaned as he whispered in her ear, turning her around. He knew what he was doing. Sophie let go of all defences and inhibitions, let herself be carried up and away from the world, into a dimension she had only experienced a few times in her life. It was lit up, the light warm and all-encompassing, and its energy was focused, stronger and more beautiful than anything . . . The warmth and light merged into one as she reached her climax. Her eyes almost rolled as she experienced *le petit mort* and she gasped with pleasure. She held him close, tightly.

Don't go . . .

Then she came back down to Earth again . . .

They gasped for breath as he stroked her body.

Lying next to Jens as the waves of pleasure died away, she briefly felt that she should stay there, close to him, just being human for a while. Taking comfort, feeling trust and a sense of belonging . . . and happiness. That she should volunteer something of herself, maybe even joke about something while they were lying there like that, because she used to be that sort of person, the sort who could make jokes. And everything would have been so ordinary, so easy . . .

But this was dangerous. The only option, when Albert's life was in danger, was to remain cold and focused. And to do that she had to be numb and hold anything emotional at a distance. She had to be emotionally shut off. She had made that decision.

Sophie got out of bed and began to get dressed.

Jens lay on his back, propped up on a pillow, and watched her.

'You can stay if you like,' he said.

'Thanks, Jens,' she said quietly, then walked out, along the corridor, to her own room.

There Sophie sat on the bed, listening to the traffic, feeling strangely calm and focused.

At three o'clock her alarm rang.

She changed clothes. Took off what she was wearing and put on the clothes she had laid out on the bed – trousers and a sweater, both black and tightly fitting.

She brushed her teeth in the bathroom. Then she washed her hands in ice-cold water, holding them there for a long time but feeling no pain.

Sophie tied her hair up in a ponytail, pulled on a jacket and did it up tightly, then left the room. She was on her own in the lift all the way down to the garage.

Jens and Mikhail were waiting for her by the car, dressed in muted black clothing.

She got in the back seat. They drove out of the hotel. There was moisture in the air, and the glow of the street lamps turned them into burning suns as the mist settled on the windscreen. The windscreen-wipers brought the world back into focus again.

Jens turned round.

'Did you get any sleep?'

She shook her head. 'No.'

Mikhail drove out of the city.

They walked across a field in single file. The moon was shining, and fog covered the countryside like a blanket.

Ahead of them a forest rose up. Imposing, quiet, dark and threatening. They walked in among the trees, and all sound shrank.

They stopped in a clearing and listened for anything that shouldn't be there.

Mikhail pointed to himself, then towards the farm, whose outside lights were glowing faintly in the distance, and walked slowly away from them. He was holding the pistol with the home-made silencer in his hand.

Jens's eyes were vibrant. She could see he was enjoying himself. Nervous, scared, anxious. But he was on familiar territory. He was in his element.

Jens glanced at the time.

'See you soon,' he whispered, then padded off like a soldier heading to war – which, in a way, he was, albeit with no weapon in his hand.

He didn't look back.

Sophie walked through the forest until she reached the look-out point where she was to stop and wait. It was close to the farm, and she lay down on her stomach, with a view of the farmhouse and the surrounding area. She saw Jens creep over to the barn and go inside. She tried to find Mikhail, but couldn't see him. Several minutes passed and nothing happened; the whole place seemed deserted.

A movement in the distance. Mikhail. He was standing with his back to her, half-hidden behind a tree, his modified gun in his hand.

He made his way towards the building and up onto the veranda, then crouched beneath a window. Jens ran over and sat down next to him. They took their tools from their jacket pockets, stood up and set to work quietly and methodically on the hinges of one of the windows, and quickly lifted it out and put it down on the veranda.

Mikhail leaped in, closely followed by Jens. They vanished from sight. Three coughing sounds. Three seconds of nothing, then the same again.

This time the silence felt bizarre. She waited.

Were they dead now? Had Hanke's men been waiting for them?

Someone appeared in the large doorway.

Mikhail waved to her.

She walked into a large, dark-wood-panelled hallway, with a big wooden chandelier hanging from the ceiling, a broad staircase sweeping up around the walls. On the stairs lay a dead man in an odd position, blood on his chest and face. Towards the other end of the room there was a second body.

Sophie stopped. Jens came down the main staircase with a small semi-automatic in his hand. Mikhail appeared from the living room – he, too, had swapped his pistol for the same sort of weapon Jens was holding.

'No one here,' Jens said.

'Not any more,' Mikhail added.

'The basement.' Sophie gestured, and headed towards a half-open door and a flight of steps leading downwards.

The basement was one single room made of smooth cement, ten

metres square. In the middle of the room was a large, square, concrete construction, like a building within a building, a building inside a room: no windows, bars, a steel door.

They looked at it.

'What is it?' she asked.

'A protective shelter,' Mikhail replied.

'Is there anyone inside?'

He didn't answer.

'Can we get in?' she went on.

'No.'

There were cameras fixed to the ceiling, pointing at them.

'I don't like this,' Jens said. 'We could get trapped down here.'

But Sophie wasn't listening. She went over to the cube, stopped and knocked on the metal door. It sounded muffled. She thudded three times with her fist, then waited. Nothing. She beat on the door, hard.

'Albert!' she cried.

A hand on her shoulder, Jens's voice.

'It's time to leave, Sophie.'

'No, we wait until they come out,' she said.

'We're leaving now.'

He sounded nervous.

'Jens is right,' Mikhail said. 'We can't stay here.' He and Jens walked away.

She was reluctant but realised they were right. She took a few hesitant steps backwards, then turned around and followed them.

They hurried out of the house, into the darkness, the same way they had come, up the slope towards the forest. Far away, beyond the farmhouse, something was glowing in the fog. She could just make out the outline of a smaller building.

'What's that?' Sophie pointed to the south.

Mikhail and Jens looked across the farmland.

'We took them by surprise, didn't we? We look everywhere, that's what we agreed,' she pleaded.

They were in the open now, between the farmhouse and the smaller building Sophie had seen. Jens and Mikhail were walking on either side of her, maintaining a fast pace.

The house grew clearer; it was made of brick and was situated at the end of the drive.

There was a light on inside, and the door was open. A car was idling outside . . .

They stopped fifty metres away. Jens crouched down and put the semi-automatic to his shoulder.

'I can see two people in there,' he whispered.

Mikhail wasn't listening; he began to shoot at the windows of the building. Then he ran towards it, firing short salvos as he went.

'Behind me,' Jens shouted to Sophie. He fired at the car, puncturing the tyres, then towards the house as Mikhail ran. The windows shattered.

Mikhail disappeared into the house through the open door. He started screaming and shouting. Then he came out again with two subdued men, forced them down onto the ground beside the car and tied their hands behind them with zip ties.

Sophie and Jens hurried over.

'Search it,' Mikhail said.

Jens went in, followed by Sophie.

It was a sort of glass security lodge, most of it shot to pieces. There was a kitchen off to their left. A smell of food. Four rooms facing one another. Solid security doors, three of them open.

Jens checked the rooms. They had been soundproofed, no windows. They were each furnished with a bed, table and chair. Secure. Cells, where people had been held captive. Sophie tugged at the door to the fourth room, but it was locked.

'Mikhail, keys!' she yelled.

Several seconds of silence. Then he came in and gave Sophie a key. She put it in the lock and opened the door.

And there he sat, in a corner of the darkened room, arms wrapped around himself. *A teenager . . .*

But it wasn't Albert, it was a different boy.

The room started to sway in front of Sophie's eyes.

'No . . .' she whispered. Repeating the word to herself, she backed out, then all her energy drained away and she sank to the floor with her legs beneath her.

Mikhail looked at her, then went over to where she was curled up on the floor and picked her up as Jens emerged carrying the boy.

The four of them left the security lodge.

39

(STOCKHOLM)

TOMMY WAS SITTING IN THE LITTLE OFFICE IN THE BASEMENT OF HIS TERRACED house. He was full of doubt and hesitation. He drank some more gin. The doubts vanished. He called the worst of the worst: Ove Negerson.

'Shall we have lunch, Ove?'

'*Yep,*' Negerson replied.

Tommy went out into the garden and down behind the shed, where the sun never shone. The biological process of decay was slower there than anywhere else, and it smelled of damp, dead matter. Covered with old leaves, probably from last year. Photosynthesis-dead, impossible to break down, brown and ugly.

He dug into the half-frozen ground with the little garden trowel. Thirty centimetres took time and a lot of work. But eventually he reached the biscuit tin. Tommy stuck his hands into the soil, digging and scraping. He pulled it out, then, holding it with one arm, put his fingernails under the lid, twisted it a little to the right and eased it open. The lid came off. The notes were packed inside. Twenty thousand euros was a nice, sizeable bundle. Tommy divided the bundle in two, then shoved them both into his pocket.

Ove Negerson was tall, broad-shouldered, with good looks. He was smiling wide, his teeth white, his eyes warm, his heart as

cold as an ancient glacier. He was walking towards Tommy between the tables of the restaurant.

'Mr Jansson,' Ove said.

'Negerson,' Tommy whispered.

Ove pulled out a chair and sat down, then looked into Tommy's eyes and sat completely still. The look on his face suggested that he remembered even more about Tommy now that he saw him again.

'Tommy . . .' he whispered, shaking off his recollections and picking up the menu from the table. 'Are we having starters?'

'Straight onto the main course,' Tommy said.

Ove turned a page of the menu.

'I think I'd like chicken today,' Ove muttered.

Ove's real surname was Ledin, after his mother. His father, Leroy Clarke, had been an American deserter from Vietnam. He arrived in Stockholm in 1971 and was welcomed by the anti-war wimps as a hero, but all he really wanted was to do drugs, fuck Swedish girls and, later on, beat up Ove's mother, Kerstin. She had a breakdown and wasn't able to look after her little boy, who was placed with a foster family out in Fisksätra.

Leroy died from a heroin overdose in 1975 in a cloakroom at the Central Station, wearing a filthy patched-up jacket and guarded by his aggressive Alsatian, Hero, which refused to let the ambulance staff near the body. Hero was put down on the spot, Leroy was cremated and the padded jacket ended up at the dump.

No one cared, least of all Ove. He grew up without a father or mother, without love or compassion, was bullied at school and given the nickname Negerson, son of a Negro. He got through it, and stayed strong and self-motivated.

Ove kept the name and made it his own. Sometimes he told it to carefully chosen individuals, as if to say: do what you like, say what you like, I can handle anything.

Tommy Jansson was one of those who had been given this confidence a few years ago. A confidence he really didn't want.

Ove looked up from the menu.

'You look beat, Tommy,' he said.

'Shut up,' Tommy muttered, keeping his eyes on the menu.

'I'm just so damned curious. This change. It's exciting . . .'

Tommy pretended to read the menu.

'What's exciting?' he mumbled.

'You . . . You were always a stickler for honesty, weren't you? A cop, a talkative, upright bastard.'

Tommy didn't answer, just kept staring at the menu, now to the point of absurdity.

'But there's something going on now, Tommy. Your old woman? I heard she was on the way out.'

Tommy didn't answer, and Ove pursed his lips thoughtfully.

'No, that's not it,' he went on. 'Grief wouldn't make you like this. You'd cut yourself off, go a bit weird and unpleasant. Mind you, you're unpleasant now, all the same. But this is something different. And I'm guessing I'm about to find out what it is.'

'Really?'

'You contacted me, Tommy. And you've changed. If you're about to ask for a favour, I'm going to find out why. If you're after inside information . . . I'd just walk away empty-handed.'

'You seem to have it all worked out, Ove,' Tommy muttered.

'True.'

Tommy had forgotten what his meetings with Ove were like. He was always on the defensive.

An over-solicitous waiter came towards them. Ove played along and adopted the same exaggerated manner as he ordered the chicken. Tommy nodded that he'd have the same.

'And some fizzy water, my friend,' Ove said.

'Fizzy water, coming right up,' the waiter said.

Ove gave him the thumbs-up.

'I'll take a beer, something strong,' Tommy said.

'OK,' the waiter said, and disappeared.

Ove watched the waiter go, then turned back to Tommy again.

'Nice guy,' he said with his eyebrows raised.

'Are you queer, Negerson? Are you going to fuck him later, or what?' Tommy asked, trying to redress the balance slightly.

'No, I like girls. What about you, Tommy, are you a bit queer?'

Tommy didn't answer.

'No one would be cross with you if you came out of the closet, Mr Jansson,' Ove whispered.

'Shut up.'

Ove chuckled.

'Tommy! What the fuck's happened? You can't even take being teased any more. Are you really that out of sorts?'

The waiter put a glass of sparkling water in front of Ove and a cold, misted beer in front of Tommy.

'And drinking beer at lunchtime? Are you completely lost, or what, man? Homer Simpson drinks beer during the day. And now Tommy Jansson?'

Ove laughed loudly to himself. He took a light-hearted view of life – and death, too.

The first time Tommy ran into him he had been a suspect in a murder investigation seventeen years ago. The victim, a man named Johan Christensson, had been beaten to death in his living room. Johan had been a bully at Fisksätra school in the '80s, a classmate of a certain Ove Ledin, and the instigator of the name Negerson. Johan had been methodically abused, every bone in his face was broken, his ribs and collarbone were snapped. It had been one of the most bestial murders Tommy had seen in his entire career. And also one of the most fascinating. Tommy remembered the revulsion he felt during the investigation, but also the fascination. Tommy had been almost bewitched by the rage that had been unleashed. And then there was Ove Ledin's calm demeanour when he was questioned. That was something else altogether. Tommy knew that Ove was the murderer, and Ove knew that Tommy knew.

'*I want you to call me Negerson*,' Ove had said.

'*No, I can't do that*,' Tommy had replied. Ove insisted, and made Tommy realise that it was inevitable, that he should see it as a compromising mix of confidence, threat, gift and understanding.

'What are you up to these days, Ove?'

'I'm working in a kindergarten.'

Tommy waited for him to drop the sarcasm. Ove noticed.

'Does it matter?' he asked.

'Yes,' Tommy said.

'Why?'

'Because I need to know.'

Ove shrugged.

'Nothing much.'

'What does that mean?'

Ove did his best to understand the question.

'Are you expecting me to answer that, Tommy?'

'Have you cleaned up your act?'

No response from Ove.

'Have you fallen in love?'

'What's that?' Ove asked.

Tommy didn't smile, and neither did Ove.

'Have you found God?' Tommy went on.

Ove gave the question some thought.

'No, God won't have anything to do with me.' His answer sounded honest, sad and considered.

'So you're as much a bastard as always?'

Ove gave Tommy a disappointed look. A nod, a truthful stare. It burned, and Tommy looked away.

Two plates appeared in front of them. Ove switched personas and joked with the waiter again. He picked up his knife and fork and dug in, and ate with a good appetite. Tommy picked at his food, concentrating on the beer instead.

'Go on,' Ove said.

'I want you on standby.'

Ove raised an eyebrow and took another mouthful.

'On standby to help me get rid of a guy . . . And possibly a girl.'

Ove stopped chewing, looked at Tommy in surprise and adopted a theatrical look of pain.

'Ow, ow, ow. The food's hot. I think I just got burned. Tommy Jansson, police chief . . . good guy.'

Tommy drank a few large gulps of beer and evaded Ove's gaze.

Ove leaned back, took the linen napkin from his lap and wiped his mouth, or rather dabbed at it, keeping his eyes on Tommy the whole while. Then he picked up his cutlery again and went on eating.

'What do you say, Ove?'

No answer. Ove just kept eating calmly. The lunch went on. Tommy realised they weren't going to get any further than that. He waved to the waiter and made a signal to indicate that he wanted to pay.

They left the restaurant, Tommy a few steps ahead. Ove walked past him.

'Follow me.'

They walked along the street, then turned into a multi-storey car park and walked down the entrance ramp.

The roof was low and all the parking spaces were occupied. Ove walked over to an AMG model Mercedes. The car flashed and unlocked. Before Tommy had time to react, Ove grabbed his arm, pulled him towards him and then pressed him up against one of the concrete pillars. Tommy felt hard pressure somewhere on his arm, and was paralysed in half of his upper body. Ove changed his grip and took hold of Tommy's neck with his big left hand, holding him tight against the pillar. With his right hand Ove searched Tommy's clothes. He found a mobile phone (switched off), keys, a wallet, an envelope and €20,000 rolled up in two bundles in the pocket of Tommy's jeans.

Ove let go.

'OK,' Ove said. 'I'm doing a risk assessment, looking for signs of any threat. The absence of any wires, the fact that your phone is switched off and this' – Ove waved the euros – 'means that I can carry on talking to you. I get it.'

'Get what?'

'Twenty thousand. I've told you before, haven't I?'

Ove gave back the mobile phone, keys and wallet. But not the envelope or the money. Tommy took his things and massaged his neck.

'Yes, you mentioned it once. Twenty thousand first, the rest later.'

'OK, Tommy. Name?'

'Two colleagues: Miles Ingmarsson, Antonia Miller. Their details are in the envelope.' Tommy pointed at Ove's hand.

Ove waved the money.

'This will only pay for one,' he said.

'There'll only be one in the end, probably,' Tommy said hesitantly.

'Probably?'

'I need to check things out first. I have to piece things together,' Tommy said.

'And when are you going to do that?'

Tommy shrugged.

'Once I've worked out a few details, I imagine you'll be able to do your thing.'

'This is a bad deal,' Ove said.

'Why?'

'Getting rid of a cop, that's dangerous territory. That makes it more expensive.'

'How much more expensive?'

Ove smiled like a salesman.

'Don't worry about that now, I'll send an invoice.'

Tommy tried to think. This wasn't going very well.

'Go ahead,' he said.

' "Go ahead," ' Ove mimicked in the high-pitched voice of a 1940s radio announcer.

'And stand by, Ove. No hasty action, OK?'

'Aye, aye, Captain!' Ove saluted, then pulled a face. An ugly face, invasive and disquieting. Then he laughed, loud and hard. Ove Ledin knew no limits. And perhaps that was what he was laughing at as he walked towards his car.

Then he turned back.

'Do you see him?'

'Who?' Tommy asked.

'There, right next to you!'

Ove pointed at nothing.

Tommy glanced briefly in that direction, at nothing.

'The devil, Tommy. He's standing there right beside you, your new friend!'

Ove laughed cheerily.

'You can stop talking so much bullshit,' Tommy said.

Ove turned away, and his laughter vanished abruptly.

'No, I can't!' he shouted back.

Feeling scared, Tommy stared down at the ground.

Ove jumped into the supercharged Mercedes and spun out towards daylight.

Tommy Jansson stood there alone and shaken, trying to make sense of something incomprehensible.

———

HIS NAME WAS NOW LARS VINGE. IN HIS HAND WAS A DRIVER'S LICENCE bearing a picture of Miles Ingmarsson.

The girl behind the counter was polite and frosty, which matched

the atmosphere of the branch as a whole. Wall-to-wall-carpet, quiet, a stagnant twenty-two degrees of heat blanketing everything.

She held out a hand, which seemed to indicate that she wished to see some form of identification. He passed it to her. She took the driver's licence, and without looking at it she turned it over and put it under the flashing red card reader. Nothing happened, so she repeated the gesture. Ingmarsson suppressed an urge to run. Instead he pointed to the licence.

'It's been damaged, as you can see.'

She looked at the code. The plastic covering had come loose.

'It's invalid,' she said in a nasal voice.

'OK,' Miles said.

'You'll have to order a new one,' she went on.

He nodded.

'Have you done that?'

'No.'

She typed Lars Vinge's date of birth into her computer. She glanced quickly at the licence twice, both sides. The queue behind him was getting longer, and Miles felt like running again.

'Are you still a customer here?' she asked.

'What do you mean?'

She read the screen.

'No activity in your account for some time.'

'Does there have to be?'

She looked up at him.

'No, I suppose not. It just seems a bit unnecessary to have two banks. Because that's what you've got, isn't it?'

'Does that matter?' he wondered.

'No, but I could make an appointment for you to see one of our advisers,' she continued.

'No, thanks. Not now.'

He was given a piece of paper, and he glanced quickly down at it: the number of the safe-deposit box.

Miles walked over to a mesh gate farther inside the office and stood there waiting. A man in a suit but no tie came up to him.

'Hi there,' he said.

The bank official ran a card through a reader. The gate clicked and he opened it.

'After you,' he said with a gesture to Miles, who walked down some steps into a narrow corridor. The bank official followed him, pushed past, apologised several times, moving submissively and ob-sequiously.

The absurdly thick door of a bank vault stood open in front of them.

'Zero eight eighteen,' Miles read from the piece of paper.

The official found the right box, inserted his key into one of the locks and turned it. Then he gave a feeble smile, unconsciously apolo-gising for his whole existence, and slipped away.

With sudden urgency Miles put his own key in the lock, turned it and pulled out a long, deep, wide plastic tray. He put it down on an empty table and opened the lid.

He looked down: a black sports bag, nothing else. Miles lifted it out; there was something inside it, something heavy. He wasn't about to open it. He was planning to get the hell out of there with it as fast as he could, before anyone got any ideas.

Miles shut the box again, locked it and went back up the stairs and rang the bell that opened the gate, walked through the calmness of the bank, opened the front door and stepped out into the cruel, wintry sunlight.

Antonia was sitting in her car on the other side of the road. He hurried towards her. She opened the door, took the bag from Miles and put it on the seat beside her, then glanced at it quickly. She was practically burning up with curiosity.

'What's inside it?'

'No idea,' he said.

Antonia pushed back in her seat, stretched her legs and pulled a folded piece of paper from her jeans.

She passed the folded note to Miles, and he read the address: *Hagagatan.*

'Roger Lindgren has a post-office box. No fixed address. But from time to time he lives with a woman in Vasastan.'

She started the engine.

'You've earned that,' she said, then put the car in gear.

'How did you get hold of it?' he wondered.

'At the dry cleaner's,' she said with a smile. 'See you, Miles Ing-marsson!'

Antonia's car started to move. Miles closed the door and took a step back, Antonia pulled away and disappeared into the traffic. Miles stared at the note. He was going to let his inner self decide this one. His dark inner self that wanted to do good.

Though he was well aware that if you let loose the darkness inside you to help put things right, everything always ended up in a complete fucking mess.

40

(MUNICH)

THEY WALKED BACK THE SAME WAY THEY HAD COME, ACROSS THE FIELDS TO where the car was parked on a secluded gravel track. The boy refused to talk, refused to answer the questions Sophie asked.

They got in the car.

'My name is Sophie,' she said. 'The boy I was asking about, Albert, he's my son.'

She saw a reaction in the boy's eyes, but he remained silent.

They took the lift up from the hotel garage. Mikhail got out on the ground floor and disappeared into the bar.

Jens, Sophie and the boy continued up to Jens's room.

Once they were in, Sophie sat down on one of the two beds. She indicated that the boy should sit down opposite her, on the other bed.

He hesitated, and for some reason he looked at Jens, as if to get the OK. Jens nodded and he sat down. Sophie looked at him carefully for the first time.

He had pale brown skin, sharp features, eyes that seemed to shift between two colours and that mouth . . . *Hang on . . .*

She leaned forward and inspected him more intently. He grew uncomfortable and looked away.

And his profile . . .

She had never seen him before, but she knew without any doubt who he was. Hector was clearly discernible in his eyes, forehead,

mouth. There was also a hard, impenetrable exterior, an intelligence, a deep courage; she had seen and felt that even during the short time she had known him. But there was something else as well, something warm and very human. Maybe that came from the boy's mother, whoever she was.

'Lothar?' she asked gently.

He looked at her in surprise. So did Jens, from where he was standing over by the window.

Sophie kept her eyes on him.

'Your name is Lothar, isn't it?' she asked quietly.

The boy didn't answer.

'What are your mum and dad's names?'

Suddenly he looked at her anxiously, then at Jens.

She leaned closer to him.

'Tell me, Lothar, there's no need to worry, we don't mean you any harm.'

His gaze flitted between Jens and Sophie.

'My mum's dead,' he eventually said.

'Your dad?'

'I haven't got a dad, I never have.'

His voice was low; he was hard as stone, this boy.

'How old are you?'

Hector had told her he was sixteen, that day they had been out on his boat in the archipelago. It had been as if he wanted to give her something, the greatest of all confidences, his biggest secret. *I've got a son,* he had said. *Lothar Manuel Tiedemann. He lives in Berlin with his mother . . .*

'Seventeen,' the boy whispered.

Sophie hadn't taken her eyes off him.

'Albert?'

He hesitated, as if he had already said too much.

'Albert?' she asked again. 'Have you seen Albert? Answer me.'

'Who are you?'

'I've already told you, I'm his mother.'

Lothar tried to read her.

'What's Albert's father's name?' he asked.

'David,' Sophie replied.

'What happened to him?'

'He got sick and died.'

'What sort of sick?'

'Cancer. Tell me now, Lothar.' She'd run out of patience.

He hesitated a little longer.

'Yes, I met Albert,' he said.

'When and where?'

'A few days ago.'

'Where?'

'Where you found me.'

She waited for more. Lothar looked at her from under his fringe.

'He was in the room next to me for a few days. We talked through an air vent.'

'Did you see him, did you actually meet him?'

'No, I never saw him.'

'How was he?'

'OK, I think.'

'What did you talk about, what did he say?'

'All sorts of things.'

'Like what?'

Lothar thought.

'His dad being dead. And you being a nurse, and his girlfriend, Anna. And the fact that he's in a wheelchair. That you live in an apartment in Stockholm . . . that you used to have a dog, a yellow Labrador, I don't remember the name.'

Rainer . . . Sophie thought.

'That you're in trouble,' he went on. 'And that's why they took him.'

'Did he have his wheelchair with him?' she asked.

'I don't know. But he thought it was a pain that there was no one to help him with the things he couldn't do for himself.'

Sophie looked down at the hotel-room carpet. It was thick, dark-blue. She held her feelings in check.

'What else happened?' she asked. 'What did he say, what did he do, how did he sound?'

'We were both scared and upset, we kept each other company. Albert thinks you're dead. I thought that too; I thought what happened to my mum had happened to you.'

Now she looked up at him.

'What happened to your mum?'

'They shot her.'

At first she didn't understand. His tone of voice was so normal. As if the significance of the event hadn't hit him yet.

'How do you know?' she asked.

'I was there,' he said.

The images came back to him. He struggled to hold them at bay.

She went on living while innocent people died around her. Sophie met his gaze. Perhaps he was asking himself the same question: *Why did they let you live, and not my mum?*

'Who took me?' he asked quietly. 'Who killed my mum?'

She knew the answer to his questions, but wasn't going to tell him. Instead she thought about the Hankes and their compulsive brutality. As if it were a language, the violence, talking to her, reminding her that she was ultimately powerless. No chance at all.

Sophie stood up and turned towards Jens.

'We leave in a few hours.'

She left Jens's hotel room. The door closed with a click behind her.

Jens sat down on the armchair. Lothar was sitting on the bed, his feet on the floor, his hands in his lap.

'How do you know who I am?' he whispered.

'Try to get some rest, Lothar,' Jens said. 'I'll be sitting here with you.'

'How do you know who I am?' he asked again, harder this time.

'I don't know who you are.'

'She knew,' he said, pointing to the door.

Jens shrugged.

'I'm not her.'

'Why did they take Albert?'

'Get some rest now, Lothar,' Jens said.

Lothar was about to protest, but Jens hushed him.

'Not now; you'll get your answers soon enough, but first you need to rest.'

With a degree of reluctance, Lothar lay down on the bed with two pillows behind his head.

Jens could see fatigue, worry and anxiety in the boy as he sat there, staring out at nothing.

Lothar came back to reality, was about to switch the television on with the remote.

'How are you feeling?' Jens asked.

Lothar thought about the question, pain and anguish on his face as he looked for an answer that didn't seem to be there.

'I don't know,' he said, clicking the remote control. A sports channel appeared on the screen. The Bundesliga. The match was fast, the play well organised, the attacks clever, the long balls hard. The crossbar – bang! The post – bang! Goal disallowed for offside. The protests not particularly vociferous.

Soon after, Lothar was fast asleep.

Jens got up from the armchair, went over to the boy and pulled the bedspread over him, then switched the television off. He sat back down again.

He had also noticed those features. The same things Sophie had seen. Elements of Hector Guzman in the boy's face.

Jens rubbed his eyes. Tiredness was taking its toll. His eyes closed and he fell asleep.

He was awakened by a noise.

Lothar was sitting up in bed and screaming out loud in terror.

41

(VILLEFRANCHE)

HECTOR GUZMAN OPENED HIS EYES.

His pupils shrank from huge to pinpricks. He stared at the ceiling for a few seconds. Then he was seized by some sort of horror and began to kick at the bed he was lying in. His movements were weak and impotent, aimed at something that didn't exist, something that was still suffusing his drowsy consciousness. There was panic in his movements; everything happened very fast and he fell helplessly out of bed, landing on the floor. He lay there, breathing hoarsely and unevenly.

He didn't know where he was, and he was scared.

Hector Guzman had been born again.

42

(STOCKHOLM)

THE SPORTS BAG ON THE COFFEE TABLE IN FRONT OF HER WAS BLACK AND UN-assuming, but Antonia looked at it as if it were something sacred, as if it contained all the answers in the world. And perhaps it did.

She leaned forward and undid the bag's zip. She peered in and took out the contents and put them on the table with trembling hands.

A plastic folder, full to bursting; a thick, heavy official folder; and a black notebook.

Antonia looked down into the bag again and ran her hand over the bottom to make sure she hadn't missed anything. There, tucked into one of the corners, was something small and plastic. She took it out.

A USB memory stick.

She looked at her coffee table. Where to start?

She might as well start with the little black notebook. She opened it. Feminine handwriting, all written in pencil, tiny writing, the pages completely covered. A lot of reasoning and theories about things that Antonia couldn't make sense of. Human behaviour, theories about what might happen. It was all too unclear, too complicated. Neither could she get any clear picture of who had written it. She closed it. The lined folder. Masculine writing, sloppy. A lot of text, again, even less comprehensible than the notebook. Antonia opened the official folder. Information about Hector Guzman and

his business dealings, including a route for smuggling cocaine between Paraguay and Rotterdam. About direct connections to other syndicates, his background, going back a long way. This was almost unparalleled evidence. Antonia went back to the black notebook and read more carefully. It was Gunilla Strandberg's notebook. Antonia read it alongside the folder. An image began to form. It was hazy, but it was enough to suggest that Gunilla Strandberg had been embezzling money from the cases she had worked on.

Antonia leafed through the pad. Lars Vinge's. Notes, confused ideas. She reached the last page.

Diagonally across an empty page of the pad Lars Vinge had hastily scrawled: *Tommy Jansson.*

Her mind was racing. What the hell?

The contents of the plastic folder spilled out. All sorts of documents: computer printouts, handwritten notes, printed photographs . . . a lot of photographs. She recognised the faces: Gunilla Strandberg, her brother Erik, Anders Ask, the police officers who were investigating Trasten before the shootout. A few photographs of Hector Guzman and Aron Geisler. And towards the bottom of the pile, masses of photographs of the same woman. Of perhaps the last person Antonia had expected to see. She held up one of the pictures in front of her. The woman was standing in a kitchen window. It was a close-up, taken with a telephoto lens. There was no doubt at all.

It was the nurse, Sophie Brinkmann.

(VILLEFRANCHE)

A CEILING FAN WAS WHIRRING SOUNDLESSLY ABOVE THEM.

Hector looked at the woman by his side who was carefully swabbing the inside of his elbow where she had just given him an injection. Her name was Raimunda; she spoke to him in Spanish, acted as if she knew him, lit up like the sun when she spoke, even laughed.

Hector tried to come to grips with the situation. He couldn't speak; he'd tried, but couldn't make a sound.

He could barely keep his eyes open, let alone lift his arms or legs. Everything felt heavy, mentally as well as physically.

He had feeling. And he could see, even if his vision was poor at a distance of more than a few metres, and he couldn't really focus. It was as if his sense of balance had been knocked out and he was drifting on waves.

The woman had checked his condition when she helped him up from the floor and back into bed. She asked yes-or-no questions about his name, family and friends to gauge his memory and general state. Hector replied with nods or shakes of his head. His hair was long, he could see it from the corners of his eyes.

The low voices and footsteps. Aron appeared in the doorway.

'Raimunda,' he said, 'leave us for a while.'

Aron sat down on a chair beside Hector.

'*Aron*,' Hector mouthed.

'Hector,' Aron said.

Hector swallowed and tried to say something.

Aron handed Hector a pad and a pen. Hector couldn't take them; his muscles weren't there, nor the signals from his brain.

Aron helped him, laid the pad on the bed and put the pen between Hector's fingers and squeezed, then he sat down, aware that his old boss would rather do it himself.

Hector tried to lift his arm, and Aron jumped up to help him again, making sure the point of the pen was resting on the paper.

Hector sat like that, motionless, incapable even of scribbling a few letters on a piece of paper. Aron was at the point of getting up again but Hector shook his head, radiating fury, fury at the loss of his dignity. He concentrated and managed to draw a line on the paper.

Aron waited patiently, knew better than to interrupt Hector, knew Hector had to do this.

Minutes passed, and eventually he managed to write a word on the page: *what*.

No question mark, just the word *what*.

The question that encompassed everything.

'We're in the villa in Villefranche,' Aron began. 'The woman you just met is Raimunda, she was a member of the emergency group of doctors and nurses that your father established some years ago.'

Hector's eyes were glued to Aron's.

'Do you remember Stockholm, the Trasten restaurant?'

Hector thought. Aron continued:

'You had a meeting with Alfonse Ramirez . . . Sophie and Jens came. Three Russians were after Jens. They came shortly after . . .'

Hector nodded a yes.

'Do you remember escaping from Trasten to Spain with Sophie on board your dad's plane?'

Hector gathered his memories. Aron went on.

'And you and Sophie were attacked on the motorway between Málaga and Marbella?'

'*Sophie*,' Hector mouthed.

'Later,' Aron said. 'At the same time, the Hankes attacked your father's house in Marbella. You got Sophie there, then you lost

consciousness. The doctors there helped you. Our security arrangements kicked in and we moved you to the house in the mountains, where Raimunda became your nurse.'

Aron stopped, scratched the back of his head hard, then met Hector's gaze again.

'Adalberto didn't make it. Your father's dead, Hector.'

There was the sound of quick footsteps on the stairs, children bouncing down to the hallway barefoot, then running straight into the room where Hector and Aron were sitting. Two boys in pyjamas. The smaller one looked terrified when he saw Hector awake, and grabbed the bigger boy's hand.

Hector squinted, unable to understand what was going on, then Angela came into the room. Then he realised, even though he hadn't seen her or the boys for many years.

'Get Fabien and Andres out of here,' Aron said.

Angela put her hands on their shoulders. But Fabien shook it off.

'Are you awake now?' he asked, wide-eyed.

Hector nodded.

'You've been asleep for a very long time,' the boy said.

Angela pulled the boys away.

'Come on, Uncle Hector needs to rest.'

She turned towards Hector, looked blankly at her brother-in-law, then left the room.

Hector wanted to say something, but Aron got up and closed the door to the room.

'*Eduardo?*' Hector mouthed.

'You've just woken up from a coma, Hector,' Aron said.

Hector waited for more.

'Six months,' Aron said without elaboration.

Hector looked down. He searched inside himself, looked up, was about to try to express something, but stopped as more questions seemed to occur to him.

'*Eduardo*,' he mouthed again.

'He was murdered in Biarritz a few weeks ago.'

That was too much. Hector stopped. But there was no sign of grief. His eyes searched for Aron's.

'The Hankes, we think,' Aron said. 'They found Eduardo . . .

Shortly after that, Daphne and Thierry were murdered in their shop.'

Hector listened.

'Ernst disappeared at the same time. I'm assuming they've got him.'

Aron was aware that another piece of bad news could have disastrous consequences. So he chose the only good news he had for his boss.

'Carlos,' he said.

Hector's eyes got bigger.

'He's been tucked away with the Hankes, he fled to them after Trasten, after he'd told them your whereabouts in Málaga, after he betrayed you.

'We found him, mainly thanks to Sonya. She saw it as her duty. She tracked him down and picked him up and took him to the house in the mountains. He saw you, and had to face up to what he did.'

Aron stopped. Hector's eyes narrowed.

'Now?' Aron said. 'Now Carlos is in hell, where he belongs.'

It looked like Hector was smiling slightly, a few brief seconds of genuine happiness.

The room was silent and still. Aron would have liked to stop there, but that was impossible.

'Sophie . . .' he said cautiously. 'I brought her in, when I wasn't sure how you wanted things. She's been working with me and Leszek, helping us . . . but . . . Carlos . . . Carlos said he'd seen her with the Hankes in Munich, they had some sort of meeting. Ralph Hanke, Sophie and Roland Gentz.'

Hector was listening intently.

'Carlos didn't hear everything, but he claimed she wanted to offer them what we've got, and give them parts of our organisation. As soon as I heard that I pulled Leszek and Hasani out of Stockholm and brought them here, along with Angela and the boys. That was when Ernst disappeared, so she must have given him to them.'

Hector began to write again, it took a long time.

Damage? Aron read.

'The authorities have frozen all your accounts and confiscated all your legal companies, seeing as there's an international warrant out

for your arrest. And the Hankes are busy helping themselves to the rest now, with Ernst's help. They're taking over all our operations and making them their own. Right now we can't do anything but watch as it happens.'

Hector pointed again to the word he'd written.

'Total,' Aron concluded.

Hector tried to absorb the information, but Aron wasn't finished.

'There's one more thing. The Hankes may have managed to track down another one of us.'

Aron leaned closer.

'Lothar,' he whispered.

Hector shook his head, as if that was an impossibility.

'Carlos said that the Hankes had found a boy they'd been looking for. I called and reported a break-in at their address. The police said the apartment was empty, no one there, no break-in. Franka isn't answering my calls. I've sent another man to Berlin, he's been looking but hasn't found anything. They're gone.'

Hector tried to think.

'Who knows about Lothar, apart from you, me and his mother?' Aron went on.

Hector looked up at the ceiling, following the anticlockwise motion of the fan. He turned his head towards Aron, and there was a sad look on his face as he mouthed: '*Sophie.*'

44

(STOCKHOLM)

TOMMY JANSSON COULD TALK TO ANYONE. HE REGARDED THIS AS ONE OF HIS greatest skills.

And now he was talking to the branch manager of the bank where Lars Shitstain Vinge had his account.

Tommy was so damned good at talking that the bank manager didn't even question the right of a police officer, simply by flashing his ID, to look through the bank's customers' transactions without either a warrant or any other appropriate documentation.

Tommy discovered that Lars Vinge had opened his safe-deposit box the previous day, was told the time and was given access to the security footage for the time in question.

Miles Ingmarsson, seen from above, in black and white, standing there confidently, talking to the cashier.

Tommy stared at the picture as one of the nerves in his left eye began to twitch.

Tommy drove through the city towards Miles's place, drinking gin and tonic from a takeaway cup.

Miles Ingmarsson's front door had seen better days. Easier to smash in than open with a lockpick. Tommy broke the lock with

a crowbar. The door flew open and he stepped into the hall, shut the battered door behind him and listened in silence – nothing but faint clicking sounds from small movements in the walls and floor of the old building.

Tommy worked quickly, like a burglar, going through every room. The kitchen, living room, bedroom, study, bathroom, hall, then back to the living room. He searched everywhere, cleared everything out onto the floor.

He was out of breath by the time he finished. Standing there in the middle of the mess, he looked around. He hadn't found any trace of what he was looking for.

THE USB MEMORY STICK IN LARS VINGE'S SPORTS BAG CONTAINED AUDIO FILES. Antonia listened to them on her cordless headphones. They were surveillance recordings of Sophie Brinkmann at her house in the suburbs . . . a dead loss. Nothing but pointless, everyday conversations between Sophie and her son, Albert. A few telephone calls. Nothing that stood out in any way.

Antonia went through the pictures again, one at a time – Sophie Brinkmann at close quarters, in various situations.

She had been scrupulously observed. *Why?*

The other material was scattered across the floor and she tried to piece everything together, all the while with the audio files playing on her headphones.

A different sound from somewhere. She lifted one side of the headphones. The doorbell was ringing insistently and monotonously out in the hall.

Through the spyhole, Tommy Jansson looked rough. He was standing out in the stairwell looking down at his shoes. He leaned forward and pressed the bell again, staring right at her.

Fear cut through Antonia and she took a step back. She didn't know why Tommy was standing outside her door . . . yet somehow she did know.

Antonia backed away silently. The doorbell rang several more times. She tried to think; should she open the door? She tried to

think of something . . . come up with a lie, some sort of explanation for Tommy . . .

The next sound she heard outside the door was quiet – a rasping, clicking sound. Tommy was trying to pick her lock.

Antonia had no time to lose. She hurried into the living room. There were photographs and notes spread out across the parquet floor, and she gathered everything together with her arms and stuffed it all into the sports bag. The lockpick was working quickly outside the door.

A loud tug at the door-handle, but the door didn't budge, and the clicking continued.

Antonia tried to gather the papers, storage devices, printed photographs, notebooks and all the other things she had found.

She thought she was going to die of the paralysing fear that took hold of her as the door opened and she heard Tommy Jansson break into her home.

Picking up Lars Vinge's sports bag and her computer, Antonia crept out of the living room. Tommy's footsteps were close.

She didn't have time to think clearly; there was only one place she could hide.

Antonia made her way quickly and quietly into the kitchen. She saw an old cupboard turned into a pantry, no door, just a curtain across the front, and she had just tucked herself inside it when Tommy Jansson stomped into the kitchen. Antonia didn't move, didn't breathe. He stopped just a couple of metres away from her on the other side of the curtain. She could hear him breathing, and could smell stale alcohol.

Then he left the kitchen and went into the living room. Antonia heard him searching as things fell to the floor and furniture was turned upside down.

Antonia was trapped. The only way out was through the living room. She waited. Her pistol was in her handbag, hanging in the hall behind her jacket.

Then everything was silent. Completely silent. Had he gone? New sounds, loud. From her bedroom. Cupboards and drawers being opened, Tommy acting like a burglar.

She stepped out from behind the curtain and started to walk

through the kitchen, passing her bedroom where, from the corner of her eye, she caught a glimpse of her boss tugging at her bedclothes with his back to her.

She carried on, out into the hall, grabbing her jacket and handbag on the way, went on out through the half-open front door and down the stairs, outside through the rear exit and then turned right, the whole time expecting to hear a voice behind her shouting at her to stop. But there was no voice. She dropped her mobile phone in a rubbish bin, left her car standing in the street and kept on walking fast. She didn't look back. After a while she realised that she wasn't wearing any shoes and was walking in just her socks.

Antonia waved down a taxi, sank into the back seat, then gave the driver the address of Ulf's apartment out in Sundbyberg.

He wasn't home. She sat down to wait on the stairs, clutching the sports bag on her lap.

TOMMY DROVE THROUGH THE CITY. THERE WAS A PICTURE OF A FACE ON THE seat next to him, a woman's face. He'd found a printout in Antonia Miller's living room, under an armchair. He wouldn't have spotted it if he hadn't put his head down on the floor. It was a printout of a photograph. He recognised it immediately. It, along with plenty more, had been in a sports bag that Lars Vinge had handed to him at Mariatorget last summer. It was Sophie Brinkmann, the nurse Gunilla had tried to use to infiltrate Hector Guzman's network . . . one of many pictures of her.

Tommy had finally made sense of everything. Lars Vinge, the idiot, had made copies of everything and put them in his safe-deposit box. Miles Ingmarsson had taken them out using a fake ID and had passed them to that bitch, Antonia Miller.

Vanessa's tree-hugging boyfriend, the cock-sucking ethnologist Mattias, was sitting in Tommy's armchair in the living room, being a twat and reading a book. There was clattering from the kitchen, Vanessa and Emelie helping their mother.

Tommy stood in the doorway. Mattias felt his presence and looked up.

'Hi,' the little Communist bastard said.

Tommy didn't answer, just nodded, barely perceptibly.

Mattias held up a paperback book.

'I found this in the bookcase.'

Tommy squinted. *The Diving Bell and the Butterfly*. One of Monica's books.

'Oh?'

'It's about a guy who's paralysed, he's got Locked-in Syndrome.'

Tommy glared at the slack-limbed boy. No muscle on him, which was presumably why he had to emphasise how clever he was. Difficult books evidently were part of all that.

Tommy didn't move. Mattias grew uncertain.

'It's quite interesting,' he said, then buried himself in the book again.

'Why aren't you helping in the kitchen?'

'They said they didn't need me.'

'They said that?'

Mattias nodded.

'Word for word?'

Mattias didn't answer.

'So you came and sat down here, in my armchair?'

'Yes?'

'It's a bit early to be taking over, don't you think?'

Tommy walked out.

He heard Mattias chuckling behind him.

Oh là là, Tommy sang silently to himself to keep from turning around and going back to strangle the boy on the spot.

He gave his daughters a hug in the kitchen.

'Hi, Dad.'

The hugs were distanced and impersonal. The atmosphere was tense and odd. Half smiles and fear of the unknown circling around their father's peculiar personality.

Monica tried to smile. Tommy noticed an oxygen cylinder on wheels beside her, a transparent breathing mask in her hand. Every so often she would take a breath from it.

'Is that new?' was all he could find to say.

Monica tried to smile in confirmation.

'Oh. Great,' he said, then pulled a bottle of wine from the rack on the wall.

As usual, the evening meal was of a high standard. They ate and made small talk. Tommy was worrying about Ingmarsson and Miller. The pressure in his chest had found its way up through his neck to his brain. It was making him stupid and sluggish. He drank his wine, quietly but quickly; it was a trick that seemed to work, he didn't think anyone noticed.

Mattias was talking about gender issues. The kid knew what he was doing, declaiming loudly and authoritatively to Tommy's women around the table.

Tommy ate, looking down at his plate, breathing shallowly through his nose. His blood pressure rose as Mattias talked about power structures, patriarchal society . . .

Tommy tried to think about something else, but the left-wing nightmare's holier-than-thou voice cut through the room at a frequency it was impossible to ignore. Phrases like *gender trap, sexism, women's football, liberal feminism, quotas, gender roles*. The words forced themselves into Tommy's consciousness.

In the end he blew his top, it was impossible to hold back. Fury burst out of his reptile brain, through his head and out from his eyes.

'You cocky little bastard,' Tommy growled as he flew up from his chair and grabbed hold of Mattias by his hair. He bit his bottom lip as he hit the boy's head hard against the table repeatedly. His plate shattered. The girls screamed, and Monica's dark, slurred, weak voice urged him to stop. But Tommy didn't hear, he was hard at work and enjoying himself. It was like finally being able to scratch somewhere you couldn't reach. The release of tension put him in a strangely happy mood, made him feel soft inside as a feeling of warmth embraced him.

Tommy stopped and looked at Mattias. Fragments of his plate were stuck to his face, along with vegetables and sauce.

From the corner of his eye he saw Monica trying to stand up to

stop him, but her paralysis prevented her. He carried on with the assault for a while longer with an open palm. Then he was done. He let go of the boy's hair and sat down on his chair again and leaned back, feeling relaxed and harmonious.

Mattias looked bewildered. His nose was bleeding steadily, his hair was on end, and his anxious eyes darted around the table, not quite aware of what had just happened to him.

The girls were crying quietly. Monica stared at her husband. He realised he was still smiling. It came from the heart.

'I'm fine, Monica,' he whispered. 'Absolutely fine.'

She said nothing, just carried on staring at him. Tommy met his daughters' gaze. They looked away, and that's when he began to doubt.

'You've got to be allowed to feel good sometimes, haven't you?'

The conviction in his voice was suddenly gone.

Tommy's mobile phone vibrated in his pocket. He took it out.

'Saved by the bell,' he said happily.

Vanessa started to cry more loudly.

He checked the number, then hushed her irritably to get her to be quiet.

'Yep,' he said into the phone as he stood up.

The reception was bad. He waved his hand to Vanessa to tell her to stop crying.

'Tommy here,' he said.

The voice at the other end was high-pitched.

'This is Roger Lindgren. Your friend Miles is here, in my apartment.'

Tommy left the table and called Ove Negerson.

THE FIRST ROUND WAS GOING TO HELL. MILES WAS LYING ON THE FLOOR. ROGER Lindgren was taking great, swinging kicks at his face.

Miles had prepared carefully, planning exactly what he was going to do.

He went upstairs in the building on Hagagatan and rang the doorbell. He pushed Roger Lindgren back into the apartment and

slapped him around a bit. Miles had expected to gain some advantage from the confusion he created. The plan was to get Lindgren down on the floor and then do what he was there for.

But Roger wasn't at all confused. Not even surprised. Miles figured that out the moment the guy opened the door.

Roger Lindgren was chewing, only without gum; he had a tense smile, a shiny druggy glow to his face and madness in his eyes. Roger Lindgren was high.

'Is your name Miles Ingmarsson?' he asked.

'How the hell do you know that . . . ?'

Roger Lindgren broke into joyous anger and quickly and violently punched Miles Ingmarsson down onto the parquet floor.

Things moved pretty damned fast after that. Seemingly endless kicks to the face. Miles sensed it wouldn't be long before he lost consciousness. Blood flew, and the violence focused on his head was brutal and remorseless. The adrenaline in his body was working hard to control the pain, but it couldn't keep up. It soon became clear to Miles that he was going to die right there on the floor.

Then, just as he felt he was about to pass out, Roger stopped kicking him. Through the fog of the assault, Miles saw Roger sit on top of him, pull a mobile phone from his jeans pocket and make a call.

Miles lay there, about to die. And he realised why.

He hadn't been angry when he stormed in, not in the slightest. He had been nervous, expectant, deluding himself compulsively that his plan would work. Which of course it hadn't. He had forgotten the most important ingredient – fury. That was why he was lying there like an idiot, just taking it.

Miles backed up in his thoughts. *Sanna* . . . Her pleading messages on his voicemail . . . her battered face in the hospital . . . How lovely she was, how honest . . .

That was why he was there, after all . . . Miles looked up at Roger Lindgren's ugly, drugged frame sitting on top of him. Roger ended the call and was about to continue his assault when Miles grabbed Roger's hair with his left hand. A hard punch with his right fist.

The blow landed just below Lindgren's eye, and Miles felt something break. Two more punches. Whatever had broken was going to be impossible to mend.

Then everything happened automatically, and time became dis-

jointed and hazy. Miles ended up on top of Roger, raining blows down on him, then grabbed his head and brought it down hard on the floor. Roger Lindgren tried to resist, flailing at the air.

Miles found his rhythm and lost track of time and space. A harmonious state of being. Apparently it was called *flow*, and there were entire books all about it.

Lindgren was finished, he wasn't coming back, was about to be knocked out for good. But he mustn't die; Miles wasn't finished with him yet.

Cold water.

Miles stood up, walked through the apartment and found the kitchen behind a locked door.

A plastic curtain, then he was met by a bright blue light, as if he were on his way to heaven. But this wasn't heaven, it was a laboratory, a meth kitchen.

Miles stepped inside. There was a heavy, acrid smell. The windows were covered with black rubbish bags, and the strong blue light came from UV lamps above an extended kitchen table. There were hot plates, cookware, heat-proof glass beakers, Bunsen burners and chemicals, benzene, acetone, petrol, sodium hydroxide, hydrochloric acid. Also lighter fluid, dismantled children's antiallergy inhalers, cotton-wool balls, coffee filters, tea towels and matches.

Miles stared.

There was a small mountain of pure white powder under one of the UV lamps. Better than cold water.

He picked up a transparent plastic bag, found a spoon in a drawer, filled the bag with amphetamine and left the kitchen.

Lindgren was lying on his back, his hands cuffed behind him. He followed Miles with his swollen eyes.

'What's that?' He sounded like he had a harelip, his voice coming from his nose and mouth simultaneously.

Miles didn't answer, and Roger realised. There was genuine panic in his voice when he started to plead.

'No, for fuck's sake, it hasn't been diluted yet!'

Miles sat astride Lindgren's chest, took a spoonful and drove it into the man's throat. Roger coughed, trying to spit it out, but Miles held his mouth closed as he looked around the living room. It

was very shabby, furnished with stuff from second-hand shops and crap from cheap trips to Asia. Ugly pictures, stupid artistic photographs. Cultural nonsense . . . Miles waited patiently for Lindgren's swallowing reflex to kick in, as eventually it did. The anguish in his wide-open eyes was unmistakable. This was high-octane amphetamine. This was a nightmare. The mother of all bad trips . . .

A new start.
Longer life.
Bang!

His whole system was working hard, pulse, heart, blood. Miles watched. Lindgren was behaving like the Hulk, mid-transformation, as his insides boiled – vomiting and writhing in pain and anguish.

Miles couldn't be bothered to hit the bastard any more. He leaned forward and whispered *Sanna* into Roger's bleeding ear. Then he looked on calmly as Roger Lindgren died of what was probably a heart attack, unless it was just the general shutdown of everything.

Miles stood up, unzipped his trousers and pissed on Roger Lindgren. It just felt right, like a sort of grand finale.

There was a noise behind him and he turned around, urine spraying across the body.

Tommy Jansson was standing there in the room with another man.

'Hi, Ingmarsson,' Tommy said.

A few seconds ticked by before Miles understood. He finished pissing, shook the last drops and tucked himself away.

'Hi, Tommy,' he said, for some reason brushing the legs of his trousers.

Miles's face and hair were covered with blood – his hands and arms, too. A butcher who had just pissed on a corpse.

'Miles Ingmarsson,' Tommy whispered. 'I didn't think you had it in you.'

No response. Miles waited for him to go on.

'It appears things have got a bit out of hand, I must say,' he continued.

Miles wiped his nose with his sleeve.

'That depends how you look at it,' Miles said.

' "How you look at it"?' Tommy let out an affected laugh. 'I'd

say it looks out of hand,' he went on, and turned to the other man. 'Wouldn't you say, Ove?'

Ove looked at Roger Lindgren.

'Things have got out of hand, no doubt about that,' he said.

Tommy scratched his chin.

'Is he still alive?' he asked, pointing at the body on the floor.

Miles turned around and tried to see any sign of life in Lindgren.

'No, I don't think so. He's probably dead now.'

'And what the hell happened to your hand?' Ove asked, staring wide-eyed as he pointed to Miles's right hand.

Miles inspected it. The knuckles of his first and middle fingers were shattered, and the bones on the back of his hand were stretching the skin like tent poles.

'I don't know,' he said.

'For fuck's sake, it's broken,' Ove laughed.

'Is it?'

Ove couldn't stop laughing.

'Yes, it's fucked.'

Miles examined his hand.

'Yes, it probably is,' he mumbled.

'You hit him so fucking hard you broke your hand!'

Ove had a chuckling laugh; it sounded genuine.

'In this short time you've won my undivided respect, Miles Ingmarsson. I want you to know that. My name is Ove, Ove Negerson.'

Miles didn't understand.

'What are you doing here, Miles?' Tommy asked.

'What are *you* doing here, Tommy?'

They stared at each other for a moment.

'What did you find in Vinge's safe-deposit box?' he asked calmly.

'Nothing,' Miles lied.

Tommy nodded, pretending to accept the lie.

'So what the fuck is this?' Tommy gestured round the room. 'Why did you kill this poor bastard?'

Miles shrugged.

Ove mimicked the shrug, exaggeratedly and theatrically.

'You can do better than that, Miles,' Tommy said.

'Does it matter?'

'Of course it matters!'

'I had to,' Miles said.

Ove put his hand over his mouth and opened his eyes wide.

Tommy glanced at Ove in irritation, then turned back to Miles again.

'Had to?'

'There was a development.'

'What?'

'A development. A personal development. I found love,' Miles muttered.

Tommy looked disgusted. Behind him, Ove was making a pantomime gesture of surprise.

'And I almost died in a car crash,' Miles went on. 'I had some sort of revelation.'

Ove was stuck in pantomime mode now, protecting his face in a car crash, then looking terrified and finally acting like Jesus on the cross.

'Then he showed up and ruined everything.' Miles pointed at Lindgren's body with his left thumb.

Ove turned into a sad clown, clasping both hands to his heart.

Tommy was irritably aware of the performance taking place out of the corner of his eye.

'Can you just stop that, Ove!' he yelled.

Ove froze like a cartoon character and looked exaggeratedly sad; the corners of his mouth hung down, his shoulders drooped and he walked with heavy steps towards Lindgren's body. Then he relaxed and straightened up. In the end he was standing perfectly normally beside the body.

'Now I'm myself again, Tommy!' Ove smiled broadly, sat down next to the body and pointed up at Miles. 'The same thing goes for your colleague. He's himself again, that's what he's trying to say,' Ove went on.

Tommy looked Miles Ingmarsson up and down.

' "Himself"? So what does that mean, then?'

No answer.

'Are you? Yourself again?' Tommy asked. 'Is this Miles Ingmarsson?' He pointed to the room once more. 'Well?'

'Maybe,' Miles whispered.

'We're all being nice and honest today, I like it!' Ove said.

Tommy scratched his stubble.

'You've committed murder here. Would that be a fair assessment, Miles?' Tommy asked.

Miles shrugged. 'Maybe,' he said once more.

'*Maybe?*' Tommy let out a crooked laugh. 'This is murder!'

Ove found the amphetamine and tasted it with his finger, then turned to Tommy.

'What the fuck are you up to, Tommy?'

'What am I up to? If we can get Ingmarsson for this murder, then that ought to be enough. That's what I'm up to,' Tommy said.

Ove snorted, then stood up with the bag of amphetamine in his hand.

'He'll sit in prison singing his heart out until someone listens to him. He's a cop. What sort of fucking stupid idea is that, Jansson?'

'I'm just trying to find different solutions,' Tommy said weakly.

' "Different solutions"?' Ove mimicked the words like a child. 'You're not looking for different solutions, you're chickening out, you haven't got the balls to go through with what we agreed. There are no other solutions, Cap'n Jansson!'

Ove took a few steps towards Tommy.

'What the hell do you know about what I'm thinking . . . ?' Tommy began.

Ove slapped him hard across the face. It made a loud noise.

Tommy was bewildered.

Miles tried to see an opportunity to run, out of the room, out of the building. But they were standing in the way. The apartment was on the third floor, so he couldn't jump out of the window. Unless that was what he ought to do? Head-first. Maybe that would be better than what was to come?

'Here, Tommy,' Ove said softly. 'Have some of this.'

He held up the bag of drugs.

'What is it?'

'Speed. Looks like absolute dynamite. It'll help with your cowardice.'

Tommy lost his cool.

'And you think it's wrong drinking beer at lunchtime!'

'Ooh, that one hit home,' Ove said.

He was smiling again now, the change in mood was striking. He offered the bag to Tommy.

'What? You think I'd take drugs?' Tommy said, affronted.

'Yes, just have a little bit and stop being such a girl.'

Ove dug out a little pile with his forefinger and balanced it in front of Tommy.

'You first,' Tommy said in a hostile voice.

Ove snorted it up his nose, pulled out some more and held his finger up to Tommy.

Tommy inhaled and pulled a face, then rubbed his nose hard.

'Tastes like medicine,' he said.

'You really do have a way with words, Tommy. Now, let's get dear old Miles out of here.'

Tommy was high, clinging to the wheel with both hands as he stared ahead, wide-eyed. Ove was grooving to the music on the radio, and Miles was sitting in the back seat with cuffs on. They drove for a good half hour, away from the city, away from civilisation. Then the car suddenly stopped. Ove pulled Miles out; they were in a dark, deserted place. He led Miles down towards a lake.

Cold, black water spread out in front of him into eternity, a few thin ice floes on its surface.

'You know none of this really has any purpose,' Ove said, pointing out into the darkness.

'What?' Miles asked.

'It's all unnecessary, completely devoid of meaning.'

Miles looked out across the threatening water.

'Lie down now,' Ove said.

The water is death.

'I don't want to,' Miles said. He heard his own voice. He sounded like a child, a frightened child who didn't want to die.

'It's OK.' Ove's voice was very close to him.

'I don't want to,' Miles replied once more.

Warmth down one leg, he'd wet himself.

'Tommy?' Miles cried.

A hard kick to his knee, and Miles's leg buckled. Then a heavy shove that got him off-balance, followed by a punch to the head. Miles collapsed. Ove grabbed his arms and dragged him to the shore. Miles saw the sky up above, the stars, galaxies.

Ove turned him over onto his stomach, Miles stared down into the water. Ove's steady hand on his head pressed him below the surface.

The water was ice-cold. Miles kicked, to no avail. He tried to move his whole body in an effort to slip out of Ove's firm grasp.

Ove called Tommy, somewhere above the surface, and Miles felt Tommy grab his legs and sit on them. He didn't stand a chance, there was no escape as the air in his lungs ran out. His ears were buzzing, his throat burned, he felt pressure building behind his eyes, his skin felt like it was boiling. His heart beat shallowly and quickly.

Then the oxygen ran out, and pain twisted through his body.

He was going to die now, and he wasn't at all ready.

But just as Miles realised that his life was coming to an end, something else appeared. Something else, between the thin veil of life and the great, dark eternity. Something that didn't exist, yet did exist. Without dimensions, without form or structure, but definitely real. A voice that wasn't speaking, a presence, invisible hands holding him, calming him.

Whatever it was, it presented itself to Miles as an alternative. The alternative that he had never made use of. The alternative that he had always shunned and avoided, that he had smirked at as something for the weak, the lonely, the slightly crazy. The alternative that wasn't real . . .

Tommy undid the cuffs and took them back.

Miles felt himself drifting slightly outside himself as Ove let go of his hair and he was pushed out into the water, gently sinking.

45

(NORTHERN GERMANY)

JENS WAS PUTTING PETROL IN THE CAR. SOPHIE AND LOTHAR WERE STRETCH-
ing their legs. The filling station shone brightly in the evening gloom.
Cars rushed past on the motorway.

Lothar had his arms around himself as he stood there shivering.

'Are you cold?' Sophie asked.

He didn't answer immediately, then muttered *yes*. Sophie put one
arm around him. At first the physical contact made him stiffen up.
Then he relaxed. Before long he started to cry. She could feel his
body shake, and held him tight as he sobbed into her shoulder.

She met Jens's gaze.

Deep inside her, responsibility, sympathy and a reflex to look
after people existed as fixed elements of her personality. They had
always been there, for better or worse. Now she had to suppress
them, shut them away and persuade herself that the exact opposite
was the right choice . . . *Keep your distance, because you're going to
betray this boy . . . horribly.*

Sophie let go of him.

Lothar walked away to be alone.

Her phone rang. Number withheld.

'Yes?' she said.

Roland Gentz's voice was very clear.

'*Have you paid us a visit?*'

'Where's Albert?' she said.

'Albert's with us.'

'Where's Albert?' she repeated.

'*Do you know who you took with you from here, Sophie?*'

She turned around. Lothar was sitting at a picnic table between the filling station and the motorway.

'Yes,' she replied.

'*We'll organise an exchange.*'

'I want that to happen as soon as possible,' she said. She kept her voice steady, didn't want to sound too desperate.

'*Get in touch with Aron,*' Roland interrupted. '*Tell him you've got Hector's son, and say you want to hand him over to them. Give us Hector. He's the only one we want. If you can do that, you'll get Albert back.*'

'Were you there?'

'*Where?*'

'At the farm. Was Albert there when we were there?'

'*No.*'

The line went dead.

She let the phone sit there in her hand. Cars raced by in both directions on the motorway.

Jens started the car.

Mikhail came out of the petrol station.

Lothar got up from the bench and walked back.

Sophie watched him. Grief-stricken and unaware of almost everything, he walked towards the car in a crouch. He didn't belong to anyone. His whole bearing radiated precisely that – abandonment.

46

(STOCKHOLM)

ANTONIA AND ULF WERE IN BED. THEY HAD LEFT ULF'S APARTMENT AFTER SHE told him what had happened, and had taken refuge just two floors above: one of Ulf's neighbours was away and had asked him to water the plants and feed the hamster for a few weeks. The hamster was dead, but the plants were still alive.

They were lying on two mattresses on the floor, under the covers. Ulf was focused but tense, she could feel it. She spooned behind him.

'I'm frightened,' she said.

'I'll help you,' he said.

'Are you frightened?'

He thought about it.

'No, I don't think so,' he said. His Dalarna accent was pronounced.

'How are you feeling, then?'

'Surprised . . . and angry,' he replied.

She couldn't really huddle up any closer, but she tried.

In spite of the peculiar decor of the apartment, and the stupid pictures of crying clowns, dolphins leaping around at sunset and a still life of a bowl of fruit, Antonia felt warm and safe there, intact.

'What are we going to do afterwards?' she asked.

'Afterwards?'

'When we're done with this. When we've done the right thing. When we've caught Tommy, when we're free?'

'Then we're going to move back down to my apartment again.'

'Really, though?' she said.

Ulf gave the question almost half a minute.

'Then I'll take you up to the cabin. We'll go hunting in the forest. We'll make food and have sex in different places . . . Would you like that?'

'Yes, I'd like that a lot,' Antonia replied.

MILES WAS FLOATING UNDER THE WATER. HIS CONSCIOUSNESS WAS BURNING like a small flame. Life was a tenacious thing.

He bumped against something. Something vertical, a chain. He came to a halt in his weightless state.

The flame inside him got some oxygen, grew a little stronger, enough for the blood in his arms to start moving. And with that minute pulse of energy he gave himself a barely perceptible push to move up along the chain.

He made slow progress as he hung there in the darkness. Then another push . . . The effort was an additional drain on a life that was close to over.

At last he broke the surface as his arms hung limply around the chain. A white plastic buoy attached to the end was bobbing beside him.

But he wasn't getting any oxygen, even though he was surrounded by fresh, cool, winter-evening air. Nothing, and he could taste blood in his mouth, an incredible pain radiating throughout his whole body and a dull throbbing in his ears.

Then all his organs turned inside out and he vomited water. Several litres of brackish, polluted Baltic Sea water gushed out of him in a steady stream.

Then he was empty, wrung out like an old bath sponge, dry as a dead twig.

But suddenly he could breathe air into his lungs. The pain was still there, worse than when death had held him in its clutches. But gradually life came back to Miles Ingmarsson. He waited until he heard what must have been Tommy Jansson's car start up and drive away. Then he swam towards land.

Miles was utterly drenched as he stood there with the lake behind him, but with solid ground under his feet and air in his lungs. He was alive.

Miles began to swear. He swore as loudly and violently as he could, right into the black night. He swore and cursed everything that was fucked up on the planet he had been left to live on. No one but the animals, nature and the punishing God listened to him. His screams died away like a drawn-out echo.

Then he walked off into the darkness.

PART THREE

47

(JUTLAND)

THE LITTLE HOUSE LAY DESERTED IN THE MIDST OF A CLUSTER OF WINTER-
naked trees. A whitewashed, 150-year-old house with a thatched
roof and pale-blue window frames.

Jens found the key in a hollow tree trunk.

He unlocked the door and showed them around, and they each
found a bed on the upper floor. Then he waved to Mikhail, and the
pair of them went back downstairs, into the library, where the old
books were lined up on built-in cherrywood bookcases. On one sec-
tion of open wall hung three rifles, one above the other. Jens un-
locked them and lifted them down one by one and passed them to
Mikhail. The first was a Winchester .22 repeater rifle, the second a
shotgun: a Spanish Aya, double-barreled, old and reliable. The third
and final one was an M1 Garand.

Mikhail held the M1 in his hands, inspecting and weighing it,
and almost smiled. The M1 Garand was a semi-automatic rifle from
the Second World War. Wooden stock, five kilograms in weight, a
metre long and loaded with an *en bloc* clip that ejected automati-
cally once the gunman had fired five shots.

'Where did your grandfather get hold of this?' Mikhail asked.

'No idea.'

Jens fetched the ammunition from a chest and passed some to
Mikhail.

'The M1 upstairs, the shotgun in the kitchen and the Winchester in the living room,' he instructed.

With the M1 and suitable ammunition in his hands, Mikhail went back upstairs and walked past Lothar's room. Mikhail hesitated, then turned back and knocked on the door with his foot, then handed the M1 to Lothar.

'Do you know how to load one of these?'

'No,' Lothar said.

Mikhail put the boxes of ammunition down on the bed, sat down on the bedspread and looked at Lothar.

'Are you OK?' Mikhail mumbled.

Lothar nodded.

'Good. Then I'll show you how to do it.'

Mikhail put some bullets and the small clips on the bedspread.

'You push the bullets in here,' he said, showing him. Lothar sat beside Mikhail and filled a magazine with more bullets.

They sat there in silence next to each other, loading bullets.

'Well done,' Mikhail said when they were finished.

'Thanks,' Lothar replied politely.

'You'll be OK,' Mikhail said. 'Time's on your side.'

Lothar looked Mikhail in the eye.

'Thanks,' he said again.

Mikhail stood up and left the room.

Jens lit a pre-prepared fire in the living room. The flame caught and the dry wood crackled.

Jens crouched down by the fireplace, letting the heat warm him. Lothar came into the room and stopped by a sideboard, looking at the framed photographs on top.

Jens turned around.

'My grandparents spent their whole lives here. Grandma died a few months ago. I used to spend practically the whole of my summers here as a child,' he said.

The fire was compact and powerful, and Jens topped it up with two lumps of wood.

'It went to her children, and was going to be sold.'

He stood up, then went on.

'I couldn't bear to see it go, so I bought it from my mum and her brothers and sisters. I don't know if that's good or bad.'

Lothar was holding one of the pictures in his hand: Grandma Vibeke and Granddad Esben standing side by side in their smart clothes, on their way to a party in the '60s.

'Why?' Lothar asked.

'If it's good or bad? It's something to do with memories. They're getting a bit hazy now that the place is mine. The exact opposite from the reason why I bought it.'

He patted Lothar's shoulder.

'It's a good house, this one; you'll sleep well tonight,' Jens said.

Sophie came into the room. Her eyes didn't seem to want to settle on either of them.

'I've spoken to Aron,' she said to Jens in Swedish.

Jens waited for her to go on, ask something, suggest something. But instead she turned to Lothar and switched to English.

'We need to talk.'

'About what?' the boy asked.

She hesitated before answering.

'About your father,' she said.

48

(VILLEFRANCHE)

A PARASOL SHADED HECTOR AS HE SAT ON A CHAIR ON THE VERANDA AND looked out across the garden towards Cap Ferrat. The parasol fluttered gently in the cool breeze.

He was physically weak. Could barely walk, couldn't lift anything. Raimunda had been forcing him to exercise since he woke up. It was irritatingly simple – humiliating to an extent – and very difficult. She said he was making progress, but far too little for him to be able to notice it. She had explained his physical shortcomings to him. Some of them would be with him for the rest of his life, others would fade in time, if he did as she told him. Raimunda was good. She was straight, honest and positive, without being affected.

His voice had returned, but his vocal cords were weak and had little strength. Sometimes his voice just faded away altogether, and then he would have to wait a while and drink a glass of water.

But Hector Guzman had changed in other ways too. Ways that he noticed, without sharing them with anyone else. Sometimes things that didn't exist could flash past at the edge of his vision. From time to time he would hear a voice saying something in a friendly tone, right next to him, even though there was no one there.

His left hand didn't obey him the way it used to, and sometimes he would find himself weeping even though he was neither sad nor in pain.

Oddly, his sight seemed to have improved, as if he saw contrasts

better. He could see colours more clearly, details, depth – everything was bolder than before. The world was lit up in a completely different way from how it had been.

The extremes of his emotions were more pronounced. He could feel deeply affected by something extremely banal and unimportant while at the same time feeling empty and indifferent towards something that was big and important. He'd been like that before, admittedly, before the coma, but now it was more tangible, as if his astonishment at some things was now as big as his indifference to others.

Hector was roused from his thoughts by footsteps approaching. Aron. He stood in front of Hector and looked at him. Then he pulled up a chair and sat down beside him. They shared the same view of the world.

'I've just been on the phone,' Aron said.

'Who to?' Hector whispered.

'Sophie,' Aron replied.

Sophie.

She was constantly in his thoughts, drifting around, out of reach, out of focus.

'She's got Lothar, she wants to let us have him.'

'The Hankes,' Hector mumbled. 'What do they want?'

'They want you,' Aron said.

'Of course. How?'

'Dead.'

'How are they going to do it?'

'Use Lothar to lure you out. An exchange, that's what Sophie's doing at the moment.'

'Does she know I've woken up?'

'No.'

Hector looked out across the bay, into beautiful infinity.

'How did she sound?' he asked.

'She sounded steady, like she usually does.'

'And?'

'I don't know, something else, too. Empty, disillusioned. Tired, maybe.'

Hector could see her in front of him, the way he remembered her . . . light-hearted, warm, no make-up, beautiful. Green eyes,

almost invisible freckles, surrounded by light. An inner light that ra-
diated outwards. But it wasn't just bright light, there was something
deeper and more complicated there.

'What did she say about Lothar?'

'She didn't say much.'

'How is he?'

'OK, she said.'

'Did you find out anything else?'

'No.'

'Is she being threatened?'

Aron shrugged.

'She passed on the information, didn't want to answer any ques-
tions.'

A propeller plane sailed across the bay.

'What does this mean, Aron?'

'That the Hankes are working hard right now. They're on a roll.'

'I know that. But why Sophie?'

'Does it matter?'

'Yes,' Hector said.

'The Hankes want to take everything from us. What could be
better than taking your son and the woman you love?'

Hector watched the plane.

'We agree to a meeting – an exchange, or whatever it is they
want.'

'Knowing that they'll do all they can to kill you?'

'Do what you can to prevent that. That's what I pay you for. Get
me and Lothar out of there. Outwit those bastards, Aron.'

'There must be some other way.'

'Do you have any suggestions?'

'I have a lot of suggestions.'

'Do you have a suggestion that keeps Lothar safe?' asked Hector.

'How could I make that sort of claim . . . ?'

'They're going to hurt him,' Hector interrupted.

He tried to move the fingers of his left hand.

'We don't have any choice,' he went on. 'I don't have any choice.
Call her, tell her I'm awake and that we agree to meet wherever they
want.'

'I'd like to ask you to reconsider, Hector.'

'I will not . . .'

Exhaustion hit. Hector quickly grew pale and tired.

Aron noticed and tapped gently on one of the sliding doors. Raimunda came out.

'Come along, I'll help you,' she said.

ANGELA HAD PUT ANDRES AND FABIEN IN FRONT OF THE TELEVISION AND WAS waiting for an opportunity. It came when Aron tapped on the door and Raimunda went out to help Hector.

Angela hurried into the kitchen, pulled the phone from its charger and went upstairs, into the bathroom, turned the shower on and dialled the number she knew by heart. The police in Biarritz.

During her years as a legal assistant at a law firm in the city she had met Gustave Peltier, a lieutenant with the Police Nationale, on several occasions. He was a tenacious detective, a career cop.

There was a click, then a voice welcoming her to the police in Biarritz.

Angela asked in fluent French to be put through to Lt Gustave Peltier.

'Tell him it's Angela Garcia Rivera, and that it's urgent.'

Thirty seconds of heavy silence followed, then two rings, crackly and hesitant. A phone was picked up.

'*Angela?*'

Gustave's voice, gruff and deep.

'Yes,' she replied.

'*You disappeared. We're investigating Eduardo's death. Where are you?*'

She spoke quietly, close to the receiver.

'I need your help, Gustave.'

Her plea, and her tone of voice, seemed to surprise him.

'*What do you need help with, Angela?*'

'The boys and I need protection.'

'*OK . . .*' He drew the word out.

'Do you know the name Hector Guzman?'

'*Hector Guzman . . .* ' he muttered tentatively to himself.

'Spanish,' Angela said. 'Son of a gangster named Adalberto Guzman, Marbella. Lived in Stockholm?'

'*Yes, now I remember. Interpol was after his father for years, without success. Stockholm, did you say? There was some sort of shootout at a restaurant last summer? Hector Guzman escaped; there's an international warrant out for him. Is that right?*'

'Yes.'

'*Why are we talking about Hector Guzman, Angela? Where are you?*'

'Listen to me, Gustave. I can give you Hector Guzman, his closest associates and a whole lot more information. In return for protection. The boys and I need protection.'

More silence.

'*What are you talking about, Angela?*'

Beside her the shower was running.

'My husband, Eduardo, and Hector Guzman were brothers.'

49

(STOCKHOLM)

THE SUN HAD RISEN BY THE TIME MILES MADE HIS WAY TO THE ROAD, AND there wasn't much traffic. He waved his left hand and stuck his thumb up, and eventually got a lift with a Pentecostal pastor with no mobile phone who thought God was cool.

'He isn't at all,' Miles said, seeing as he'd just met Him.

'You look like you could do with a hospital.' The pastor smiled.

'No, that can wait. What I need first is a phone.'

Forest and fields. Signs with strange place names, little wooden houses with obsessively neat gardens with no fences. This was a world Miles didn't recognise.

He got out in a hamlet with no name.

'God bless you,' the pastor said.

'And you,' Miles said.

He found a roadside café. A smell of fried food, friendly atmosphere. 'I need to borrow a phone,' he said to the woman behind the counter. She lent him her mobile phone, an old one with buttons.

'How are you doing, dear?' she asked.

He knew he looked terrible, assaulted, broken hand, dead and resurrected, filthy and in a wretched state generally.

'I'll survive, thanks.'

'Your hand?' She pointed to his limp right hand.

'It's broken, I think, but not to worry.'

She was about to say something else, but Miles stepped aside and called Antonia Miller. Her voicemail clicked in immediately.

'Disappear and go underground,' he said, then hung up.

Then he called his brother, Ian – a congenitally unfaithful bastard with a secret fuck-pad in Birkastan that he used whenever he wasn't at home playing daddy and loving husband out in Åkersberga.

'I need the apartment, your secret one,' Miles said.

He hadn't spoken to his younger brother for a very long time. He was soon reminded why.

'*I don't know, it's not convenient right now.*'

'Ian, I'll call your wife and kids.'

'*Piss off and go to bed, Miles.*' It was like he was twelve again, perhaps he always had been.

But before Miles could say anything, Ian backed down in the face of the threat.

'*I'll unlock it and leave the keys on the kitchen table, but you'd better not break anything.*'

Miles ended the call, then handed the phone back to the kind woman. She passed him a bandage from the first-aid box.

'Wrap it up for now, and make sure you get to a doctor.'

Miles took the bandage. He was so grateful he could have kissed her.

Miles travelled by bus, commuter train and underground. He was returning to reality and Stockholm at the same time. He tried to remain calm, but it didn't work.

He bought a new pay-as-you-go mobile phone from a news-stand, and hurried to Birkastan.

The fuck-pad was a two-room apartment, registered to a company that was owned by a friend of Ian's. Evidently they shared it. The friend was in the telecom business, and was keen on young girls. Miles had no idea what Ian was keen on, and didn't want to know.

Miles was surprised by the furnishings. The apartment was very tastefully laid out. That wasn't thanks to Ian, he knew that much. And at a guess, it wasn't the telecom paedophile, either. Perhaps it had been bought already furnished.

On the coffee table there was an old Chianti bottle with a can-

dle in it, and an eternity of wax had run down and solidified in the woven basket that covered half the bottle.

He sat down on the sofa, a big velvet thing. It was supposed to look old but was new. And expensive.

He searched for Antonia Miller's home number on his new phone. She didn't have one. He tried to find someone related to her. He called people named Miller, but no one knew her. Perhaps she wasn't even still alive.

He searched his memory. The man in her kitchen popped into his head. With the Dalarna accent, with the football T-shirt . . . Real Madrid . . .

What was his name? *Ulf.*

Miles had seen him at blue-light events, he'd been a patrol cop for years. Then he got promoted and went into surveillance. Miles didn't know anyone in Surveillance. He didn't really know anyone at all. He dialled the number of the internal police exchange.

A male voice answered.

'Surveillance, please,' Miles said.

'Putting you through,' the voice said.

The line bleeped a few times. Then another voice, female this time, who answered by giving the department number.

'Uffe?' Miles said.

'*Sorry?*'

'I'd like to speak to Uffe . . .'

'*Uffe who?*' She sounded annoyed.

'Yes, what is his surname? Big guy, from Dalarna, I think. Arrived at Surveillance a couple of years ago, used to be in a patrol car . . .'

'*Oh, I know who you mean. But no one calls him Uffe. He's just Ulf. His surname's Lange.*'

The call was put through, then redirected and the tone changed – presumably he was being put through to Ulf's mobile phone. It was switched off.

Voicemail clicked in, and a pre-programmed voice said: '*The person you are calling is not available. Press 1 to leave a message, hold to be transferred to the operator.*'

Miles held the phone in front of him and pressed the number 1. There was a beep, and Miles gambled everything on one throw.

'Antonia Miller?' His voice sounded rusty, as if he hadn't spoken all day.

Silent a moment too long. He went on.

'Hello from the worst cop on the force. In all categories.'

Miles gave his new mobile-phone number, then ended the call.

Ten minutes later his phone rang. Antonia sounded agitated.

'Are we safe on this line?' he asked.

'I don't know, I think so.'

'Where are you?'

She seemed to hesitate.

'Staying with a friend.'

'Are you safe there?'

'Yes. But I don't know how long for; there's a warrant out for me.'

'What for?'

'Don't know, a load of fabricated crap, it was issued yesterday. But that doesn't matter. I'm blown, I can't be seen in public.'

'Get a taxi and come here, can you do that?'

'Yes.'

'Use one of the smaller companies, the ones that don't take pictures of their customers,' he said. 'One more thing . . .'

'What?'

'Maybe you'd better warn Ulf, I don't know.'

'I already have,' Antonia said.

Miles told her the right street but the wrong house number.

He wandered restlessly round the apartment for a few minutes, then he went and stood by the living-room window, carefully nudged the closed curtain aside and looked down at the street.

Twenty minutes later Antonia arrived in a taxi. She got out and walked to a door on the opposite side of the street. Then she stopped and got a mobile phone out of her pocket. Miles looked around. He wasn't sure what he was looking for. Someone or something that shouldn't be there, perhaps. The street was dead, apart from an elderly lady who was patiently waiting for a terrier that appeared to be suffering from constipation.

His phone vibrated in his hand. Her number on the screen. He looked at her down in the street before answering.

'The door opposite, third floor,' Miles said, then gave her the door code and the name on the door.

The doorbell rang out in the hall. It was a two-tone, ding-dong model that sounded almost pleasant.

Miles paid particular attention to the distorted extremities of the peephole – nothing. He undid both locks, opened the door, let her in, then shut and locked the door just as quickly.

She was white as a sheet. She looked at him, his facial injuries and his bandaged hand. But she said nothing and walked into the apartment with the sports bag in her hand.

Antonia sat down on the sofa, and in a few quick sentences told him about Tommy breaking into her apartment. Miles told her about his and Ove's attempt to murder him.

Tommy . . .

'Dear God, Miles,' she said.

He was standing leaning against the doorpost.

'I thought you were dead,' he said.

'I'm not. Where's Tommy now?' she asked.

'Looking for you, I guess.'

She looked hard at him.

'And he thinks you're dead?'

Miles nodded.

'And Roger Lindgren?'

'Dead,' Miles said.

'How?'

'I killed him.'

Antonia tried to figure out Miles's feelings from those bald words. He pre-empted her.

'That was when Tommy turned up. He's been watching us. He asked about the safe-deposit box, about Lars Vinge.'

They both looked at the bag on her lap.

'Have you found anything?' he asked.

Antonia unzipped the bag and took out the big folder. She stuck her hand in and pulled out a bundle of papers, the printed photographs and dropped it all on the coffee table.

Miles left the doorway and sat down in an armchair in front of the coffee table, leaned over and saw a woman in her forties on a

bicycle. Then working in a garden, walking out of the main entrance of Danderyd Hospital, standing in the window of a villa looking straight at him. Lots more photographs of her in various situations. All taken with a telephoto lens.

'She was under surveillance,' he muttered.

He leafed through the pictures.

'So who is she?'

'Her name is Sophie Brinkmann,' Antonia said.

Miles studied the pictures.

'Her name cropped up in the Trasten investigation,' Antonia went on. 'She's a nurse, she looked after Hector Guzman when he was in the hospital after a hit-and-run incident.'

Miles looked up.

'Oh?' he said, curious.

'I met her briefly, asked her a few questions, but she didn't know anything. I wasn't expecting that, either . . .'

'But?' Miles said.

'No buts. Apart from these pictures, the bag contained a bunch of audio files.'

'Audio files of what?'

'I haven't really had time to go through them all properly. But they're surveillance recordings.'

'Who of?'

Antonia pointed to the pictures of Sophie.

'Why was she being bugged?'

'I don't know.'

Miles picked up the pile and leafed through the other pictures. He saw Gunilla Strandberg, Lars Vinge and Gunilla's brother, Erik Strandberg, a bearded man in his sixties, flushed and blood-pressure red. Then Hector Guzman and Aron Geisler. Then a photograph taken from a distance. He looked at it closely and saw a blond man sitting on a bench. Another picture, the man had turned his head and Miles could see his face.

'That's him,' Miles said.

'Who?' Antonia asked.

Miles held the picture up to her.

'The Mexico man.'

'What?'

'It's him, the man I picked up from Arlanda, the one who was freed.'

Miles looked at the man who had saved his life after the car crash. He wiped his face with his left hand. He put the heap of pictures on the coffee table.

'Who knows?' she asked.

'Tommy knows,' he replied.

'Apart from Tommy?'

Miles looked across the table, as did Antonia. An excessive amount of information about the nurse, Sophie Brinkmann – so many pictures, pictures, pictures . . . and so many recordings.

'We've got to get hold of her.'

They got to work. Sophie Brinkmann didn't exist anywhere. No address, nothing. She no longer worked as a nurse, seemed to have no connections anywhere. A complete absence of social contacts, even on the Internet.

They left the apartment. It was cold and dark, and snow crunched beneath their shoes as they walked a few blocks before Miles flagged down a taxi that drove them out towards the smart suburbs to the north of the city. Eighteen minutes later they pulled up outside Sophie Brinkmann's villa in Stocksund, where Antonia had met her six months ago. It was a wooden house, painted yellow, well maintained. It was rather quaint. There was a warm glow from inside.

They asked the driver to wait, then went through the gate and up the gravel path to the front door. Antonia remembered that the veranda where she had met Sophie and her son Albert last summer was at the back of the house.

Miles rang the doorbell.

A man in his fifties opened. He looked sporty, and was wearing a smile that said *Don't disturb me*.

'We're trying to find Sophie Brinkmann,' Miles said.

'She doesn't live here any more.'

'Do you know where we could find her?'

His strained smile was still in place.

'Who wants to know?' he asked bluntly.

Antonia held up her police ID.

He leaned forward slightly and looked at it.

'We bought the house from Sophie Brinkmann a few months ago; I don't know where she moved to.'

'No idea at all?' Antonia asked.

He was curious now.

'What's this about, has something happened?' he asked.

'No, we just want to get hold of her, ask her a few questions. So you haven't had any contact with her since you moved in?'

'No, not at all,' he said. 'If there was something, we'd have gone through the estate agent. But I don't think there was.'

'What was the estate agent's name?' Miles asked.

The man thought for a moment.

'Peter Nilzon . . . with a *z*,' he said.

'Do you have his number?'

'No,' the man replied bluntly.

'Is there anything else you remember? It's very important that we get in touch with her.'

'I'm afraid not.'

Miles and Antonia turned and walked down the porch steps. The door closed behind them. They were heading down the gravel path towards the gate when the door opened behind them again. They stopped and turned around.

'This might be a bit of a long shot,' the man said. 'But I think that estate agent was doing a double deal. Selling this house and sorting out a new place for her at the same time. But I'm not really sure.'

'What makes you think that?' Antonia asked.

'I just got that impression. He seemed very eager to please, all nervous and submissive whenever she was around on the few occasions that we actually met.'

'But you don't really know?' Miles asked.

'No, no idea, just a feeling.'

They were driving through the suburbs in the taxi. Antonia dug out the estate agent's home address. He lived in the same district, on the other side of the motorway.

'We could just phone, couldn't we?' Miles suggested.

'No, they just hang up. Face-to-face confrontation is better,' she said.

The taxi pulled up in front of a four-storey block in a small residential estate. They got out and walked towards the door.

She took hold of Miles's arm.

'Are we doing the right thing, Miles?' she asked.

He stopped.

She thought hard about something, then went on: 'I had Tommy in my apartment, and I had my pistol. I could use that and turn it against him, bring him in. We could talk to the senior bosses. You can tell your story as well. We could get him that way.'

Miles looked at her sceptically.

'What's changed?' he asked.

'Nothing's changed,' she said. 'I just get worried sometimes. It's just how I am.'

It was obvious she was telling the truth.

He nodded.

'Me too. But we've got little enough chance as it is, Antonia. This isn't going to end well. Our lives will never be the same as they were.'

'So what are you saying?' she asked.

'That there's no way to make it any easier for ourselves. Let's just carry on along the path we've already started on.'

'Which is what?'

He gave the question a few moments, then said: 'Suppose you'd drawn your pistol and aimed it at him?'

Antonia listened. Miles went on.

'Could you have pulled the trigger?'

She looked down, then shook her head.

'In which case it was good that you walked away,' Miles said. 'Because Tommy will kill us the moment he gets hold of us. We're going to get out of this alive, Antonia.'

Miles turned away and walked towards the illuminated entrance.

Peter Nilzon was about to go to bed, and opened the door in his robe. His hair was neatly combed and full of gel. Antonia and Miles held up their police IDs.

He showed them into the kitchen.

'Can I get you anything?' he asked.

'No thanks,' Antonia said.

They sat down at the table, and Miles took over.

'You sold a villa in Stocksund a couple of months ago. Sophie Brinkmann. Do you remember?' Miles said.

Peter put his hands on the table.

'Yes, of course I remember. I remember all my jobs. Why?'

'Tell us about the sale,' Antonia said.

'There was nothing special about it. It was quick, but houses out here always sell fast. We've got a long line of potential buyers. And her villa fulfilled a lot of the criteria that our buyers – '

Miles interrupted.

'You didn't help her find a new place to live?'

'No, I didn't. I just sold the house.'

'Do you know where she moved to?'

'No, no idea.'

'Did she already have somewhere lined up?' Antonia asked.

'I don't know.'

'Isn't that the sort of thing you'd talk about?' Miles asked.

'What?'

'As an estate agent, wouldn't you want to know? Try to get another sale out of it?'

'Well, it does happen.'

'But not with Sophie Brinkmann?'

Peter shook his head. He was trying to act normal, that much was patently obvious. Antonia and Miles went on staring at him until he became uncomfortable.

'Do you know what surprises me?' Antonia said.

'No, what?' Peter replied.

'That we've showed up to see you late in the evening, and you're acting all relaxed and calm, as if this meeting was entirely normal.'

He laughed.

'That's what I'm like,' Peter attempted. 'I'm very easy-going, I have to meet people all the time—'

'My colleague works with the Economic Crime unit,' Antonia interrupted, pointing at Miles. 'I'm a detective with the National Crime division. We can examine your work and all your sales down

to the last krona. We'll dig up a whole load of shit there, enough to make your life extremely difficult. And then the taxman will come knocking on your door and . . . well, you can imagine.'

Peter was about to protest, but Miles got there first.

'So tell us, did you arrange something for her? Off the books? Did you sell her a new place? We really don't care about that. We just want an address.'

'I don't know, and I think you should leave. And I don't think police officers should be making that sort of threat . . .' he said feebly.

'Tell us what you know, and we'll leave.'

'I've sworn an oath of confidentiality,' the man in front of them said.

Antonia laughed.

'What did you say?' she asked.

He didn't answer. He was looking away from the pair of them.

'Peter Nilzon with a *z*,' Miles said very clearly. 'You're not a psychiatrist, you're an estate agent. Now, tell us what you know.'

Peter sat there in silence, staring down at the table.

'Peter, you haven't got a choice. We're not going to give up,' Antonia said.

'I made an agreement,' he said quickly, and glanced up, as though surprised at his sudden admission.

'What kind of agreement?' Miles asked.

Peter regretted saying anything, and sat there motionless.

'An agreement not to say anything?' Antonia asked.

He looked up at her briefly, then back down at the table.

'Were you given money?' Antonia asked.

Peter Nilzon seemed consumed by doubt.

'What were the terms of the agreement?' Miles asked.

Peter was grappling with a mass of thoughts. He bit one of his fingernails. 'No,' he said. 'I can't do this. I want you to leave.'

Peter Nilzon gave them a crooked smile and tried to sound stern.

'Did the money come with an unspoken threat?' Antonia asked.

They were close now; both Miles and Antonia could feel it.

'I'm going to ask you some questions,' Miles went on. 'A *no* is a *no*. A *maybe* is a *yes*. And, as my colleague said, we're not going to give up. We want an address where we can contact Sophie Brinkmann.

This is your best opportunity to get this out of the way; we'll walk out of here and you'll never hear from us again.'

The estate agent sat there in his robe and neat hairstyle, staring down at the table. Someone had scared the life out of the poor sod.

'Did you help Sophie Brinkmann find a new place to live?'

Peter Nilzon looked up, met their gaze, cleared his throat and said, 'Maybe . . .'

ANN MARGRET WAS WORRYING ABOUT HER WORK AND FEELING GUILTY. SHE FELT she wasn't getting any real feedback.

She had taken some work home. Her laptop, a printer and a few files were lined up on the kitchen table. She wanted to dig deeper, give Tommy something more, show her appreciation for his faith in her, know that she had been important, good at her job . . . someone who could be trusted. She needed it . . .

Ann Margret was drinking a glass of wine, her fourth. Wine boxes – such a good invention.

Bosses liked summaries. That was what she was busy with at the moment, a clear overview of the situation, neatly gathered now in one file.

Eros Ramazzotti's hoarse voice was playing on the old stereo from the last century. Ann Margret put some printouts in the file, then drank another glass.

If she had been sober, analytically minded or had looked at her summary with so much as a hint of doubt and curiosity, she might have seen a pattern, if only a small one.

But Ann Margret was instead driven by a desire to show how clever she was, which had its roots in self-interest. That sort of personality trait often involved a degree of tunnel vision.

Then she called him, and – emboldened by drink – apologised for calling so late in the evening. She said she'd been working at home on a summary, and she was wondering if he'd like to see it sooner rather than later. He was welcome to come over to her place and go through it, have a glass of wine, or else he could see it at work tomorrow?

'*I'll come over,*' Tommy said gruffly.

Ann Margret brushed her hair in front of the bathroom mirror, put some lipstick on, checked her underwear wasn't visible through her white slacks and sang along phonetically with Eros's Italian, seeing as she didn't actually understand a word of it. She sprayed some perfume on the right side of her neck, rubbed it in with her wrist, then pulled a self-deceiving attractive face in the mirror. Then she drank a bit more wine from the box, which was suddenly and inexplicably empty. She was just as surprised every time.

Ann Margret found another one in the fridge, opened it with a practised hand and topped up her glass.

Half an hour later the doorbell rang. She glanced quickly around the apartment to make sure everything was decent.

Tommy was half-smiling, his eyes hazy, when she opened the door.

'Hi, Maggie!'

He was evidently half-drunk as well.

She did a rather sexy walk as she led Tommy into the kitchen.

They sat down next to each other at her kitchen table. The candles smelled of violet. She offered him some wine and began to explain her summary. She realised that she was actually laughing, and was pleased to see Tommy wasn't angry.

Tommy wasn't listening, he was staring at the wall. Some letters had been stuck to it. *Carpe Diem*. He looked at the words, but had forgotten what they meant.

He leaned forward, picked up a folder from the table and put it on his lap, then leafed through it. Ann Margret was babbling on about Antonia Miller.

'She makes repeated calls to her mum, who lives in Falköping, to a Japanese restaurant, to that Ulf, and makes occasional calls to a friend . . .'

Tommy went on reading, and Ann Margret kept going. An echo of something appeared in his consciousness.

'Ulf who?' he interrupted.

Ann Margret stopped talking, considered his question and went back in her mind.

'Ulf,' she said. 'He's in Surveillance! Ulf Lange.'

Ann Margret leaned over to the wine box and pressed the magic button. Her glass filled up.

'You had information about him in previous reports.'

Ann Margret drank some wine.

'Antonia talks to him by phone a few times a week,' she said. 'They might be in a relationship, I wrote that I suspected as much. I haven't got any evidence, but it seems quite likely. So I wrote it down for you. My own analysis, if you like.'

'Do they talk to each other during work time?' he asked.

'What?'

'Do they talk at work, or privately?'

'Let's see,' she said, then cleared her throat and tried to hide her nerves.

Ann Margret leafed back through the folder on Tommy's lap, leaning close to him, ran her finger down the list of contents and pushed it in by one of the numbered tabs.

It took time. She had to move the folder from Tommy's lap to the table as she looked for the phone number and times.

'Mm-hm, as I thought,' she said weakly. 'Outside working hours. They mostly talk in the evening . . .'

'And you say they're in a relationship, Ulf and Antonia?' Tommy asked.

'I don't know for sure, but I looked at a number of factors and eventually concluded that –'

'You're a star, Maggie,' he interrupted, without any feeling.

Her face broke into a crooked smile.

'Well, thank you.'

'One last thing,' he said. 'Could you get hold of something for me?'

'What?'

'Lange's phone calls. A list of calls he's made and received over the past two weeks.'

'Ulf Lange?'

Tommy smiled. What the fuck was wrong with the woman? 'Yes.'

'No problem, that's easy,' she said merrily.

Ann Margret got to work at her computer.

Tommy took the folder and looked back through it, then started again from the beginning. He scanned page after page.

He was almost taken aback by what he read. Surprised that the

image that emerged was so clear. In purely structural terms, the folder was a fucking open book about what Tommy had been up to.

He glanced at the woman beside him, still banging on, trying to show how clever she was. Did she really not have any idea of what was going on? It was all there, after all, and in the right order, too. Anyone who spared it more than a passing thought would realise that Tommy Jansson, as a result of the questions he had asked her over the past six months, was in all likelihood involved in the deaths of Gunilla Strandberg and Lars Vinge.

Was she completely stupid, the woman sitting next to him?

'Here you are, Tommy,' she said with a smile.

Ann Margret turned the screen towards him, and he read through Ulf Lange's call history. One number of particular interest stood out. It appeared many times at odd times of the day. Ulf had received the first call from that number the day after Tommy had searched Antonia's apartment.

'Can you check to see who owns that number?'

She tapped at her keyboard.

'I'm afraid not. It's an unregistered pay-as-you-go mobile phone.'

Bingo.

Tommy copied the number from the screen on a page of the file.

'Well, we should celebrate this!' he said, closing the folder noisily.

She laughed. 'Celebrate?'

He emptied his glass.

'You've done a remarkable job, Ann Margret. Let's go out!'

She laughed, not quite understanding.

'What?'

Tommy hid his irritation, he hated having to repeat himself.

'Let's go out and celebrate!'

'Now?'

'Yes! But let's have another drink first.'

Ann Margret's laughter bubbled happily.

'Goodness! Right, then!'

Tommy and Ann Margret, in her tragic little kitchen. He made sure she carried on drinking wine until she was completely drunk and lost the fragile hold on reality that was all she could possibly have. And she did. Ann Margret got to her feet and danced badly

to the music, looking up at the ceiling with her arms held out from her body.

She lurched forward and tried to kiss him. Her judgement was screwed. *Perfect.*

Tommy found a carton of orange juice and a bottle of Campari in the fridge door, and a clouded bottle of vodka in the freezer. He mixed a lethally strong cocktail in the Campari bottle – not much juice and a hell of a lot of spirits. He found two glasses.

'One for the road,' he said in English.

She tried to figure out what he was saying, but it was too hard.

They were sitting in his car, she was drinking the cocktail, spilling it on the seat and kept fiddling with the radio: she wanted music. 'One Night in Bangkok.' She sang along, and he cast a disgusted glance at her. She was making this so easy for him.

It was a long drive, but Ann Margret was hammered and had a very weak grasp of time.

They turned off where Ove had killed Miles Ingmarsson, Ove Negerson's favourite place for drowning people.

'Where are we?' she asked. She was slurring her words, and sounded grouchy.

'Out in the countryside, we're going to have a little picnic,' he said.

Ann Margret jerked her head to look at the impenetrable darkness. Then she looked back at Tommy.

'Here? But it's dark, and winter?'

'Yes, but you can't really complain about the weather – come on!'

Her mood suddenly changed.

'No, I don't want to. I want to go home now, Tommy.'

'Don't be so fucking boring,' he said with a laugh, then opened the car door and got out and walked around the bonnet towards her door.

Ann Margret panicked and locked the door, trying to hide her growing unease with a forced smile through the window.

Tommy tapped on the glass, then bent down closer to her.

'What's the matter, Ann Margret? Open the door!'

'I want to go home now, Tommy. It's late, I'm freezing and I'm tired.' She had sobered up in an instant.

He knocked hard on the glass.

'Stop being silly, come on, let's have a drink.'

She looked down at her lap, her lips pursed tightly.

Tommy used the remote key in his pocket to unlock the door and quickly opened it. She tried to move across to the driver's seat, but he grabbed hold of her arm. Ann Margret screamed as he dragged her out of the car. Her white trousers got splattered with muddy snow, and he let go. She tried to get up and run, but he caught her easily. The water was some way off. He decided it would have to happen here instead.

Tommy pushed her down on her back in the grass, put his hands around her throat and pressed hard. She was silently mouthing his name. He looked away, breathing into his arm.

As Ann Margret struggled and shook beneath him, Tommy Jansson decided to stop drinking.

50

(JUTLAND)

THE FIRE WAS BURNING IN THE LIVING ROOM.

'Why Malmö?' Mikhail asked from his armchair.

'I don't know,' Sophie said. 'Roland said the location was a multi-storey car park. That I should take Lothar up to the top floor . . .'

She was standing up, arms crossed, and was fiddling with the rug with her foot, staring down at it.

'And what did Aron say when you told him the location?' Jens asked from the other armchair.

'Nothing, he just said yes. That they would be there.'

'No objections?'

'No . . .'

'What else did you say?'

'That Hector was to wait on the top floor, like Roland had told me.'

'And Aron just accepted that?'

'Yes.'

'How is the exchange supposed to happen?' Mikhail asked.

'I'm to wait until Hector shows up. Hand Lothar over to him and leave. Albert will be waiting in a car on the floor below.'

Jens and Mikhail exchanged a glance. Sophie saw it.

'What?' she asked.

'Nothing. I just think the whole thing is odd,' Jens replied.

'Tell me something that isn't odd,' she said.

'It's difficult,' he whispered.

They paused.

'Well, now we're here, Jens,' she said.

'Where?'

'You said that even if I could give Hector to the Hankes, you doubted that they'd let me have Albert back.'

'Mm . . . Yes, I said that.'

'Do you still think that?'

He didn't say anything.

'So what's your advice?' she said.

'I haven't got any advice, Sophie.'

'Stop it, Jens. Tell me what to do!' She sounded upset.

'Can you choose not to go?' he asked.

She shook her head.

'No, I can't do that.'

'Well, then.'

'We'll have to assume the exchange is going to take place. And that we'll be leaving there with Albert,' Mikhail said.

Sophie closed her eyes, then opened them again.

'What do we do?' she said.

'I mustn't be seen,' Mikhail said. 'I'm Hanke's former body-guard; both sides would start shooting at me. I'll wait nearby with the getaway car. Jens can keep an eye on the floor of the car park where Albert's going to be left. You and Lothar do as you've been told.

'There are three groups,' Mikhail went on. 'Us, the Hankes and Hector's gang. Let them fight it out, not us. Just quick in, quick out, and don't upset anyone we don't have to.'

Sophie stood for a moment with her arms clasped around herself, her head bowed.

'I'll go and check on Lothar,' she whispered, and left the living room.

The wood on the fire crackled and hissed. Mikhail scratched the back of his neck.

'They're going to kill Hector on the roof of the garage,' he said to Jens.

'Aron must have realised that?'

'Yes. He'll have snipers set up nearby.'

'How are the Hankes thinking?'

'That depends on who's taking care of this for them. Kill Hector . . . or capture him. I don't know.'

The fire went on burning, and the next day got closer.

51

(STOCKHOLM)

SOPHIE HAD PAID FOR AN APARTMENT IN STOCKHOLM VIA TWO FALSE BUSINESSES AND A FAKE name. The estate agent, Peter, had been bribed, threatened and frightened by an unknown man of Polish origins. Antonia and Miles had eventually managed to get the address out of him.

It was three o'clock in the morning when they reached Eriksbergsgatan and stopped outside the door to Sophie Brinkmann's building. The newspaper delivery showed up fifteen minutes later, brought by a girl in a tracksuit. Miles and Antonia pretended to be a bit drunk, said they'd forgotten the code and followed her into the stairwell, stumbled a little, then took the lift up, passing the girl as she was on her way back down.

Brinkmann's apartment was on the third floor. Antonia looked through the letter box – there was a metal grille inside, impossible to force open. On the floor was a pile of papers and post.

'Impossible,' she said.

They went back down and out into the street. Miles took a few steps backwards, then looked up at the façade and pointed.

'That balcony belongs to her apartment.'

His eyes went to a drainpipe attached to one corner of the building.

'You could get across fairly easily.'

Antonia looked. It was high.

'Me?' she asked.

Miles raised his bandaged hand.

She bit her lip, kicked off her shoes and dropped her coat on the ground.

She tugged hard at the drainpipe a couple of times, then started to climb up it. Her arms were strong, and she made her way farther and farther up with her legs locked around the drainpipe to support herself.

Miles lit a cigarette.

Antonia was getting close. She stopped for a moment to gather her strength, then she grabbed the lower part of the balcony railing. The balcony shuddered. She hung there swaying for a moment.

Miles watched her from below, smoking to calm his nerves. Antonia pulled herself upwards, caught hold of the top of the railing, heaved herself up and over and landed on the balcony. Antonia stood up, kicked through one of the windows in the balcony door and disappeared inside the apartment.

Miles stood there waiting, chain-smoking cigarettes; he said hello to a young couple going by, waved to a solitary dog. A half-drunk young man wove his way past and asked for a cigarette.

'*Watch out!*'

Miles looked up, something was flying towards him. A plastic bag. It was falling through the air at high speed. His instincts kicked in and he caught the bag like a goalkeeper, with his cigarette still in his mouth.

Antonia made her way down the drainpipe.

She picked up her grey coat and put it back on, then slipped her shoes on.

'OK, let's go home, Miles.'

They emptied the contents of the bag on the floor of the fuck-pad.

Antonia had gathered together anything connected to Sophie. Even things that at first glance didn't seem to offer any useful information at all.

She went through every object, thoroughly and carefully, then passed it on to Miles. Her concentration was infectious. Miles double-checked everything.

Handwritten notes, an address book, receipts, bank statements,

photographs, a napkin with a handwritten number on it. Information about her son Albert's school, handwritten scribbles on a newspaper, a stack of old bills and other documents.

'OK,' Antonia said to herself, looking at the pile on the floor in front of her. She held her hand out.

'So this is Sophie Brinkmann.'

Miles looked through the address book.

'We're going to have to make some calls,' he said.

'It's still the middle of the night,' she said.

'At least people are at home then,' he said.

They worked their way through Sophie's address book, pretending to be colleagues from work or old friends. Sleepy answers, nothing useful.

Antonia Miller looked at the handwritten number on the napkin. A German country code. She dialled the number.

A ring. A very long ring . . . then another one.

The phone was picked up at the other end, and a mumbling male voice answered.

Antonia took a chance.

'Sophie,' she said simply.

'*Hello, Sophie,*' the voice said in broken English.

'Who am I talking to?' Antonia said in a neutral voice.

'*It's me, Rüdiger.*'

'I want to get hold of Sophie,' she said quickly in English.

'*I can't help you,*' the man replied.

'Her life is in danger.'

'*That's not enough,*' he said calmly. '*I'm going to hang up now, don't call back.*'

'Wait!' Antonia cried. 'Are you in touch with her?'

The man didn't answer. Antonia decided to go for it.

'My name is Antonia Miller, I'm a Swedish police officer, her life is in danger, mine too. I'm in hiding, and I think she's doing the same. I have to get hold of her.'

The man remained silent, but he hadn't hung up.

'I'll give you my phone number,' she said.

No answer.

She told him her number. Then, when she was finished, the man hung up.

STEFAN ANDERSSON WORKED IN FORENSICS. HE WAS A COMPUTER SPECIALIST who kept an eye on racehorses.

Tommy was sitting in his car, talking to Stefan on his mobile phone, hands-free.

'Saturday, Stefan. Which ones do I bet on?' Tommy asked.

Stefan started babbling about horses, jockeys, results and his own complicated theories about who would come in first, second and third.

Tommy wasn't listening. He waited until Stefan had finished, then said, 'Thanks. And what can I do for you in return?'

'*I want that forensic IT job, but you already know that.*'

'I know, and I've spoken to your boss about it, just be patient.'

'*Thanks, Tommy.*'

'Don't mention it . . . Actually, there was one more thing.'

'*Oh?*'

'I could do with some help tracing a mobile phone – '

'*You just have to download the right app.*'

'I don't want a fucking app,' Tommy said.

'OK, give me the number.'

Tommy read the number out. It was a little while before Stefan spoke again.

'*I'm not getting much. The GPS is switched off.*'

'So what have you got?'

'*That the phone is probably somewhere in Vasastan. But it's a big area. I'm localising it from the towers used to make the last call.*'

'You can't say where it is, then?'

'*No, not at the moment. But I'll keep an eye on it, Tommy, in case the GPS gets switched back on. Then I'll be able to locate it, down to the nearest metre. I'll be in touch.*'

'OK, thanks, Stefan,' Tommy said.

'Good luck this weekend.'

'With what?' Tommy wondered.

'The races.'

'Sure.'

52

(MALMÖ)

LESZEK WAS SITTING ON THE ROOF OF AN APARTMENT BLOCK, TAKING THE pieces of the dismantled rifle out of his bag, fitting them back together and unfolding the little two-legged support at the end of the barrel. He lay flat on his stomach next to an air vent and tucked the rifle in against his right shoulder. Through the telescopic sight he had a full view of the multi-storey car park.

To his right, fifty metres away, Hasani was busy putting his own rifle together.

'*Two?*' The voice in Leszek's earpiece belonged to Aron.

'Two,' Leszek said into the microphone by his cheek.

'*Three?*'

'Three,' Hasani replied.

'*Start looking,*' Aron whispered.

Leszek looked. The garage, cars, nearby buildings, every floor, every window. Every nook and cranny he could reach with the telescopic sight. But there were a lot of blind spots, places he couldn't see, places where snipers could have been posted.

At the sight of the first flare from a barrel, all three of them were to aim their weapons at that point. But by then it might be too late. And it wasn't even certain that things were going to turn out like that anyway. The Hankes' intention could be to take Hector with them . . .

Leszek didn't have a clue. Neither did Aron or Hasani. And Hector certainly didn't.

This was a crazy idea. But Hector had been impossible to talk to as soon as Lothar's name was mentioned. It was as if he were no longer governed by common sense . . .

THEY WERE TRAVELLING IN A NEW OUTBACK, STOLEN BY JENS ON A TEST DRIVE from a Subaru dealer in Jägersro.

Sophie and Lothar got out of the vehicle on the street outside the car park. As they walked over a pedestrian crossing, Sophie glanced over her shoulder and saw Jens and the car disappear.

Sophie had been surprised by how few questions Lothar had when she told him about Hector. Instead, he had asked if he could have some new clothes. So they had gone shopping. It had all happened in silence. A bizarre experience. She had a feeling that she was dressing him for his funeral. That he was sick and was going to die, but that she couldn't tell him.

Sophie felt terrible when she was around Lothar. She was forced to behave neutrally towards him. But he was still going to be sacrificed. And she had been the person who made that decision. He sought her out occasionally, trying to talk, and had even managed to slip in a joke or two. But she kept her distance – a cold, inhuman distance from an innocent boy who was in an appalling position, having seen his mother murdered, and now left entirely alone to be used in a game he didn't understand. And Sophie wasn't helping him. Quite the reverse . . .

The ground floor of the car park was damp, dark and full of cars. The lift that slowly ground its way upwards was cramped, made of shiny aluminium.

Her nerves were eating her up from inside. Lothar was nervous as well, but in an entirely different way. He was cheerful, in a restrained way, happy. He was going to see his dad, after all.

He had chosen his new clothes with care. Jeans, sneakers, a striped shirt, a dark-blue V-neck cashmere sweater.

'You look very smart,' she said.

' "Smart"?'

'You look fine, Lothar.'

He gave her a clenched smile. Sophie looked away.

The air was cold and raw when they got out at the open-air top floor of the garage.

Lothar's face was anxious and tense. He was quiet and introspective now. She stayed close to him, unconsciously protective.

Sophie looked at her watch. It was twenty minutes past the arranged time. There was a rumbling sound beneath them. A car drove up the ramp and out to where they were standing, and found a free space a short distance away. A man got out. He was wearing a jacket, opened the boot, pulled out a leather briefcase and walked away. She followed him with her eyes until he disappeared towards the lift.

'*Hello.*'

A voice, off to one side behind her.

She turned around. Hector was sitting there, leaning between two parked cars.

She looked him right in the eye. He looked calm, almost amused.

'Hector?' she said.

He was thinner than when she had last seen him, his hair longer and he was wearing far too few clothes for the climate. In spite of the circumstances she felt happiness bubbling up inside her. A warm giddiness that shouldn't be there, not now. But she remembered it, recognised the colour and shape of a feeling she had only ever shared with Hector. And she imagined she could see something similar in him, the same sort of warmth, the same recognition of something gone but not finished. But there was also indifference and coolness, sorrow, perhaps. But with that as a sort of bedrock for his personality, he also radiated certainty, as if he owned this situation in spite of the fact that he was completely exposed on the roof. But he had come, nonetheless. As if he were happy to be there. As if he had realised more about the nature of life since they last met.

'I think it's probably safest if you both sit down too,' he said.

They did so, between two cars, just a few metres away from Hector.

'Hello, Sophie,' he said. His voice was rough and deep.

'Hello, Hector,' she replied quietly.

His eyes turned to the boy beside her.

'This is Lothar,' she said.

Hector soaked up the boy's appearance.

'Hello, Lothar,' he said.

Lothar didn't answer.

'You know who I am?' Hector went on.

Lothar nodded.

Hector read Lothar's face, then said, 'I'm sorry about everything, about your mother. About the way everything has turned out.'

Lothar looked down.

There was a sudden rise in air pressure. Sophie looked up at the sky; it was bright blue. Then she did as she had been told.

'Stay here, Lothar, and keep down,' she said.

She stood up and started to walk away. Left the two of them to their fate. She steeled herself and didn't look back.

Lothar's voice behind her.

'Sophie?'

She speeded up as she crossed the open roof of the car park, towards the lift they had arrived in.

Then she heard him behind her, and turned around. He was standing up.

'Where are you going?' His voice was uncertain, lost.

'Stay there, Lothar, and sit down! Do as I say!'

She sounded strict, but without conviction.

'Why?'

'Lothar!' Hector said. 'Sit down!'

He turned towards his father. Sophie hurried away, her eyes fixed to the floor, with pain in her heart.

A rapid whining sound flew past her, followed by something hard hitting flesh and tissue with a heavy thump.

Hector collapsed and lay flat on the ground. More shots followed, all from guns with silencers, quiet before the bullets hammered into the car that Hector was lying next to.

She took cover behind a parked car.

The shooting stopped. There was silence.

Sophie stared down into the ground as if she was frozen solid there for a moment. Reality came back suddenly. She looked up.

Lothar was lying in the same place, curled up by a car tyre. Some ten metres beyond him she could see Hector. He'd been hit. It looked

like his left leg, the side of his thigh. Blood was pumping hard from the wound, a lot of blood. She realised he had been hit in an artery, and that he would die unless he . . .

Then the same sound again, but somehow different. Weapons with silencers, spluttering some distance away. But no more bullets came in their direction. Instead the projectiles were whining above their heads, in the blue sky, passing above them in two different directions.

She looked over at Hector. He was still lying in the same position, now with a pistol in his hand as blood pumped from his thigh.

'You need to bind the wound, stop the bleeding!' she called to him.

Hector pulled his belt from his trousers and fastened it around the top of his thigh.

'Pull as hard as you can,' she said.

More bullets hit the car where Hector was hiding. Then more from a different direction, thudding into the metal, in a regular pattern and in long bursts.

He stayed down, completely still, trapped from two directions, the slightest movement and he'd be hit.

The shooting stopped, leaving a strange silence.

Everyone caught their breath and stayed very still.

'Lothar!' Hector called hoarsely.

'Yes!'

'Are you OK?'

'Yes . . .'

'Just stay down, and keep still, do you understand?'

'Yes,' Lothar replied.

She looked around cautiously. She couldn't see where the shots were coming from.

'Sophie?' Hector went on.

'Yes?' she replied.

'How are you?'

'What do you want me to say to that, Hector?'

He said nothing for a moment, then said, 'I was thinking of you when I woke up from the coma.'

She looked down at the ground.

'I've missed you too, Hector,' she said.

Lothar was in between them, listening, even though he didn't understand a word of their Swedish.

'What are you doing here, Sophie?' Hector asked.

She just sat there.

'Have you betrayed me?' he went on.

'What does that mean?' was all she could manage to say.

'Have you betrayed me?' he asked again, this time stressing the word *me*.

'No, Hector,' she replied. 'I haven't betrayed *you*.'

'What are we doing here?' he asked.

The question hung in the air.

'Our children, Hector,' she replied.

'Albert? Is he OK?'

'I don't know.'

Hector could hear how helpless she was.

'Where is he?'

A fresh shower of bullets slammed into the car where Hector was sitting. From two directions. Gunmen working together. It stopped abruptly. Then, as before, someone shooting at the gunmen. Once again, there was a muffled exchange of fire above their heads.

Hector curled up as much as he could and seemed to understand his fate. He wasn't going to get out of there alive.

'Take Lothar and get out of here, now!' he cried.

Then more bullets hit the car, still not reaching Hector. It was unlikely to stay that way, Sophie knew that. The snipers just needed to find the right position.

'Can you get up and run?' she asked Lothar.

A car windscreen exploded above her. A bullet flew past from behind, brushing against her hair and thudding into the tarmac.

She froze, unable to move at all.

ARON LAY WITH HIS SNIPER'S RIFLE ON THE ROOF OF A BUILDING ON THE OTHER side of the multi-storey car park, opposite Leszek and Hasani. He was higher up than they, had a better view and was searching the buildings around the car park through his sights.

The man who had shot Hector was hidden in a church tower. Aron told Leszek and Hasani to fire in that direction. They blew him to pieces. But it was too late, Hector was hit and they had revealed their positions. After that it was almost impossible to find the Hankes' men. They were intelligently deployed and kept moving, trying to get closer to Hector. The Hankes had the upper hand, and Aron had to change his aim many times, as well as his location. Every second, every shot fired, could mean the difference between life or death.

But now he abandoned his primary task for a while to carry out the second thing he had planned for, without anyone else's knowledge.

Aron switched off his radio, made himself unreachable. He lay there stretched out on his stomach, his eye glued to the telescopic sight, examining the car behind which Sophie was hiding, and found her head.

He breathed out, held his breath and squeezed the trigger. The rifle lurched, the car window exploded. He couldn't see Sophie, didn't know if he'd hit her. He kept the rifle aimed at the car, waiting for her to show herself.

Aron switched the radio on again. Leszek's voice in his ear.

'*Come in, One, come in, One! Require assistance! Number Three shot. Unable to hold them.*'

Aron aimed his sights at the rooftop opposite and saw Leszek disappear from his post. Aron swung the rifle to the left. Through the telescopic sight he could see Hasani lying flat on his stomach beside his rifle, blood everywhere, badly shot up, dead.

'One here. Must have been interference,' Aron said into the microphone.

Leszek's voice, breathless.

'*I'm getting out of here, I'm going to try to reach Hector.*'

Aron looked towards the roof of the car park again. He could see firing around Hector's location. He couldn't see the gunmen. Quickly he tried to find Sophie. She wasn't visible anywhere.

A car came driving up the ramp at high speed, a Subaru. Aron looked at the driver through the sights.

Jens Vall.

SOPHIE WAS LYING DOWN. A CAR WAS HEADING UP THE RAMP FAST, ITS ENGINE revving hard. It stopped, doors opened.

She felt her panic growing. Her stomach clenched. There was a shrill screech as the car reversed at high speed behind her, rounded a corner, hit some parked cars and dragged them with it. She glanced out quickly.

Jens's Subaru was heading towards her with its hatchback door open. Sophie didn't think, just stood up and threw herself into the boot; the seats were folded down and she rolled forward, hitting her shoulder but without feeling any pain. Jens carried on in reverse, towards Lothar. He did the same as Sophie, and threw himself in.

'Keep going back!' Lothar yelled.

Jens hesitated.

'Do as he says!' Sophie cried.

Shots hit the car.

Jens reversed at high speed towards Hector and crashed into the shot-up wreck. Hector was lying there, curled up.

Lothar lay on his stomach; Sophie held on to his legs and he reached out a hand to his father.

Hector grasped it and pushed off. Lothar dragged him into the car, then screamed something to Jens, who accelerated forward at high speed.

Hector was lying half inside the car as Jens aimed for the downward ramp. Bullets were still slamming into the roof and sides, shattering the windows. Each moment seemed endless.

Jens swerved onto the ramp, got under cover and kept on going down at high speed.

'Albert?' Sophie shouted to Jens.

'He's not here. No one is . . . just shooters.'

KOEN DE GRAAF WAS DRESSED AS A BICYCLE COURIER. HE'D BEEN FOLLOWING the drama from his position on the top floor of an office building.

Koen was feeling the after-effects of the smack. He worked well like that. His emotions were contained, the world was soft and man-

ageable. Everything had gone well to start with. Then he had lost control, both of the situation and of his men.

Hector's men had stayed well away from their boss. Koen had been counting on the exact opposite – that because they knew Hector, and Hector alone, was the target, they'd try to protect him as closely as possible.

Instead Hector had stood there alone, with the woman and the boy. One shot seemed to have hit him. But that wasn't enough.

A car had burst in on the situation. Sucking up Sophie, Lothar and Hector like a fucking vacuum cleaner.

Koen's gunmen had opened fire on it, but it had disappeared down the ramp.

Koen scratched his cheek hard, watching developments with deep concentration. When he realised they weren't going to stop the car, he left the office, took the lift down, walked out and went around to the back of the building. His bicycle was parked there. It was pale blue, with drop handlebars and studded tyres – very advanced, and very fast.

He zigzagged between the cars, cycled through the middle of a traffic jam, went through red lights, rode on the pavement for a while, predicting other people's behaviour. Heroin was made for cyclists . . .

He had studied in this city. The University Hospital was up ahead. That was Koen's only chance. He took it.

———

JENS FORCED HIS WAY THROUGH THE TRAFFIC IN THE SHOT-UP CAR. IT WAS TOO light, too everyday. People were staring at them. He called Mikhail on his phone.

'Meet us at the University Hospital.'

He hung up.

Sophie bound Hector's wound as well as she could. He was suffering badly, losing a lot of blood and getting weaker. Lothar was holding his father's hand.

'Hanke's people are after us,' Hector said weakly. 'Call Aron.'

'No, not now.'

Hector didn't understand.

'We'll drop you at the hospital, then we'll call Aron.'

Now he understood.

'Lothar comes with me,' he said, trying to sound stern.

'Lothar comes with me,' she said.

He looked at his son, and was on the point of asking him in English.

Sophie noticed.

'No, Hector. That's not going to happen, don't make it any worse than it already is.'

The car stopped abruptly in front of the main entrance to the hospital. The back door opened. Mikhail was standing there, big and solid. He took hold of Hector, who whimpered and flashed an icy look at Sophie.

'He's my son! Do you understand what I'm saying?' Hector said.

She looked away. Mikhail pulled Hector out, and he let out a scream of pain. Mikhail put him down on the ground.

They changed cars, and all got into the Passat that Mikhail had stolen.

Lothar turned around as they drove off, and watched as hospital staff came rushing out and crouched down next to his father.

Sophie was sitting in the passenger seat. Her heart was pounding in her chest. She closed her eyes, tried to bring her pulse rate down, tried to breathe calmly. She managed to call Leszek's number, and he answered after two rings.

'We've left Hector at the hospital. You should get there right away.'

'Lothar?' he asked.

She ended the call.

Shock at what she had been through crashed over her like a tidal wave. Sophie's hands began to shake. She tried to stop them by holding them tight.

SONYA TURNED INTO THE BIG GARAGE IN FRONT OF THE HOSPITAL. SHE PULLED up a little way from the entrance.

Leszek and Aron left the car and hurried into the building.

They stopped in the large entrance hall with no idea of where they

should go. They looked at one of the plans on the wall, but it wasn't very clear. They quickly decided to head to the A&E department. Chaos there. A car accident had occurred, many cars involved. Relatives thronged at the reception desk and wanted answers. A lonely confused nurse tried to oblige. Leszek and Aron crept past. They found the corridor where the operating theatres were. But the glass door was locked. Access code needed. Aron looked around, stressed, glanced at his wristwatch.

Doors to the right of them opened with a bang. Two paramedics came in with a stretcher, a nurse ran alongside and held up a drip bag. They came towards Leszek and Aron. The nurse called out four numbers to Aron. He pressed the code, the door swung open, they hurried past with the bloody patient. The door closed itself.

Aron looked through the glass, waited until they disappeard into an operating theatre with the patient. The corridor was empty. He pressed the code again, went in with Leszek.

Hector was in theatre number 7. He was lying on a stretcher under sterile green covers. Dazzlingly bright lights were shining down on him. His eyes were closed, he was sedated. The trauma team around him was wearing green gowns and caps, with masks over their mouths. Three of them. A surgeon, an anaesthetist, a nurse. They all stared at Aron and Leszek.

The surgeon protested behind her mask and told them to get out.

Leszek pulled an automatic pistol from his jacket pocket and stopped by the door.

'Sew him up now,' Aron said, glancing at the time. 'You've got two minutes.'

Dressed in green surgical outfits, Aron and Leszek pushed Hector into the corridor outside the operating theatre, then found an empty hospital bed and wedged it against the door to the theatre behind them and locked the wheels.

They pushed Hector in the opposite direction from the one they had come from, hurrying through a glass door to a lobby containing stairs and two wide lifts. The lift arrived. The doors opened; it was empty. They pushed Hector inside. Leszek pushed the button for the ground floor and the doors slowly closed.

Rapid footsteps outside, an arm pushed between the doors, which opened again automatically.

The man who stepped in was out of breath and smiled gratefully. A bicycle courier, rucksack, tight clothes, helmet on his head. A strange look. Something about his eyes.

He stood where he could find room, by the edge of the bed; he looked down at Hector, then up at the ceiling.

The lift slowly made its way down.

There was a brief moment of nothing, a moment of mental relaxation, and Leszek looked down at his shoes.

Suddenly a quick movement from the courier.

'Pistol,' Aron said. He pronounced the word calmly and clearly.

Leszek grabbed Koen's wrist with both hands, forcing it up and back. Aron took hold of Koen's left hand and they forced him down onto his back, still holding his arms up. Aron put his left shoe on Koen's throat and pushed with all the strength he could muster. The lift was approaching the ground floor and Leszek pressed the emergency Stop button. The lift stopped with a jolt.

Aron pressed down with all his body weight. Koen de Graaf struggled in vain. After a minute the pistol fell from his hand and he tumbled helplessly into the dark depths of hell.

The ground-floor lobby was empty as they pushed Hector out. Sonya was waiting at the back of the hospital. They lifted the unconscious Hector into the car and Aron got in beside him in the back seat, while Leszek got in the front. Sonya pulled away.

Aron turned to Hector and checked his pulse. It was regular but weak.

He sighed, then rubbed his face with both hands.

'What a fucking mess,' he muttered as he looked behind to see if anyone was following them.

'Hector's alive,' Leszek said.

Yes, Hector was alive. But Hasani was dead. Because of him, perhaps, Aron thought. He settled into his seat.

Sophie, he'd been so close.

Thoughts swirled through his head as Sonya drove steadily out of the city.

Why Malmö? he asked himself.

They made their way through the traffic and emerged onto the motorway to Copenhagen, then headed across the Öresund Bridge on their way back to France. Aron went on pondering as he looked out at the flat Danish landscape.

Denmark and Jens Vall. He had been there today, at Sophie's side again. *Denmark and Jens Vall . . .* there was a common denominator there, but what? Aron was stressed, his thoughts confused, he tried but couldn't find the right memory.

Aron sighed loudly, then rubbed his face again.

'Leszek,' he said.

Leszek half-turned around.

'Help me. Denmark and Jens Vall? What's the connection?'

They both thought hard. Leszek got there first.

'Do you remember When we first encountered Jens?'

'The ferry in Rotterdam harbour last summer, wasn't it?'

'Yes,' Leszek said, and went on: 'After the shootout with Mikhail . . . We went out to the ship, then we dropped Jens off on the west coast of Jutland, when the rest of us left the ship.'

Aron remembered. That was it, he should have remembered. Jens had called his grandmother from the ship. She lived on Jutland.

Sweden was behind them, Denmark in front of them. Aron weighed things. Exhausted or not, he wasn't done, and now he had an idea.

'Drop me off there,' he said, pointing towards Kastrup Airport, up ahead of them at the end of the bridge.

53

(VILLEFRANCHE)

THE BOYS WERE SWIMMING IN THE POOL, EVEN THOUGH THE AIR TEMPERATURE couldn't be more than fourteen degrees Celsius. Raimunda was watching them from a lounge chair as she read a book.

Angela was by the window of her room upstairs, looking on as Andres splashed water at Raimunda, who put her book down, stood up, pretended to be angry and walked towards him. He laughed in panic and swam off. Fabien did the same in the shallow end, hooting in delight and fleeing even though he wasn't being chased.

Angela left the window, grabbed the two packed suitcases from the bed and quickly made her way downstairs, where she stashed them away on top of each other in a cleaning cupboard. She stopped for a moment, took a deep breath, then walked across the cold marble floor of the hall to the heavy oak front door and unlocked the three locks, then walked into the living room with its wall-to-wall carpet.

The French doors to the pool area were open, and the linen curtains fluttered in the afternoon breeze. Angela stopped in the darkness of the house, looking out into the daylight. Raimunda was now sitting at the edge of the pool with her trousers rolled up and her legs in the water, splashing the boys, who tried to do the same back.

Angela glanced at her watch. A minute or so passed. Then she heard the front door open carefully, and footsteps moved inside the house.

Angela didn't turn around; she knew whose they were. Instead she went out into the sunshine and forced herself to smile.

'I'll take over now, Raimunda. Thanks. There's some lunch for you in the kitchen.'

Raimunda stood up from the edge of the pool.

'Thanks, that's kind of you,' she said, then turned towards Andres, who was still in the water, and faked a stern expression.

'And that little monster needs to learn how to behave.'

Andres laughed, and any sternness on Raimunda's face melted into a smile. She walked off.

Angela waited until Raimunda was inside the house, then she beckoned the boys over and fetched their robes from the table they'd been left on. They protested. She made it clear that now wasn't the time for that, and they were taken aback by her sudden harshness. They did as they were told, got out of the pool, put the robes on and took their mother's outstretched hands.

Angela led them into the house through the living room, wet footprints across the carpet. Police officers were moving around inside the villa.

'Mum?' Andres said, looking around curiously.

She didn't answer, just guided the boys with her through the hall and past the kitchen. Two uniformed officers were watching Raimunda, who was sitting on a chair at the kitchen table. Angela met her gaze, there was a mixture of derision and security in Raimunda as she looked at Angela. Derision because Angela was the traitor. Security because that was precisely what Angela lacked.

Angela found Gustave Peltier in the dining room. He looked just like she remembered him: harassed, in a jacket, jeans, calfskin shoes, mid-length greying hair, a scarf around his neck, the scruffy vanity of the middle-aged.

'Angela, everything's been arranged. Where are your bags?'

'The cleaning cupboard under the stairs.'

Gustave snapped his fingers at a uniformed officer and gestured to him to fetch them. He shepherded Angela and the boys ahead of him, out through the door to a waiting police car.

A plain-clothes officer was already sitting at the wheel, a young man with a look of intense concentration in his eyes.

Gustave got in the front. They drove off at once, and Gustave began talking quickly into a walkie-talkie. The villa was already behind them.

54

(DENMARK)

THEY HEADED WEST THROUGH DENMARK. SOPHIE'S PHONE VIBRATED IN HER pocket.

'Yes?'

'*What happened?*' Roland Gentz's voice was unmistakable.

'Why are you asking me?'

'*Is Hector alive?*'

'I don't know.'

'*Was he alive when you and the boy took off?*'

'Where's Albert?'

'*Answer my question.*'

'Answer mine,' she said.

'*Albert's OK. Is Hector alive?*'

'He was alive when we left. I want to talk to Albert. Why didn't you bring him to me?'

'*Where's Hector now?*'

'I don't know where Hector is. We had an agreement, and you broke it.'

She was trying to stay calm.

'Give me Albert now,' she begged in a low voice. 'There's nothing to be gained from this. I want my son back . . .'

'*We need to know if Hector's alive.*'

'What for . . . ?'

'*We'll be in touch.*'

Her mobile phone went quiet. He'd hung up.

She was shaking inside. An overdose of grief and despair, frustration and rage was taking complete control of her whole existence with paralysing force. She let her discomfort wash over her and push her down. Let it hurt, torment her, suffocate and sting. Sophie just kept breathing and waiting, there was nothing else she could do.

'There's a police officer looking for you, Sophie,' Mikhail said.

She didn't follow.

'What did you say, Mikhail?'

He looked at her in the rear-view mirror.

'A Swedish police officer has been looking for you, a woman, Antonia something, she wants to talk to you.'

'How do you know that?'

'From Rüdiger.'

Antonia, Sophie thought. Antonia Miller. She remembered the policewoman who had been investigating the murders at Trasten. Antonia had visited her at home in the villa in Stocksund, asked questions. She seemed reserved but curious.

'What did she say?'

Mikhail sat back, then glanced in the mirror again.

'Don't know. Rüdiger just passed the message on.'

'She called him?'

'Yes.'

'What did he say to her?'

'Nothing, I guess.'

Mikhail felt in his pocket and pulled something out, then reached his hand back towards her, a note between two long fingers. A Swedish mobile-phone number.

Jens had turned around. He didn't say anything; perhaps he was waiting for a decision.

Sophie put her mobile phone in her lap and looked out the window, searching for an answer.

'Call her. Hear what she's got to say, you've got nothing to lose.' Jens turned around again.

She dialled the number on the scrap of paper. It rang twice, then a woman answered.

'*Yes?*'

'You've been trying to get in touch with me.'

'Yes, I have.'

The woman sounded almost relieved.

'What for?'

'*Where are you?*' Antonia asked.

The world racing past outside the car, it was all a blur.

'I'm going to hang up if you don't tell me what you want,' she said.

Another silence, as if the woman at the other end was considering what to say very carefully, afraid of saying the wrong thing, afraid of missing her chance.

'*I'm on the run as well,*' Antonia said.

'Explain.'

'*Things are happening.*'

'What sort of things?'

'*You know Lars Vinge?*'

'What about him?'

'*You know who he was?*'

'Yes.'

'*He left a bag. And I've got that bag.*'

'Oh?'

'*You're rather over-represented among its contents.*'

Antonia's voice became steadier.

'*I need to know why, so I can put an end to this.*'

'Put an end to what?'

'*I don't know yet.*'

'You said you're on the run. Who's after you?'

'*I've gone to ground. I can't say more.*'

'What do you know?' Sophie asked.

'*A bit.*'

'What don't you know?'

'*A lot more.*'

Sophie's eyes met Jens's.

'So what do you want my help with?' Sophie asked.

'*I need to get a clearer picture.*'

'What of?'

'*The people who died six months ago, what happened to them, what they knew, what you know from Trasten. What happened*

there. There are two of us in hiding now, we're both police officers, and we're onto something big.'

She thought for a moment.

'Sophie?' Antonia sounded like a friend now.

'Yes?'

'What do you need help with?'

'I need to find my son,' she whispered.

55

(VILLEFRANCHE)

LESZEK AND SONYA HAD BEEN TRAVELLING NON-STOP AFTER DROPPING ARON off. The ferry from Rødby to Puttgarden, then straight through Germany to its southern border, across the Alps and down towards Lugano. Hector woke up there. They pressed on through Italy until they reached the Mediterranean, then turned west towards the French Riviera and Villefranche. A journey of twenty hours.

Considering the circumstances, Hector felt reasonably OK. Soon Raimunda would be able to look after him.

Villefranche was asleep when they arrived early in the morning. They drove up the winding road towards the villa.

Leszek looked up at the house, scanning the façade. A blind pulled down in one of the guest rooms facing the road: a signal that everything was OK . . . in the afternoon. But not now, not early in the morning. Now the blind should be pulled up and a nightlight switched on inside. That was what they'd agreed, and Raimunda was a very conscientious person.

'Keep going. Drive past,' he said to Sonya. 'Hector, lie down and take cover,' he added.

They drove past the villa. Leszek couldn't see anything else unusual, and they kept on going up the road and stopped at the crown of the first hill.

'Wait for me here,' he said, then got out of the car and disappeared into a garden.

He made his way quickly back down to the villa. There he climbed over the wall and landed feet first on the lawn beside the pool, where he stopped and listened. Complete silence. Toys and an inflatable mattress floated in the pool. That never happened. Raimunda usually kept things tidy.

Under cover of the trees and bushes in the yard he made his way around to the front. There was a car parked there. The little Peugeot Raimunda used when she went shopping. Leszek kept going, to the side of the house, where he crouched beneath the big living-room window, then peered into the gloom. All the furniture was exactly where it should be. He moved on to the dining room. Same thing there, just dormant furniture in a peaceful room.

Leszek crouched down again and went on to the kitchen, and peered in cautiously. There was someone sitting at the kitchen table in the darkness, the red glow of a torch gave the man enough light to read a book by. Beside him on the table was a flask, a mug, a French newspaper and a glistening black pistol.

Leszek craned his neck. Two people were asleep on the floor over by the kitchen cupboards, in sleeping bags on top of camping mats. One of them had a black rucksack beside him. It had the emblem of the Police Nationale on it.

Leszek backed away, then ran off silently, across the wall, through the neighbour's garden, back up to the car.

'The police are in there waiting for us,' he said as he got into the back seat next to Hector.

Sonya started the car and drove off.

'The others?' Hector asked.

'I didn't see any of them. It looks like they left in a hurry.'

They all thought hard.

'How did the police find us?' Hector asked.

'Raimunda or Angela?' Leszek replied.

'Angela,' Sonya said. Neither of the others disagreed.

'What does she know?' Hector asked.

'Enough,' Sonya said.

'Enough, how?'

'She was married to your brother, Hector.'

Sonya steered the car along the winding road.

'Where are we going now?' she added.

'We need to disappear completely,' Hector said tightly.

'We haven't got any money,' Sonya said. 'And without money we haven't got any friends.' She tried to find Hector in the rear-view mirror.

'No friends, no money,' he said to himself. Then he smiled, as if there was something funny about that.

They started suggesting names. Names of business partners, friends, acquaintances, people from the past. None of them was suitable, they all entailed too much risk.

Leszek eventually said, 'Your father's cousin, Hector.'

'Who?' Hector asked.

'Every year Adalberto used to send money to the monastery in Tuscany; he kept it going, don't you remember?'

Hector searched his memory, yes, he remembered. *Roberto . . .*

'Head towards Tuscany,' he said.

56

(STOCKHOLM)

THE PASSPORTS WERE STANDARD EU ONES.

Marianne Grip from the laundromat was sitting behind the wheel of her silver Jaguar XJ6, inspecting them like a customs official.

'It took him a day and a half to do these after you called me, Antonia. Some forgers really do deserve their reputation,' she said, handing them to Antonia and Miles, who were sitting in the back seat.

Miles and Antonia opened their new passports, looked at their pictures, the fake names, the fake signatures.

'This isn't exactly standard-issue stuff, as I hope you appreciate.'

Miles and Antonia stared at her uncomprehendingly.

'This is a miracle,' Marianne said. 'Fake ID cards and passports that work . . . Don't take any of this for granted.'

Marianne fixed her eyes on them.

'And finally: This is a '76; I got it from Assar. If you so much as scratch it I'll never forgive you.'

She opened the car door; it was big and heavy. Marianne got out, then leaned over and looked in again. She let out a sigh and her sternness vanished, and her face went back to normal.

'Be careful, whatever it is you're going to do,' she said, and closed the car door.

Miles and Antonia climbed into the front, Miles behind the

wheel. It was wide and thin. He turned the key. The old car started. The engine purred reassuringly. Antonia switched on the GPS on her mobile phone, opened the maps and keyed in the address in the little village in Jutland that Sophie had given her.

She held the phone up to Miles, who read it.

'Ten hours' driving ahead of us,' he said, pulling out of the parking space.

'Do you want to play I Spy?' she said flatly.

TOMMY WAS LYING ON THE SOFA AT HOME WITH HIS HEAD AGAINST MONICA'S breasts. She was stroking his hair. The movement was minimal, barely perceptible.

'You've been good to me, Tommy.'

Her voice was thin and slurred, her speech deteriorating, drawn out, almost dark. She struggled with the words.

'Always, ever since the first time I met you. Towards me and the girls, everyone you know. Even your enemies.'

He tried to find some sort of symmetry between the ceiling and the top of the open door.

'But then you turned bad, Tommy.'

With one eye closed he managed to line up the top of the door with the corner of the ceiling.

'You stopped talking to me, you got quiet and depressed. And sometimes you got angry, as if your depression had found an outlet. You changed. I wanted to help you, but I couldn't reach you, Tommy . . . You cut yourself off, and disappeared.'

Tommy looked away from the corner and stared blankly up at the ceiling instead.

'Perhaps that's finished now, Tommy? Over?'

Monica broke off abruptly, breathing shallowly, then she went on in a weaker voice. 'You should talk to your daughters, explain yourself. Give them a chance not to have to carry your problems. You used to be able to talk to them. Do it again . . . Do good, Tommy.'

Tommy listened. He heard what she was saying, but he didn't understand. He used to understand. But that was then, and this was

now – completely different things. He had been someone else then, everything was different. He used to be a policeman, a husband, father, colleague. Down-to-earth, considerate, and he used to try, in spite of a fairly negative view of the world, to do the right thing. Now he was still a policeman, a husband, father and so on. But he was also a criminal, a murderer and now, with the same negative view of the world, he was actively trying to do wrong. That was the path he had chosen. He couldn't change it, no matter how much he might want to. The consequences would be too great.

Monica . . . She meant everything to him. Perhaps that was his underlying driving force. It ought to be nothing but good, but it wasn't; it was nothing but bad.

He looked at his wife.

'I've stopped drinking,' he said.

She looked deep into his eyes.

'That's good,' she whispered.

'I love you,' he said.

She believed him, he could see that. That was a big thing, now that he no longer believed in himself. Tommy turned his head away.

'I love our girls,' he went on.

Monica stroked his head.

The sun disappeared behind a cloud and the living room turned darker.

'I wish I could turn back time, Monica. But I can't.'

She went on stroking him.

'No, Tommy, you can't.'

Her voice was so thin, so weak.

Time passed by around them. He wanted to stay there, to stay with his Monica. Where life was safe and normal.

'Tommy?' she whispered.

He waited.

'I want you to promise me one thing.'

He tried to pre-empt her. 'I'll take care of everything, I promise.'

'No, not that,' she interrupted.

Monica turned his face so he was looking at her.

'Help me go when the time comes.'

Tommy didn't know what to say.

'Promise to help me if I get trapped inside myself. I don't want to end up there, I don't want to be scared. Promise to give me a bit of help along the way.'

He stared at her. But she just looked calmly back at him. Tommy stood up and walked away, into the kitchen, walked around the kitchen table, his hand on his head . . . What the hell was he doing in the kitchen?

Then down into the basement, down the steep, narrow steps.

The bottom drawer of the desk was empty; he'd emptied the bottle of gin down the toilet earlier.

There was a humming sound in his head and he bit his thumbnail.

His mobile phone buzzed in his pocket and he answered it.

'Yes?'

'Stefan here.'

'Stefan who?' he shouted.

'Stefan Andersson, Forensics!'

Tommy scratched his head hard.

'What is it?'

'I've managed to locate the mobile phone. The GPS has just been switched on.'

'Where?'

'Norrbackagatan, Vasastan – Birkastan.'

Tommy unlocked the gun cabinet where he kept his hunting rifles and took out an old snub-nosed revolver, a .38 he stole during the search of an embezzling lawyer's home four months ago.

He checked the gun – fully loaded, silver-coloured with a mother-of-pearl handle – and weighed it in his hand.

Tommy grabbed his winter jacket in the hall. He tucked the revolver away in a hidden inside pocket, pulled the jacket on and headed off into the vile world outside.

He called Negerson from his car and gave him the address in Birkastan. Tommy drove fast, his car straining around him.

———

Ove Negerson was already there, at the address where Antonia Miller's phone was supposed to be, leaning against the bonnet of his Mercedes when Tommy drove past, looking for somewhere to park.

Ove was standing at the back of the car when Tommy walked up. He opened the boot with the remote. All of Ove's guns lay spread out on a blanket. He waved his hand.

'Voilà.'

Tommy saw two pistols, two rifles – one shorter, with a sniper sight, the other old and rusty – three knives (two butterflies and one bowie) and two silencers.

'So what's it to be?' Tommy asked.

Ove scratched his chin, as if he were only allowed to pick one chocolate from a full box, then pointed at a modern black pistol and one of the silencers.

He leaned in and screwed the silencer onto the pistol, then held it up like a trophy.

'What about you?'

'Nothing,' Tommy said.

Ove opened his mouth theatrically and stared at him, wide-eyed.

'Living on the edge, Tommy?'

'Fuck off.'

Ove shut the boot and they walked towards the entrance to the building. A man with a young dog was walking towards them.

Ove stiffened as he stared at the dog.

'Scared of dogs?' Tommy chuckled happily.

'Yes,' Ove said. 'I've always been frightened of dogs, ever since I was little.'

They were on their way in through the door when Stefan from Forensics called again.

'What the hell is it now?' Tommy answered.

The signal vanished, then popped up again. They are heading south on the motorway.

'Damn.'

Tommy turned and ran towards his car.

'Let's take mine,' Ove called after him.

57

(JUTLAND)

THE WEATHER HAD TURNED VICIOUS. IT WAS BLOWING A STORM, AND THE TREES outside were bending under the wind as sleety rain lashed the windows. Lothar was standing looking out of the leaded window of his room.

Sophie was leaning against the doorpost. She didn't know if he was captivated by the storm or just letting his thoughts roam free.

She leaned heavily to one side, her body weight pressing harder on the door jamb, and the old wood creaked.

Lothar turned around. He looked at Sophie for a few moments before saying, 'Am I going to have to escape from here?'

'No, you won't have to escape from here, Lothar.'

'What are you going to do with me?' His voice was firm.

'I don't know,' she whispered.

'Have I been kidnapped again? By you this time?'

'No, you haven't.'

'So I can take my things and just walk out?'

'No, you can't,' she said.

'So I have been kidnapped?'

She wrapped her arms around herself. Sometimes it was cold, even though it was warm.

'I want to be with my dad,' he said, almost in a whisper.

She didn't want any more of this, couldn't do any more of this. She turned to go back downstairs.

'Albert said you think you're not allowed to make mistakes,' he said to her back.

Sophie stopped and turned around.

Lothar went on: 'He said you think you're not allowed to make mistakes. So you always think you're doing the right thing instead.'

'I know I make mistakes,' she said in her own defence.

Lothar shook his head slowly.

'He didn't mean it as a criticism. He didn't know if you were alive. I'd told him about my mum, about them killing her. He was frightened the same thing had happened to you.'

'So?'

'That's why things are the way they are.'

'Because of that? Because I'm not allowed to make mistakes?'

He shrugged.

'Maybe.'

'Did Albert say that?'

Lothar nodded.

She felt like snorting. Felt like saying he didn't know what he was talking about . . . But she knew he did.

'What else did Albert say?'

'It doesn't matter.'

He was calm. Matter-of-fact.

'Why are you telling me this, Lothar?'

'Because my mum's been murdered. Because I'm being dragged around in a world that's got nothing to do with me. I have no voice. I met a dad I didn't know existed, and then I was dragged away from him just as abruptly.'

He paused.

'And the whole time, you're the one who decides the outcome, Sophie.'

'No, it's not like that . . .' she attempted.

'Yes, it is. My life is in your hands, but you wouldn't dare admit it.'

She looked away from him. Rain and snow lashed the window, and the wind made a sucking sound as it tried to find a way into the old house.

'What do you want me to do, Lothar?'

She felt awful.

'Rise above it.'

' "Above it"?'

'Above all the wrong.'

Hector's son. The spitting image of his father just then, that much was obvious. The sudden ability to put something into words, to overturn your view of yourself, make you see something as it really was. Unafraid, courageous, wise. Boundless.

'How?' she whispered.

'Tell me what you're thinking, and what's going to happen to me. I have to know.'

'You know,' she said.

'No, how could I know if you don't tell me?'

Sophie wanted to flee. But she remained where she was. She swallowed twice, then said: 'I want my son back, and I'll do anything to make that happen.'

'Anything?'

She nodded. Her jaw was clenched.

Then Sophie turned and went downstairs, into the kitchen. She went and stood by the sink, leaning on it heavily with her hands, breathing hard with her eyes closed.

Lothar came down behind her.

'Would you like a drink?' she asked with her back to him.

'A drink would be good,' he said, sitting down on a chair.

———

MIKHAIL HUNCHED FORWARD AS HE MADE HIS WAY ACROSS THE SQUARE, fought against the wind and rain.

The silver Jaguar was parked in front of the café.

He approached the car from behind, read the number plate and without looking around pulled open the back door and squeezed into the back seat.

'Drive,' he said to Miles at the wheel. Antonia glanced back at him from the passenger seat. Mikhail indicated that she should look forward.

They drove away from the square and out of the town. Mikhail directed them onto a main road and they speeded up. Mikhail leaned

back, pulled a walkie-talkie from his jacket pocket and pressed the Talk button.

'How does it look?'

There was a crackle. Jens's voice.

'I can't tell, can you?'

Mikhail looked back. The weather was still bad, and visibility poor. He could barely make out Jens in the Passat, three cars behind.

'There's no one following us,' he said.

'We'll take a few detours, then carry on.'

Mikhail directed Miles to drive in circles, around and around, this way and that.

Half an hour later they headed up the drive to Jens's grandmother's house. Miles parked in front of the entrance and they got out.

Antonia looked around. In spite of the storm, it was beautiful. A chalk-white, half-timbered house with a thatched roof.

Mikhail had already opened the boot and taken out the sports bag, and now he walked up to her and gestured that she and Miles should lean against the car. Mikhail hurried Miles along, pushing him towards the car, and Miles put both hands out to brace himself, wincing at the pain in his broken right hand.

'Stay like that,' Mikhail said, then frisked him. He did the same to Antonia.

'In my handbag,' she said. 'My service pistol's in my handbag.'

Mikhail indicated that they should go in.

Sophie met them in the hall. They were wet and cold after being made to stand in the storm while they were searched.

'Hello, Sophie,' Antonia said, brushing the wet hair from her forehead.

Sophie didn't respond.

'Miles Ingmarsson.' He introduced himself.

'Follow me,' Sophie said, and walked into the kitchen.

Miles and Antonia sat down at the kitchen table. Sophie leaned back against the counter, radiating watchfulness.

Mikhail walked in behind them and put the bag on the table, then pulled out a chair, put it over by the wall and sat down, legs wide apart.

'Thanks for letting us come,' Antonia said.

Sophie waited.

Antonia reached for the bag. She pulled out all the copied photographs and dropped them on the table, and gestured for Sophie to take a look.

Sophie saw herself in various situations in her house out in Stocksund. She saw Albert before the accident, standing in the kitchen behind her. She saw herself riding a bike, driving a car, working in the garden.

'There are hours and hours of audio recordings of you as well,' Antonia said.

'I know,' Sophie said.

Miles and Antonia were taken aback.

'How do you know?' Miles asked.

'We found the microphones,' she said.

'How? Why?'

'We scanned the house,' Sophie replied bitterly.

'Who installed them?' Antonia asked.

'You did,' Sophie said.

'No, not us,' she said.

'Yes, you, the police. Gunilla Strandberg had them installed.'

Antonia's mind was spinning.

'What for?' Her eyes were blazing.

Sophie recognised that eagerness from their first meeting, that thirst, that curiosity . . . that urgency. There was something compulsive about it, something Antonia Miller tried to hold in check.

Sophie snatched up a photograph of Albert.

'Tell me what you know, and why you're here,' she said.

Antonia looked at Miles, as if to ask: *Can you help me?*

'This is your show, Antonia,' Miles said.

'Could I have some water?' she asked.

Sophie took a glass from the shelf, filled it from the tap and gave it to Antonia, who drank half of it in one gulp.

She put the glass down on the table, then stared into it as if her story were floating around in it.

'I was the first detective to arrive at Trasten after the shootout and murders in August last year,' she began. 'I started to investigate

but couldn't make any progress. Not long ago I was pulled from the case, and Miles was brought in instead.'

She pointed at him quickly, then went on to tell them how Miles had been told not to do anything, and how she kept on looking, but without finding any answers, only more questions. How she eventually started looking outside the case itself, at the police officers who had been investigating Hector Guzman, Gunilla Strandberg and her brother. Nothing there, either. And then how she suddenly got a lead from an unexpected source, a small-time Stockholm gangster named Håkan Zivkovic, who gave her some scant information but mentioned Lars Vinge as someone she ought to take a closer look at. And how that had led to the safe-deposit box and the bank, and the bag in front of them on the table. And then Tommy's attempted murder of Miles, and how she and Miles had gone to ground. And how they had managed to contact Sophie thanks to the napkin they found in her apartment.

'And now here we are,' Antonia concluded.

Sophie pointed at Lars Vinge's sports bag.

'Go ahead and ask,' she said quietly.

———

THE GROUND WAS WET, AND TOMMY WAS LYING ON HIS STOMACH LOOKING through a pair of binoculars. Next to him was Ove, with a rifle equipped with a telescopic sight. Tiny needles of ice were being thrown by the rain, simultaneously cold and wet. The visibility was atrocious. Denmark really was a fucking dump . . .

Through the binoculars Tommy could see into an old-fashioned country kitchen, four people in total . . . Sophie Brinkmann and a big bastard on a chair by the wall. He scanned around; Antonia Miller was sitting at the table. Beside her was a man with his back towards Tommy . . . *That couldn't be right*. The man turned his head.

That profile . . .

No doubt about it. Miles fucking Ingmarsson, risen from the dead.

'Do you see what I see?' Tommy muttered.

'Four people,' Ove said.

'Do you see the man at the kitchen table?'

Ove looked through the rifle sights.

'Yes,' he said lazily.

'You're no good at drowning people, Ove.'

'I'm hurt, Tommy,' he said sarcastically.

'Can you get them both?'

'Maybe,' Ove said.

'*Maybe?*'

'Who's most important?'

Tommy thought. Antonia Miller. She was the driving force behind this, she was the one who knew the most; she knew what was going on, she had to die first. That was why he was there. But on the other hand . . . Miles . . .

'Come on, Tommy, you're the customer. Tell me what you want!'

ANTONIA WAS OVER THE MOON. SHE WAS ENJOYING HERSELF, SHE LISTENED, she understood. She now finally had the whole picture there in front of her. The murders at the Trasten restaurant, every step, every word, every detail. Sophie and Mikhail gave her everything. Antonia could see the chain of events in her mind's eye. Who was there, what was said, what was done. The murders, how they were committed and by whom. The whole of the case that she never got to finish was replayed in front of her, all the questions she had been asking were finally answered. Faces that she had only seen in two dimensions on paper came to life.

She saw how Hector and Alfonse Ramirez from Colombia were sitting in a meeting at the Trasten restaurant. How Sophie and Jens took refuge there when they were being chased by three drugged-up Russian gangsters. Sophie had thought they had shaken them off, but the Russians stormed the restaurant and held everyone at gunpoint. The leader of the Russians subjected Jens to a brutal assault. Then they got it into their heads to shoot everyone in the restaurant. They were all saved at the last minute by Mikhail and Klaus Köhler, who burst in and emptied their weapons into the Russians.

Antonia and Miles looked at Mikhail, who was sitting there on his chair, apparently calm and relaxed.

'Then the police arrived,' Sophie said. 'Anders Ask and Hasse Berglund. They worked for Gunilla; they were all corrupt. They'd tracked Hector down and had come to extort money from him. There was supposed to be some sort of transfer of money from Hector to Gunilla's gang. They were going to supervise the transfer at the restaurant.'

'And was the money ever transferred?'

'No, I don't think so. Hector and Alfonse Ramirez had just finished off the last of the Russians in the kitchen . . . Dmitry, that was his name. When they were done, Hector came and got me, and we left Sweden in a plane from Bromma Airport, flew to Málaga. We were attacked on the motorway. Hector was shot. Simultaneously his father was murdered in Marbella.'

'Who by?' Antonia asked.

'One of Hector's enemies. A German businessman. Ralph Hanke.'

'How did he get hold of you?'

'The man who ran the Trasten restaurant worked for Hector. Carlos Fuentes, he was there. He betrayed Hector, told the Hankes where we were.'

Antonia and Miles listened, soaking up every detail.

'And Gunilla Strandberg?' Miles asked.

'She was corrupt, her brother was corrupt. Everyone in their group was, apart from Lars Vinge. He figured out what was going on and was about to stop them . . .'

Antonia absorbed it all.

'Vinge? Who's he?' Antonia asked.

Sophie brushed some hair from her face.

'He was the one watching me, he took those pictures. He got too close. Then we caught him. He started to talk, and revealed how corrupt Gunilla and her colleagues were. He claimed they'd murdered his girlfriend . . .'

'So that's why he shot Gunilla, and then himself?' Antonia asked.

Sophie paused to think.

'Perhaps not.'

'Why not?'

'Because he was getting somewhere. He was very keen, in spite of everything.'

'In spite of everything?'

'Vinge was different,' Sophie said.

'Different, how?'

'He was broken, obsessed in a rather unfortunate way.'

'And people like that don't kill themselves?'

Sophie didn't answer that.

'There must have been a third person there,' she said. 'Someone who knew everything.'

Antonia and Miles looked at each other.

'Yeah. Tommy Jansson,' Miles said.

'Head of the Violent Crime unit. Close friend of Gunilla Strandberg,' Antonia explained. 'He's the one we're hiding from. And he's the one we're trying to stop . . .'

Silence descended on the kitchen, as they all tried to digest what had been said.

Sophie rubbed the tiredness from her face.

'How are you doing?' Antonia asked.

Sophie looked at Antonia in surprise.

'How am I *doing*?'

'Yes, how are you doing?'

'I don't know how to answer that.' She almost smiled.

'Your son?' Antonia went on. 'You said you needed help finding your son?'

Sophie was trying to figure Antonia out. She felt safe with her. That would have to do.

'Go on,' Antonia said.

Sophie began to talk about Albert. About his accident, when Gunilla's thugs ran him down and left him confined to a wheelchair. About how he had adapted to his new life, and having to live in hiding with Sophie, how she had tried to protect him, then how he was snatched from her, kidnapped by the Hankes and used to blackmail her.

'Where is he?' Antonia asked.

Sophie could feel her sympathy.

'I don't know where he is,' she said.

The kitchen fell silent again.

'We'll help you find him, you've got my word on that,' Miles said.

'Thank you, for everything,' Antonia said, feeling relieved and

liberated by all the questions that had now been answered. She was enjoying this new knowledge. She took hold of Miles's good hand and held it in hers.

'We're going to do good now, Miles Ingmarsson, aren't we?'

'Yes, we are, Antonia,' he replied.

A window shattered behind Antonia. A bullet flew through the kitchen and pierced the back of her neck, shredding her carotid artery.

Antonia Miller died instantly.

More shots followed, breaking the remainder of the kitchen window and slamming into the walls. Glasses and crockery flew off the shelves, and splinters of wood and lumps of plaster filled the air.

They all threw themselves down. Mikhail and Sophie flat on the floor, Miles on top of Antonia, protecting her, pressing a hand to her neck as the blood poured between his fingers, thick and dark.

Mikhail passed Antonia's service pistol to Sophie, then ran upstairs.

'Protect Lothar,' she called after him.

Sophie pulled herself across the floor to Miles.

'Miles!' she cried.

But he was in shock, out of reach. She grabbed his arm and squeezed hard. He looked up at her.

'She's dead,' Sophie said.

She held Antonia's gun out to him. He stared at it, then at Sophie. She pressed the gun into his hand.

'We've got to defend ourselves. Do you hear me?'

Miles looked down at Antonia, who lay dead beneath him.

From upstairs came the muffled bursts of five distinct shots as Mikhail emptied the M1, followed by a clattering sound as the cartridge ejected itself.

Rapid footsteps outside the kitchen window, the door was yanked open and someone came into the hall, heading for the kitchen. Miles grabbed Antonia's pistol from Sophie's hand and readied it to fire.

'No!' Sophie cried out, and managed to push Miles's gun towards the floor.

Jens entered the kitchen, crouching down. He was out of breath as he slid down and sat back against the wall, the rifle in his hands. He looked at Antonia Miller's dead body, then at Miles.

'There are at least two men out there,' he said, breathing hard. 'One hundred metres to the east . . .' Jens swallowed and went on. 'I think there might be a third among the trees to the west.'

He looked at Miles more closely.

'We know each other,' he said.

Miles said nothing; he picked up a blanket from the sofa and laid it over Antonia's dead body.

Mikhail's rifle clattered once more from up above.

'Either we stay here and defend ourselves,' Jens said. He double-checked that the rifle was loaded. 'Or Miles and I go out and find them instead.'

Sophie looked at the two men. Jens: afraid, curious, excited. Miles: quiet, blank, empty.

'We go out and find them,' Miles said flatly.

There was no more to say. Miles walked towards the hall.

Jens followed him but stopped in the doorway and turned back towards Sophie.

'Stay close to Mikhail,' he said.

'Stay close to Miles,' she said.

Silence . . .

'Fear is what keeps me alive,' he said.

The words came out of nowhere.

'What fear?' she asked.

'This, among others.'

He stood there with the rifle in one hand, and gestured vaguely with the other to indicate the situation they were in. It was ridiculous of him to start talking now. But she wanted to know more.

'I don't believe that,' she said.

He looked at Antonia's body, then at Sophie. There was something painful in his eyes.

'So what are you saying, Jens?'

'I want to be with you, free, together. Not like this. I'm tired.'

Jens turned around and left the house.

She watched him go, gathered herself for a moment, then went and sat a few steps up the staircase – it had walls on either side, she was protected there.

Mikhail was sitting below a window upstairs, with the rifle between his legs.

'Lothar?' she asked.

Mikhail pointed to his left.

'I'm here,' Lothar said, showing himself. 'I'm helping Mikhail reload.'

'Lothar,' she said.

He looked out again.

'Don't worry,' she said.

He realised she meant their last conversation. He smiled at her, then sat down behind Mikhail again.

There was a crack from outside and Mikhail stood up and fired three aggressive shots back.

At the same moment the shots rang out, a hand clamped over Sophie's mouth. She was pulled backwards and dragged down the stairs. Someone held her in an iron grip, pressing her down onto the kitchen floor.

Another two shots from Mikhail's rifle, and the man who had her in his grasp kneed down on top of her back. For a brief moment, just before he put his hand over her mouth, Sophie's face was side-down to the floor. She got a quick glance at the man's face.

It was Aron.

The rattling sound again as the magazine hit the floor. It sounded so close, she wanted to call out, call Mikhail to come and help her. But Aron Geisler's strength was phenomenal, the body that was holding her down and the hand over her mouth that had her in a vice-like grip. She caught a glimpse of a blade flashing. Not very long, a large field knife. It thrust into her right side. It had looked so sharp, but it didn't feel sharp as it forced its way through layers of skin and tissue. More the opposite, in fact: that she was being stabbed with something blunt, thick and long. As if something was being hammered into her. The pain flashed through her whole body. She screamed into Aron's hand as Mikhail fired more salvos above them. Aron twisted the knife to cause as much damage as he could. She felt paralysed. The knife was pulled out of her body.

Sophie lay there immobile, saw his shoes as he moved silently through the kitchen, then his whole body as he stopped at the kitchen table, still covered with photographs. Aron quickly gathered them in the sports bag and left the house.

Blood filled her eyes and she was sucked backwards into something dense and empty.

THE WIND AND MIXTURE OF SNOW AND RAIN MADE FOR POOR VISIBILITY. JENS was making his way through the vegetation of the garden. Miles was off somewhere to his right. They were planning to flank their target from both sides.

A sound, a short distance away, Jens stopped, crouched down, listened. His heartbeat was pounding in his ears.

A gash in time. A powerful car started up in the distance and drove off. Jens remained still, saw movement to his right and Miles emerged from the storm, calm and ice-cold.

He squatted down beside Jens and they listened together.

'There's no one here any more,' Jens whispered.

Jens saw Sophie as soon as they got back, the blood, her eyes closed. Mikhail was crouched beside her at the foot of the stairs.

'No, no, no,' he muttered to himself as he rushed over.

Mikhail was working fast, trying to stop the bleeding. A pale and frightened Lothar appeared, bringing towels.

'She needs medical attention urgently,' Mikhail said.

'I'll call an ambulance; carry her out to the car and I'll drive and meet them,' Miles said.

Mikhail and Jens carried Sophie out to the Jaguar and laid her in the back seat, and Lothar followed with the towels. Jens got in beside her, and pressed the towels over the wound that was still pumping out blood. Miles hurried over, his phone clutched to his ear, got in behind the wheel and drove off.

Mikhail and Lothar watched the car as it disappeared at high speed. They stood there until they could no longer see or hear it. It was completely quiet. They knew what they had to do. Mikhail patted Lothar on the shoulder.

'Come on,' he said.

In a shed behind the house they found a couple of spades. They

strode out onto the lawn, dug their spades into the ground and began to dig a grave for Antonia Miller.

The Jaguar sped along the road.

Miles was hunched over the steering wheel, and Antonia's handbag was on the seat next to him. He stuck his hand in, dug around and found the forged passport that Marianne had given her, then passed it to Jens.

'Will this work?' he asked.

Jens took the passport and glanced at the photograph.

'Yes,' he said, and stuck the passport in the pocket of Sophie's jeans.

Swirling blue lights from an emergency vehicle ahead of them. Miles flashed it down as it got closer.

The exchange happened quickly. The paramedics put Sophie on a stretcher and wheeled her into the back of the ambulance. Jens followed her in and the doors closed. The ambulance drove off with its sirens blaring.

Miles stood there watching it until it disappeared from view. The storm had died down.

He looked back at the Jaguar. Open doors, blood on the back seat.

He jumped in, turned the car around and drove off, looking for a lake on the map application on his mobile phone.

There was one very close.

Miles sat behind the wheel as the Jaguar purred in neutral. A sandy beach and a long jetty stretching out into the water. The sun was going down. Darkness came quickly at this time of year.

Antonia . . . Miles could see her in front of him. She shouldn't have died. She shouldn't have taken that bullet . . .

Miles called his brother. Ian Ingmarsson answered.

'*Hello?*'

'Listen, now, little brother. I don't exist, I've disappeared, gone missing. I need your help, I really do. Can you do that?'

'*Tell me what's happened.*'

'No. I want to know if you'll help me.'

The sound of Ian breathing.

'*Yes, I will.*'

'Good. Who runs the embassy in Copenhagen?'

'*An idiot, that dyslexic bastard who was on the Defence Committee and molested that intern –*'

Miles interrupted him.

'I need to get hold of someone in authority at one of the nearby embassies, someone good, trustworthy, someone who's prepared to bend the rules and won't talk.'

'*I don't get it . . .*'

'Berlin, Warsaw, The Hague, Brussels, Prague, Vienna? Second and third in command would do as well.'

'*I don't follow, Miles.*'

'Someone decent! What don't you understand about that?'

Ian ran through a list of names; most of them he claimed were idiots. Like most people, in his view of the world.

'*But Prague . . .*' he said.

'What about Prague?' Miles wondered.

'*The ambassador there is that woman, that old Social Democrat cow, what's her name? Solveig Svensson.*'

'OK . . .'

'*Well, she's useless, of course, and her number two is that moron from Småland who's trailed after her for years, used to write all her speeches. But if I remember rightly, the third in command is a good guy. Wessman. Clued up, made of the right stuff, Foreign Office down to his core, an old hand, makes sure things that need doing get done in that embassy. He's been to dinner several times at Mum and Dad's. You've met him.*'

Clued up, the right stuff, Foreign Office . . . Miles thought. That was how the Ingmarssons talked about their colleagues.

'Can he be trusted?'

'*Yes, if you can give him something he wants.*'

'What does he want?'

'*Money and influence, just like everyone else.*'

'In what order?'

'*Influence first, then, if that doesn't work, money.*'

'Can we give him both?'

'*We?*'

'Yes, we,' Miles said firmly. 'Is there anyone else I know at that embassy?'

'*No, not as far as I know. I don't think so.*'

'I want a job there, at the Swedish embassy in Prague, as soon as possible, under a fake name with a fake CV, mid-level, no diplomatic crap, no public role, just a guy no one really cares about. Get it sorted out with Wessman.'

Joyless laughter from his brother.

'*Hang on, Miles, what the fuck do you think–*'

Miles interrupted him.

'No, none of that crap, just show me that *you're* made of the *right stuff*, Ian, and that you can pull off something like this.'

Miles could see his little brother in his mind's eye, sitting there trying not to explode.

'One more thing, Ian,' Miles said.

'*What?*'

'There's a woman in intensive care at Södermalm Hospital, Sanna Renberg. Go and see her, make sure she's got everything she needs.'

Miles opened up a bit.

'I really need your help this time.'

Ian heard the change in Miles's voice and suddenly understood the situation.

'*OK, Miles. I'll see what I can do.*'

They ended the call.

Miles lit a cigarette and wound the window down slightly.

Antonia was dead. He took another drag on the cigarette, his hand shaking.

Tommy Jansson . . .

Miles took his mobile phone, wallet and packet of cigarettes from his jacket, opened the car door and put them on the ground.

A few deep drags, then he shut the door and revved the engine.

Tommy Jansson . . . You fucking, fucking bastard.

Miles pressed the pedal to the floor, the Jaguar's six-cylinder engine roared, the car accelerated hard and he veered out onto the jetty, the tyres clattering over the planks. He was rapidly approaching the end.

The Jaguar flew over the edge, heavy after a moment of sudden weightlessness, and hit the water front-first. A cascade of water over the windscreen. Miles hit his head on the hard steering wheel. The car was floating but was taking in water fast.

He got the door open, slid out into the cold water and swam away from the car. It sank behind him, lit up for a moment beneath the water, before the water short-circuited the electrics and the car disappeared into the depths.

He emerged from the water, picked up his mobile phone, wallet and cigarettes, and started to walk through the woods towards Jens's house.

Miles called Ulf, Antonia's boyfriend, to tell him that Antonia was dead, murdered.

Ulf cried.

———

A PARAMEDIC IN A FLUORESCENT JACKET WAS SITTING BY SOPHIE'S SIDE. THE water-resistant Gore-Tex was wet with rain, sparkling in the light.

There was a muffled high-frequency noise – the ambulance siren. Blasting into the dark night along with a harsh, cold blue light that found its way into the back of the vehicle where Sophie lay. She was strapped onto a stretcher, rocking in time with the motion of the ambulance.

A voice somewhere inside the ambulance penetrated her consciousness. The shape of a man sitting on a fold-down seat. Jens.

'What did you say?' she whispered.

He moved closer to her.

'I'm here with you. Try not to worry.'

'Aron,' she whispered. 'Aron Geisler stabbed me.'

Jens stroked her cheek with his hand. He hushed her. His eyes looked sad.

Sophie felt the speed of the vehicle again. The ambulance was driving very fast. Unbelievably fast.

She looked down at herself for the first time. Blood on her chest, arms, stomach, blood everywhere. Cold and damp.

'How bad is it?'

The paramedic leaned in front of her face and looked into her eyes.

330

'Just take it easy, don't try to talk,' he said in Danish.

Don't try to talk . . .

Then she understood. She had said the same thing to countless patients. *Don't try to talk.* That's what you said to patients who were on the way out, to the ones whose life force was draining away uncontrollably.

The vehicle braked hard. The siren started again. This time it seemed louder, pressing in on her consciousness.

A prickling cold embraced her, nausea weighed down by a physical weakness that spread out from her neck. Then a sense of being upside down, weightless. That she was about to topple over the edge of a cliff and lose everything. She couldn't hold on. The cold got worse, cutting through her entire body. Then shaking, hard and remorselessly.

The paramedic was suddenly standing over her, holding her body to the stretcher, trying to hold her still. She looked into his eyes and saw fear.

She heard her own voice cry out *'no!'* several times. *No*, she thought, *dear God, I can't die now!*

'I BET YOU A THOUSAND KRONOR MY COCK'S BIGGER THAN YOURS, TOMMY,' OVE said.

They had stopped to have a piss in a patch of woodland.

'I'm not going to take you up on that,' Tommy muttered, pulling his zip down.

'No, very sensible,' Ove said. 'Because then you'd have lost a thousand kronor. And who wants to lose a grand just because they've got a tiny cock?'

'At a guess, no one,' Tommy said.

'Quite right. No one!' Ove said, then started to pee.

'I've stopped drinking,' Tommy said.

'Way to go, Captain Jansson! Very sensible for a handsome man like you. You do know that you're very handsome, don't you, Tommy?'

'So I've been told plenty of times.'

Ove lit up.

'Tommy! You're joining in the joke! Jesus Christ! This is getting better and better. You and me, Tommy, shit, we have a good time together.'

Ove chuckled, whistled the theme to *Rocky* and concentrated on peeing.

Tommy put his right hand inside his jacket, took out the snub-nosed .38 from the hidden pocket and weighed it in his hand.

'In the winter I usually piss "Ove" in the snow. Big or small letters, joined-up or not.'

Tommy took a firm grip of the revolver, raised his arm and shot Ove in the cheek. The blast was incredibly loud. Ove's head shook from the force of the bullet and he fell where he stood. With his pride and joy still hanging out of his fly.

Tommy finished pissing, shook his cock, put it away, then went over to Ove, who was lying on his side staring up at Tommy. He was breathing fast and shallow, with a gaping hole in his cheek. His upper jaw was shattered, loose teeth scattered in his blood-filled mouth.

Tommy Jansson looked at him without saying anything, raised the gun and emptied the magazine into Negerson, into his crotch, chest, shoulder, neck and forehead. Six shots in total.

THE WATER IN THE WASHBASIN TURNED A GRISLY PALE PINK. ARON WASHED Sophie's blood from his hands. He had checked into a motel beside the motorway at the Danish-German border.

In the bedroom he opened the bag he had taken with him from Jens's house, emptied its contents onto the bed and started to go through everything. It was all about Sophie, and the fact that she had been under surveillance, that the police who had been watching her had been corrupt. All of which he already knew. But it was possible to discern something else now too: that she might have talked to the police, or had at least been in contact with Gunilla Strandberg, who had been hunting Hector. It wasn't all clear, and she could have been innocent. But there was enough material to give a general impression that Sophie couldn't be trusted. A good enough impression to make Hector understand, help him let her go.

Aron divided the contents of the bag into two piles. The first was filled with compromising material about Sophie. The next was for everything else.

He put the first pile back in the bag. Then he sat down on the bed and destroyed everything in the second pile, shredding paper, destroying storage devices, tearing up photographs and pictures until they were unrecognisable. Removing every shred of evidence against Hector and his organisation that Gunilla Strandberg had committed to paper.

Then he put it all in a plastic bag, tied it up and threw it in a skip behind the motel restaurant.

58

(MUNICH/VALLE DEL CAUCA)

'ARE YOU SITTING COMFORTABLY?' CHRISTIAN ASKED.

Albert nodded.

The private plane, a Bombardier Challenger, furnished in beige leather and walnut wood, had room for eight passengers but was carrying only four. Albert, Christian and, behind them, Ernst and Roland.

'Do you need anything?' Christian went on.

Albert shook his head.

'Are you thirsty?'

'No,' Albert said gruffly.

'Hungry?'

Christian was smiling. Albert looked away.

The Challenger cruised sedately at 12,000 metres, carried by the jet stream. Albert ate, read, tried to kill time. Night came and he fell asleep and drifted off into a dream. He was back in the farmhouse, in the room where he had been held captive. The door was open. Albert stood up from the wheelchair and walked out of the room, on foot. He walked outside, the sun was shining. Then he started to run away from there. His legs were strong, carrying him at high speed, his shoes pounding on the ground. He was on his way

home, home to his mum, to his girlfriend and his friends. On his way home to his old life . . .

He was torn from the dream as the plane touched the ground. Albert tried to figure out where he was as he looked out the window. They had landed somewhere in the darkness to refuel, and took off again. He didn't go back to sleep, and just sat there in the darkness, alone with his thoughts, which told him it was highly unlikely that he would ever go home again.

Daylight came and the plane sank through the clouds, looped around a city, found the right course and descended for landing. It was a private airstrip, with a small control tower from a bygone age. The plane landed, braked hard and taxied towards two waiting silver Cadillac Escalades.

The sun was white-gold and was shining mercilessly; the heat shimmered. It was a long way from home.

'Where are we?' Albert asked.

'Come on, let me help you get out,' Christian said.

They drove through open countryside, then into a jungle-like forest. A barrier across the road, an armed guard, then more forest. Snipers among the trees with their barrels trained on the vehicles as they passed. Then the forest opened out to reveal a castle, an animal park, pools, waterfalls, tennis courts.

The car turned and pulled up outside the main entrance.

When Albert's door opened there was already a wheelchair waiting. Christian lifted him out.

A man came down the steps, a radiant, broad smile on his face. His shirt was loose, his jeans new, his hair black and shiny.

'Christian!' he said. 'Welcome! And you too, Albert.'

The man stopped in front of Albert.

'I know your mother. My name is Alfonse Ramirez. My uncle is Don Ignacio; this is his house, and he asked me to say that you are all very welcome here.'

Alfonse studied Albert's face carefully.

'You're very similar, you and your mother. You're lucky.'

He laughed. Then he pointed at Christian to indicate that he

should join in. Then, standing on either side of the wheelchair, they carried Albert up the steps and in through the main door.

They brought Albert to a large, open hallway. It was marble and gold, with life-size porcelain animals. Over-the-top. There was a cage up by the ceiling containing a chimpanzee that ran around nervously and shouting. A couple of servants in livery went past, as did some guards. It was like a film. A bad one.

A man walked towards them. He was about fifty-five, black hair, pale skin, poor posture.

'Uncle, this is Christian Hanke and Albert Brinkmann,' Alfonse said.

The chimpanzee screamed again.

Don Ignacio looked at Christian and then at Alfonse.

'What's this?'

He pointed at Albert.

'This is Albert,' Christian replied.

'A kidnapped child in a wheelchair in my house? Where's Hector Guzman's child?'

'We no longer have him,' Christian said.

'I see. So what are we going to do with *him*?'

'He's with me, until further notice,' Christian said.

' "Until further notice"?'

The chimpanzee was shrieking and running around its cage. Don Ignacio ignored it, but Christian couldn't. The animal unsettled him.

'Yes, until further notice,' he said, almost irritably.

'What about you, then, how long are *you* going to stay? Until further notice?'

'We'll stay until we know what's going on with Hector.'

Ignacio gave him a disapproving look.

'You came here to hide?'

'We're going to get Hector, sooner or later. We just need a bit of time to gather our strength.'

Don Ignacio flared up.

' "Until further notice," "gather our strength" ... What sort of crap is that? You and your father want to get Hector Guzman. That's what our collaboration is based upon. We helped you to find his son, we helped you with assets and men. We helped you to the

point where you actually had Hector in your sights. And even then you managed to mess things up. And now this?'

'Our collaboration goes on until we're done with Hector; that's how we see it.'

Don Ignacio opened his eyes exaggeratedly wide.

'That's how you see it?'

He turned towards Alfonse.

'That's how they see it, Alfonse.'

Albert was listening to all this. Ignacio's voice was dripping with sarcasm. The chimpanzee screamed above them.

Christian stared at the floor.

'But that's not how *I* see it,' Ignacio said. 'And that's the only thing that matters.'

The chimpanzee was rushing around.

Ignacio held up a hand, and a bodyguard walked over to Christian and indicated that he wanted to search him. Christian held his arms out. The guard found a mobile phone and put it in his pocket.

'I've done the same to Roland and Ernst,' Ignacio said. 'You are my guests, until I decide how things are going to develop. If you try to leave, I will take that as an insult and my men will hunt you through the forest and shoot you in the back. We'll leave your bodies with the hippopotamuses. They'll trample and piss on you until you're beyond all recognition. And then you'll be thrown to the pigs.'

The bodyguard took hold of Christian's arm and led him away.

'And what about you, little boy?' Ignacio said. 'What happened to you, why are you in a wheelchair?'

Albert looked at Ignacio, then at Alfonse and then back to Ignacio.

'I was run down by a car,' he said.

There was no trace of sympathy from Don Ignacio.

'When?'

'Last autumn.'

'Are you going to be stuck in it for ever?'

'It looks like it,' Albert replied.

'Can you manage?'

'Yes, most of the time,' Albert replied.

Don Ignacio's tongue moved around his mouth, a new thought.

'Did they treat you well, the Hankes?'

The questions came thick and fast.

'I've got nothing to compare it to,' Albert replied. 'I've never been kidnapped before.'

Ignacio smiled, as did Alfonse, who intervened.

'Answer Don Ignacio's question, Albert.'

'No, I can't say that they did.'

Ignacio grunted something inaudible but wasn't finished.

'I've never liked Germans,' he said.

He seemed to get caught in his thoughts, and one vein on his forehead grew as bitterness bubbled up inside him. Ignacio snapped himself out of it.

'Alfonse, I'm sick of the Hankes, I'm sick of Guzman, sick of the fact that those bastards are incapable of killing each other.'

He sighed irritably.

'See to it that the boy gets some food.'

Then Ignacio Ramirez walked away.

59

(NICE)

A HOTEL ROOM. THE TOWN OF NICE WAS SHIMMERING OUTSIDE.

They had been working all day. Angela, Gustave and a thickset female prosecutor, as well as one of the prosecutor's assistants.

Angela had given them what she had.

Her story had started in Marbella when she met Eduardo, Hector and their father, Adalberto. She had realised early on that the family was engaged in illegal activities. She and Eduardo decided to make a life of their own, on their own terms. Over the years they had only sporadic contact with the rest of the family, until Hasani appeared after Hector had been run down in Stockholm. Everything had carried on as usual until, out of nowhere, Eduardo was murdered. She told them how she, the boys and Hasani had been flown up to Sweden, where they were kept hidden and protected. Then Daphne and Thierry were murdered and they had to take refuge in the apartment on Norr Mälarstrand, until one day they had been forced to flee from there as well, when Hasani told them to go with him and they were driven down through Europe to the French Riviera and Villefranche.

The prosecutor's assistant typed any names Angela mentioned into a computer, where the databases did their job and pictures of the people appeared and were pinned up on a sort of bulletin board that was leaning against a sofa. In the centre: Hector Guzman. In

a circle around him: Aron Geisler, Leszek Smialy, Hasani, Sonya Alizadeh, Ernst Lundwall and Sophie Brinkmann.

The prosecutor was sitting in an armchair, Angela and Gustave on chairs.

'What do you think happened there? Why didn't Sophie Brinkmann and her son go with you?'

'I don't know,' Angela replied. 'It all happened so quickly. Hasani came up to the apartment and fetched us, told us it was urgent. We were bundled into his car and driven south.'

Gustave was studying the board and pointed at a photograph of Ernst.

'This one, the adviser, Ernst Lundwall. Where was he?'

'He came and went; he didn't live there. I don't think he was there that day. I don't know.'

'Was his name ever mentioned by Leszek or Hasani?'

'No, they never talked about anything, just short phone conversations with Aron during the journey.'

Gustave scratched his head.

The prosecutor had been sitting there listening, and now she smiled apologetically at Angela.

'You've given us more than anyone could hope for, Madame Garcia. But there's one thing missing. And you yourself are aware of what it is.'

Yes, Angela knew. There was no specific event that the prosecutor could build a case around.

Gustave went on again.

'We had been hoping we might be able to begin an investigation of Guzman from here. But we need to take a different route.'

'What route?' she wondered.

He pointed to the bulletin board.

'Sweden. That's where the only investigation of any real significance into Hector Guzman has happened. A shootout at a restaurant in Stockholm six months ago. That was when he vanished.'

Gustave stood up, walked over to the board and pointed at Sophie.

'If Ernst is the *adviser*, Hasani the *bodyguard* and Leszek the *middleman* . . .' He turned to Angela. 'How would you describe her?'

Angela thought for a moment.

'I don't know. She was there because she had been forced into it. That's what it felt like anyway.'

'Threatened?' Gustave asked.

Angela pursed her lips.

'Maybe. But on the other hand, she was also working for them. Sometimes she would disappear and then come back, and then have quiet meetings with Leszek. She was initiated into the secret things that were always going on around us. She had some sort of active role.'

Gustave turned back to the board and pointed to Sophie's picture again.

'An active role? A central role?'

'Maybe,' Angela replied.

'What's her connection to Hector?' the prosecutor asked.

'They had a relationship.'

Gustave raised his eyebrows.

'Hector was run down on a pedestrian crossing in Stockholm by a rival criminal gang that he was feuding with – Germans, I think they were. He was taken to the hospital, and spent a while there. Sophie Brinkmann was one of the nurses on his ward. That was how they met.'

Gustave made a noise to indicate that he was curious.

'Then what?'

'As I understood it, their relationship continued.'

'What sort of relationship?'

'I don't know, but they were very close to each other. Sophie was in the same car as Hector when they were attacked on the way to Marbella. She's been working closely with Aron and Leszek while Hector's been in a coma.'

Gustave turned to the prosecutor and pointed at the board.

'I'll organise an international warrant for her.'

'Because . . . ?' the prosecutor asked.

'Because if we were to target one person in this group . . .'

The prosecutor nodded.

'Of course. Madame Brinkmann.'

(STOCKHOLM)

THE JACKET AND NEW SHIRT MONICA GAVE HIM FOR HIS BIRTHDAY WERE HANG-
ing in the bedroom.

Tommy got dressed in front of the mirror on the inside of the wardrobe door, buttoned the shirt, thought he looked fairly smart. The absence of drink hadn't exactly made him better-looking, but more sturdy. There was something solid about him. And he was planning to keep it that way.

Monica was sitting by the large terrace window with the oxygen tank to her right, staring out at a magpie hopping around in the snow looking for food. She pressed the mouthpiece to her face and breathed.

He went and stood in front of her, holding the lapels of the jacket.

'This is the one you gave me. Smart, isn't it?'

He tried to smile, offer a little of himself. It didn't work. Monica looked away.

The front doorbell rang out piercingly. The nurse aide stepped into the hall. She was a Thai woman, about a metre tall and a metre wide, chirruping as usual. Tommy could never remember her name.

Then a nurse came in, bringing with her a new wheelchair, and shook Tommy's hand.

'Hello, I take it you must be Monica's husband?'

'Tommy Jansson,' he said quickly, and made to leave.

'We're supposed to be having a talk.'

'A talk?'

'Yes, we did inform you about it.'

'I see, I must have missed that. So, what's the latest?'

'First, Monica's going to get this wheelchair. Then we need to talk about respiratory care, and the fact that we're probably going to have to put Monica on a permanent respirator soon,' the nurse explained to Tommy.

'I see,' he said.

They sat in the living room, the nurse, Tommy and Monica. Monica in the new wheelchair.

The Thai woman was making coffee in the kitchen. The nurse laid out brochures and talked about the various procedures and options as far as respirators were concerned.

Tommy looked at his wife, and Monica met his gaze. They both knew what this meant.

Help me to go when the time comes . . .

She looked so gentle sitting there, Monica. How could he possibly do that? His Monica . . .

He felt sick.

Tommy excused himself when the aide came in with coffee on a tray.

He hurried into the bathroom and leaned over the toilet. He retched, but nothing came up.

(JUTLAND/PRAGUE)

THE OPERATION TOOK SIX HOURS. SOPHIE HAD BEEN FIGHTING FOR HER LIFE.

Now she was lying awake but out of reach, heavily sedated, drifting through an in-between world.

'Will she be OK?'

The question came from Ejnar Larsen, a police superintendent from Kolding. He was standing at the foot of Sophie's bed with her doctor, Vibeke Steen, in his police overcoat, because of the bad weather, but otherwise in plain clothes.

'The patient was technically dead when she arrived. Brain activity had ceased,' the doctor said. 'We managed to revive her. Her injuries were extremely complicated. Whoever stabbed her knew what he was doing.'

'He?' Larsen wondered.

'Yes, *he*. When was the last time it was a she?'

'You can never be sure,' Larsen replied.

'Yes, you can. And I'm going to carry on saying *he* when we're dealing with extreme violence like this.'

Larsen laughed. He knew women were capable of just as much.

'OK . . .'

Larsen was holding the passport that had been in Sophie's pocket, as well as a pad he proceeded to read out loud from.

'Two men in a car handed her over to the paramedics on a road, and one of them went with her. Have you seen him?'

'No.'

'Have you seen anyone who might have anything to do with the woman?'

'I'm afraid not . . . According to her passport, she's Swedish,' Vibeke said.

'Yes, so I see,' Larsen said.

'And she shouldn't have made it.'

'How do you mean?'

'She was dead when she came in, but something brought her back.'

'That honour belongs to you, surely?' Larsen said.

'Hmm,' she said, without conviction. 'Well, it's not over yet. We'll have to see how she recovers.'

Larsen looked down at the passport.

'Are we done?' Vibeke asked.

Ejnar seemed absorbed, but looked up.

'Yes, yes. Thanks very much for your help,' he said.

She walked towards the door. He went on staring at the passport.

'Excuse me,' Ejnar called after her.

'Yes?' Vibeke turned around.

Larsen held the passport up to her. 'Is this really the same person?'

She was taken aback by the question, but retraced her steps into the room.

Vibeke looked at the picture of Antonia Miller, then at Sophie in the bed.

'Hard to say,' she said.

Ejnar Larsen seemed irritated, and kept looking from the passport photo to Sophie.

'It might have got through customs OK,' he said, 'but this isn't the same person. The nose! Look at the nose.'

She shrugged.

'You're the policeman,' she said. 'I'm here all night if there's anything else.'

She left the room.

Ejnar Larsen remained where he was, frowning to himself with the passport in his hand. He pressed the radio microphone that was attached to his left shoulder.

There was a crackle, then someone answered.

'Ejnar here. I want to check a Swedish ID number,' he said, then read the number out from the passport.

Denmark and Sweden shared their databases.

Ejnar Larsen waited, then was told that there was no such ID number.

'Try again,' he said, and read the number out once more. Then he asked them to search by name.

The same answer: there was no real person listed under either the number or the name.

'OK, thanks.'

The noise from the radio stopped.

Larsen sat down on a visitor's chair and inspected the passport, holding it up to the light, checking the numbers and the way the photograph was laminated. He couldn't tell if it was a forgery or not.

It would soon be evening, and he had no desire to do any overtime. He wanted to go home and play with the kids, pinch his wife's bottom and watch television. That English series about the country house . . .

Ejnar looked up at the woman in the bed. Who was she? Why was she lying there? Who wanted her dead?

He looked at her carefully. There was something classical about the way she looked. Privileged, perhaps. But something else, too . . . something good-hearted. Ejnar liked to think he could see things like that. Even if he knew how unlikely that was. But he still thought it . . . a sort of conviction that he could actually tell a lot about a person's inner self just by looking at their exterior. And this woman had been a victim of something. Something she didn't have any control over. He could tell. And in his world, people like that needed protection . . .

Well, that decides it, Ejnar thought. He called the duty officer at the station and explained the situation.

An hour later, two men from Forensics rolled in and photographed the patient, took DNA samples in the form of saliva and blood and scanned her fingers to get some good, old-fashioned fingerprints.

A recently graduated police constable showed up half an hour after that and mumbled that he was going to be on guard at the door.

'Go ahead,' Ejnar Larsen said, gesturing to an empty chair. 'Take that with you and go and sit outside the door. You know what to do?'

'Don't let anyone in except hospital staff, and call in anything suspicious.'

'Good,' Larsen said authoritatively.

The constable went out, the pair from Forensics carried on for a few more minutes until they were finished, then they packed their equipment away in their cases.

'What happens now?' he asked one of them.

'We run everything through our system and then send it on to the Swedes. We'll see if we get a response anywhere.'

JENS WALKED SLOWLY ALONG THE CORRIDOR. A POLICE OFFICER WAS SITTING on a chair outside Sophie's room a short distance away.

Two plain-clothes officers emerged, each carrying a rectangular case.

Forensics . . . Jens thought as he passed them. Dangerous. He assumed that Sophie's fake ID had been blown. And if they were any good, they would soon figure out her real identity . . .

Jens passed the policeman on guard, then walked to the end of the corridor and out the other side.

KENNET WESSMAN WAS SHORT AND HAD CROPPED HAIR. HE SHOOK HANDS WITH Miles Ingmarsson at U Malého Glena, a pub a few blocks away from the Swedish embassy.

'Welcome to Prague,' Kennet said with a smile. 'So you're Miles, Ian's brother. They say we're supposed to have a met a few times.'

He said this without any great conviction, then pulled out a chair and sat down at the table.

'But that's totally fucking irrelevant right now, isn't it?' he went on.

'Completely irrelevant,' Miles said, sitting down opposite him.

'OK,' Kennet said, putting his hands on the table. 'You seem to be in a bit of a mess. Personally, I'm not interested in knowing anything. But according to your brother, you need a job, apartment and anonymity, is that right?'

'That's right,' Miles said.

'What job do you want; what do you want to do?'

'Research. I need access to pretty much everything.'

'Internationally or just for Sweden?'

'Internationally.'

'This is going to be expensive. And you say "access to pretty much everything" – what do you mean by that?'

'Intelligence.'

Kennet looked surprised.

'I see. Well, that's going to be even more expensive. And fucking risky.'

'What's Ian told you?'

'He said he'd help me with the next step up the career ladder. But that I should take up the money side of things with you.'

'Give me a price for the job, anonymity, access to most files and somewhere to live,' Miles said.

Kennet thought for a moment, turning things over in his head. Then he gave Miles a hefty six-figure number.

'OK,' Miles replied. 'We need to sort out a doctor as well.'

'A doctor?'

'Yes, a general practitioner of some sort. With access to equipment and medication, someone who'll keep their mouth shut. Can you do that? Then I won't argue about the price.'

'Are you sick?'

'No, not me.'

Kennet Wessman didn't ask anything else.

'I'll see what I can do,' he said.

'That's not enough.'

A pause.

'I'll find a doctor,' Kennet said. 'When, and for how long?'

'I'll get back to you about that.'

They stopped talking, and everything else just lay there unsaid.

'Do you have your passport, Miles? The fake one?'

Miles handed him the passport. Kennet tucked it away in the inside pocket of his jacket.

'Good, I'll employ you under this name. You're an IT technician, and will have access to pretty much everything in the embassy.'

'I don't know anything about computers; what do I do if anyone asks?'

'You used to be a diplomat, didn't you?'

Miles nodded.

'Then lie, for fuck's sake. That's what we do best.'

The Swedish embassy was just a few blocks north from the pub. They walked up the cobbled streets towards the Castle District.

Kennet pointed to a building to their right.

'You'll be living there; a friend of mine has an empty apartment, I've booked it for you.'

Everything was nice and close. Miles liked Prague.

Kennet Wessman led him into the embassy, then sorted out the details of his employment and a pass card. Everything was prepared, and went very smoothly. Miles was starting to like him.

Then down into the basement, a dark corridor with a room at the end. No windows, three computers, standard-issue Swedish public-authority furniture, several servers, a kettle and some instant coffee.

'Will this be OK?' Kennet asked.

The room was claustrophobic and nondescript.

'Couldn't be better,' Miles said as he hung up his coat.

62

(JUTLAND)

JENS AND MIKHAIL STRODE INTO THE HOSPITAL AT TWENTY MINUTES PAST three in the morning. The blue-shirted policeman outside Sophie's room was pouring coffee from the flask he'd brought with him. In his lap were a pen and a book: *Kamikaze Sudoku.*

He started to get to his feet when he saw the two big men rapidly approaching him.

'Stop,' he said loudly, fumbling for his holstered pistol. He went for his radio instead and tried to press it, realised that time was running out and switched to the pepper spray kept in a leather pouch on his belt. His panic was the cause of his downfall. Mikhail grabbed him and dragged the police constable into the sickroom and laid him down on his stomach, taped his hands and mouth with electrical tape, then took him into the bathroom. He removed his pistol and radio, then closed the door.

Jens had released the brakes under Sophie's bed and they rolled her out into the corridor and set off towards the rear entrance of the hospital.

Dr Steen bumped into them as she emerged from the staff room.

'Stand still,' Jens said in Danish.

Vibeke froze, and looked first at Mikhail's huge bulk and then at the policeman's pistol in his hand. Jens took her by the arm and led her to a medicine storeroom.

'Unlock it,' he said.

She did as she was told, her hand trembling as she found the right key on her key ring, put it in the lock and opened the door.

Jens grabbed the keys from her hand and shoved her into the storeroom.

He was about to close the door when Vibeke said, 'She's in a very weak condition; she won't make it if she doesn't get treatment.'

'She's going to get treatment,' he said.

Jens began to close the door.

'When?'

'In ten, fifteen hours,' he said.

'That could be too late . . .'

Jens studied the doctor. She seemed genuinely concerned.

'We're going to take her away from here, come what may,' he said.

'She mustn't wake up for the next twelve hours,' Vibeke said, and began to take things off the shelves in the medicine storeroom, still talking as she read the labels and put the medication into an empty box. 'Make sure you keep her sedated the whole time. And she absolutely mustn't lose any more blood. Keep her on a drip, and monitor her pulse.'

She went on giving him instructions about how to care for Sophie: what medication to give her, how often and by what means. Jens picked up the box of medication and drip bags and walked out of the storeroom.

'Someone will come and let you out in a while,' Jens said, then shut the door on her, locking it with a loud click.

They rolled the bed through the corridor, following their pre-planned route, towards the fire-escape stairs, where they folded the wheels under the bed and carried it down two floors and rolled it out on to a loading dock in back of the hospital.

A Chevrolet Express was standing there with its back doors open. Lothar was waiting in the back of the van.

Sophie was pushed inside the Chevrolet. They locked the bed, fixed it to the floor and walls with cables, then drove off, quietly and carefully.

The back of the van rocked as Lothar and Jens worked to attach the drip, while Jens gave Lothar the information he had just been given inside the hospital by the doctor.

'I'll manage,' Lothar said.

'Good,' Jens said. He stopped for a moment. 'You're a good kid,' he said, and patted Lothar on his shoulder.

Lothar didn't reply, and arranged the medicines in a plastic tray on the floor.

Jens made his way to the front of the van and slipped into the seat next to Mikhail.

EJNAR LARSEN WAS CONFUSED. HIS TIED-UP COLLEAGUE HAD BEEN FOUND early that morning by his replacement. The female patient with no identity was missing. As was the bed she had been lying in.

None of the surveillance cameras had registered anything.

Ejnar was reading a computer printout from Sweden. The DNA hadn't brought up any matches, and neither had the fingerprints. The woman was still anonymous.

He scratched his head, the way he sometimes did when he needed to think. And there was something else bothering him.

Ejnar went through the events of the past few days – the reports and investigations. He had seen something, noticed something in passing . . . recently . . . very recently.

Something about the Copenhagen Police working on a report from the Malmö Police on the other side of the Sound. They'd asked for help . . .

What the hell was it, again?

Ejnar searched his papers. The piles were large and unsorted. He cursed himself for being so untidy. But eventually he found what he was looking for.

He skimmed through the report. A remarkable gunfight at a multi-storey car park in Malmö. No witnesses to speak of, the Swedish police suspected the use of guns with silencers. It was all very sketchy . . . But it wasn't the shootout itself that caught Ejnar Larsen's interest. It was an occurrence at the hospital shortly afterwards . . .

He searched his desk again and found a report of a man with a gunshot wound being admitted to the University Hospital in Malmö.

The man, who hadn't had any ID on him, was operated on, then was picked up by two men and disappeared.

Exactly what had happened here? . . .

He scratched his head again.

'*Hello!*'

Ejnar looked up from his desk. Vibeke Steen was standing in front of him. He made an attempt to stand up.

'Please, have a seat. Did you get on OK with the artist?'

She sat down.

'I don't know. The memory cheats . . . But I hope the pictures will help you.'

Ejnar interviewed her. Vibeke told him about the men, how they had looked when she encountered them.

'They cared about the patient,' she said.

'Friends of hers?'

'Maybe.'

'Did they say anything?'

Vibeke thought.

'They said she'd be looked after in ten, fifteen hours.'

'Anything else?'

'The one who talked to me spoke Danish. But it felt a bit odd.'

'How?'

'You know when someone's lived abroad for a long time, the way they speak . . . their mother tongue is a bit old-fashioned?'

Ejnar Larsen made a note on his pad.

'I've got one more question,' he said.

'Fire away.'

'Why would someone do that? Take someone from a hospital?'

'How do you mean?'

'Has it happened before? Someone doing this sort of thing?'

She almost laughed. 'Yes, it's the third time this week.'

He smiled at the joke.

'No, it hasn't happened before,' she said.

But it had, only the other day, on the Swedish side of the Öre-sund. Exactly the same thing.

He said goodbye to Vibeke Steen, then sat down and continued thinking.

Why would anyone do that, and take such a risk?

Presumably if you were on the run, or if there was a warrant out for you.

A warrant . . .

Ejnar Larsen dug around on his computer. He couldn't get into the Swedish system, so he started with the Danish one. That was fairly straightforward, because there weren't that many women on it. But there was no one who looked like the missing patient. He moved on to Europol, then Interpol.

After scrolling down for a good half hour, staring at far too many pictures of women who had warrants out for them, he recognised her straight away. The warrant had been issued by the French police, and was marked as low priority.

The woman was named Sophie Brinkmann, and she was Swedish, registered in Stockholm.

Ejnar picked up his phone and dialled the number of the detective in charge of the case, Gustave Peltier at the Police Nationale in Nice.

63

(TUSCANY)

DRESSED IN A BLACK BENEDICTINE HABIT, HECTOR WAS SITTING ON A BENCH under a cypress tree, looking out at the world in front of him.

The monastery was on a plateau. The view from the garden was immense: rolling landscape, forests, villages, farms, mountains, the horizon.

Next to him was a small patch of garden, where two monks were working, pulling out dried-up plants and turning the soil.

Aron walked towards him; he had a bag in his hand, a black sports bag. He sat down beside Hector.

'How did you manage to pull this off?' he asked.

'Roberto, a cousin of Dad's,' Hector said.

'It is secure?'

Hector looked around at the tranquil scene.

'This is the safest place right now.' He turned towards Aron. 'Where have you been?'

'Denmark.'

'Did you find them?'

'Sort of,' Aron replied.

'Lothar?'

'I don't know, he wasn't there when I got there,' Aron said.

'What happened?'

A breeze blew through the trees around them.

'Sophie's dead,' he said.

Hector flinched, albeit slightly.

'I found her on the floor inside the house. They'd been attacked.'

'Lothar?' he asked again.

'No one else there. It was empty.'

Hector was trying not to feel anything, but somewhere in his chest . . .

'Apart from . . .' Aron began.

'Apart from what?'

'Another body, a woman.'

'Who?'

'I'm not sure, but I think it was the detective who was investigating the Trasten case; we read about her in the papers, if you remember?'

Hector thought, and remembered.

'Yes. Miller?'

'Mm-hm. Antonia Miller.'

'What was she doing there?'

Aron passed the bag to Hector.

'Look through this.'

Hector glanced warily at Aron, then opened the bag.

What he read gave him an indistinct impression that Sophie had been in contact with the police ever since their first meeting, that she had been supplying them with information.

'She betrayed us very early on,' Aron said. 'She betrayed us, Hector. And she continued to betray us, right to the end.'

Hector leafed quickly through the photographs and notes, but couldn't deal with it and handed the bag back to Aron.

'Who was at the house, who killed Sophie and Miller?'

'Difficult to say. Jens, Mikhail and Lothar were gone. I don't know.'

Hector looked at Aron. He had fought tirelessly for their survival, but there was something odd about him, something different. The conviction in his eyes was gone. As if he were hiding something. As if he were trying to hide that fact too, by keeping his eyes steady, not blinking, overemphasising that he was exactly the same as usual. But on the other hand, he was exhausted, just like everyone else.

'Thanks, Aron,' Hector said.

'What for?'

'For everything.'

Some church bells started to ring a short distance away. Hector stood up and walked towards the monastery. The two monks in the garden were already on their way. More were approaching from other directions.

Aron remained seated and watched him go.

Hector walked into the chapel and sat down on a wooden bench. The monks started to sing. It was beautiful – melancholic.

Sophie was dead. He was seized by longing and despair, a sense of incredible loss and loneliness.

The monks' singing echoed around the cool stone vaults of the chapel.

Hector could see her clearly in his mind, as if she were right in front of him, and he dared to let himself hold on to that.

One thing grew clearer to him. A dream, almost unconscious, but a dream that had grown inside him since the very first time he met her. That she was the woman, his salvation, his life, that she was the one who would bring to pass everything he hadn't managed to achieve on his own. Finding happiness, and sharing it.

A sob escaped from his throat. He clamped his hand over his mouth. He could feel the racked sobbing that was on its way, could feel despair welling up and threatening to turn everything upside down. But Hector fought against it, struggling to hold the tears and anguish at bay.

It worked. After a while he was able to remove his hand from his mouth.

She betrayed us. Aron's words came back to him. Yes, she had. But had she betrayed him? Did he really care, when it came down to it?

She was dead.

Gone.

And he would never see her again.

The monks' singing rolled back and forth through the room.

If he had believed in what they believed in, he would have prayed for her soul. But Hector didn't know how.

The only thing he had in common with the men in front of him

was that he, like them, was penniless, didn't even own the clothes he was wearing. But the men singing had made an active choice to become penniless. Hector had made an active choice to be the exact opposite.

Alongside his grief was rage. It had carried him through life, deeply embedded in a black little world he had kept hidden ever since he was a child. And it took hold of him now. Oddly enough, the rage kept him calm, fended off his grief, helped him to think and make decisions. And that's what he did. He made the decision that he was going to find his son Lothar, that he was going to take back what was his, with interest, and that he'd kill all the fuckers who had had the nerve to fuck with him.

But most of all he planned what he was going to do to the person who had killed Sophie. And thereby also his dream.

64

(PRAGUE)

SOPHIE OPENED HER EYES; THE ROOM WAS WHITE, THE CURTAINS THIN. THE ceiling was high. She remembered the trip in the ambulance, she remembered Jens sitting beside her. He was sitting there now, on a chair beside her bed.

'Where are we?' she whispered.

'We're in Prague,' Jens said.

'Why?'

'We're hiding here.'

'Albert?'

'No . . . nothing new.'

A large wardrobe in front of her, open. Her clothes were hung up inside.

'Mikhail unpacked your case,' Jens said.

On the bedside table were neat rows of medicine, cotton-wool balls and antiseptics.

'Lothar . . .' Jens said. 'He's taken on the responsibility of being your nurse. He gave you your medication during the journey, kept you sedated.'

'How did we get here?'

'By road from Denmark. You were operated on in the hospital there. But the police started to take an interest in you and we were forced to act quickly.'

'Whose apartment is this?'

'Miles has organised everything, even a doctor who's been keeping an eye on you.'

Lothar peered through the door. He was overjoyed to see her, as if her awakening was a miracle, a resurrection.

She found his positive energy infectious.

'Thank you for looking after me, Lothar,' she whispered weakly.

'Is there anything you need?' he asked.

'No, thanks. Is it OK, being here?' she went on.

'I've looked at a map. We live in the centre. If you go down the street you come to a square, and then the Charles Bridge over the river. That's where the Old Town is. In the other direction' – he pointed behind him – 'there's a big park with an observatory.'

'Then one day we'll walk there,' she whispered. All the talking and listening had worn her out.

'We will,' Lothar said, then let go of the door frame and disappeared.

Jens waited until Lothar was gone, then said, 'He's happy. He's changed; he's been looking after you the whole time, giving you your medication. He's proud of being part of your survival. He couldn't have handled it if you'd died. That was obvious when you got hurt. Lothar's very fond of you. He's drawn to you, sees you as someone he can rely on . . .'

'Stop it, Jens,' she said.

'Can't you allow yourself to let him in?'

'I am,' she said.

'No one knows what's going to happen tomorrow,' he said.

'I can't,' she said. 'I mustn't.'

'Says who?'

'Please, not now . . .'

She shifted slightly in the bed and pain from the knife wound cut through her.

MILES HAD BEEN WORKING TIRELESSLY FOR FOUR DAYS, ALMOST AROUND THE clock. Searching, investigating, analysing. He had become a police officer again.

An embassy was as good as being an espionage centre, with close connections to the Swedish Intelligence Service.

In years gone by, during the Cold War, all eyes had been on the East, towards the Russians. Now it was mostly about promoting Swedish companies in the country where the embassy was based – in other words, primarily industrial espionage. It all happened in a nice, incognito way, and only a few people in the embassy were involved. In Prague, that meant Kennet Wessman.

He knocked on the doorpost.

'What have you found?' Miles asked.

Kennet stepped in with a bundle of papers in his hand.

To get hold of the information Miles was after, Kennet and Miles had concocted a case involving questions from the telecom company Ericsson. Whenever Ericsson was involved, the Intelligence Service was always very obliging. Kennet had spoken to the intelligence agents himself. He told them their client wanted information about some German competitors regarding what meetings they had, what their travel arrangements were, as well as when and where.

The Intelligence Service was in a position to help; that sort of thing was routine for them.

Kennet Wessman waved the documents, then handed them to Miles.

'Hanke GmbH owns a number of planes, and has several more on long leases. This is a list of most of them, as well as what routes they've flown over the past few weeks.'

Miles took the papers.

'Passengers?'

'We can never get those lists.'

'How about regular flights?'

'No, they'd have to dig much deeper for those. This is what we've got to go on.'

'OK. Thanks, Kennet,' Miles said, and started to go through the documents, crossing some flights out and circling others.

There were plenty of trips, in all directions. But one stood out immediately from the others.

Miles Ingmarsson ran out of the embassy and down the cobbled street towards the apartment. He had a cigarette in his mouth and the bundle of papers under his arm. He almost slipped several times.

Mikhail opened the door for him.

Miles was out of breath. He walked in past Mikhail.

'Jens!' he called out.

Jens looked out of Sophie's room. He waved Miles to him, and Miles headed past the kitchen, where Lothar was sitting at the table with two piles of playing cards.

'Hi, Lothar.'

Lothar raised his hand.

Sophie was awake when he entered the room.

'Welcome to Prague,' he said.

'Thanks,' she said weakly.

He passed the sheaf of papers to Jens, who immediately began to scan through them, top to bottom, before moving on to the next one.

'Have you found something?' Sophie asked.

'Maybe,' he replied.

'What?'

He pointed at the documents Jens was working his way through.

'Information about where the Hankes have flown to recently.'

She waited for more.

'It could be a long shot. But a private plane belonging to one of the Hankes' daughter-companies took off from Augsburg, a small airport west of Munich, and flew to Colombia, Cartago, a military airfield.'

'When?' she asked.

'Within the timeframe I'm looking at.'

'I flew to Cartago when I went to see them,' she whispered.

'I know,' Miles said.

'Passengers?'

Miles shook his head.

'We can't find that out.'

Jens looked up from the papers.

'I can go over there,' he said quietly, almost in passing.

Lothar's voice from the kitchen, happy, playfully teasing.

'*Warning to everyone! Mikhail is cheating at cards!*'

They were getting closer to what none of them wanted to acknowledge.

Miles understood.

'I'll put some coffee on,' he said, and left the room.

They could hear Lothar laughing now, chuckling happily.

'Take him with you,' Sophie said. Cold and direct.

The atmosphere in the room darkened.

She and Jens both felt a shame that neither of them knew how to share.

'It feels wrong,' he whispered.

She sat there motionless.

Jens stood up and walked out.

The sky outside the window was winter blue. Clear and fresh, open and broad. Sophie stared out at it.

Everything had been leading up to this.

She could no longer justify anything to herself. She wanted to change places with someone, hide away, stop feeling. But that was just as much of a deception as anything else. Aron's knife cutting into her had given her a liberating pain. As if that evened things out somehow. But it was only temporary. Nothing could liberate her from this.

She had struggled to keep Lothar at a distance. It was like trying to convince herself that she wasn't thirsty or hungry. It was impossible.

Emotionally, he was a constant presence inside her. Not only as the embodiment of her guilty conscience but also as a child. A child who had looked for her, needed her, trusted her. And had helped her, saved her life, had done nothing but good, as if that had been his duty, his conviction. Lothar was a good person.

'Hello . . .'

He was standing in the doorway.

Every hour Lothar gave her painkillers, checked her wound and took her pulse and temperature. He stepped into the room.

'Mikhail cheats at cards,' he said as he made sure the drip was working the way it should. 'And he refuses to admit it, the damned gorilla.'

Lothar met Sophie's gaze and laughed quietly.

'You're going away with Jens tomorrow,' she interrupted.

'Where to?' he asked.

'Sit down.'

He hesitated but did as she said. He was no longer smiling.

'Where am I going?' he asked again.

'That doesn't matter,' she said, looking sadly at him. Lothar seemed to understand where this was heading. As if the situation he was in became clear again, as if he had forgotten where he was. There and then it seemed to dawn on him that these people really didn't wish him well, that he was a pawn in a game and possibly the loneliest person on the planet at that moment.

He looked down at the floor, rubbing his legs with the palms of his hands.

'OK,' he said, trying to sound happy and cheerful, almost grateful.

'Look at me,' she said.

He did, and their eyes met. She started to cry, large, heavy tears that ran down her cheeks. Sophie went on talking as though she weren't crying.

'You've got to be strong, Lothar. You've got a lot of strength inside you, and now's the time to use it.'

She wiped her cheeks with the palm of her hand.

'Do you understand what I mean?'

He was looking at her steadily.

'No,' he said in a toneless voice. 'I'm afraid I don't.'

His straightness and honesty disarmed her. Sophie was struggling with her sense of shame. But it was impossible. Whatever she said, it wouldn't make any difference. There was only one word left. One single word to sum up an entire attitude. An attitude she had been fighting to hold at bay, deny, suppress.

'Sorry . . .' she found herself saying. Like a whisper. 'Forgive me . . .' Then once more: 'Forgive me, Lothar.'

She couldn't stop crying.

Lothar got up from his chair. He stood there, looking at her. Instead of answering and saying *I forgive you,* he said, 'It'll be OK.'

Then he left the room.

An empty feeling of nausea spread through her.

65

(NICE/JUTLAND)

GUSTAVE PELTIER WAS STILL IN NICE WHEN HE RECEIVED THE CALL FROM HIS
Danish colleague, Ejnar Larsen.

The conversation took him by surprise. Sophie Brinkmann had
appeared with a life-threatening knife wound at a hospital in a small
town on Jutland in Denmark, and was picked up by armed men.
And Ejnar Larsen had theories about some shootout in Malmö. But
that would have to wait.

'Take what you've got and catch a flight to Stockholm,' Gustave
said, then booked a flight for himself.

The lead investigator in the Trasten case, Tommy Jansson, met
both men outside the airport and drove them into the city in his
Volvo.

Jansson talked about things that were typically Swedish. Elves
and trolls, reindeer and the Sámi people, midsummer and drinking.
Boats in the Stockholm archipelago, the Eurovision Song Contest
and painted wooden Dala horses.

He tried to sound lively and alert when he spoke, but it didn't re-
ally work. Tommy Jansson didn't seem to be terribly well. Gustave
looked at Ejnar. He also seemed to find the situation rather odd, and
had crossed his arms defensively. He tried to be light-hearted with
Tommy, but Tommy didn't seem to notice.

On the island of Kungsholmen in Stockholm they parked outside

Police Headquarters. Tommy led them inside and up to a conference room.

Ejnar filled their coffee cups to the brim. Tommy took a cinnamon bun and pushed it into his mouth, breathing through his nose as he chewed, then topped himself up with coffee and took another bun. It seemed to calm him down slightly.

'OK,' Gustave Peltier said. 'Thanks to both of you for agreeing to meet at such short notice. I was contacted by Hector Guzman's sister-in-law, and she's given us information about Hector. Unfortunately we missed him. During our conversations with her, one name began to loom large, a Sophie Brinkmann. We don't have a clear picture of her, but she seems to be close to Hector, both personally and professionally. We decided to focus on her, and issued a warrant for her, which Ejnar here dug out when she appeared under a false ID at a hospital in Jutland with a serious knife injury.'

Tommy listened as Ejnar took over.

'There could be a link with a shootout in Malmö a few days before. Once again, in that instance the injured person was removed from the hospital.'

'Who was that?' Tommy asked.

'The description suggests that it could have been Hector Guzman. But that isn't certain,' Ejnar said.

Tommy looked at the men. Now he was going to start lying to them. It was one of his more accomplished skills. Tommy adopted a fresh attitude, calmer, more focused, more cop-like.

'We're in a hell of a mess up here,' he said.

The Dane and the Frenchman looked curious.

'We've been the victims of lengthy deception. Two of our close colleagues have been killed.'

Gustave Peltier raised his eyebrows.

'And we're in a mess because both of them were working on the Trasten investigation.'

'Explain,' Gustave said.

'It's a long story. But Antonia Miller led the investigation from the start. I thought she was mishandling it and not making any progress – she was simply doing a bad job. I said I wanted to try someone else. She fought to keep the job, then suggested Miles Ingmarsson, who she thought was good. I already knew him, and thought, *Why*

not? But I deeply regret that decision. It turned out that both detectives, Antonia Miller and Miles Ingmarsson, were working together, and were totally corrupt. They were blackmailing the culprits and making a fortune from their activities. When I began getting close to them, they went up in smoke. They must have realised. This was just a week or so ago.'

'Last contact?' Ejnar asked.

Tommy sighed.

'It's a fucking tragedy . . . Miles Ingmarsson killed an amphetamine dealer here in Stockholm, Roger Lindgren. We found his DNA, blood and prints at the scene. As we now realise, they were doing business together.'

Tommy looked distraught. Ejnar sympathised.

'It's impossible to predict everything, Tommy,' he said.

Tommy pursed his lips and met Ejnar's gaze in a tacit *thank-you.*

'How has this affected the investigation?' Gustave asked.

'No change. It's ground to a halt, of course. And is seriously compromised.'

Gustave leaned back, coffee cup in hand.

'We'll pool what we've got,' he said. 'Investigate what we can, and look for a way forward. Hector Guzman is going to be arrested. And Sophie Brinkmann is our ticket to him. There's an international warrant out for her, so she's bound to show up on the radar soon.'

'Sounds good,' Tommy said.

'Very good,' Ejnar said.

It had gone better than Tommy had expected. He had created an image of himself as rather naïve, regretful, upright. Now he was going to invite Ejnar and Gustave home to his modest little terraced house and force them to endure a socially awkward dinner with him and his fatally ill wife and their two well-behaved daughters. And with that, their impression of Tommy would be complete.

He would be free to stroll on through the blazing inferno he had created for himself.

66

(VALLE DEL CAUCA)

THEY LANDED AFTER A BUMPY DOMESTIC FLIGHT FROM BOGOTÁ. JENS, MIKHAIL and Lothar stepped out into the new world. Blinding sun, heavy heat and new smells.

The taxi was an old Nissan, its shock absorbers long since dead. Everything shook, and the driver was drinking a can of beer.

They checked into a hotel in the centre of Cartago.

The room was neither big nor small: two beds, and a television on top of a bureau with a minibar underneath.

Mikhail stretched out on one of the beds. Lothar did the same on the other and switched the television on.

Jens dialled the number of an old business acquaintance who had a direct line to Alfonse Ramirez.

A voice answered.

'Contact Alfonse Ramirez and tell him that Jens from Stockholm is in town and wants to meet. I'll call again in three hours.'

They ordered room service and stared at peculiar television programmes. Three hours passed very slowly. Lothar passed out.

Jens dialled the number again. The man with no name gave him an address.

'*You can go right now,*' he told Jens.

He nodded to Mikhail and left the room, hanging the Do Not Disturb sign on the door.

It didn't look like much. A stuccoed building on a busy road, not many windows, surrounded by a low wall.

Jens opened the door. It was a restaurant, with music and a lively atmosphere. The ceiling lights were bright. Children were running around playing while the adults drank and danced.

Alfonse Ramirez walked up to him. He held out his hand and leaned close to Jens's ear to make himself heard over the noise.

'You look better than last time.'

Alfonse laughed at his own words, then indicated with his hand that Jens should follow him.

Last time . . . Jens lying half-dead on the floor at Trasten. Alfonse Ramirez and Hector had killed Jens's assailant. They beat the bastard to death in the kitchen. Alfonse Ramirez's face had been beaming with joy when he emerged, Jens remembered.

They made their way through the sea of people, and reached a table where a pale, sweaty man sat watching Jens with a blank look in his eyes.

'Don Ignacio,' Alfonse said by way of introduction, and gestured for Jens to sit down opposite him.

Don Ignacio. Jens hadn't been expecting that.

There was an energy field surrounding the man. A shield everyone in the room seemed aware of. No one came too close, no one let on how scared they were. They were all playing a game: this was a party, and they were all happy. Because that's what *he* had decided.

'You already know each other,' Don Ignacio said, pointing briefly at Alfonse.

There were no bodyguards in sight, but they were there, everywhere, all the time.

'We met very briefly,' Jens said.

'Trasten . . .' Alfonse said. 'I still count that day as one of the best of my life.'

Jens didn't.

'So, tell me why we're sitting here,' Don Ignacio said.

All traces of friendliness were gone.

Jens took a chance.

'I've come to take Albert home.'

Neither Ignacio nor Alfonse said anything. Jens tried to discern a reaction, any clue. But they just sat there with blank expressions, waiting for more. And that was enough for Jens. They had him, they had Albert.

Alfonse broke the deadlock.

'That day in Stockholm, Jens . . . when you were lying on the floor in the restaurant, after that Russian had kicked you black and blue. You were half-dead, but you kept goading him. In hindsight, that was probably what saved the lives of the rest of us. You dragged things out. It made me curious about who you were, so I checked you out when I got home. It wasn't easy. It was very difficult, in fact. It took time, and people were unwilling to help me. But a picture started to emerge.'

Jens didn't like this.

'You have a track record,' Alfonse went on. 'You've worked with a lot of people. You're good at what you do. Possibly the best smuggler around at the moment. And so why don't we know you?'

Alfonse laughed theatrically. Then a pause, and he leaned forward.

'So, tell us, how were you thinking of getting what you want?'

'I want to exchange Albert for Hector Guzman's son, Lothar.'

Ignacio and Alfonse exchanged a glance.

'Lothar,' Ignacio said. 'That kid's been subject to a lot of inflation. Like everything in this particular affair. Do you know the background?'

'Half,' Jens said.

Music, laughter and partying around them.

'To start with,' Ignacio began, 'it was all about business: the Hankes hurt Hector Guzman in Stockholm, ran him down in a car. As a warning. Hector raised the stakes and blew up Christian Hanke's girlfriend in Munich, even if his target was probably Christian Hanke himself. So it all got very personal. And when things get personal, they usually go to hell, wouldn't you agree?'

Jens didn't answer. Ignacio Ramirez wiped his face with the palm of his hand. He had dark rings under his eyes, and a five-o'clock shadow was starting to appear on his pale skin.

'How did you get hold of Lothar?' Ignacio said.

'Why do you want to know?'

Ignacio shook his head as if to say that there was no ulterior motive behind the question.

'I just want to hear how it happened,' he said.

Jens leaned back in his chair.

'We were looking for Albert,' Jens said. 'We assumed that the Hankes had taken him, and started looking in Munich.'

'Who are *we*?'

'Sophie Brinkmann, me and Mikhail . . .'

'Mikhail?' Alfonse asked.

'He used to work for the Hankes. You met him at Trasten. He was the one who saved our lives there, not me.'

'The big Russian?'

'Yes.'

'So you attacked that farm?' Ignacio said.

Jens nodded.

'How many of you were there? Who else?'

'No one else. Just the three of us.'

The men were quietly astonished.

'Weapons?' Alfonse wondered.

'Mikhail had an old pistol.'

'And you?'

Jens shook his head.

'Nothing?' Alfonse asked.

'No, nothing. We decided to get hold of weapons when we got there,' Jens said.

Ignacio laughed at this, followed by Alfonse.

'So you were able to just go in and take him?' Don Ignacio asked.

Jens didn't answer.

Don Ignacio made himself more comfortable in his chair.

'They got that wrong; thought there were more of you,' Don Ignacio explained. 'They assumed it was Guzman's people attacking in force. But Albert had been moved the previous day. Ralph and Roland set off minutes before you arrived, and Lothar was going to be moved out, along with the remaining guards. You were lucky.'

Jens shook his head.

'No, we weren't lucky. We were there to get Albert. We didn't succeed.'

'You got Lothar, and without him you wouldn't be sitting here now.'

Ignacio changed tone.

'We'll give you Albert, on one condition,' he said.

Jens waited.

'That you're part of the deal, that you stay here and work for us.'

Jens wasn't prepared for that. This was bad . . . Really bad.

Alfonse and Ignacio sat there in front of him. Smiling slightly. *Bastards*.

'What guarantee do I have that Albert will be taken safely to his mother?' Jens asked.

'We'll work that out,' Alfonse said.

'He has to get back to a European country without being noticed; he can't travel on his own passport.'

'There are several ways. He'll probably be flown out on a military flight. We often use those when we have to travel.'

'I want it organised as a diplomatic consignment.'

Alfonse nodded.

'It will be a diplomatic procedure, no problem.'

'And the exchange?' Jens asked.

'There again, you can decide how you want things. But you and Lothar stay here with us . . .'

Jens looked down. He had a fucking dark path in front of him; it sloped down somewhere ahead of him, probably straight to hell.

———

MIKHAIL WAS PACKING LOTHAR'S SUITCASE, PUTTING BACK ALL THE THINGS Lothar had taken out and put in the chest of drawers in the hotel room. The boy clearly liked to keep things tidy.

Lothar came out from the bathroom, toothbrush and toothpaste in his hand, and gave them to Mikhail, who put them in the case.

Lothar sighed. A nervous sigh, as if the oxygen in the room were running out.

'Sit down,' Mikhail said, holding up a pair of handcuffs.

'I'm not going to run.'

It was non-negotiable. Lothar sat down on the bed, and Mikhail cuffed him to the metal frame.

Mikhail finished packing the case and zipped it up. He turned to Lothar.

'I've met your father,' he said. 'I ran him down with a car in a pedestrian crossing in Stockholm. He broke his leg and ended up in the hospital. I was working for Ralph Hanke back then.'

Lothar tried to get his head around what Mikhail was saying.

'Then I returned to Sweden a few weeks later and threatened Hector Guzman with a pistol, and told him to back off. It didn't turn out as we'd planned. Everything went to hell and we were overpowered. The man I arrived with, Klaus Köhler, had a gunshot wound in the stomach and I assumed he was going to die. But your father spared Klaus's and my life.'

Lothar had relaxed slightly as he listened.

'Later on, I got a chance to repay him when I came to their rescue in a restaurant in Stockholm.'

'Trasten? Sophie told me,' Lothar said.

'Yes, Trasten . . .'

Mikhail rubbed his chin with the palm of his hand.

'All the way through, your father remained strong, dignified and he never allowed anything or anyone to get the better of him. The same goes for you. You're his son; never forget that you're strong, and never let anyone else get the better of you, no matter how much power they may have over you.'

Lothar sat there, thoughts rolling around his head.

'Did you hear what I said?'

Lothar didn't answer, instead he said: 'I played football a few weeks back. I was studying for a maths exam. I had just started texting with a girl in school. We were about to go out soon. I had bought tickets to a football game, then we would go out for Asian food and I would walk her home. I was happy. Life was normal. Everything was good . . .'

'That's in the past.' Mikhail's words were a cold statement.

'Am I doomed to this, then? Being part of something that . . .'

'It doesn't matter, Lothar. Let it go.'

Lothar was quiet. Mikhail continued: 'Did you hear what I said about your father?'

'Yes,' Lothar said after brief pause.

'Are you going to take that with you?'

Lothar thought a moment.

'I don't know,' he said.

Mikhail studied Lothar.

The hotel-room phone rang, cutting through the silence. Just once. It meant it was time to go.

'My dad will come and get me, eventually,' Lothar said.

'Good. Hold on to that.'

'What about you, Mikhail? Will you come and get me?'

'You just said your dad will be doing that.'

Mikhail looked hard at the boy.

'Goodbye, Lothar Guzman,' he said, then left the hotel room.

Mikhail walked through the lobby and out into the dark evening. It had just stopped raining. The air was heavy with dampness and moisture.

He felt depressed. He'd rather be angry. But anger didn't seem to want to appear, just sorrow and emptiness . . . He liked Lothar, and didn't like what was happening.

Mikhail walked a few blocks, got in a taxi that drove him to the appointed meeting place and was dropped off at a little square in the slum district. There was a smell of food, rubbish, and exhaust fumes. A spiderweb of electricity cables above him. And everywhere the sound of cars, mopeds, people, dogs and music, together creating a jumble of impressions. But Mikhail couldn't shake off his sadness.

Shit . . .

A gleaming drug dealer's SUV stopped abruptly in front of him.

Mikhail got in the back seat. It was cool and quiet.

Alfonse grinned at him.

'This is like a reunion, a Trasten reunion.' He laughed unpleasantly.

JENS WAS WAITING AT A BUS STOP ON A BUSY STREET IN THE EASTERN PART of the city. People drove like idiots here; the mopeds and motorbikes appeared to have no fear of death.

A large silver Cadillac stopped at the bus stop. Jens opened the back door. Albert was sitting in the back seat, and Jens got in. Albert was suntanned, and his hair had grown.

'Jens?!' Albert practically shouted his name. 'Mum?' he went on, fear and anxiety flashing across his face.

'She's fine, Albert, don't worry.'

Jens held Albert tight, as if he didn't dare let go of him.

'You're going home to her now . . .'

Albert relaxed, and Jens could feel his body trembling. As if the struggle to hold his fears and anxieties at bay was finally at an end. The dam had burst. But there were no tears; his body just shook as if he were frozen right down to the marrow.

Jens held Albert tighter.

'What's going on?'

The car pulled out into traffic.

Albert was worried, he looked around as if he was searching for something.

'Everything's OK, Albert,' Jens said quietly.

Albert was different, he was stressed and anxious. Foreclosed and distant. Jens had expected something else. Perhaps an angrier Albert. But this was a boy torn by inner turmoil. Shocked, confused . . . broken.

'Are we going home?' Albert asked.

'No . . . not yet. You're going to Prague. You'll be living there for a while.'

'And Mum's there?'

'Yes, she's safe, don't worry.'

But Albert was no longer listening. A new thought had just struck him.

'How did you get me out?'

The Cadillac was thundering along the two-way street, forcing its way through, bullying, running traffic lights. Jens let go of Albert, reached for his seat belt, pulled it across him and fastened it.

'Does it make any difference?'

'Yes, it makes a difference,' Albert said.

'Albert. We're on our way out of here now. You're going home to your mum, that's all that matters.'

The driver blew his horn, then accelerated.

'I heard them talking about it,' Albert said.

'Who? Talking about what?'

'That I was going to be exchanged for someone.'

Jens said nothing, and Albert turned towards him.

'Lothar?' Albert asked.

Jens was staring in front of him.

'Yes . . .'

'Did anyone think to ask me about this?'

'No.'

'I want to stay here,' he said.

Jens turned towards him in his seat.

'Listen to me now, Albert.'

Albert's eyes wavered.

'Your mum's been hurt.'

Albert froze.

'She was stabbed,' Jens went on.

Albert struggled to say something. Eventually he said, 'How is she?'

'OK, under the circumstances.'

A thousand thoughts.

'Who stabbed her?'

'Aron Geisler,' Jens replied.

A look of surprise. 'Aron? Why?'

'We don't know yet . . . but that doesn't matter. We're all being hunted, Albert, tracked down and searched for. There's no space to accommodate your individual wishes. You're going to your mum, that's what's going to happen. Do you understand what I'm saying?'

Albert seemed lost in thought.

'Do you understand what I'm saying?' Jens repeated.

'Yes,' he replied.

'If it's any consolation to you, I'm going to be staying here with Lothar,' Jens said quietly.

'Staying?'

'Yes.'

'Why?'

'I'm part of the deal. But that's nothing for you to worry about.'

Albert lowered his head, as if he were ashamed.

'I don't know what to say,' he whispered after a while.

'You don't have to say anything. And don't feel guilty. This is just the way things have turned out.'

It was raining as the car turned into the military airfield and drove out onto the apron. A 737 bearing the insignia of the Colombian Air Force on its tail was waiting with its engines running, a movable flight of stairs leading up to the rear entrance.

Another Cadillac pulled in ahead of them. Jens watched it as it stopped. He saw Mikhail get out in the rain and walk towards them.

'Come on,' he said to Albert. 'Let's get you out of here.'

Jens helped Albert out from the SUV, the driver waited outside with Albert's wheelchair.

Mikhail and Albert shook hands. Then the three of them headed towards the plane.

'What are you going to do after this, Mikhail?' Jens asked.

'After this?'

'When you get back. Are you going to leave Prague?'

'No, I'll stay for a while.'

'Why?'

'Various reasons.'

'Give me one.'

Mikhail glanced at Jens, then said, 'I don't think Lothar should have to live in this country with these people. Nor you, Jens.'

He fished out a piece of paper.

'You can contact me via this website,' he went on, and tucked the note into Jens's pocket.

The two men carried Albert up the steps in his wheelchair. When they reached the top they put Albert down inside the door of the plane.

Jens held out his hand to Albert, who took it.

'Look after yourself, and your mum,' Jens said, then turned around, gave Mikhail a pat on the shoulder, then jogged down the steps and over to the car, where Alfonse was waiting.

———

Mikhail rolled Albert into the plane. The rear section was open cargo space, with seven rows of old first-class seats from the '80s towards the front.

He helped Albert into one of the seats.

A pilot came out from the cockpit in a green Air Force uniform. He folded Albert's wheelchair away.

'We'll be landing in Prague. While we're taxiing, we'll have to put the boy into a wooden crate in the hold. It's marked as a diplomatic consignment. You,' he said, pointing at Mikhail, 'will leave with us. You'll have time to peel off once we're through.'

JENS WATCHED THE 737 AS IT HEADED TOWARDS THE RUNWAY. THE FLASHING of the navigation lights cast a harsh glow through the rain-drenched car windows.

Then the howl of the engines, and the plane accelerated along the wet runway, took off steeply and banked away from him into the darkness.

Albert, on his way to Sophie . . .

'The address of the hotel?' Alfonse said beside him in the back seat.

Jens felt an urge to break Alfonse's neck, strangle the driver, then take Lothar and run.

But Alfonse had a pistol in his hand, and the driver had one on his lap, in full view.

It would have to wait.

Alfonse went with Jens up to the hotel room, his pistol swinging from his hand.

Jens released Lothar's handcuffs and picked up his case, and the three of them left the room.

Once they had been driving through the countryside for a while, Jens turned to Lothar.

'I'll be staying here with you.'

Lothar didn't understand at first.

'I'm going to be working for these people. I'll have to do quite a bit of travelling, but I'll come back to you as quickly and as often as I can.'

Lothar seemed absorbed in a particular thought, then relaxed and lightened up.

'OK,' he whispered.

Their new home. A prison. The drugs castle in the jungle appeared as they emerged from driving through the dense forest.

They looked at the animals in their enclosures, the tennis courts, swimming pools, waterfalls and the helicopter pad, all lit up in the evening.

The car didn't stop in front of the main building but carried on beyond it, through another patch of jungle and along a gravel road.

At the foot of a verdant hillside lay a row of white, single-storey buildings, with small gardens, an orangery and two more buildings without windows. It looked like a miniature suburb, but it was all surrounded by a three-metre-high metal fence with signs warning of extremely high voltage. There was a barred gate in the middle, and guards patrolling outside.

They pulled up in front of the gate; Jens could see some men sitting on the illuminated veranda of one of the houses. They were dressed in casual clothes, almost as though they were on holiday, sitting around a table, perhaps they were playing cards . . .

In the front seat, Alfonse turned around.

'Do you recognise them?' Alfonse asked, nodding towards the veranda.

They were some distance away, but Jens recognised one of them, at least.

'Ernst Lundwall, Hector's adviser,' he said.

'That's right,' Alfonse said. 'The other two are Christian Hanke and Roland Gentz.'

Ralph Hanke's son and his right-hand man.

Don Ignacio Ramirez was collecting people. Just like the animals in the enclosures. And now he and Lothar were collector's items of his as well. The picture was becoming clearer. Alfonse and Don

Ignacio had the right people in their possession to take over whatever they wanted to from Hanke's or Guzman's businesses. Possibly everything. Because they had their sons.

Jens looked at Lothar. He sat there beside him, his expression not revealing anything of what he thought about things.

'You're not going to be living here. You're guests in the main house,' Alfonse said.

'What does that mean?' Jens asked.

'That we start up there. If you behave yourself, Jens, and if you're cooperative . . . well, you understand. Then Lothar will have a decent life here.'

67

(STOCKHOLM)

TOMMY WAS PUSHING MONICA IN HER WHEELCHAIR. IT WAS COLD. SHE WAS looking at the wildlife, it was always beautiful. However grey and miserable it was, she always enjoyed looking at things.

She had stopped talking to Tommy. He thought it was because of her illness. She could talk, sometimes really well. But she was never going to talk to him again. She had made her mind up about that. And then he had begun to talk to her, properly. Their walks, like this one, were unbearable. He pushed her ahead of him in her wheelchair and told her one appalling truth after the other. As if he were unburdening himself to her. As if that was what she was for, now. The truths were partially camouflaged, but she understood. Tommy was a murderer, a mass murderer, who used his warped sense of honesty to justify everything with wise words and childish psychology. And all the while he reminded her that it was for her sake that all of this was happening, because he was going to make her better.

He was so sick, her Tommy. He didn't even have the decency not to say that, not to try to lay the blame on her.

'Do you remember Denmark?' he said. 'That was our best holiday, wasn't it? The girls were so happy. They loved that beach, and the restaurants. We're going to go back there again. We'll stay at the same place, and it will be just as much fun.'

He sounded so convinced of everything he said. As if every

thought in his head were a truth. She couldn't even remember Denmark.

And Monica knew that Tommy would never help her with anything again, and certainly not help her on her way. The biggest thing she had ever asked from her husband, after a lifetime in his service.

But Tommy was only capable of helping himself the whole time, over and over again, sucked in by centrifugal force towards the centre of his own self-obsessed and warped universe.

And she could no longer do anything but pray for him, pray hard and intensely in the vague hope that one day he would come to his senses and put a bullet in his own head.

68

(PRAGUE)

KENNET WESSMAN SHOWED HIS DIPLOMATIC PASSPORT TO THE CUSTOMS OF-ficial at Václav Havel Airport in Prague. He signed to acknowledge receipt of a large wooden crate sent from the Swedish diplomatic delegation to Colombia.

The crate was loaded into his van.

Miles was sitting behind the wheel as Kennet jumped in. They drove away from the customs office. But instead of heading towards the centre of the city, they steered around the building and drove a short distance until a large man in just his shirtsleeves emerged from the darkness.

Mikhail pulled the back door open and climbed inside.

'God, it's cold,' he said, shivering.

With Kennet driving, they sped off. Miles clambered into the back and helped Mikhail to open the crate. The lid came off.

Albert was sitting inside the box, his legs tucked beneath him.

'I'm Miles Ingmarsson,' Miles said, sticking his hand in the crate.

'I'm Albert Brinkmann,' Albert said, taking his hand.

She was lying in bed and heard the door open, heard Miles talking, heard Albert answer. Then the sound of rubber tyres on the wooden floor of the apartment. Albert's wheelchair.

He came into her room. They looked at each other. Albert looked the same, but was different in a way that she couldn't quite put her finger on. Something in his eyes.

Tears were running down her cheeks. She held his hand and leaned towards him. And in spite of the pain from the knife wound, she managed to hug Albert. She held him tight. He felt a long way away.

'Hello, Mum,' he said.

'Hello, darling,' she whispered.

EPILOGUE: TWO WEEKS LATER
(STOCKHOLM/PRAGUE)

THE HOUSE WAS QUIET WHEN TOMMY OPENED THE DOOR. HE WALKED THROUGH the hall and into the living room. It felt clean, as if someone had been hard at work.

'Hello?' he said cautiously.

In the kitchen, at the table, Monica was sitting in her wheelchair, her head lolling sideways, dead; staring eyes, arms hanging limply. On the table a glass of water and an open bottle of pills.

Tommy stood there motionless. The afternoon sun was shining on her. A scene of calm. He took a few careful steps closer. He took hold of a chair and realised he was moving quietly, as if he didn't want to upset her spirit, which he knew was still in the kitchen. Tommy sat down beside Monica.

Her hand was cold, but he held it in his, tried to warm her up.

'Monica,' he whispered.

He had shared parts of his secret with her during their walks. Not everything, but small fragments. It had felt good. And he hoped it had given her something, a feeling of trust, perhaps. But mainly it had helped him. And now she was going to disappear? Unless she already had? He needed her . . . as the bearer of his guilt.

So Tommy began to explain in graphic detail to his dead wife how he had shot, strangled and murdered people around him, then talked about his self-awareness and self-control, seeing as he had managed to stop drinking all on his own. After that it just kept coming. Tommy

talked about his view of life. Lots of truths, they just kept coming, they sounded good. They made him sure that everything he had done was right, and that he had to keep going along the same path.

And Monica seemed to agree with him, because she didn't say anything, just sat there listening and concentrating, keeping her eyes on a single point.

Then Tommy cried, lots of heavy tears, his body shaking as he wept. He was crying because he was free. It felt so good . . .

Tommy let go of Monica's cold, stiff hand, and called to report his wife's death.

Some uniformed colleagues arrived, went through the routine for suicides, passed on their condolences. The paramedics waited until they were done, then came into the kitchen and carried her out to the ambulance.

Tommy watched them drive away. Then he packed all of Monica's clothes and belongings into some moving boxes and carried them down to the basement. There, in his little office, his refuge, his hiding place, he looked at his desk. Piles of papers; it looked messy.

He began to tidy up, organise, sort things . . . It was mostly to do with his surveillance of things that could come back and bite him, expose him. So Tommy looked at it in a different way. He started to investigate himself, like the brilliant detective he was. He looked at it all from every angle, to see how the intense events of recent weeks could be traced back to him. Only then could he block the holes. And once again, Tommy was surprised by his own skill, both as a detective and as a perpetrator.

He worked, wrote, sketched . . . evaluated risk. Two names leaped out at him. Miles Ingmarsson and Sophie Brinkmann. Otherwise he was untouchable.

He was going to make it, he was going to put a stop to this, he would work hard, always one step ahead, and be seriously goddamn dangerous. Tommy felt strong . . . invincible.

———

MILES WAS WAITING IN THE ARRIVALS HALL AT PRAGUE AIRPORT. HE SAW HER walking towards him. His brother Ian by her side, pulling a case. She

was wearing a shawl, sunglasses, a scarf. But it wasn't enough. The recent operations to her face were clearly visible.

She speeded up as she got closer to him, crept into his embrace and stayed there. They stood like that for a long while. Ian waited at a distance.

'Now we're together,' Sanna said.

He pulled out of the embrace and looked at her.

'It'll heal,' she whispered. 'The doctor said so.'

He patted her gently on the cheek.

Ian walked over.

'Hello, Miles,' he said.

'Hello, Ian.'

Miles looked at his younger brother and thought he must have grown a metre or so since he last saw him, in terms of his character at least. There was a sort of honesty to him, a stability. As if he had stopped trying to hide his poor self-esteem, and had thereby got rid of it.

'Thanks for all your help, Ian,' Miles said.

Ian shrugged, as if to say that he didn't know what Miles meant. But Miles was serious. Ian had worked tirelessly on everything Miles had asked him to do. First on protecting Sanna at the hospital. And now he had accompanied her here, had even bought new clothes for her so she'd feel she looked OK. Now he was going to turn around and fly home again.

Ian hugged Sanna, then held his hand out to Miles.

Before Miles took it, he said, 'I hope we'll soon be able to sit down, the two of us, and just eat, drink and talk.'

'About what?'

'About nothing,' Miles said.

'I hope so too.'

Miles shook his hand. Ian smiled, turned around and walked away.

They ate together in their shared home, the apartment in Prague.

Sophie, Albert, Mikhail, Miles and Sanna. There were two empty

places. That was what they had agreed. Lothar and Jens would sit there again. No one knew when, but that wasn't the point.

Sophie looked at the people eating, drinking and talking to one another.

She was starting to recognise Albert again. He was talking, wanted to understand, wanted to know what was going on. She had told him everything, without any evasion, without softening or glossing over anything. It had been hard. But he had demanded it of her. He had demanded her honesty, not so much for his own sake as for hers. And it had been a relief . . . like the start of her own process of accepting herself for who she was, and of getting better.

The same applied to everyone around the table. It was as if that was their tacit understanding: to get better, each one of them on their own terms. Because they had each chosen to.

Miles looked radiant, in a way Sophie liked. Sanna was good for him. She was aware, honest, wise and warm, and created harmony around her. And Mikhail, he was more and more human with each passing day. But perhaps he always had been.

But they were also sitting there for a reason that none of them had any power over. They were all hunted, with death constantly lying in wait around the corner. None of them was free.

And none of them could simply accept that. They were going to fight for their survival. For their freedom.

Albert was sitting on the other side of the table from her. He laughed at something Miles was saying.

His laughter was infectious, and she started laughing too.

ACKNOWLEDGEMENTS

THANKS TO MY EDITOR, ZACHARY WAGMAN, EDITORIAL GENIUS, FRIEND AND advocate; Molly Stern and the brilliant team at Crown; Elizabeth Foley, Alison Hennessey and everyone at Harvill Secker; Neil Smith, translator extraordinaire; and all of my dedicated publishers around the world. Finally, gratitude to all the inspiring authors and storytellers out there.